SPARTAN
NEGOTIATOR

PRESS

A Superior Publishing Company

P.O. Box 115 • Superior, WI 54880
(218) 391-3070 • www.savpress.com

SPARTAN
NEGOTIATOR

John F. Saunders

First Edition

First Printing

Copyright © 2013 John F. Saunders

Cover design: Debbie Zime / DeZime Graphics

Fear and Retribution Photo used in the composite of the front cover, Copyright Mark Krajnak, JerseyStyle Photography.

This book is a work of fiction. Names, characters, places, and incidents either are products of the author's imagination or are used fictitiously. Any resemblance to actual persons, living or dead, events, or locales, is incidental and coincidental.

ISBN - 13: 978-1-937706-07-4

Library of Congress Catalog Card Number: 2013931640

Published by:

Savage Press
P.O. Box 115
Superior, WI 54880

Phone: 218-391-3070
Email: mail@savpress.com
Website: www.savpress.com

17 16 15 14 13 9 8 7 6 5 4 3 2 1

Printed in the United States of America

To
Jan,
Fear the Spartans
Not your dentist. I
hope you enjoy it

Dedication

To my beautiful wife, Lynn. It takes a very special woman to love a knucklehead like me.

To my sons John and Jake. I am proud of the men you have become.

To all the honorary Spartans out there who know that life is obligation and some debts can only be paid in blood.

SFFS. Straight roads. No cages.

Hard it is on earth,
With mighty whoredom;
Ax-time, sword-time, shields are sundered,
Wind-time, wolf-time, ere the world falls,
Nor ever shall men each other spare.

— The Elder Edda

Prologue

Three men were dead. Murdered.

No, that wasn't the right word, Dennis thought. They had been executed. Even when he closed his eyes, he could still hear the roaring of the guns; see the dark splashes of blood on their clothes, even smell the acrid stench of gunpowder. It was a waking nightmare, and he couldn't escape it. Dennis closed his eyes again. His world seemed to have gone insane.

The dark blue unmarked Ford Crown Victoria turned slowly into the driveway. The tires crunched on the bits of debris on the old concrete. FBI Special Agent Richard Redding shifted the car into park but didn't turn it off. He looked to the man in the passenger's seat.

"Dennis, we're back. Safe and sound just like I promised you. Now go inside and get some rest. Tomorrow is going to be another big day."

Dennis opened his eyes and looked around. He saw the silhouettes of the two cops in the black and white police cruiser parked at the curb in front of the house.

"Will we be coming back here after I meet with the grand jury again?"

"No. After you testify, we'll move you to a new safe house. Now get inside and lock up tight. I'm going to check in with the officers down there on the street before I head back. I'll see you at eight o'clock sharp. Wear a clean shirt and a tie if you have one."

Dennis nodded. He hated being chaperoned like a child. He got out and walked to the door just off the small one-car garage. The house was a small two-bedroom, two-bath bungalow. It was painted a muted tan and white. The front hedges were neatly trimmed just below window height. The yard had been recently mowed. There was nothing remarkable about the house. It disappeared from memory as soon as you looked away. Maybe that was the point. A safe house had to be invisible to provide safety.

He could just hear Redding and the two cops talking beside their squad car.

"All quiet here, fellas?"

"Yes, sir."

"I'm Special Agent Redding."

"I'm officer Van Horn. This is officer Middendorf."

They all shook hands.

"Good to meet you both. Nothing out of the ordinary tonight? Nobody walking their dog around? No late night joggers?"

"Nothing. Not even a stray cat. You would have to have some big brass balls to approach a house with a police car parked out front."

"Keep your eyes open. The Bureau doesn't want anything to happen to our boy. We're counting on his testimony to put away some very bad guys for a very long time."

Dennis couldn't hear the rest as he went inside. He locked the door behind him. More babysitters. He walked down the hallway to the back bedroom. The master, they called it, but it wasn't much larger than the other bedroom. The only difference was the en suite bathroom. He reached to turn on the overhead light, forgetting there was no switch. He walked to the bed and turned on the lamp by the bed and farther in, the tall lamp beside the reading chair. Like he was going to do some fucking reading with people trying to kill him.

In the bathroom, he turned on the light and shut the door. He took a much-needed piss and let out a long sigh of relief. A good piss was definitely under-appreciated by most people. He flipped the overhead fan on and knelt beside the Kleenex dispenser. He opened it and removed a half empty pack of Camel cigarettes and a book of matches hidden inside. He saw the two joints. They were tempting Sirens calling him. He thought better of it. Dennis tapped out a cigarette and lit it instead, drawing the smoke deep into his lungs. Held it. Finally, he blew the blue smoke up at the fan. Then waved his hands dispersing the cloud that remained.

The cops said no smoking in the house. Against the rules. Fuck 'em, he thought. And fuck the rules. And fuck Katy too. Damn bitch. This was all her fault anyway.

He took his time smoking. Savored the cigarette down to the filter. He tossed it and the burnt match into the toilet, flushed and hid the cigarettes. You couldn't be too careful with cops. They did everything by the rules. They might search his room tonight after he went to sleep looking for his weed. He would have to remember to sneak the cigarettes and joints out with him tomorrow. He switched off the light in the bathroom as he turned back into the bedroom. He jumped when he saw the man sitting in the reading chair.

The man was large like a body builder or pro football player. He wore gray coveralls, paper shoe-covers, black gloves and a black balaclava. Only his blue eyes were visible. The eyes seemed to glow in the lamplight. The big man motioned with the gun he held in his right hand. It looked almost like a prop from some movie with its large noise suppressor. Dennis knew it was real.

"Sit," the man said.

Dennis did not move. He couldn't. His body wouldn't respond. His brain was locked up.

"If you want to live, you need to sit down."

Dennis fought for words. "You've got the wrong guy," was all he could think to say.

The man smiled. Dennis could see it through the balaclava. See the material change shape at the mouth. The big man's voice was calm with a touch of humor. "You are Dennis Torney. You are twenty-eight years old. You have one sister, Evan. She is married and lives in Kentucky where she raises horses. Both of your parents are dead. You graduated from Louisville with a degree in business. You, until recently, were working as the manager of an American Auto Parts store. Your long-time girlfriend, Katy, just moved out of your apartment. Now, if you need me to, I can give you your social security number and birth date. But I would have to go back to my car to check the numbers and to tell you the truth it would be easier to just shoot you in the head."

Terror crept through Dennis. His mind scrambled to find a way out. He could make a break for it. He might make it.

The big man read his mind. Shaking his head he said, "You'll never make it, Dennis. This is a Kimber, arguably the best handgun in the world. I am very good with it. And since it is loaded with 147 grain, 9mm Ranger SXTs that will shred you like you were hit with a chainsaw, I don't even need to be too accurate."

The truth was, in almost every way, the Kimber was a perfect killing weapon. It was accurate. It was expertly designed. It used the finest steel for its frame. And it was embarrassingly beautiful. The big man's only complaint with it was that it was hard to clean. Glocks and Sigs took seconds to break down. Hell, he could do it blindfolded, but the Kimber had to have a special Allen wrench inserted in the spring. It was a pain in the ass.

"If I yell, the cops will hear and come check it out. You'll be caught."

The hint of the smile showed again through the balaclava. "It's nice of you to worry about me. If you shout and the police officers do hear and respond, then their wives will become widows. Their children fatherless. In any case, I promise, you will not be alive to witness the outcome."

"What have I got to lose? You're going to kill me anyway."

"That is not true. You will decide what I need to do, Dennis. The only way you can survive is if you do as I ask and listen to what I have to say. Now, please, sit down. I don't like to ask more than once. It shows a certain level of disrespect for me."

Dennis sat on the edge of the bed.

"On your hands, if you don't mind. And cross your legs at the ankles."

Dennis did as he was told. The position kept him off balance enough to impede getting to his feet; it also helped condition him to do as he was told without asking why.

"What did you tell them, Dennis? At the preliminary grand jury hearing?"

"I didn't tell them anything," he lied. "I don't meet with them until tomorrow."

The man chuckled to himself. He shook his head. "I usually don't tolerate lying, but I understand your situation, Dennis. You have to try certain things, so I will not punish your lapse in judgment. Let me rephrase my question. I have seen the transcript of your testimony...."

"How...?"

"Dennis, we know everything. We own everyone. We have people everywhere. That's why I could find you so easily. Now tell me your story. I want to be sure I understand exactly what happened. Exactly what went wrong."

Dennis sighed. "I'll tell you, but I don't understand it all myself."

"Fine. I will try to explain what you don't understand as well if I can. Start from the beginning."

"I had broken up with my girlfriend, Katy. It was all my fault. I was a jerk. The breakup was killing me inside. I started drinking more than I should have. A lot more."

"That's why American Auto Parts let you go?"

"Yeah. I was spending a lot of time at the Hideaway. It's a dive bar in town. Drowning my sorrows like some god damn cliché."

"We've all been there. That's why they're clichés. Go on."

"I drank the place closed as usual. I went to my car to go home. Just feeling sorry for myself. I started to drive and realized how drunk I was. I couldn't keep the car on the road.

"Your statement left that fact out."

"They told me not to mention it. I think the cops thought it would make me look bad. Anyway, I figured that, with my luck, I would get pulled over for a DUI or total my car. I saw a closed gas station and pulled in. There were a bunch of cars parked at the side. I figured I could park there, catch a few hours of sleep and be gone before they opened."

"That explains why you happened to be there."

"I crashed in the back seat. Sometime later I heard a car pull in. I'm thinking it's the cops, so I laid low hoping they'd drive by. But the car stops. I peeked out the back window just as three big motorcycles roared up. They parked facing the car. It was a Caddy. The guys in the car get out. There's a giant black guy and he's got a shotgun across the crook of his arm. He's not even trying to hide it. There's also a young Asian guy with some kind of machine gun, and another older Asian guy gets out of the back. They look like businessmen. All nice suits."

"That would be Mr. Lei and his bodyguards. What did the three motorcycle men do?"

"The black guy with the Asians hollers that he wants to see they are unarmed. One of the bikers is real skinny. He's got this white wife-beater on and baggy jeans. He lifts his shirt and turns around slow. The second one is wearing a shirt with a confederate flag on the front. He protests, but I can't hear what he says. The lead biker says something and the flag guy raises his shirt and turns around. The black guy points the shotgun at the leader of the bikers."

"The one you identified to the police, correct?"

"Yes. He had this long white scar down the right side from his ear all the way down his neck, and a mostly white beard. The police said he was Robert Ziglar."

"Bobby Z. Zee Money. Blanco Grande. His scar is very distinctive. It is hard to miss. You couldn't identify the other two with him?"

"No. The cops showed me a lot of photos, but I couldn't be sure."

"What happened next?"

"The one called Bobby was wearing a leather vest with a red T-shirt beneath it. He lifted it up and turned around. The big black guy nodded and said something. The older Asian and Bobby approached each other. They talked for a few minutes and then the Asian laughed. It was a really weird laugh. High like a girl's. They stepped apart and the Asian walked back to the car."

"Do you know why they were meeting, Dennis?"

"The police said they didn't know why."

The big man laughed.

"They knew. Or at least they had a very good idea. Mr. Lei, with the backing of a Vietnamese Triad, was trying to move into the area to sell heroin. It was an area controlled by us. Although we had no heroin trade ourselves, it was our territory so we requested a percentage of their profits to allow them to operate."

"It was a drug deal?"

"At the most basic level. Protection for access to a new market. A fair business arrangement. Unfortunately, Mr. Lei did not wish to pay for this privilege. He felt he should be exempt from such things. He thought he was too well connected for such considerations. Which was why he was laughing. What happened next?"

"The bikers started to leave when the one with the confederate flag seemed to get mad. He started screaming that he wasn't going to let some nigger tell him what to do, and that the next time he would kick his black nigger ass. Things like that."

"What did Mr. Lei do?"

"He laughed at first. The same girly high-pitched laugh. The black guy was getting angry and started toward the white guy. Lei put his hand on the guy's chest to stop him. The two of them started to argue. That's when it happened."

"What exactly? I am very interested."

"Out of nowhere, the one with the scar has a big gun in his hand and starts shooting. It sounded like a fucking cannon."

"It was a 45. A very loud weapon. Causes some people to freeze up."

The big man smiled at Dennis' description, "out of nowhere." He knew that Bobby Z had a special upside down holster in the back of his vest. It was almost invisible. The big man had designed it himself. Bobby Z was a regular fucking boatman. Not as good as The Jake, but damn good. The Jake now, that was another story altogether. He was almost as good as the big man himself. Almost.

"What happened then, Dennis?"

"The black guy fell first. Lei and the other Asian with the machine gun turned toward the shooter."

"Did they open fire?"

"Before they could do anything, the skinny guy had a gun out and he shot the Asians three times real fast."

The big man knew the gun had been hidden in an ankle holster. It had happened as he had drawn it up. The racial taunts distracted the black man and Mr. Lei so the Spartans could draw their weapons.

"Lei looked stunned. He started begging in Chinese or something. The guy with the scar walked right up to him and shot him point blank in the front of the head. Blew his brains out all over the hood of the Caddy. Then he turned to the black man on the ground. He may have still been alive. He said something and shot him again."

"The black man was called Big Tom," the big man said. "He and Bobby had been friends at one time."

"Friends? They had been fucking friends? He killed him."

The big man shrugged. Without emotion he said, "You stand against the Spartans, you get hurt. Big Tom made his choice."

"Spartans. Those bikers were Spartans? They weren't wearing colors or anything."

"Cops forget to mention that to you?"

"Fuck. The Spartans." Dennis stared wildly at the man with the gun. "Then you're the guy."

"What guy?"

"The guy. The guy the Spartans send. The killer. That guy. Kane. Frank Kane."

The big man laughed. He was enjoying himself.

"Kane? I'm not him. He's a monster, some kind of brutal, relentless, killing machine. Thank your gods they didn't send him tonight. If Kane shows up to negotiate, people die. Lots of people."

"Then why did they send you if not to kill me?"

"I have a certain amount of seniority within the Spartans. It gives me leeway in these matters. I was told you were a problem and that I was to make you disappear, permanently. How was not specified. The logical implication was that you were to be killed."

"Fuck."

"Relax, Dennis. First of all, I respect what you did. It takes a lot of courage to stand up for what you believe in. I've checked you out. You're not a bad guy. Unfortunately, I can't let you testify against Bobby Z. He's like a brother to me. He is a good warrior and I stand by him. So we have two options. We can do this the easy way or the hard way."

Dennis leaned forward, intense. "What's the easy way?"

"That's not too good for you. I put a bullet in your forehead and slip away."

"What's the hard way?"

"I was hoping you would ask. You have to disappear. Vanish. You call your sister. Tell Evan you couldn't identify anyone at the shooting. Tell her the police were forcing you to identify a guy that you hadn't seen. Tell her you are going away for a while, then go."

"Won't the cops come after me?"

"At first. But without you there to corroborate your earlier testimony and with your sister's allegations that you were coerced, it will blow over. The charges will be dropped. Bobby will be released. And you get to stay alive."

"How long do I have to hide out?"

"Forever. After tonight, you can't call anyone. In a year or two you can call your sister, tell her you're okay, but you can't visit her."

"Why not?"

"Someone might see or hear."

"But you said the cops wouldn't care in six months."

"The Spartans won't forget. The Spartans never forget. Someone will see. The word will be sent. They'll send someone else, Bobby Z or even Kane, to make you disappear again."

"What about my sister? Is she in danger too?"

"The Spartans do not make war on the families of our enemies, there is no honor in it."

Dennis stared at the big man, confused by the answer. "Shit. It won't work. I don't know how to disappear."

"It is easy. You walk out the back door. Cross through the neighbor's yard. There's a red Acura TL 3.2 parked in front of their house. The key is in the ignition. There's some money under the front seat in an envelope. And be careful, there's another patrol car cruising the block. Head east for half an hour. Stop and call your sister. Her phone records will show from where the call originated. Then head west. The Feds won't be back before eight. You'll be long gone by then."

"What then?"

"Just live. Oh, I would dump the car when you get settled. Don't try to sell it. Once you're on your feet, just park it somewhere and leave it."

Dennis looked at his shoes. He started nodding. "Okay. I can do this. I can do it. There is nothing for me here anymore anyway."

"Then I have your word?"

Dennis stood and stared once more into the bluest eyes he had ever seen. "That's all you need for a guarantee?"

"It's enough between men of honor," the big man said.

Honor was a powerful word for those who believed in it.

For those who didn't, it was like a gambler's tell that they would remember and hope to exploit against you later. Ironically, the big man believed fully in the power of the word.

"You have my word."

The big man stood and walked to the bedroom door, saying only, "Good. Get up."

Dennis rose, unsteadily. "Wait. If you're not Frank Kane, who are you? What do I call you?"

"Nothing. I'm a ghost. I was never here."

"I hope I never see you again."

"As long as you keep your word, you won't. If you don't, I'll be the last thing you do see."

"I won't break it."

"Go in the bathroom and spark up one of those joints before you start your new life, then go, before you have time to chicken out."

Dennis turned toward the bathroom and suddenly stopped. "How did you know about the joints?" he asked, turning around, but the man was gone. Dennis listened to the night. Everything was silence.

Chapter 1

Seven Years Later

Bruce Burns' hand trembled as he lifted the telephone to his ear. He could smell the stench of his own fear as he punched in the number. He thought he could even taste it, sour and strong with an odd hint of metal. He fought to control his rising panic. What else could he do? There was no one else he could call. Not the cops. Not about something like this. His brother was the only one who might be able to help. In his heightened state, the phone seemed to ring ominously as he waited for someone to answer. The silence that followed each ring lasted an eternity. For God's sake let him be in, Bruce thought. His brother's unlisted private line was answered on the third ring.

"Elliott, thank God, you're there."

"You know me, little brother. I'm a workaholic. Where else would I be?"

"I need your help."

The terror in his brother's voice shook Elliott.

"What is it? What's happened?"

"They've taken her. They've taken Judy."

"What are you talking about? Who's taken her? When?"

"I was taking a shower before work, when I got out she was gone. Vanished. No sign."

"Maybe she had to run out. Get the morning newspaper or something."

"At 5:30 in the morning? It's still fucking dark outside. Her car is still here. I checked the house. I even called her cell. Nothing. They must have taken her."

"What are you talking about?"

"I'm in bad trouble. Some men. Russians, I think. I was supposed to deliver something for them, but I don't have it, so they took her. I don't know what they'll do to her."

"Settle down, Bruce. If they did take her, then we can figure out how to get her back. It's just a business deal gone south. It happens. We can figure something out. There's always a deal that can be made. You know that. You may have to pay some restitution, but it will work out. You'll get her back. There's no reason for them to harm her."

"That's right," Bruce stammered, a glimmer of hope in his voice. "That's what I need, someone to figure out the best angle. A negotiator. Somebody who can act as an intermediary for me. Can you help me? Do you still know anyone from the old days you can send?"

Elliot paused.

"I'll send, Frank."

"Frank? Frank Kane? I thought he was dead."

"He was."

"I don't know, Elliot. Frank was an enforcer. *The enforcer.* I don't know if this is something he could handle. It might require some finesse. These are serious guys…."

"I heard Cyrus say once that Frank was the best negotiator the Spartans ever had."

"Really? Cyrus said that? Cyrus was the top guy. He wouldn't have said it if it wasn't true. Would he come?" A distant, muffled noise reached Bruce. "Wait. I hear someone downstairs. It might be Judy. She might be home. Maybe I just panicked. I've been pretty jumpy lately. Listen, I'll call you right back."

"Call me right back."

"Okay."

Bruce hung up and hurried downstairs. His mind was slow at processing the information it was receiving. The noise was wrong for his wife. It was too loud. He knew it wasn't Judy, but he kept moving toward the sound. He was drawn to it like a swimmer to a distant shore. Someone else was in the kitchen. He could hear them going through the refrigerator. Even as his mind sorted this out his feet still drew him relentlessly into the kitchen.

A giant in a bad blue suit leaned against the sink. He was close to three hundred and fifty pounds easy. He wasn't fat. He was just huge. There was a sense of enormous power in his barrel chest and thick legs. His huge arms were crossed over his chest. His face was blank. The heavy dark brows were furrowed as if in annoyance. A second man leaned out from the refrigerator where he was cradling an open carton of milk. He was thin and wore an ill-fitting gray suit with a white knit Polo shirt underneath. His long black hair was oiled and combed straight back. This man smiled. He had small cruel eyes that did nothing to reinforce the smile. He looked like a ferret in a suit. He took a drink of milk. Bruce did not move.

"Good morning, Mr. Burns," the thin man said as he wiped his mouth on his jacket sleeve. "I trust we are not disturbing you with our early morning visit."

"Who are you? What are you doing here?"

"You know who we are, and you know why we are here," the man said. The smile stayed on his face.

"Where is my wife? What have you done with Judy?"

The thin man smiled again. "We have her. She is safe. For now."

Without thinking, Bruce lunged for the man, hoping to grab him and shake the information out of him. Before his fingers reached the thin man, the giant moved. The giant took only a half step, and the punch was small. Yet to Bruce it was like an avalanche. It tore him from his feet and crushed him to the floor. Bruce struggled for air his lungs seemed unable to find. The big man stepped back against the sink and spoke in Russian to the thin man. Bruce understood nothing except the name of the thin man, Dimitri. The giant spoke for a minute. Dimitri nodded. He knelt beside Bruce on the floor.

"We apologize for that. We truly do. It is a crude tool for communication. But these outbursts will not do, Mr. Burns. You must remain calm if you hope to see your wife again. You want your wife back, do you not?"

"Yes," Bruce croaked. He made no attempt to get to his feet.

"Good. We have to make proper arrangements to be sure this occurs."

"Sure. Just let me know what you want."

"The Greek is not happy with you, my friend," Dimitri said and made a clucking noise with his tongue. "You have failed to deliver the contracted merchandise. You have implied to him that you are hesitant to fulfill your obligations in this matter. This will not do."

"No. That's not it at all. He misunderstood me. It just hasn't arrived yet. I was understandably concerned. That's all. You'll get the merchandise. We had a deal. That's how I get paid."

Dimitri seemed to ponder this information. He seemed confused by this response. He had thought there would be denials. He spoke to the giant. Afterward he turned back to Bruce.

"This may be true, Mr. Burns. Have you contacted your driver to determine the reason for his delay?"

"I can't. That's part of the safeguards I use. He can only contact me when he arrives in the U.S. Once he's safely across the border."

"That is unfortunate for you. And your lovely wife."

The giant grasped Bruce by the back of his silk Hermes robe and jerked him to his feet. He did not release him. Bruce could only reach the tile floor with the tips of his slippers.

"Please, I'm doing all I can," Bruce whimpered. "You just have to be patient a little longer. It will get here in a day or two at the latest. I promise. You'll see."

Dimitri smiled. "I hope you are right, Mr. Burns. Time-critical plans have been put into motion. The Greek has instructed us to begin taking out the interest if we are forced to delay much longer."

"Sure. As much as you like."

Dimitri leaned in close. He breath was harsh. He pulled out a long bladed knife from a sheath hidden under his arm. He placed it beneath Bruce's right eye. The polished steel gleamed. Bruce tried to pull away, but the giant held him firmly. Dimitri pressed the tip in just below the surface. Dimitri's hand flashed and a thin pale line appeared down James' flesh. It reddened, and a thin tear of blood crept down his cheek.

"Your wife has beautiful skin, Mr. Burns. It reminds me of fine Russian porcelain. It is so firm and cool. I would hate to have to remove her pretty pink nipples to motivate you."

Bruce struggled. The giant seemed not to notice.

"Please, don't hurt her. Please. She hasn't done anything."

Dimitri slid the knife back into its sheath.

"I hope it will be unnecessary. But I warn you; the Greek is not a patient man. There are schedules that must be kept and, as you Americans say, the clock is ticking. Now go and finish dressing. I would like for you to be on time for the work. Our shipment may be coming today. Many lives depend upon it. Not the least of which are yours and your pretty wife's. And you may wish to put a bandage on that."

The giant released Bruce and he crumpled to the floor. He tried to struggle to his feet. His legs didn't seem to be able to work. They seemed like alien limbs attached to his body. Dimitri smiled and set the milk carton on the black granite countertop. He knelt beside Bruce and helped lift him to his feet with a hand beneath each arm.

"We are not barbaric men, Mr. Burns, but sometimes we are forced to act that way. We understand each other now, do we not?"

"Yes."

"Say it. Say you understand."

"I understand."

"Very good."

The giant barked something in Russian. Dimitri nodded like a trained dog. "We must stop at Starbucks on the way. You have one nearby?"

"Yes. Sure. Lots of them."

"Good. He likes the Starbucks. The very strong, sweet American coffee, it makes him happy," Dimitri smiled and shook his head slightly as if to say such a thing was silly. "You should always try to see that he is happy. He can be very unpleasant if he does not get his coffee in the morning. Once, when we were in Afghanistan…."

The telephone rang. The two Russians stared at it without moving.

"Who would be calling you so early in the morning? Your driver perhaps?"

"No, he knows to call me at the office. He doesn't have this number."

"Then who?"

"I don't know."

The telephone stopped ringing. A few moments later it started again.

"Have you called anyone, Mr. Burns? Told them your wife was missing? That would prove unfortunate."

"No. Who would I call? I just found out she was gone."

"Let us see. Answer it."

Bruce reached for the telephone. It had to be Elliott. He prayed Elliott would play along. He lifted the receiver to the drone of a dial tone.

"Probably a wrong number. One of those robo-calls. I get those all the time." He cradled the telephone.

Dimitri did not seem convinced. "For your sake I hope you are telling us the truth. A meddling friend would be an...inconvenience."

"I told you. I didn't call anyone."

Dimitri smiled. He lifted the receiver and pressed the caller I.D. function. Bruce held his breath. The number came back as blocked. Dimitri hung up.

"Get dressed."

Bruce pulled his silk robe tighter and went back upstairs. He had met Frank Kane only twice, but he scared the hell out of Bruce. Any man who had looked into those cold blue eyes knew he had seen the face of death. He prayed Frank would come. He knew it might already be too late.

2

Frank Kane ran five miles each morning before work and five miles after work. He ran at a comfortable pace in his work clothes. He called this combat running. He knew that when and if he had to run, he would not be dressed in loose shorts and tennis shoes. He would be dressed as he was now in long pants, long-sleeved shirt and work boots. Frank was six feet four inches tall and weighed a tight two hundred and twenty-five pounds. He trained his body every day with a strict regime of push-ups, sit-ups, pull-ups, and squats, using his own mass for resistance. He varied the route of his morning runs because routines could get you killed in the bad old days. Yet he would admit, if pressed, that he liked this route the best.

If he timed it right, he could see her for a minute before work. It was weak and self-indulgent. Frank was neither of these. Yet there was something so beautiful and innocent about her that he did not try to resist this small temptation. Frank moved along the chipped and broken sidewalk without any variation in his stride. He saw her waiting ahead, standing by the bus stop. Her name was Rosa. He did not know her last name.

Frank slowed when he reached her and she smiled a beaming display of white teeth and dimples. She was happy to see him. She was six years old. She stood with her Uncle Carlos. He was very protective and always waited for her at the bus stop. Four or five other children stood nearby talking.

"Good morning, Rosa, Carlos."

Carlos nodded.

"Good morning, Mr. Frank," Rosa said. "I was hoping you would come before I had to go to school."

Frank squatted before her. He looked into her eyes.

"Have you been studying hard in school?"

"I made an A on our spelling test yesterday," she said proudly.

Frank looked up toward Carlos who smiled.

"She is very bright. And she works very hard at school. We are very proud."

"I am going to be a doctor when I grow up," Rosa said confidently.

Frank noticed the weathered face of her grandmother at the nearby window. The old woman never spoke to Frank, but she watched him with Rosa. She was suspicious of all strangers, especially gringos. Overprotective. That wasn't a bad thing in this neighborhood. Frank's parents hadn't worried or cared much about what he did growing up. Frank turned his attention back to little Rosa.

"That is very good. Good grades will open a lot of doors for you. You can be anything you want to be."

"Did you make good grades, Mr. Frank?"

"No. That's why I have to work so hard now. I wish I had studied more when I was your age."

"You could go back to school like Uncle Carlos."

Carlos looked embarrassed. A hint of red blushed his cheeks. "It is nothing. Some night school classes, that is all."

"That's great, man. Good luck," Frank said, and meant it. "I brought Rosa a treat. Do you mind if I give it to her?"

"It is all right."

"What did you bring?"

Frank reached into his cargo pants and pulled out a lollipop and offered it to her. It had a red wrapper. "Always take red. It's the best color."

"Thank you, Mr. Frank. Did you bring any for my friends?"

Frank surveyed the other children who watched him expectantly. Tiny tongues licked tiny lips in anticipation. He liked the way Rosa was always willing to share.

"Have they been studying hard too?"

Rosa nodded vigorously. Frank reached into his pocket again and pulled out a lollipop for each child. He handed them to Rosa to distribute. The other children surged around her for their treats. It was a ritual they did each time he met her at the bus stop. He noticed Carlos smiling.

"Rosa has given you a new nickname."

"What?"

"She calls you Angel con Ojos Azules, Angel with Blue Eyes. She thinks your eyes are very kind and gentle like an angel's. She says they are also pretty like the blue of the ocean."

Frank smiled. He noticed the man across the street. The man had been standing on the corner watching them. The man checked to see there was no traffic and crossed over to where they stood at the school bus stop.

"Yo. Yo. You the candy man?"

Frank turned but did not speak.

The man was Latino. He was dressed in baggy jeans with expensive tennis shoes. He wore a plaid long-sleeved shirt with the top three buttons closed over a blue t-shirt that winked out beneath the buttons. He was all smiles and loose joints. His arm movements were almost like those of a bird flapping its wings. The nostrils on his long nose even flared up like a bird's.

"You got a lollipop for me, candy man?"

"Sorry. All out."

The smile vanished. "Fuck, you say, Paco? Run them pockets out, puta, and show me."

Frank did not move or respond.

The plaid shirt seemed unsure of what to do next. "Don't be givin' me no eye, puta. Santos will straight fuck you up. You know who you dealing with here?"

When Frank didn't answer, the man pulled down the collar of his shirt, revealing a tattoo on his neck. It was a paca. It read MS-13. Frank knew the gang sign. Mara Salvatrucha. Mara meant gang; Salva meant El Salvador where the gang had originated, trucha meant fear us. The number represented the thirteenth letter of the alphabet, M, for the gang's association with the Mexican Mafia. Frank hadn't realized MS-13 had cells in Greensboro. Frank had read that the FBI had formed a special task force to deal with the gang's rising. They had formed a similar task force to take the Spartans down. After showing the tat, the man pulled his collar back up and started nodding as if that answered all questions. For him, it probably did.

"That's right, puta. Baddest del mal. Baddest of the bad. Santos ask you for something you give it up if you know what's what. You come with that attitude," he said as he reached behind his back. He pulled out a 9mm automatic. It was a Glock. He flashed it quickly and then reseated it behind his back beneath his shirt. "I smoke yo punk gringo ass."

Still Frank did not answer. He never understood why people spoke of themselves in the third person. He also found it odd that a South American gang member chose to mimic the speech patterns of black American gangbangers. Another couple of life's mysteries, he thought. He had no doubt he could kill the plaid-shirted Santos before he could redraw his weapon. There was another man dressed in similar clothes standing a little way down the connecting street. A third man sat on the porch in a metal folding chair. Frank knew this man kept a weapon under the towel he kept folded beside him. It was a Tek-9 machine pistol. Frank had watched him secret it there during previous runs. He recognized the distinctive perforated barrel shroud. The assault pistol was easy to convert to full auto and, with a fifty-round clip, it could do a lot of damage. A fourth man worked the crack stash inside the house. Four men. All probably armed. Difficult, but it could be done, if a man was quick enough. And Frank was very quick. But then what? Police? Possible collateral damage to the kids or Carlos. Those days were in the past.

Frank did not answer.

Carlos spoke in rapid Spanish to Santos. Santos hollered back at him in

Spanish and began moving from side to side like a fighter bobbing from one foot to the other. Carlos was not backing down. Santos' eyes seemed to spin in his head. Latin machismo.

Frank remembered Spanish Johnny's favorite saying. Every child of the gun knew that one day he would be a fraction slow. He would duck when he should have rolled. He would zig when he should have zagged. He would miss a shot he had to make. Before a fight when his life was in the balance, knowing that this might be the day he died, Spanish Johnny would say, 'Hoy no ese dia.' Today is not that day.

Frank placed a hand on Carlos' shoulder to calm him. "Hoy no ese dia."

Frank took a lollipop from his pocket and tossed it toward Santos. The man's hands came up in reflex and he caught it. He seemed as surprised as Carlos. Santos started nodding his head to some inner monologue.

"That's right. That's what I'm talking 'bout, hombre. Don't nobody fuck with Santos. MS-13 for life."

Santos unwrapped the lollipop and stuck it into his mouth. The cocky smile returned. He moved back across the street as a car approached and slowed. Morning rush hour for a drug dealer. Santos pulled the lollipop from his mouth and hollered back at them.

"That little girl wants a real lollipop, you tell her to come over across the street. Santos got a big lollipop for her. An all-day sucker." Then he began to cackle at his humor.

Frank could still feel the tenseness in Carlos' shoulder muscles.

"Let it go. It's not worth it."

"Bastards. MS-13." He spat on the ground. "Former soldiers come up here from El Salvador and Colombia, selling their shit out in the open and no one does nothing."

"You try calling the cops?"

"Yes. They don't bother to come. Just took the information. The house over there is abandoned and they deal that poison from there. Something should be done. It is not right."

"The cops did nothing?"

"They don't care about here. Working people don't mean anything to them. If it was Irving Park, or that Starmount, they would be here pretty quick."

"Give it time. This stuff tends to work itself out."

Carlos nodded as the school bus ground to a halt at the stop. Needed to get those brakes worked on, Frank thought. Pads were loose on the front wheels. Rosa and her friends waved to Frank as they climbed on board. He watched her face at the bus window until it pulled away. Blue Eyes. That was sweet. Him and Frank Sinatra were in the same club now. There was something about her innocence that touched him. He would have to figure out a way to encourage the MS-13 gang to relocate. That shouldn't be too hard. Frank turned and continued on his morning run, Rosa's smile bright in his mind. Her grandmother's face was tight against the window behind him. Always watching.

Maybe he was getting soft, Frank thought as he parked his old truck at Elite Motorcycles. There was something about little Rosa that always seemed to lighten his heart. For a brief moment Frank wondered what it would be like to have taken a different path. Gotten a wife, a kid, a couple of good dogs. He had only been in love once, with a girl he barely new.

Her name was Helen. She was beautiful and brave and smart. But that was back in the day, and she had sacrificed their love and herself to keep them both alive. She had given herself to Cyrus, the leader of the Spartans. It was the right move. The smart thing. The only choice they had to survive. It had nearly killed Frank.

Frank dismissed the daydream. No point in regrets or second-guessing. You played the hand you were dealt or in his case dealt yourself. Helen was gone. Had been for a long time. They had probably killed her when everyone went down. He liked to hope she had made it somehow. Figured a way out, like always. Made the smart play. He never tried to find out. The Spartans were gone now. Ancient history. Every door led to a different path. This was where he was now.

Anthony waved as he approached the truck. He was a twenty-year-old Rasta wannabe that worked with Frank at the motorcycle shop. He fumbled absently with a fallen dreadlock. He looked worried.

"What's up, man? Everything ire?"

"No, mon, no cool runnin's here. Elliott be having da break down or sum shit. He wanna see you as soon as you get in. He already call down here tree times to see if you be in yet. He say tell you it be important. Mumbled something about de old times."

Frank nodded. He got out of the truck and went to Elliott's office. Elliott was the owner of Elite Motorcycles. He had started out as a fence and bike repairman for the Spartans motorcycle club. They had protected him as they grew and kept him secret from everyone else except the innermost circle. When the Spartans had been destroyed, Elliott had reinvented himself as a businessman. He formed Elite Motorcycles, a company that sold, built, rebuilt and customized motorcycles for its clients. It quickly made him a rich man. It was becoming so well-known there was talk of franchising the business to other states. He knew Elliott had been looking at opening a store in Pennsylvania. After prison, when Frank had decided on a new path, he had called Elliott and asked for a job. There was only one answer possible, but Elliott was happy to do it. Frank knew bikes.

The office was small, but tastefully decorated. There were a few pictures of renowned riders and famous custom bike builders praising him. There was a large mahogany desk with the required computer and a funky lamp with a motorcycle motif. Frank supposed the lamp was very expensive. Some of the upper-end clients that they worked with probably liked it. Frank thought it was one of the silliest things he had ever seen.

"Thanks for coming, Frank," Elliott said and extended his hand, very formal.

Frank shook it and took a seat in one of the high-backed red leather chairs across from it. He shifted around in the soft leather to find a comfortable spot. Frank had heard a hint of fear in Elliott's voice. That was unusual.

"What can I do for you, Elliott?"

Elliott had known Frank for a long time, so he just told it. Straight through, without comment, leaving nothing out. When he was finished he just stopped talking and waited. Frank sat quietly as he processed the information.

"This the same brother who used to do some side work for the Spartans?"

"Yeah. Bruce handled some logistics on some of our shipping concerns. Specialty items. He came up with the idea of smuggling in dog food trucks. The cops never trusted their dogs' noses around that stuff. And the lawyers had a field day with whatever was found. Fruit from the poisoned tree, I think they called it."

"I remember. Clever fellow. He got us into running cigarettes to New York from North Carolina. That scheme alone made the Spartans hundreds of millions. What's he into now?"

Elliott turned away and stared out the only window in the room.

"I got to tell you, Frank. We aren't as close as we used to be. He was a little younger and wanted to cut his own path. We had some words. Lost touch. You know how it is."

Frank nodded and waited for Elliott to continue.

"Anyway. He was good at import-export, got into the lamp business." Elliott must have seen or suspected that Frank was surprised and hurried to add, "He makes a ton. It's a high markup business or so he used to say. You ever hear of Frederick Cooper? He's a famous designer of lamps. He made that lamp." Elliott pointed toward the motorcycle lamp on his desk. "One of a kind. Each handmade. Bruce sells a ton of his shit."

"So your brother's not in the game anymore?"

"That's what he claims. But I hear things from some of our old contacts. Word is he's doing some gunrunning like he used to do for us. They say he's using the lamp business as a cover."

Frank nodded. "I'll see what I can do?"

Elliott turned and Frank could tell he was struggling to keep his emotions under control. Frank was glad about that. He didn't like emotional outbursts.

"I can't tell you what this means to me."

"Not a problem. I'll go home, get things squared away, and leave today."

"I got you covered with transportation. I'm having a car brought up for you to take."

"Good. Which one? The big Lincoln?"

"No way. The Mercedes. It gives off a better vibe. Makes the cops think twice about hassling you. The VIN and license plate are legitimate; they just don't match the VIN on the engine block. It's fully outfitted. The cradle is underneath, on the driver's side with eight screws, two on each side. I had a guy I trust repack it so everything you need is in there. The glove box combination is 480," Elliott said and paused to see if Frank remembered the significance.

"Thermopylae," Frank said.

It was the famous Spartan last stand against overwhelming Persian forces. They had fought to the last man. The date had been 480 BC. Frank had read somewhere they had figured the exact date to be September 17th, 18th and 19th.

"Exactly. It's the same for the combination on the briefcase. It's welded shut, but the combination triggers the charge if you need to dump the car."

"C-4?"

"Two pounds. Ninety-second delay." He opened the desk and pulled out an envelope. It was packed with cash. "Here's ten grand to help cover expenses."

"This isn't about money, Elliott."

"I know that, Frank. Hell, you probably got more tucked away than Croesus. I figured you might not have time to access it. This is just for expenses. Might need a good hotel room, or supplies. I know how you always hated a paper trail."

He offered the envelope to Frank. Frank tucked it into the front of his cargo pants. He ran a thick finger over the lamp as if trying to discover its hidden value. He looked up at Elliott.

"You surprise me, Elliott. I would never have guessed you would still keep a vehicle and weapons stash from the old days."

"You always told me to expect the worst. I hoped I would never need it. The driver is bringing it over from Tennessee when it's ready, so you got a few hours. I'll have DC drop it off. I know you guys got a history and you trust him."

"I do."

"Look, if there is anything I can do…I mean, he's my only brother…." Elliott paused. Finally, he extended his hand again. "Thanks."

Frank grasped him at the wrist in the old Spartan handshake. "Brothers in arms."

Elliott smiled. "Until death."

3

Frank parked behind his two-story house. It was white with black trim. The yard was neatly mowed and the hedges cut. The driveway had been swept. The large green city garbage can sat empty at the curb. He shared the three-bedroom house with two girls, Jenny and Caron. He had rescued them from some bad business in Atlanta and they had come back with him to Greensboro. They were still in high school and, although both had been awarded the legal status of emancipated adults, Frank served as an ad hoc guardian for the girls. This was their senior year and both were preparing for college. Neither had yet decided where they wanted to attend and seemed in no hurry to make the decision.

Frank wrote a note to the girls explaining that he would be away for a few days on business, and that if they were suicidal they should use this as an excuse to throw a party. He knew they wouldn't, but thought they might like the idea of Frank worrying about them. Teenage girls were a complete mystery to Frank. He reminded them to call DC if they had any problems.

He packed a couple of changes of clothes; pullover shirts and khakis as well as a pair of light tan colored Oakley boots. He normally wore Timberlands, but lately he had tried the Oakley boots on a whim. It was supposedly the same boot worn by Special Forces teams in Iraq. It was tough but very comfortable. Plus, the Timberlands were becoming too much of a fashion statement with kids two decades younger than Frank. If he was anything, Frank was anti-fashion. He packed four red nylon t-shirts. The ancient Spartans always wore red battle cloaks. This was as close as he could come. He got out a nice suit bag and put a navy blazer inside. He also grabbed a couple of dark dress shirts. Frank changed into a lightweight silk Armani suit. It was black with a thin red chalk line. Armani was usually cut close to accentuate broad shoulders and narrow hips, but this one was a little big to help hide Frank's build. He even slipped on a good pair of conservative black wingtip shoes. You couldn't drive a hundred and ten thousand dollar car dressed like a deadbeat. It just begged a highway patrolman to stop you and check you out.

He tossed in his toilet case and razor and added an electric screwdriver. Better safe than sorry and it could come in handy. He slipped a small lock pick kit into the bag. He never traveled without one. He also packed the usual universal repair kit of duct tape, superglue, WD-40 and a clothesline. Finally, he added a small but powerful LED flashlight made by Surefire.

Frank knew he had to do something to disguise himself. It was an old habit. You always prepared for the worst scenario. He removed a board from beneath the vanity in his private bathroom. He took out a contact lens case. It contained a pair of small prescriptionless contact lenses. They were tinted to change the color of his blue eyes to a pale, almost milky color. He placed one in his left eye. It made the eye look dead without affecting his vision. He pocketed its mate. He found a tube of hair gel. An old friend of his had worked in Hollywood doing makeup and she had taught him a few tricks. He wore his hair cut very short, but this gel would give it a light gray tint. He worked it in for two minutes and washed the excess out. It was a subtle change, but it added ten years to his face. The tint would last three or four days depending on how well he washed his hair.

He used a special blend of FX glue to create a small hairline scar just above and beneath the left eye. The glue held the skin pinched together so it created the impression of a scar. He used a razor blade to cut a small path through his left eyebrow that connected the scar. The scar and blind eye ensured that whoever he met would notice them, but would probably be too polite to stare. The final touch was a pair of thick black-rimmed glasses hung from his neck on a thin keeper. The lenses were clear, but Frank thought they softened his face and gave him a slightly scholarly look.

He opened a small box. There were several rings inside. He removed a gold wedding band he had bought at a pawnshop. It was dented a little like a real ring should be. It looked like it had a history. He slipped it on his ring finger on his left hand. The ancient Greeks called gold the skin of the gods because it never tarnished. Frank smiled at the memory. Inside was an inscription that said simply, Honor. He liked that. It was a good omen.

Someone making the money to afford a Mercedes and wearing a nice suit would have gone the whole nine yards. He would have a wife tucked away back home. Frank looked at his big rough hands thick with calluses. They didn't look like the hands of an executive. They looked like what they were, the hands of a laborer. There wasn't anything he could do about that.

Frank closed the secret compartment under the sink and repacked the items that sat upon it. He took one of the dark hand towels and walked into the spare bedroom. It was his reading room. There was an old fireplace along one wall. There was a small woodbox filled with kindling and three medium-size logs off to one side. The hearth was covered with a metal fire screen. He moved it to one side. Inside the fireplace was a black iron grate filled with black ash and partially burnt logs. He slid the fire grate over to one side. Frank took out his knife. He pried up a section of bricks beneath it. Inside was a metal fireproof box.

He took it out and lifted the top. The lock wasn't used. If someone found the box, then they could pick the simple lock anyway. Inside were half a dozen identical packets. Frank chose one and slipped the rubber band off. He opened the packet and examined the contents. There was a current passport, driver's license and credit card in the name of Frank Nomin. There was also a silver card-holder with embossed business cards, which identified him as Vice President of Acquisitions, whatever that was, for Aegis Corporation, whoever they were, and a fake telephone number. Frank put the passport back inside and closed the box. He repositioned it in the hidden recess and then replaced the fire grate. He spread ashes back to conceal the false bottom. He used a small broom to sweep away the evidence that the ashes had been disturbed. He replaced the fire screen and wiped his hands on the towel.

Frank had an attorney, Evan Hamric. They had worked together for years. Hamric renewed the cards and passports when necessary. Frank had helped him out of a jam when the Spartans were still riding tall. The attorney had agreed to help handle certain legal and business matters in return. They corresponded now only through a company that ran a drop box service, and by secure telephone. Frank only trusted him so far. After all, he was an attorney. Frank didn't want anyone knowing where he lived. The home addresses on each packet were different. None were real. They all led away from North Carolina to blind locations that had no connection to him.

Frank knew he was too memorable to be completely invisible. He also knew that most straight people were predictable. They didn't pay attention. They didn't need to. When someone described him, he would be reduced to a set of easy-to-remember features. He would be the big geeky guy, about fifty, blind in one eye, with a scar and glasses, all features that could be changed in a short time. If someone was very observant, they might notice the wedding band. Frank didn't plan to need a disguise, but he wasn't sure what he was walking into.

It could be nothing. It could be bad. Elliott knew that. That was why he hadn't suggested a flight. Frank's credentials were good, but it could be dangerous. Airports kept detailed records of travelers. They had armed security patrolling the concourses. They had security checks. They were blanketed with security cameras. There was no safe way to bring in what Frank would need on a commercial airplane. He liked that Elliott hadn't even suggested it. Time might be important, but going in unarmed was suicide. You had to mind the details. In the bad old days, the red days of riding with the Spartans, it was Frank's attention to details that had kept him alive. He went to wash his hands a final time.

He took his knife out of his pocket. It was a distinctive blade made in Japan by a master knifesmith. Japanese letters spelled out 'Death Before Dishonor' on one side. It was very light and ruthlessly sharp. The blade was made from a composite that was reportedly ten times sharper than steel. Some very enterprising Fed might be able to trace it back to Frank if it went missing in Texas. He placed it in the medicine cabinet.

His preparations complete, he settled into his reading chair and turned on the lamp. It wasn't a designer lamp. He had picked it up at Target for twelve bucks. It worked fine for him. He had started re-reading Herodotus' History of the Persian-Greek war. Herodotus was not, by strict standards, the most objective historian. Frank liked him because, as a Greek, his bias was apparent from the first chapters. Frank found the chapter where he picked up to be a good omen. Herodotus described a battle with Argos in the early days of Sparta.

The Argives and Spartans had met on the battlefield outside Thyrea. Each army consisted of three thousand warriors. In a rare nod to prudence, they had both agreed to send three hundred hoplite warriors to determine the battle. Each army agreed to accept the outcome and withdrew out of sight of the battlefield to deter any temptation to join the battle if their side was losing. The battle was evenly matched and raged throughout the day. At dusk, only one Spartan, a man called Othryadas, and two Argives still survived. The Spartan was wounded and his spear was shattered. His shield was lost and his Lakonia was notched from the hard fighting. The Argives assumed that their numbers would guarantee them a victory so, not wishing to risk the potential for any further injuries, they withdrew to the main body of their army to report their victory. The last Spartan found himself alone. Since his enemies had quit the field of battle, Othryadas considered himself the victor. He built a small shrine to the god Apollo in honor of the victory. He stripped the armor from the fallen Argives as was the custom after victory and rejoined his army.

The next day both armies returned to the battlefield and claimed victory. They disputed each other's claim. Words fell to blows and they refought the battle with their entire armies. The Spartans slaughtered the hoplite warriors from Argos to the man. It was because of that victory that the Spartans, who had previously worn their hair short, made a law to wear it long for as long as they ruled Thyrea. The warriors of Argos likewise cut their long hair short and promised never to grow it long until they reclaimed their lands. They never did.

The blaring car horn pulled Frank from his book. DC was outside. Time to go. He closed the book and placed it on the reading chair.

DC stood beside the car beaming like a kid on Christmas morning. The Mercedes 550E glistened in four thousand pounds of black armor. Frank had never seen a black that was at once so dark and yet seemed so brilliant. Her black was as dark and lustrous as polished onyx. It drew the eye as naturally as a beautiful sunset did.

The Mercedes had been a new addition just before things started to fall apart for the Spartans. Frank had never driven the car, but he knew her. He knew that big engine. She was a seven speed automatic and carried a V-8 with 400 horsepower. She could reach sixty miles per hour in just under five and a half seconds. Even with all this raw power she looked sleek and elegant.

"I got her filled up and ready to go," DC said.

"Thanks."

"Elliott wanted me to tell you about some minor modifications he had made. It's now all-wheel drive instead of just front. He goosed the engine for more power because of the added weight."

Frank nodded as he approached the car. DC reached in and popped the trunk for him. Frank placed his suit bag and small suitcase inside. There was a three-gallon empty plastic gas container. He noticed the silver attaché case resting to one side. The C-4. A thick hidden strip of Velcro secured it to the carpet in the trunk. He opened the rear door and laid his suit coat out across the back seat before moving around to the front door. The inside was all cream colored leather and burled walnut wood trim.

"The car is a super smooth ride. It has all the bells and whistles you would expect. Ten-way power front seats, ABS, digital sound system, sunroof, front seats that circulate air to keep you cooler, a command center steering wheel..."

"What's that?"

"You know. You can control a bunch of shit from the steering wheel, wipers, radio stations, volume, cruise, that stuff."

"Command center?"

"I made that name up. Just thought it sounded cool."

Frank smiled. "It does, DC. Has she got a GPS?"

"No. That was one of the modifications. Elliott had it taken out. He said you're a stickler for keeping your trail clean."

"What's that got to do with using a GPS to find where you are going?"

"You can back trace on it. Everyone knows that. GPS tells where you want to go but also where you've been and where you're coming from. You might be able to trick it by not programming your destination until you got out of Greensboro. The GPS would just pick you up on the road, not where you started from. Which brings me to one of the modifications. Elliott installed a locator chip in the car, sort of a mini GPS."

He handed Frank a controller. It was about the size of a garage door opener with a small two-inch wide screen.

"This is your backup. A contingency. Keep it with you all the time. If you get separated from the car for any reason, you can track it with this. Just press this button to turn it on and the car's position shows up on the screen. Just scroll to follow the map on the screen and you can get back to your car, no problem. This is also a keyless remote to start the car. Press the green button and it will work just like the original key." He handed it to Frank.

Frank pocketed it. "That's a good thing to have. Anything else?"

"The driver's side door is reinforced with thin Kevlar strips. If someone takes a pop at you in the car, that's where they'll shoot."

Frank nodded. It made sense. "Does it affect the handling?"

"A little. Mostly on braking. Takes a tiny bit longer. She also pulls a little to the left."

Frank noticed the file folder on the passenger's seat. "What's that? Reading material for me?"

"Yeah. I got a file put together on everything I could think of. It's got information on Elliott's brother, Bruce. Home address. Business address. Telephone numbers. There's a computer-generated map to get you to Fort Worth by the fastest route. It's broken down into miles and time. There's a city map of Fort Worth and a Texas tour book that I picked up from AAA on the way over. I figured you could use them."

Frank eased into the seat and adjusted it for his size. He had a lot of driving to do and needed as much comfort as he could get. The lumbar support might seem frivolous to some, but on this trip it would be critical. He strapped his seat belt into place. "Look after the girls while I'm gone. I'll be back as quick as I can."

"You can count on me."

"I know."

"One more thing. Under the file."

Frank lifted the file up. There were three CDs resting in thin Mylar wraps. One was labeled "I", a second one "P", and the other "M".

"While I waited for the car, I burned you a couple of CDs. The one labeled 'I' is mostly instrumental and classical shit. Beethoven, Mozart, Bach the stuff guys who drive a Mercedes listen to. Might need it for your cover. The one labeled 'P' is punk and the one labeled 'M' is metal stuff. They are both hard-core in case you need to get jacked up for something. Its got Soil, Five Finger Death Punch, Black Flag, Unearth, Dope, Drowning Pool, and to top it off a cut from Amon Amarth. Way cool shit."

"What, no Pennywise or Blood Simple?"

"Dude. I am impressed. They're there. They're both represented. That's good shit. You surprise me. You know your stuff."

"I am a man of many surprises."

"Dude. If you say so. Look after yourself, Frank. I got your back here."

"I will. You have my private cell number if there is an emergency."

DC nodded. Frank's cell phone was registered under DC's name. In turn, he paid both his and DC's bill. It also gave him a look into whom DC might be contacting.

Frank glanced at the clock in the dashboard. It was time to go. Elliott had asked him to go because he knew there was no one better than Frank Kane. Frank could accomplish what other men couldn't because the laws of a civilized society did not encumber him. He would do whatever was necessary and may the gods help anyone who stood in his way. A part of him, the old part, was looking forward to the trip. His demons murmured and whimpered at the red thoughts. They wanted to be free again. They shook their bars and rattled their chains in anticipation. They missed the sounds of gunfire; the smell of blood; the feel of bodies broken; the sight of his enemies destroyed. His mind flashed to the name once more. Bruce Burns. He had met a man long ago in prison with the same name except he called himself only Burns. He said most his friends on the outside called him Fire Starter because he got things started.

Frank slipped the CD labeled "M" into the disc player. Chrome Division warned their listeners about a Raven Black Cadillac with the Reaper at the wheel. It was bad ass rock and roll. It was also another good omen. He backed the car out of the driveway and headed toward I-85.

4

Frank estimated it would take something like eighteen hours to drive to Fort Worth from Greensboro. Even in a slick ride like the Mercedes, he knew it would be physically and mentally challenging. He was going into an unknown situation against an unknown number of enemies. He had done it many times for the Spartans. Still, it would have been nice to have some backup. Someone he could trust. Of course, his judgment on that subject was not infallible. He had trusted Spanish Johnny for a decade. They had even saved each other's lives a time or two. That changed when Frank met Helen. Spanish Johnny had wanted her killed. Frank refused. It was a line in the sand. She became a wound between them that never healed. Frank lost Helen and forgave Spanish Johnny's treachery. The years crept on and Frank assumed they were past their conflict. It was an assumption that nearly got him killed when Spanish Johnny had plunged a knife into him. Fuck that shit, he thought. It was over. Water under the bridge. Spanish Johnny was dead. Frank had killed him.

Frank knew if he had a choice he would have brought Apollo. Apollo was not physically imposing at less than six feet and one hundred and sixty pounds, but he was one of the toughest men Frank had never known. Apollo claimed to be a former Navy SEAL. A specialist. A sniper. He had been one of the founding members of the Spartans and Frank's closest friend and mentor. Frank smiled at the memory of all the things he had learned from Apollo. It wasn't just the obvious things like weaponry and hand-to-hand combat and military tactics. Apollo had taught him the importance of logistics, offshore banking, how to establish false identifications, and about the critical importance of exit strategies.

After Helen had left him, Frank had spent a great deal of time at Apollo's compound on the Western coast of Costa Rica near the small town of Nosara. The compound consisted of eighty acres on an isolated stretch of the Nicoya peninsula. A simple chain link fence circled the outer boundary of the property. A small security building occupied by an unarmed local secured the single, long winding gravel driveway that led to the sprawling home. The house was six thousand feet of stone and stucco and native wood fronted by an elaborate swimming pool. It had been constructed from local materials as a way to help funnel money back into the local community. Staying on good terms with the locals was the first step to good security. There was a huge garage that housed a Range Rover, a couple of quad bikes, a John Deere Gator for lawn care, a truck, and a late model Suburban for the staff to use. A short gravel drive off the main driveway led to the beach. There was a boathouse, which contained three jet skis and a twenty-four foot Grady White sport fisher.

Apollo kept a permanent staff of five at all times. The staff consisted of all young females, except for the cook who was in her fifties. They all rotated duties, taking turns at maintaining the inside and outside of his estate. Apart from the old cook, the staff all happened to be very attractive young Ticas.

Frank remembered his last trip to visit Apollo at his compound. They had been sitting in white wicker rocking chairs on his huge balcony drinking Flora de Cana, the flower of the sugar cane, a premium Nicaraguan rum. Apollo was only wearing a pair of thin brown linen pants. His black skin glistened with a fine sheen of sweat. He bore a number of tattoos on his body.

Above his heart was a Navy SEAL tattoo. It showed an eagle reaching around an anchor and clutching an old flintlock pistol in its left talons and a trident in its right talons. The insignia showed that the SEALs were part of the Navy and fought on land and sea. The cocked weapon and trident showed they were always ready for battle.

In an arch-shaped tattoo across his stomach was the simple word, Spartans. It identified Apollo as a first citizen in the motorcycle club. The Hells Angels motorcycle club numbered about six thousand members worldwide. The Outlaws, Bandidos, and Mongols only numbered about a thousand members each. The Warlocks topped out at about five hundred members worldwide. In contrast, at its largest the Spartans numbered more than two hundred thousand members. However, only three hundred were granted the distinction of becoming a first citizen.

On his right forearm was a ritual scar in the shape of a lambda, the Greek letter L. Frank could not see it, but he knew that Apollo also had a brand on his left shoulder of the Greek letter Ά, alpha. This ritual scarring was a special privilege enjoyed by only the founding members of the Spartans. Cyrus, their leader, had given each founding member of the Spartans the name of a Greek god. Cyrus had said it was because they were not mortal men any longer. The alpha on Apollo's shoulder represented the Ά of the Greek god Apollo. By coincidence, his birth certificate identified him at birth by the same name.

Frank bore the exact same tattoo and ritual scars. However, on his left shoulder was the Greek symbol Π, Pi, for the letter P. P was for the Greek god Poseidon. Poseidon was the younger brother to the God Zeus. He was the god of the sea and often called the earth shaker. The god Poseidon was described by the poet Homer as a moody and vengeful god. Frank was aware of the similarities.

A ceiling fan turned the thick, warm air above them. Frank swirled the smoky amber liquid in his glass, lost in his thoughts. The ice clinked. He felt restless. Somewhere out in the darkness the howler monkeys began screeching. The peacocks sounded the alarm. Everything alarmed peacocks. Alexander the Great had taken the Egyptian trick of using them as watchdogs. Apollo copied his lead. Frank had tried repeatedly to sneak out at night without alerting them. He had never succeeded.

"You have any trouble coming down?" Apollo asked.

"No. It was smooth. Flew directly into Liberia with Phil Bullington. The kid is young, but he's a damn good pilot. I took a van from there."

"He still a coke head?"

"I think so, or he's got chronic allergies. Only way to explain the runny nose and bloodshot eyes."

Apollo laughed.

"Claudia set it up for you?"

"Yeah. Just like usual. She is something else."

Apollo sat for a while, then added, "She is an amazing lady. She has the largest brown eyes I have ever seen. Look right into your heart. I think everybody who met her fell in love with her a little."

"True."

"But not you."

"Not me."

"You were above that shit, right? All business. Not taking a little somethin' somethin' on the side."

"Nope."

"Probably why Claudia fell in love with you."

"Probably. She was a gem. The Spartans were lucky to find someone with her unique set of talents."

"Glad you didn't have to whore her out."

"Me too. It would have been a waste. We had a lot of whores. Not many women can run a business like she can."

Minutes crept past without another word. Apollo toyed with his Navy SEAL signet ring that he always wore. Finally Frank spoke.

"Why so quiet, Apollo?"

"Just thinking. We've had a pretty good run, haven't we?"

"Absolutely. Some great years. More ahead. I don't see anything that can stand before us."

"I don't know, Frank. I got a bad feeling. Like something bad is coming."

"You're starting to sound like an old woman. Something bad is always coming for men like us."

"You remember the story about Croesus, the King of Lydia."

"Remind me."

"Richest man in the world. The most powerful. He asked a visiting wise man who was the happiest man in the world, assuming the wise man would name him. The wise man named someone else and Croesus got mad. The wise man said all things change. The gods were fickle. Those who were mighty fell. He told Croesus to wait and reexamine his life at the end to see how happy he was."

"And bad things happened to him?"

Apollo smiled. "Predictably, he lost his kingdom, his family, his wealth and was taken prisoner. He became a slave to the Persians."

Frank thought a moment. He was an amateur historian. He knew the story well.

"I think you're leaving out the most important part of that tale."

"What part, brother?"

"As I remember, King Croesus was placed on a pyre to be burned alive by the Persians. He railed against the gods for abandoning him. Apollo sent a storm and quenched the flames. He told the fallen king that his fate had been written long ago, but because he was such a devoted supplicant they had granted him extra years of prosperity although even they could not alter fate."

"Your point, Frank?"

"Enjoy the time you have. None of us live forever. Men like us don't get to retire to a quiet life, even in Cost Rica. We have cheated fate for a long time. Some day we will have to pay. It won't be pretty."

"I don't know if that's the best point for the story."

"All right. How about, trust in Apollo if you want to live. And keep your guns loaded."

Apollo laughed. "I like that better. A little dark, but to the point enough."

A dark haired Tica girl arrived with a silver platter covered with a handful of cigars and cigar paraphernalia. Frank took one and breathed in its rich aroma. The band looked odd, but said it was a Cohiba. Cohiba was the best-known and most counterfeited brand in the world. Frank used the silver tip cutter to remove a small portion from the back tip of the cigar, than passed it to Apollo. He took the silver lighter from the tray. It had the Greek letter alpha engraved across its face. He lit the tip, rolling it in the flame, and inhaled the rich smoke. Apollo did likewise. The two men sat for a few minutes in silence, the ash lengthening on their cigars. The fine tobacco of the hand-rolled cigars burned slow and evenly.

"This has to be the real deal," Frank said. "It smokes so smoothly. Got to be Cuban."

"Better than that. These are Fidel's own private stock."

"I thought Castro smoked the super big ones like Bill Cosby. I think I saw it in a picture one time."

"Those are called Churchills. They're seven inches long, a good two inches longer than these. These are called Coronas. Fidel told me personally that he preferred the Corona size."

Frank gave Apollo a skeptical look. "You met Castro?"

"Absolutely."

"I thought he gave up smoking a long time ago. For his health."

Apollo took another deep draw from his Cohiba and blew a cloud above his head. The fan swirled it away.

"He did. Do you know the story of the Cohiba?"

"No, I don't think I do."

"The legend is that Fidel saw one of his bodyguards smoking a wonderfully aromatic cigar. The man told Fidel that a friend of his made them. One thing led to another and sometime in the early '60s they built a factory, the El Lago, in Havana. This man was put in charge. The cigars were hand rolled from the finest mixture of leaves to achieve the perfect taste and burn. It's still one of Cuba's largest exports."

"So these are real Cohibas from Cuba?"

"Patience, Poseidon. Eventually, the man became dissatisfied and left the company. I think the cigar master became a farmer or something. Anyway, he continued making cigars on his own. Fidel was always granted the finest of the fine. These were the most perfect leaves for a special blend that only Fidel was allowed to smoke. A very small stock of special cigars was created just for him. These are also hand-rolled just like the originals. The band is distinctive too. Normally, it's black block lettering on a white field. As you probably noticed, these are black on a gray field. Almost black on black. They are never sold and their existence is even denied."

"And these are from that special reserve?"

"You catch on fast."

"How did an old pirate like you get your hands on them?"

"I was waiting for you to ask. It is the most logical next question, but not the most important. A year or so ago I was asked to do a favor for Raul Castro. A distant relative, an expatriate, was causing him some trouble. I made the man disappear. It was beautifully done, if I may be so bold. He disappeared off his yacht while fishing with his young mistress and some friends. They assumed he fell overboard. In payment I asked for two things. The first was a lifetime supply of these cigars which Raul was only too happy to give."

"And the second?"

"That's what I wanted to talk with you about, Frank. It's why I asked you to come see me. You remember what I said about exit strategies? About before you get into something figure out how you would get out?"

"I remember. That's why you got this place in Costa Rica. No extradition treaty with the U.S."

"Exactly. When we formed the Spartans and the money started coming in, I started building my escape clause. Criminals are like the Special Forces in the military. Once you're in they don't like to let you out. It's easier to lose a man in battle than let him retire."

"I paid attention, like you taught me. If I need to get out, I can. Maybe I'll come down to CR and crash with you."

Apollo laughed. "You would be welcome, my friend. That was why I asked for the second part of my payment."

Apollo signaled to the girl standing off to their right. She hurried forward with a manila envelope and handed it to Apollo. He opened the flap and reached inside.

"Listen, Frank, you can never be too careful. Always have a fallback option if you can. That's what I got for us."

He handed the contents to Frank. There was a diplomatic passport and another document identifying Frank as a special assistant envoy for the nation of Cuba. The picture was recent.

"This is your get out of jail free card. If the shit hits the fan you can get out to Cuba. It's a legal sanctuary. You have full diplomatic immunity. The Feds can't touch you. There is no expiration stamp on the passport. It's good for life. It was a bitch to set up, but it's done. I got one too."

"Who else knows about this?"

"No one. I only got the two. The Spartans don't know about my side work for Raul."

"Not even Cyrus?"

"No one. Don't let them know. All men are suspicious and covetous. You can't trust them. Any of them. Remember that."

"I will. And thank you for this."

"Don't get all sniffly on me. You would have done the same thing for me."

"Are you going to tell me how you made the man disappear in the middle of the ocean?"

"Sometime. Maybe. The key to betrayal is always a woman. Remember that advice. Now finish up that cigar, the girls are waiting for us inside. Little Cleo has been eyeing you all night. You must be the kind of man she likes."

"What kind is that?"

"Big and ugly, I'd say."

Frank toasted him with the glass of rum and followed it with a deep draw on the cigar. Apollo called out something in Spanish and was rewarded with the musical sound of the girls' laughter. Apollo laughed too. Maybe, Frank thought, Apollo had been wrong. Had misread the omens. Accepted the dark signs too easily. Given in to his own melancholy without check. Here, thousands of miles from the United States, surrounded by the lush jungles of Costa Rica with Apollo, Frank felt at peace. He was safe here. What could touch them?

The squeal of tires snapped him out of his daydream. A red Nissan Pathfinder swerved in front of him and accelerated. Frank saw that the "a" in the word Pathfinder had been replaced with a Greek lambda. It was a similar shape to a capital "A" without the crossbar. Some marketing nerd probably thought it looked cool even though it really meant "L". Frank smiled to himself. Still, it was a good omen. And on top of that the SUV was red. It seemed obvious. He took it to mean that he was following the right path for a Spartan. He glanced at the clock. He had been driving for six hours. It was a good time to refuel and push on.

5

FBI Special Agent Richard Redding was eating a turkey sandwich at a nondescript desk, in a nondescript office, in a nondescript building on an unremarkable street. The sandwich was nothing special either, only turkey and lettuce and a little mayo. It didn't even have a nice slice of ripe tomato to jazz up the flavor a little. Redding washed each dry bite down with a sip of bottled water. Not exactly the kind of life he had envisioned when he first joined the Bureau. He picked up the approach of the other agent in the periphery of his vision. He turned when the other man reached his desk.

"Special Agent Redding?"

"I'm on my lunch break."

"I'm sorry to bother you, sir. I was told to report immediately."

Redding looked him over. He was a poster boy for the FBI. He was young. He was six feet tall, trim, with that fresh-scrubbed wholesomeness the Bureau loved. His suit was appropriately dark blue, with a white shirt and conservative red striped tie. The black hair was thick, but neatly trimmed. There was a small American flag pinned to the left lapel. He looked like any of a thousand other new recruits.

"You just graduate from the Academy?"

"Yes, sir."

"You a Mormon?"

"I don't see what bearing that has on…"

"Just answer the question."

"Yes, sir, I am."

It figured. The Bureau seemed to have a hard-on for Mormons. They had that wholesome, farm-bred, all-American, small-town, strict value system that turned out the best agents. They embodied the FBI motto, Fidelity, Bravery, Integrity. It was a "dignified" abbreviation. Easy to remember. A perfect spoonful of crap for the American people. Everything by the rule book. Well, the newbie would learn soon enough the damn manual didn't have all the damn answers in the real world. Redding pasted on his most fatherly smile.

"What can I do for you?"

"I'm Special Agent Edward Harris. I was told to report to you."

"Why?"

"Why, sir?"

"Yeah, why? Why were you told to report to me? No one told me anything about a newbie. What am I supposed to do with you?"

"It's the Spartans, sir."

"What about the Spartans? They're old news. We busted them up half a dozen years ago."

"Didn't you get the memo from the Director? There's some concern that the Spartans are trying to rebuild."

"I got it. It's pure bullshit."

"I was told you were the authority on the Spartans for the Bureau. You were the Agent in Charge of the original task force. The Director wants you…I mean us to see if there's any truth to the rumors."

"What rumors exactly? And who's saying them?"

"Low-level informants are my understanding, sir. Street-level chatter. The usual suspects."

Redding leaned back in his chair, a genuine smile covering his face.

"So the rats think the lions are coming back to the jungle. What are they saying?"

"The talk's that Frank Kane is back. Tying up loose ends, taking care of those that betrayed the Spartans. Our boys in the Atlanta bureau say they think he's tied to an outlaw biker club that got wiped out there."

"One percenters?"

"Sir?"

Redding shook his head and sighed. Rookies didn't know shit.

"Never mind. They got any evidence?"

"No. Only circumstantial. The hit was professional. Whoever did it sterilized the site. That's one of the reasons they think it was Frank Kane."

"And the other?'

"The other?"

"The other reason. You said one of the reasons. I assume there is at least one more reason."

"Two actually. Kane was apparently seen in the area by members of the Jokers motorcycle club. Now no one seems to know anything more."

"Simple enough. We'll interview the Jokers and get to the bottom of this."

"Can't, sir. That's the other reason. The Jokers are all dead or in hiding."

Redding's mind sorted through his vast knowledge of the Spartans. He didn't speak, but reached to his unread memos in their tray. He found the one about the Spartans and read it quickly. Harris stood rigidly before his desk. Redding took a final bite of the turkey sandwich and tossed the rest of it into the wastebasket under his desk.

"You any good with computers, Harris?"

"Yes, sir."

"We aren't in the Army, Harris. Call me Redding, everybody does."

"Everybody at the Academy called me..."

"I don't care what they called you. Let's just stick with Harris if you don't mind. Now log in and pull up everything we have on Frank Kane. He did some time after the Spartans came apart. See where he is now."

Harris came around to the computer on Redding's desk and began working the keys. Redding slipped his coat on. He opened the top drawer where he kept his pistol. The Glock 23 in 40 caliber was a damn fine weapon. It had the same envelope as the Glock 19, just harder hitting. But at thirty-one ounces it was too damn heavy to wear all the time. He secured it in his belt holster. He wore two spare magazines on the other side of his belt.

"What you got, Harris?"

"Nothing, sir. I mean Redding. There's nothing in the system."

"What are you talking about? He's there. You just aren't looking for it right."

"It's not there. I accessed the records and his are gone. They've been deleted."

Redding moved Harris aside and started punching keys. He got the same result. He tried a different heading. Nothing.

"This is weird. He was the Spartans' chief enforcer. He had a sheet a mile long. We had a file on him six inches thick. It's all supposed to have been transferred when the system was updated last year."

"Maybe it hasn't been updated."

A strange look came over Redding's face and he started typing again.

"Fuck."

"What?"

"There was another hitter for the Spartans. Redneck named Robert Ziglar his file is gone too. We almost put him away once for murder. There was another big time enforcer they used. Jake something. I can't remember. They called him The Jake. He was a killing machine. They said he was a true boatman. Oh, shit." He continued typing. A look of something close to fear showed in Redding's face. "They're all gone. Somebody has wiped their files clean."

"Who?"

"Cyrus, Helen, Spanish Johnny, Ares, Apollo, Helios, all their top guys are gone. This is bad. This is real bad. You got to have some strong juice to pull this off. Call the I.T. guys, see if there's any backup of the files. There's always multiple backups, right?"

Harris started dialing.

"And see if they can trace how this was done. If the Spartans still have a high-evel mole in the Bureau, maybe we can track him."

Redding kept working the computer. He shook his head. How could this happen? There were still hard copy originals. There had to be hard copies. The Bureau was meticulous with its record keeping. They wouldn't commit totally to computer data.

"Harris, get the originals copied and couriered over from Archives. We have to have those complete files."

"I'm on it."

Redding stood with his hands on his hips. He had one ace in the hole. He had a C.I., a confidential informant, who would know. The man had been one of the founders of the Spartans, but he had a weakness that would have gotten him killed. Redding had used it to turn him. Redding had gotten valuable intel and in turn protected him. If the Spartans were coming back, he would know.

Harris hung up the phone.

"They're checking."

"Let's go."

"Where to?"

"I got someone we need to see."

"We need to log our destination."

"No, this is off the radar. I can't risk my C.I. being compromised."

"Is this an undocumented C.I.?"

"No. Just top classified. The Director and the U.S. Attorney General know who he is. Nobody else."

"Didn't the Attorney General die of a stroke last year?"

"Yeah. The circle of knowledge got a little smaller with his passing."

"No hint of foul play?"

"None. But you never know. These are serious cats we are dealing with."

They hurried to the elevator. Redding punched the button and they stood waiting for the car to arrive. Redding turned to Harris.

"This is a good assignment for a rookie," Redding said.

"Thank you. I was tops in my class at Quantico."

"Not good enough."

Harris actually blushed. "My dad is a U.S. Senator."

"Senator Harris from Ohio? The same Senator Harris who oversees the committee that controls all funding for Homeland Security?"

"Yes, sir. I am afraid so."

Redding smiled. "Nothing to be embarrassed about, Harris. My dad's a Democrat."

The elevator chimed its arrival.

"You want me to drive?" Harris asked.

"Fuck no."

6

She couldn't help but notice the two strange cars in the driveway. One was a new BMW sedan and the other a new BMW SUV, both a soulless black. She opened the garage door and parked her silver Lexus inside. She got her Prada tennis bag from the back seat, patted her face with the white cotton towel and steeled herself.

She unlocked the door and went inside on long muscular legs accentuated by the very short white tennis dress.

Three men were seated around the central dining room table. Two other men stood off to the side watching. The men sat up straighter. They smiled as she entered. She had that effect on men.

"Did you have a nice game, Helen?"

"It was fine."

"Did you win?"

"It wasn't about winning, Cyrus. It was about getting some exercise. Seeing my girlfriends."

"It is always about winning," Cyrus said.

Helen smiled her perfect intoxicating smile. "Of course I won, darling. I never lose. You know that."

"Good. That's one of the many things I love about you."

Helen went to the refrigerator and got out a glass bottle of Perrier. "I see you have business. I'll just grab a shower and leave you boys to your schemes."

The newcomer, the one with his sunglasses still on, smiled. He was very handsome but wore those damn sunglasses. Still, it was a charming smile itself. It was a smile full of swagger and sex appeal. It was nearly as irresistible as her smile, but not quite. He nodded his head in her direction. His desire for her was almost palpable. She ignored it, nodded back, and turned from the room. She knew what they were talking about, Frank Kane. It was the only thing that would have brought the others to her home. It was the only thing they all feared.

Upstairs, she threw her tennis bag on the bed. She went to the master bathroom. It was larger than some homes she had lived in. She turned on the shower and let it warm up. The shower had two separate nozzles. She undressed and stepped beneath the hot water. She let the water soothe her muscles as it washed the sweat of the tennis match away. Helen stayed under the water for a long time. Her mind was empty. She finished showering and stepped out. She lifted a thick towel made from Peruvian cotton from the heated towel rack and patted her body dry. She wrapped the towel around her long blonde hair. She started to get a second towel, but stopped before the mirror. She wiped the fog from the mirror with a well-manicured hand. She admired herself.

She had aged well. Her body was still trim and firm. Frank had told her that was what separated Spartan women from the other women of Greece. Spartan women were educated and trained physically like the men. They had their own Olympic games. Other Greeks called Spartan women "thigh flashers" as an insult because they were unashamed of their bodies.

She traced the almost imperceptible tattoo just above her navel. Her navel piercing hid it almost completely. She had been the first woman elevated to the inner circle of the Spartans. It had saved her life but cost her everything else. Cyrus had bent the rules with her body art because he hadn't wanted to spoil her beauty. On her right forearm was a tiny ritual scar, burned in the shape of a Lambda. It looked like an upside down V. She turned slightly and gazed upon the Greek Ἀ on her left shoulder, the mark of a Spartan goddess. The Ἀ stood for Aphrodite, the perfect woman of Greek mythology. She turned once more to look at her body.

Helen was still beautiful. Her stomach flat. Her breasts firm and high. Perhaps her face couldn't launch a thousand ships like the Helen of ancient Sparta, but she was possessed with an unmatched natural beauty.

She wondered if Frank was still alive. She remembered how he smelled, strong and clean. She remembered the way his rough hands had felt on her smooth skin. She remembered the way his lips had nearly driven her mad. She remembered how he struggled to be gentle. His body radiated primordial strength and raw power, yet he held it in check to not hurt her. She had never felt such a connection before or since. In their short time together she had loved him completely.

Helen shrugged on a fluffy robe and cinched the waist tight. What would it mean if Frank Kane really were still alive? Part of her prayed it was true. Part of her prayed it wasn't. If Frank Kane was alive, he might kill her. She wasn't sure she didn't deserve it. Could he be searching for her even now? If he was still alive, she had to find him first.

7

Frank felt the ache in his knees and hips. A man his size wasn't meant to sit so long. He pulled into a gas station in Mississippi to stretch his legs. He parked at the pump on the far side. He went inside to pay cash for the gas and rummaged through the stock of supplies inside. In the old days he would have been popping speed by now or doing a few lines of coke to keep the buzz going. Frank didn't do drugs anymore. They were a crutch. He would rely on his will. It would be a good test, he thought. He settled on a few bottles of water and some Jack Link beef jerky. He liked the teriyaki.

As he was filling the Mercedes' tank a pair of motorcycle riders pulled up. They were in their late forties, early fifties. Their beards were long and streaked with gray. Their jeans were well worn. They wore dusty, buckle-style leather motorcycle boots. The tips of the left boots were worn thin from years of changing gears. Maybe decades. Their leather jackets were weather-stained and scarred. They also wore the proud colors of an outlaw motorcycle club. It was the classic three-piece patch. The upper rocker identified them as Mongols. Their club logo filled the center. The lower rocker said only California. The lower rocker was a proclamation of the territory they claimed. Most bikers' colors only proclaimed a city or small area. The California rocker had brought them into conflict with the Hells Angels, who felt the state was their domain. There had been a war. Some kind of truce was drawn up. Then the Mongols were infiltrated by the cops and nearly brought down. Frank didn't remember all the details. That was the West Coast. The Spartans ruled the East Coast. The Spartans had even taken the concept of "colors" to another level. They rarely wore them. But when they did there was only a Spartan Lambda branded into the leather. The Lambda for Lacedaemonia, Sparta. There were no club insignias sewn onto a jacket or vest. The branding was permanent, like membership within the Spartan world. The Spartans had also abandoned the concept of rockers. The arrogant message was that the Spartans ruled the world.

Frank wondered if the Mongols were expanding into Mississippi now. Their saddlebags were loaded, but that didn't necessarily mean anything one way or the other. Maybe they were just on a road trip. He didn't really care.

He didn't know if they were carrying guns, but he knew they were armed. One percenters were always armed. He noticed the clasp of a knife concealed in each man's front pocket. A blue bandana hung from the back pocket of one of the Mongols. Bikers often attached a bandana to a large padlock. It was as lethal as a mace in a fight, but if a policeman discovered it, you could explain it was used to lock up your bike. The other Mongol sported a large black Maglight flash-light hanging from a loop on his right pant leg. Bikers called them kill lights. The Hells Angels had been infamous for their preference for the devastation you could cause with a ball-peen. Again, it was just a tool, easily explained.

Like true gear-heads, they were drawn to the black Mercedes. They couldn't help themselves.

"Nice ride, brother."

Frank put the nozzle back into the pump. "Thanks. Nice looking bikes."

The Mongols smiled. "You know something about bikes?"

"Not really. I just recognize classic Harleys. Nothing better. Nothing more American."

"Got that right," one said. "Fuck a bunch of crotch rockets."

American motorcycle clubs had rules for joining. Foremost among them was that you rode an American-made bike of a certain size. An American motorcycle was not inexpensive. Riders often spent additional tens of thousands of dollars customizing their bikes. Frank recognized the wheels on one of the bikes. They sold them in the shop at Elite Motorcycles for about six thousand dollars. It was funny, he thought, most outlaw motorcycle clubs claimed ownership of your bike when you joined. You were only allowed to ride your own bike. The Spartans had abandoned that tenet. It didn't matter what type of bike you rode. You didn't even have to ride to be admitted. What was important was your loyalty and serv-ice to the Spartans. Nothing else.

Most outlaw motorcycle clubs limited membership to whites only. The Spartans abandoned that concept as well. Black, white, Asian, Latino, it made no difference. It opened access to new markets. The only core value was loyalty to Sparta.

A final difference with the Spartans and the other designated outlaw groups was also critical to their success. Motorcycle clubs wanted respect more than anything. They became involved in crime as a means to sustain their lifestyle. The Spartans wanted money. Crime was business. Making money for them was a key to staying in their good graces. If someone was caught and faced time in the Graybar Hotel they were expected to stay silent. Betraying other Spartans was punishable by death.

Frank tried a smile. He had been practicing a lot. It was not too scary anymore.

"Take care on the road, guys."

"You too, brother."

He got into the Mercedes and pulled out. He was confident they hadn't recognized him. He hadn't done any work on the West Coast. Plus, the car had all of their attention. To them he was just the guy who got to drive it.

Frank passed a KIA dealership. The A was another lambda. The sight buoyed him. The omens were still good. He felt confident. Frank didn't run different scenarios in his head. He didn't try to guess what he would find in Fort Worth. It was a waste of his time. There were too many unknowns. He would find what he found. He would assess the situation and then do whatever he needed to do to resolve it. He had made a promise to Elliott. He was bound by his honor to see that promise carried out. This was familiar territory for Frank.

The Mercedes cruised along down the black highway, like a shark in deep water. Pennywise sang about "being hardcore until the day they died." Frank sang along with them. His voice was more lion's roar than harmony. Still, he enjoyed the act of singing when no one could hear him. The ancient Spartans had felt that, next to warfare, singing was the most important skill for a man.

The predators noticed as he passed them on the highway. They fell in behind. They knew they were invisible as they stalked him. They would be patient and wait for the right opportunity to strike. They could be swift and brutal when necessary. This was a prize worth hunting. They wondered and plotted. They had done this before and were very skilled at the hunt. They would watch for the opportunity and act accordingly. One of the predators turned on the radio. It was an old sixties song by The Tokens, *The Lion Sleeps Tonight*. They sang along.

"In the jungle
the mighty jungle,
the lion sleeps tonight.
In the jungle
the quiet jungle
the lion sleeps tonight.
A-wimoweh, a-wimoweh
A-wimoweh, a-wimoweh"

They laughed as they sang the refrain, oblivious that, tonight, they hunted the lion.

8

Jenny read the note from Frank out loud. Frank was appropriately laconic, she thought. She chuckled at her clever humor. Laconic. Laconia. Sparta. Get it? Caron stood listening. She blew a bubble and popped it. She wrapped the strand around her index finger. She stuck it back in her mouth and started chewing again. A second bubble followed the first. She wrapped it around her finger and stuck it back into her mouth.

"What do you think, Caron?"

Caron smiled a devilish smile.

"I think we should have a party."

"You have to be kidding."

"I am. Relax, tight ass. I think it means what it says."

"I mean about why Frank's gone. You think it's dangerous?"

"Of course it is. Does he do anything for anyone that isn't dangerous? Hello… he rescued us and killed some bad guys doing it."

"We don't know that for sure."

"How do you think he got us out of there? And DC told me Frank shot the guy who burned his feet. So he killed at least one of them."

"I don't want to talk about that."

"Just saying."

"I know. I just don't want to talk about it. We have to be careful while he's gone."

"What are you talking about? When the cat's away the mice can play."

"You heard what he said about having a party."

"Not a big party. I bet DC would get us some beer and wine. We could have a little party of our own."

"I don't know, Caron."

"I bet DC can even score us some weed if we want. You know he smokes bud. You can tell."

"Frank would die if he found out."

"Who's to tell him? Not us and not DC if he gets it for us."

"You think DC would really buy us some?"

"Sure. He kind of likes me. I can tell."

"Caron."

"It's true. He's just afraid of Frank is all. And he's got a really cute butt."

Jenny punched her friend in the shoulder. "You're so bad."

"Used to be. Now I'm just boring. School and work and zero fun."

"That bad stuff is behind us now. School and work are fine for now. We got a second chance. Those don't come too often."

"I know. It's just that Frank scares all the cute boys away. I wouldn't mind a little action."

"It would be nice to go out on a date again. Go to a movie or something."

"Or get laid," Caron said, laughing.

Jenny punched her again. "You're so nasty."

Caron ran her hands over her own body. "Oh, baby. Oh, baby," she cooed.

Jenny laughed.

Caron started dry humping the air. "Give it to me, baby. Uh huh, uh huh."

Jenny shook her ass around. "Oh, baby. It ain't enough if it ain't rough."

Caron laughed and shoved her friend. "Now who's being nasty?

"Well, you made me."

"That's what you always say. Come on, we've got to get ready for work or we'll be late."

The girls worked together at an Applebee's restaurant. It wasn't fine dining, but it was a step up from fast food, and the tips were better. Most of the kids at Westchester Country Day School, their private school, didn't work. If the other students didn't approve, they were smart enough not to make fun of them. Frank made work a requirement for Caron and Jenny staying in Greensboro with him. They shared a car Frank gave them. It was a Volkswagen Bug. He let them pick out the color and didn't complain about the yellow or the stickers they decorated it with. He promised to give them a second car after graduation as a reward, if they worked hard.

Jenny hurried to their bathroom, but Caron shut the door before she got there.

"Come on, Caron. I've got to pee."

"Too slow," she called through the closed door. "Use Frank's if you have to go so bad."

Jenny went to Frank's room. She felt a rush of nerves. She felt like she was trespassing. She went in the bathroom. She was about to bust. She finished her business and flushed. Jen was washing her hands when she saw it.

Frank's knife winked out at her from the half closed medicine cabinet. She opened the cabinet. She had been there when DC ordered it for him. She had watched his pride at such a well-made knife. She reached in and took it. The knife was almost weightless in her small hand. She traced a finger over the delicate Japanese scrollwork. She pressed the button and the blade appeared. It was virtually silent. The blade was polished to a satin finish. Frank said it was a composite, not even metal, but ten times sharper. She reloaded the blade and reopened it. She did it again. The knife felt good in her hand. It fit perfectly in her small grip. It gave her a tingle. It seemed so deadly. She slipped it into her back pocket. Jenny felt safe and dangerous herself.

9

Special Agents Redding and Harris eased the car to a halt in front of the small house. It was once white, but the paint was starting to peel. It needed a new roof. Black tears crept down the worn tarpaper. The carport was empty.

"Why didn't you want to call ahead?"

"Because he would have known something was up. I was afraid he would bolt if he knew I wanted to talk with him."

"Looks like he isn't home anyway."

"Let's have a look around, Harris."

They got out of the car. Redding checked his gun. Harris copied the senior agent's movements, obviously looking to the older agent for direction on field-work. They approached the front door. Redding took a quick glance inside through the front window. Nothing. The house was dark and still. Redding sensed no one was home. He knocked anyway. He waited three seconds and knocked again, this time identifying them as FBI agents. Only silence from within. The agents exchanged looks.

"Lets try around back," Redding said.

The back of the house was overgrown. The grass needed cutting and the bushes needed trimming. The small flower garden was choked with weeds. There were spider webs in the corners of several windows. The back door was locked. Peering inside, Redding saw nothing.

"I'll call a judge I know. Get a search warrant."

"I don't know if we have grounds. Just because he isn't home...."

"Listen up. This C.I. is critical to our task. If something has happened to him, we need to know, and the sooner the better."

"I just meant that legally, it might be hard to persuade a judge to sign a warrant."

"I know some judges who are a little more lenient about probable cause. We can work through the details. Not much more to do tonight. I'll get the warrant and we'll try again tomorrow."

"Shouldn't we notify the local authorities?"

"So they can compromise the situation? I don't think so. I'll call them tomorrow. Maybe you aren't ready for field work if you're going to question everything the Senior Agent in Charge does."

Harris looked away, then back again. "I apologize. I realize I have a lot to learn."

"That's better."

Harris said, "Can I ask you something?"

"Shoot."

"Earlier you referred to the Spartan hit men as boatmen. What does that mean?"

Redding smiled his fatherly smile even though he had never had children, at least that he knew of. "Boatman is a term the Spartans themselves use. In ancient Greece when you died they put a coin in your mouth. I know what you're thinking, that it was over the eyes, but it wasn't. It was in the mouth. The coin was for Chiron the boatman. The boatman would ferry you over the river Styx to the world of the dead. If you see a boatman, you're already dead."

"Wrapping what they do in mythos doesn't make them better than any other killers," Harris said.

"These guys, the boatmen, weren't just killers. They were more than that. They were unstoppable. It was almost like they were superhuman. They could get to anyone. They got through any security."

"It sounds like you bought into it."

"If you'd seen the things I did, you wouldn't be so quick to be a smart ass."

Harris shook his Mormon head, "I'm sorry. It just sounds so comic book. A killer is just a killer."

"If you're lucky you'll never find out how wrong you are. Come on, we got work to do."

10

Frank Kane hated to admit it. He was tired. His butt and knees ached. His eyes burned, and he caught himself drifting off as he drove. The black car followed his distraction as it drifted into adjoining lanes of traffic. He thought back to Claudia Murphy. She was exactly as Apollo had described her, "someone everyone fell in love with." But not Frank. Maybe she had fallen a little in love with him.

Claudia had worked as the manager of one of the Spartans' strip clubs, The Mirage. It also operated as an escort service. The local Spartan captain wanted to put Claudia's ass on sale along with the other girls. She had refused and complained that she was more valuable as a manager. Frank had been sent down to evaluate the situation and negotiate a settlement.

They met in the office of the club. She was five feet tall with long brown hair. She was very pretty; small nose, thin mouth with a touch of strength, high cheekbones, everything in proportion except her eyes. Her dark eyes were huge. That was her best feature, and she knew it. Her makeup highlighted their size and shape. She used dark eyeliner to accentuate them even more. Men looked into their depths and became lost. They commented that she was a good listener, or compassionate, or she seemed trustworthy. Frank saw none of those artifices. They were carefully applied lures to control men in some way or another. What Frank did see was a calculating intellect. She was smart and not just in the street-smart way of grifters and whores. She used the strip club to feed men's fantasies further by running an escort service with the dancers. It had been her idea. Profits were high from The Mirage Club, and Cyrus loved profit.

Claudia had been prepared to flirt and praise and even barter her body if it let her stay out of the rotation. When Frank seemed unmoved by her subtle and not so subtle advances, she appealed strictly to the logical business advantages of keeping her separate. Frank agreed. Good managers were hard to find, not impossible, but hard nonetheless. Their talk turned to what she had done prior to working for the Spartans. She had a background in travel. She had been a stewardess for USAir and then moved into corporate work, first as a reservationist and then as flight manager. Frank listened and began making mental calculations.

The Spartans needed someone to arrange private travel for them. Claudia knew the ins and outs of the airline business. She was sure she could do it off the books. They discussed what would be necessary. She would need a front business, a travel agency, to run the off-radar trips through. So in a smoky strip club in Charlotte, North Carolina, V.I.P. Travel was born. The possibilities were endless.

His negotiations were over. He had made his decision. No Spartan captain would dare to question it. It was easy to find a new Spartan captain.

A horn blared and Frank pulled the Mercedes back into his lane. Fuck. He had to take a break. He rolled the window down and let the hot, dry air slap him awake. He had to find a place to pull over. And maybe some food and coffee would help.

11

Jenny and Caron came home from work tired and dirty. Working in a restaurant you came home smelling of the food you served. It seeped into your clothes and the pores of your skin. It wrapped around the strands of your hair. It was a greasy, fried smell, a mix of chicken and steak and cheeseburgers and French fries. Jenny parked the little Volkswagen in the driveway. Caron was first to the door, her key already in hand.

"Dibs on the first shower," she called as she hurried inside.

"No fair, Caron. You got first shower yesterday."

"You snooze you lose."

"Ok. But don't use all the hot water."

Caron posed dramatically on the stairs. "You can use Frank's shower if you want."

"I'll wait."

"Chicken. You're afraid he'll find out and be pissed."

"Bitch."

Caron laughed and hurried into the bathroom. Jenny smiled. The house seemed strange without Frank waiting for them. He had always been there. Sometimes there was only the glow of his reading light from under his bedroom door. But it was reassuring just the same. She knew he was awake and waiting up for them. He didn't need a lot of words to let them know he was looking after them. There was a hollow echo as she walked into the living room and turned on the TV. Why was she afraid to use his shower? Was she afraid of him? Or was it something else? Maybe it was respect. He didn't bother their things. It didn't seem fair to use his. No. That wasn't it. That was just a way to rationalize the lie. She felt the knife in her back pocket as if to remind her of her hypocrisy. She took it out and flipped it open. It thrilled her on some elemental level. Some core cells recognized it as a weapon and it gave her a little surge of power. It was good to feel powerful.

The doorbell chimed.

Jenny jumped at the sudden sound. Her heart pounded. She closed the knife and slipped it into her pocket again. She walked to the door. She turned on the outside light and looked out through the peephole.

DC stood on the stoop holding a box of Krispy Kreme donuts. She opened the door with a smile growing on her face. DC knew they both loved donuts, but Frank rarely allowed sweets in the house.

"What are you doing here?"

"Just checking on you. I promised, Frank. Thought I might bring a little temptation for you girls."

"You are so bad. You know they go right to our hips."

"Well, if you don't want them, I can take them with me."

"Get in here," Jenny said grabbing his arm and pulling him inside. "I would hate to have to hurt you."

DC laughed. "Do you have any milk? These cats are hot and cry for the taste of cold milk."

"Put them in the living room. I'll get something for us to drink. And no sneaking any until I get back."

"Where's Caron?"

"She's in the shower."

"More for us."

DC flopped down on the sofa and picked up the remote. Something in a man's genetics drove him to take control of the television remote as soon as he entered a room. He flipped through channels trying to find something good. Jenny returned from the kitchen with two tall glasses of cold milk.

"Caron can get her own if she ever comes down." Jenny turned and shouted up toward the stairs. "Caron, DC's here. He brought donuts."

No reply. She probably couldn't hear over the shower.

Jenny sat in the La Z Boy and grabbed a donut from the box. She took a bite and used her index finger to scoop the warm sugar from the corner of her mouth.

"God, that is so good. It's like sugar air. It doesn't melt. It evaporates."

"Yeah. I hate most donuts. Too heavy, like eating lard. This is pure pleasure."

"The company is out of Winston-Salem. So we're supporting local business by eating these."

"Fuck that. We're eating them because they're so good. I think I need a second one while they're still hot."

They heard the door to the bathroom open and Caron come out.

"DC's here. He brought donuts."

The quick, light slap of feet on the wooden stairs announced Caron's approach. She was fresh from the shower and her shoulder length brown hair was swept back and held with a black scrunchy. She hadn't put on the robe that Jenny knew was hanging on the back of the bathroom door next to her own. She was wearing a thick pale blue towel. It wrapped her breasts just barely above her nipples and managed to press her breasts together and upward slightly. She had taken the time to put a small cross necklace on that hung to just above her cleavage. It drew the eye naturally to her breasts. The towel stretched down to miniskirt length, accentuating her long tanned legs. She had, surprisingly, opted not to wear six-inch stripper heels. Maybe she thought it was too much, Jenny thought. DC's wide-eyed stare and slightly open mouth showed that her stratagems had not been wasted.

She scooted beside DC on the sofa and demurely tugged the towel down. She picked up a donut between two dainty fingers and nibbled at it.

She beamed at DC. "You are so sweet."

"I try to be. Frank, told me to check in on your girls while he's gone."

"Frank must think a lot of you to ask you to look after us."

"I guess he does. You girls mean a lot to him. It's the least I can do for a friend."

"See, Jenny, I told you he was sweet."

"So, you did."

Caron seemed to become suddenly aware of her lack of dress. "Oh, me." She said. "I better run upstairs and get some clothes on."

"Don't on my account," DC said.

She patted him on his arm. "Don't be wicked," she said in a voice implying he should be.

She hurried up the stairs and stopped and turned. "DC, will you do me a favor while Frank is gone."

"Sure," he said sitting up like a well-trained poodle.

"If it's not too much trouble."

"What? Just name it."

"Could you bring some wine next time?"

Lust battled fear. "I don't know what Frank would think."

"He doesn't have to know. We won't tell if you don't."

"I guess it would be okay. What kind do you like?"

"You pick," Caron said.

"We don't know much about wine," Jenny added. "It might be fun to drink a little wine and rent a movie."

DC nodded. "Sounds like a plan. I'll see what I can do."

Caron winked at Jenny. When DC turned to watch Caron go upstairs, Jenny stuck her tongue out at her.

12

Helen hurried down the stairs toward the front door. She futzed with her purse searching for the keys. She didn't see the man in the den.

"Where are you off to, angel?"

"Dinner with the girls. It's our night. You know that, Cyrus."

"That's right, darling. I forgot. Will you be out late?"

"No later than usual. It's just dinner."

"Where this time?"

"Anton's."

"Anton's. They serve excellent veal."

"I wouldn't know, Cyrus. I am not a fan of veal. The sauces are too rich. I'll probably get one of their chicken dishes. I have to keep my girlish figure or you'll lose interest in me."

"I fear that would be impossible. You are as beautiful now as the first time I saw you. Maybe more so."

Helen smiled her perfect smile of warmth and love. "You say the sweetest things for such a bad man. You must be wearing rose-colored glasses, darling. I am slowly turning into a hag."

Cyrus chuckled. "If all hags looked like you, it would be a beautiful world to behold."

"If you need me, I have my cell."

"Have a good time."

Helen waved a flitty wave and was gone. Cyrus heard her car start and pull away. He turned back to the darkness. A cigarette flared in the blackness to his left.

The man in the sunglasses spoke first. "Do you think she knows where he is?"

"I don't know. I doubt it."

"You're certain?"

"How can I be certain of anything? She's always had her secrets. As do we all," Cyrus said.

"Yes, we do."

Cyrus said, "But you think me naive to trust her."

"Perhaps. We can't take the chance that they're in contact."

"No, we can't."

"We have to be sure."

"Yes, we do."

"Then we are in agreement at least."

"Your men are pursuing the other leads we discussed?"

"Yes. The few remaining Jokers were hesitant to aid us, but with sufficient encouragement they verified the information. It was Frank."

Cyrus steepled his hands before his face and stared into the dark. Finally, he spoke.

"Follow her. Don't let her know."

"And if she meets him?"

"Then kill them both. We can't afford loose ends. It would be too dangerous. Either I can trust her or I can't."

"There will not be any loose ends. I'll let you know what I find."

"Do that."

13

Frank saw the sign for the Bob's Super Truck Stop five miles before the ramp off the interstate. Bob's was a classic truck stop set in the middle of nowhere. There were a couple dozen big rigs parked on the side reserved for long-haul drivers. There was also a large parking lot for regular automobiles. The building itself was a flat one-story monstrosity crouched like a toad in the middle of the asphalt lake. The outside was white with a bright red trim. The abundance of windows tried to make up for the scarcity of fresh paint. Frank parked to the side of the building where the car would be visible from the inside. He locked the car and went in. He carried the papers on Frederick Cooper from the file DC had made.

A rack of newspaper dispensers stood sentry by the front door. Inside the main entrance was a large sign; to the left you could find the store and showers, to the right the restaurant. Frank glanced left. The convenience style store was large. There were the customary shelves of food and snacks. A gigantic cooler covered one wall with the usual assortment of beverages. A sign indicated the showers were deeper in the back. The Spartans had run some truck stops. Good place to run whores and sell speed. Truckers loved them both.

Frank turned to the right and entered the restaurant.

The restaurant was huge, designed in a diner motif. The booths were all well-worn red vinyl. The tables in the center had the chairs upholstered in the same red vinyl. There was no hostess, so Frank found a table facing the door and took a seat. The menus were already on the table clipped to the napkin dispenser. Salt and pepper dispensers rested in their wire nests on either side. Frank lifted the menu. It was old and had a greasy feel that for some reason comforted Frank. He liked when things were as they were supposed to be. A truck stop diner needed to be a little worn down and serve food with a little grease. The confederate battle flag on the wall was a statement as much as a decoration. Nothing politically correct about it.

He scanned the menu. It was the back elbow of the night, what did he want to eat? Breakfast seemed appropriate. As he considered his choices, a young couple came in behind him. The girl was carrying a red purse the size of a small suitcase. It was old and worn, but she clutched it like it held the Hope Diamond. Maybe it did. She was young, twenty-four, twenty-five. She had long black hair, parted not quite in the middle, so the left side hung partially over her eye. It was a nice effect. She had a nice oval face with pretty dark eyes, a thin pointed nose, and a cruel chin. She was slim. No, that was not accurate. Frank prided himself on accuracy. She was waifish. Like that model Kate Moss. She looked like she was one good meal from starvation. It was not a look that appealed to Frank, but she may have just been hard up. She had an innocent vulnerability about her that drew your interest. Other men noticed her as well. He noticed how some of the diners set up a little straighter when they saw her.

The man with her was lean like a wolf. He had a hardness that usually came from time in prison. He didn't try to look hard, he just radiated it. Tattoos peeked out from the edge of his short-sleeve shirt. He was about five feet ten inches tall. He wore dirty jeans and nice new Nike tennis shoes. He sported an expensive looking watch on his left wrist. He scanned the diner and pointed her toward a table. The girl's eyes swept over Frank and lingered just a second. Unexpectedly, it sent a small electrical shock through his system.

"Help you, hon?" the waitress asked.

She was not nearly as pretty as the young girl. She was past fifty with iron-gray hair and about fifty pounds too much of Bob's food. She had the weary look of a woman who has seen hard times and didn't expect them to come to an end anytime soon. Frank could smell cigarette smoke on her. He forced his practiced smile and spoke softly. He ordered eggs and bacon with hash browns and a short stack of pancakes. At the last minute he decided against the coffee, and ordered sweet tea instead. The waitress nodded her approval as she wrote it all down on her pad.

"Like to see a big man eat like a big man," she offered.

Her smile was as false as Frank's. She saw a lot of big men and, judging by the size of the current crop, they liked to eat. Frank had read somewhere that in the United States one in five men weighed two hundred and fifty pounds or more. For women it was like one in eight.

She brought him the tea first. He drank it and got an immediate refill. She smiled. Maybe she liked to see a big man drink a lot too. He noticed the couple had only ordered coffee. The girl cradled hers in both hands and blew and sipped almost in one motion. The man seemed angry. He leaned toward the girl and snarled words that Frank couldn't hear. The man would point at her and shake his finger. She seemed to cower a little, like she was afraid he might hit her. Might have done it before. Probably had.

Waiting for the food to come, Frank opened the file of lamp information DC had printed out for him. He read until his food came and he turned his attention to it. Somewhere during the eggs, but before the pancakes, the wolfish man started shouting at the girl. Something about her being a whore and he was done with her shit, blah, blah, blah, fuck you, blah, blah, blah. Then he threw some money on the table, turned and stormed out. The girl didn't move. She was marooned at the table with her worn suitcase purse and pretty face. Frank watched her from the corner of his eye. She didn't move. She sat still, like she was in shock. Frank returned to his eggs.

Thirty seconds later a trucker approached the girl. He had come in shortly after the couple. He wore the outfit of a truck cowboy. He had a cowboy hat, cowboy boots, black leather cowboy vest and a big rodeo belt buckle. Frank wondered if maybe he had a horse tied outside. He was six feet tall, and about a buck fifty. He seemed to be asking if he could help. The girl looked to Frank and back at the man. She shook her head no. The cowboy went back to his seat.

Frank was finishing the last of his pancakes when she came over. She was carrying the giant purse in front of her with two hands like a shield. Her eyes were damp, like she was trying not to cry. She stood looking at him, but Frank made no indication that he noticed her. Finally, she spoke. It was a good voice. Clear and strong with just a hint of school girl.

"Excuse me, mister."

Frank put his fork down and looked up. "Yes?"

"I hate to bother you, but I'm in a fix and need help."

Frank watched her face. He saw the emotions play over the smooth skin. He liked the way her ears blushed. He wiped his mouth with a paper napkin. She would have to ask.

"I seem to have gotten myself stranded. My boyfriend ran out on me and I need a ride."

Frank wiped his mouth and then his hands with another of the paper napkins. They were cheap and thin.

"I think there are a great many men here who would be happy to give a pretty young lady like you a ride."

She shifted from foot to foot. "Some of them don't look too trustworthy and I don't want to get myself into a worse mess than I'm already in."

"Why me?"

"You've got an honest face."

She smiled. It was a beguiling smile. Frank was sure she had beguiled many men with it. He knew he did not have an honest face. He looked like a gorilla dressed in a dark suit. He stared at her. The seconds crept past.

"I'm sorry. I can't help you. I have business."

"Please, mister. I just need to get away from here. Drop me wherever you're headed. My sister will wire me bus money to get home."

Frank opened the bill on the table. He took some money from his pocket and tucked it inside. He looked into her eyes. She had scars inside; there was no doubt about that. But it wasn't his problem.

"I'm sorry. You'll have to find another way. Now if you will excuse me."

Frank got up and went to find a bathroom. A long ride still loomed ahead of him. When he came out the girl was gone. He went outside. The cowboy trucker followed him. Frank scanned the parking lot, as was his habit before leaving any building.

He saw the girl standing near some big rigs parked off to the side. She saw him and turned, like she might call out to him. Behind her a man appeared from the dark shadows. He grabbed her and jerked her into the darkness between the trucks.

Frank didn't have time for distractions. He hesitated. The cowboy trucker spoke from his left shoulder.

"Hey, fella, did you see that? We got to do something. We got to help that girl."

Frank sighed. He ran to where the girl had disappeared. He heard the trucker's boots behind him trying to catch up and a barely audible metallic click. Frank didn't hesitate. He moved fast between the trucks. The girl was standing in front of him. The boyfriend was standing behind her. He held a large bladed Bowie style knife against her throat. He was smiling, showing his teeth like a wolf.

The purpose of the girl was to lure Frank into the trap. There's always free cheese in a rattrap. The image of the girl in danger was meant to hold him. He was supposed to yell something threatening. Try to scare the boyfriend off. Frank could hear the cowboy trucker closing fast. Reinforcements were coming, just wait.

Frank knew how the trap worked. He glanced to his left, saw nothing and spun hard to his right. The other man was just stepping from behind the cab of the truck. He had a pipe in his hand. The man was big. He probably went six three and two twenty. Frank spun and swept the pipe arm away with his own right. He struck him two savage blows to the kidneys and as he crumpled, Frank followed with a powerful right forearm to his face.

The cowboy trucker slowed at the action. He was supposed to close the back door of the trap. Maybe give Frank a little shove to knock him off balance for the pipe man. Frank caught his mouth with a hard left hook. The cowboy hat went flying and Frank felt the jaw shatter. The cowboy trucker fell stiff like a statue toppling.

Frank turned to face the two still standing. The look of triumph on the boyfriend's face had been replaced with a look of feral rage. The moment held, then Frank smiled. He blew him a kiss. The boyfriend shouted and charged. He held the knife with the blade down in a stabbing position with his arm raised high.

Frank divided knife fighters into four distinct categories. The first was what he called the housewife. This was someone who picked up a knife or hammer or any potentially lethal weapon in a moment of stress. They held it out in front of them like a talisman to warn you away. They hoped it would work like a cross was supposed to work on a vampire. They had no intention of using it and, unless you tripped and fell on it when you approached them, you were under no risk of injury.

The second category was thug. Frank placed himself in this category. A thug used a knife or any weapon in a brutal, unskilled way. They hit you with a club. They stabbed you with a knife. They choked you with a rope. Even though Spanish Johnny had tried to teach Frank the finer points of knife work, Frank had been a poor student.

The next level was where it got scary. A professional knife man was a thing to be feared. They did not stab. They cut you. They bled you. They toyed with you like a cat with a mouse. Spanish Johnny had been a professional. He may have been the fastest man with a knife that Frank had ever seen. And he had seen a lot of knife men.

The final category was the assassin. These men had some unnatural affinity for a blade. They felt a nearly sexual pleasure in using a blade. Their skills were beyond comprehension. A life had to be devoted to this art. Frank had only known two. He had killed one of them.

The boyfriend was a thug. He attacked with his rage leading him. Frank waited patiently. He blocked the down stroke at the wrist. He caught the wrist and snapped it around behind the boyfriend's back as he spun him. He leveraged it up until the pain made the boyfriend drop the knife. Frank locked his left arm around the man's neck in a chokehold. The boyfriend tried to struggle, but he was helpless.

"Smoke him, Cherry," the boyfriend croaked.

The pretty girl dug into her big purse and produced a snub-nosed Ruger LCR with a crimson trace-sight. She fumbled getting it out of her purse and raising it into shooting position. Frank waited some more.

"Shoot him you dumb bitch. Shoot him, Cherry."

Frank applied a little pressure and shut off the boyfriend's ability to talk. The girl lowered the pistol and spent long seconds finding the laser switch on the bottom of the gun butt and flipping it on. This done, she pointed it at Frank. The red dot danced between him and the boyfriend. It was a hard shot for her. Easy for Frank. The red dot took the guesswork out of it. It reduced skill to just waiting until the dot touched the target, then a quick squeeze of the trigger. But the LCR had a twelve-pound trigger pull. A hard pull for a frail girl. Frank just looked at her. It was her call. Their eyes met.

She hesitated and the moment was gone. She put the gun back into her big red purse.

"Fuck him," she said. "Break his fucking neck for all I care."

The boyfriend struggled in Frank's grasp. Frank choked him out and let him fall to the pavement.

Frank looked up at the girl. She looked back. She looked like she might run. "Still need that ride?"

"Sure," she said and smiled.

Frank picked up the knife and patted the boyfriend down. He found a pair of brass knuckles and tossed them under a truck. There was a small walkie-talkie on the ground near his body. Frank searched the pipe man. He kicked the pipe away and casually broke the man's right arm with a short vicious twisting move. Using the pipe was overkill. It was one thing to rob a man. This was something else. It hinted at some deep-seated sadism. The pipe could kill someone. Frank checked out the cowboy trucker last. He had the other walkie-talkie. The metallic clicking Frank had heard was the cowboy trucker alerting his friends that they were on their way. It was still in his left hand. Frank stomped the hand and the walkie-talkie with his expensive shoe. It sounded like celery snapping. The cowboy trucker also had a sheath knife in a boot and Frank tossed it away.

"Show me your car," he said.

She hesitated, and then nodded, leading him across the parking lot to the far side. It was an old Saturn missing its two front hubcaps.

"Anything you need from here?"

She shook her head no. Frank used the boyfriend's knife to cut all four tires, then tossed the knife into a drain. He looked back at the girl. Her eyes were huge under the halogen parking lot lights.

"Let's go."

He led her to the Mercedes and held the door open for her. She got inside. He climbed in the other side. The headlights flashed over the three unconscious men between the trucks and then they were gone into the darkness.

14

Helen arrived at the restaurant. A valet gave her a slip with a number and took her car. Wearing an understated blue Versace dress with comfortable shoes, she went inside. It was a small intimate place with only sixteen tables. It had a trendy vibe with lots of local art on the wall and a huge teak bar. The tables all had linen tablecloths and a small central candle. The candleholder was crystal. The vase with the single flower was hand-blown glass. The napkins were Balinese. Helen's friend saw her and waved.

The friend's name was Johanna Godwin. She was about eight years older than Helen. She was a tall, smart redhead. Johanna ran a small expensive art gallery and was an accomplished tennis player and local philanthropist. Johanna was a very attractive woman, but her beauty was eclipsed by Helen's, making her appear merely nice looking.

Helen hurried over and the two women embraced.

"I was so glad you called, Helen."

Taking her seat, Helen said, "It has just been such a long time. I thought we could catch up on things."

"That is so sweet. I was just thinking about you too."

"Your hair looks spectacular. I really like it long."

"You're sweet. I just needed a change."

A female server drifted up like a bit of flotsam on the bay. She was painfully thin with darting eyes, but attractive like a model. Her blonde hair was tied back.

"Good evening. I'm Erika. I'll be looking after you tonight. Can I get you ladies something to start with?"

"How about some wine? What do you suggest?" Helen asked.

Erika started in on the long list of wines available.

The handsome man in a suit at the bar watched them through the mirror behind the bar. He nursed a drink and absentmindedly fumbled with his cell phone. He looked like a bank vice president, successful, but not overtly. He seemed bored, like he was waiting for someone who was late.

The women renewed their friendship over wine and small Caesar salads. They chatted about a new artist Johanna had recently discovered. Over an entrée of herb-crusted salmon and asparagus, they agreed to meet for tennis soon. Predictably, both women declined dessert. The dinner crept past two hours before they had finished. Over a final glass of wine, they said their goodbyes. Erika was attentive all night without being too aggressive, the mark of an experienced waitress. She brought the final bill, which Helen took over Johanna's objections.

"At least let me split it with you," Johanna pleaded.

"No. It's my treat. I've been meaning to call you for such a long time, and you were sweet to come on such short notice."

"I'm always glad to see you. You know that. And I'm serious about tennis."

"I'll call. I promise."

Erika drifted back again to collect the payment and bill. "Thank you. I enjoyed serving you tonight."

"Thank you. It was wonderful. I left a little something extra for you inside. I apologize for monopolizing your table for so long."

"Thank you, very much," Erika said as she collected the bill. "You stay as long as you like. I'll be right back."

The man at the bar was still there. Still nursing his second drink. He was still alone. He politely rebuffed a young blonde's offer to sit. He watched the two women leave. He didn't follow. He opened his cell phone and dialed.

"Yes, sir. It's just as she told you. She met Johanna Godwin. They had dinner. Their talk was about tennis and art. Nothing of any importance. No one made contact. She's on her way home now. Carter will pick her up outside and follow her home, just to play it safe."

Erika took the bill to her station. She entered in the payment and tip. Written on the copy of the bill was: Frank Kane is alive. Find him. A.

Erika crumpled the note and slipped it into her skirt pocket. She would have to be very careful. She would contact some of her friends. If Frank Kane was alive, one of them would know where he was. She would do what she could. She owed Helen her life.

15

The waif sat silently as the Mercedes roared down the Interstate. Frank asked, "Is the gun yours?"

"What?"

"The gun, the Ruger, is it yours?"

"You don't understand."

"Is the gun yours? Did you load it?"

"It's Kevin's gun. I guess he loaded it. I don't know. Why?"

Concealing his move, Frank pushed 4-8-0 into the keypad. The glove box popped opened. It was empty.

"Put it in there."

"Why?"

"Police have to have a warrant to search the glove compartment. And I don't want you packing around me. Now do what I tell you or I'll put you out on the side of the road."

She started to speak, but didn't. She placed the gun inside and he closed it. She was prettier than she had appeared under the harsh diner lights. In the soft glow of the dash, there was a certain quality in her features that made you want to like her. It was a nice mix of innocence and wisdom. He liked her nose and eyes.

"My name is Frank. What's yours? Your boyfriend called you Cherry."

She smiled. "Kevin called me Cherry Red because of the lipstick I use. My real name is Catherine. My friends call me Cathy. My special friends get to call me Cat."

It was a well-practiced answer. It was said in an honest, slightly mischievous voice. Frank knew it was a lie. He was too tired for this.

"Fine. Tell me when you're ready."

"What do you mean? My name really is Cathy."

Frank ignored her plea. "Who were the other two?"

"The trucker's name is Clay. The big guy is named Will. He likes to be called Thumper because he likes to thump people."

"Nice friends."

"They aren't really my friends. We just kind of hooked up."

"Where are you going?"

"It doesn't matter. But let me explain about back there. So you don't get the wrong idea."

"What's to get wrong? It was a honey trap. It was exactly what it looked like."

"I mean…it wasn't personal. Kevin just wanted your car. He saw it and had to have it. It was like crack to a crack-head. We followed you for a long time trying to work it out."

"You do this often?"

"Not the carjacking. This was a first. Been running cons for the last year. It seems to work pretty good."

Frank smiled. "You always run it the same way? Always run the honey trap?"

"No. We change it up. We try to focus on married men. Traveling alone. They're pretty easy marks. But I'm pretty good at spotting the lipstick lesbians. You know, the women that might want to try it with a girl, but haven't."

"I know what it means. You go back to their rooms with them, then close the trap."

"Yeah. Get it compromising until the guys can show up. They take pictures. The mark always pays so no one finds out."

"How do your friends find you? You go to the shower and make a quick call?"

"Something like that. I text where we're at. What kind of businessman are you?"

"The kind that pulled your ass out of that stuff back there."

"Sorry. No need to get mad. What do you do? Security work or something?"

"Lamps. I sell custom lamps. You ever hear of Frederick Cooper?"

She shook her head, no.

"It doesn't matter," he picked up a business card from the console, handed it to her. She reached up, pushed the overhead light on, read our loud, "Frank Nomin, Vice President of acquisitions. Aegis Corporation." She clicked the light off, "Cool. Where we headed?"

"Fort Worth. Ever been there?"

"No. But one place is as good as another to me."

Frank nodded. He understood the sentiment. The car rolled on. Frank waited. She didn't disappoint.

"Sometimes if the guy's hot, or the woman's really pretty, I don't text the location until afterwards."

Frank didn't respond. It was a common ploy. She was trying to shock him. Show him her worldliness. Get on top again. Look for an angle. It was how criminals were wired.

They rode in silence for more than an hour before Frank felt exhaustion gripping him again. All the adrenaline had burned off and it left him feeling drained. He was in Texarkana, burning up I-30, still three and a half hours from Fort Worth. If he pushed on, he would still have to kill time until the lamp store opened. He decided to stop. What difference could a few hours make, he reasoned. He knew how she would respond.

"I'm going to stop up ahead at the Country Host Inn. I'm too tired to go any farther tonight."

From his peripheral vision he could see her smile. He liked her smile.

The Country Host Inn was a small, neat, functional motel. Frank parked around the back so the car wasn't visible from the road. It was late, but the office was open. A sleepy middle-aged woman eventually came to the desk.

"You folks need a room?" The woman smiled knowingly. She had probably rented to stranger couples many times. She didn't seem surprised that Frank would be with such a young woman. She tried hard not to stare at his blind looking eye.

"Will a king be all right?"

He saw Cherry smile again. It made sense to her. To control your situation you had to understand it. Frank was hot for her just like all the marks. She could play him.

"No," Frank said. "We need two rooms. First floor."

"We can share a room," Cherry said. "It's cheaper. Just get a couple of doubles."

"No. We need two rooms."

The clerk seemed as surprised as Cherry but got out two keycards and coded the magnetic strips. "Cash or credit?"

Frank paid cash for both rooms. He got his bag out of the trunk and walked Cherry to her room. He handed her the key card.

"I'm trusting you. If you contact your friends, I will hurt them."

"Hurt them? What do you call what you already did? If that's not hurting them, I don't know what is."

"That was a lesson taught. If they come again, I won't be so gentle."

"Hey, I'm not going to contact them." She dug her cell phone out of her purse. "Here, you can take my cell if you want to."

Frank shook his head no. "I'm just saying. So we're clear." He turned and went two doors down to his room and let himself in. He didn't look back.

He tossed his bag onto one of the beds and hung up the suit bag and his coat. He went into the bathroom and brushed his teeth. It felt like something was growing on them. He stripped off his clothes and started an abbreviated nighttime workout regime. He did two hundred and fifty push-ups and then two hundred and fifty sit-ups. His muscles stood out like steel cables. His skin dripped sweat in the hot dry air. He turned the air conditioner up to high. He sat on the edge of the bed. He didn't feel sleepy any more. He turned the TV to a FOX twenty-four hour news channel. An Israeli tank was shooting at something in a cloud of dust.

There was a lambda on the side of the tank. Maybe it was a chevron or some kind of identifier for this type of tank. Frank didn't care. It was another good omen. Spartans going to war. He turned the television off.

He looked out his window. Everything was dark and still. He watched silently. His skin felt dry and brittle. He knew what he needed. He pulled on his boxer shorts and grabbed a towel from the bathroom. The god of the sea needed water. He slipped outside. He waited. Nothing. He walked to the outdoor pool and slipped into the cool water. The pool sign warned that there was no lifeguard on duty and you were swimming at your own risk. Frank smiled. He would chance it. There was something magical about swimming at night. He began a slow silent breaststroke from one end to the other and then back again. Suddenly he was back in Costa Rica with Apollo. He hadn't thought of the twins in years.

16

Frank could see why Apollo loved Costa Rica. He was treated like a king. The new cook was uncommonly good even if she didn't talk much. One of the girls hurried to gather up their dishes and the remnants of banana pancakes and eggs.

"I heard you trying to sneak out last night," Apollo said.

"It's those damn peacocks. I can't slip past them."

"That is saying something. And it's why I have them. They don't miss much."

"What's the plan for today? We going spear fishing again?"

"Yeah. I got a new spot I want to try. An undersea mount that's reported to be swarming with fish."

"Sounds good to me."

"Currents can be a little tricky."

Frank laughed. He was a powerful swimmer and completely at ease in the water. He wondered if somehow Cyrus had known this when he had named him Poseidon.

"What do I have to fear from the sea?"

"Well, just as a precaution, I will stay on the boat."

"You were always cautious."

"Only when my life is at risk. Get your gear and meet me at the dock in ten minutes. And no stopping for a morning quickie with Pilar."

Fifteen minutes later they were skimming across the ocean. A school of spinner dolphins danced across the waves around them. They jumped and spun and fell back into the embrace of the sea. Frank even saw a pair of Wright whales, all black with their broad heads rolling just beneath the surface. They reached the waypoint on Apollo's GPS and slowed. "It's too deep to anchor on the pinnacle so I'll cruise around and watch for you," he said.

The air temperature was in the upper 80s and the surface water in the lower 80s, but Frank donned a full 3mm wet suit. He pulled on gigantic three foot long Mares free diving fins and rolled into the water. He wore a twelve-pound weight belt. He grabbed the side of the boat and Apollo passed him a spear gun. The gun was made of mahogany. It was forty-five inches long and fired a forty-two inch steel shaft. The sling was released by a pistol grip located two-thirds down its length; as primordially simple as it was deadly.

Frank drifted down toward the pinnacle eighty feet below. The water was colder here. The deep blue was dark and silent. It was a world as prehistoric as when it was formed. There was something about being in the ocean that made him feel whole. It renewed his soul in an unexplained way. He had heard scuba divers say they felt like outsiders allowed to look into the ocean. Frank didn't feel that. He felt like an insider. He belonged here.

There was a rhythm to the ocean. It was an unseen vibration. There was a tempo to the currents. He hung at sixty feet, waiting. He felt the schools of fish before he saw them. They were fast moving Amber Jacks. He did not pick a target. He did not fire. He merely drifted, reveling in the sensations. Weightlessness. Frank felt the cool drift of the current. He heard the silent steady pulse of his heart. He moved down to the pinnacle. There were fish everywhere. He still didn't fire. He just watched. He returned to the surface and signaled Apollo that he was all right.

He hyperventilated and dove again. A thirty-pound grouper picked at the coral in a small outcropping. He raised the sling and took the fish just behind its head just distal to the gill plate. They would eat well tonight.

The fish struggled against the line, then fell into a series of death spasms. Frank moved to the surface trailing the fish. It was never safe to linger after a kill. The vibrations and blood called other predators. He surfaced near the boat and Apollo drove over. Frank reeled the fish in and passed it to Apollo.

"This should do for dinner."

"You got that right. How does the pinnacle look?"

"Incredible. There are lots of schools. I'm going back and see if I can shoot something really special."

"A mahi mahi would be nice."

"I'll keep that in mind."

Frank dove down to the pinnacle again. Schools still swarmed beneath him. A large sea turtle was busy foraging in the coral. Frank watched, mesmerized. The turtle was oblivious to his presence. Suddenly the turtle stopped feeding. It was almost as if it heard a warning. The turtle turned and swam away. The schools of smaller fish vanished. Frank got an eerie sensation. In the distance he spotted a large shadow at the edge of his vision. He strained, trying to identify it, but it stayed just outside his vision. Then, as if answering his gaze, it moved closer. It was a shark.

The shark was a tiger. It was at least twelve feet long with the dark stripes of its species. On a deep level he appreciated its simplicity. It knew nothing of fear. Everything was prey, or it wasn't. It drifted elegantly thirty yards away, its movements hypnotic. The thick body seemed to move in slow motion. The long tail swung back and forth in a gentle rhythm.

There was an odd series of scars above its right eye. It watched Frank as Frank watched it. He could easily have hit it with the spear gun, but he knew he couldn't kill it with a spear shot. Maybe if he had a bangstick. Frank never saw the second tiger shark until it bumped him from behind.

A moment's flash of terror seized him. It was identical to the first shark. The second shark even had the same scars above its right eye. They were twins. Frank knew at that moment that he was dead if they wanted to kill him. There was nothing he could do to prevent it. He slowed his heart. He had been down nearly four minutes and knew he had to surface soon. He also knew that surfacing might trigger an attack. He was more identifiable as prey on the surface.

The tigers moved into a pattern of circles like a noose. They tightened it closer and closer. Frank stayed calm. The sharks moved in. One passed within inches of him. Their skin looked like melted honey beneath the dark stripes. Frank felt compelled to reach out and feel the sandpaper rough skin as it passed. The second shark mimicked its twin and Frank let his hand trail across it as well. The sharks repeated their moves, but this time rolling onto their backs exposing their pale undersides. It was unheard-of behavior. Frank rubbed their undersides. They were acting more like tiger cubs than supreme predators. The clock in Frank's head clicked past six minutes. He was out of air. He wasn't going to make it to the surface.

One of the sharks rose from beneath him and placed its huge flat head against his fins and gently pushed him toward the surface. It rolled away. The second twin did the same. Frank's head swam with darkness. He felt at peace. There was a sense of being safe, the same sensation a child finds in his own bed.

A giant head nudged beneath his arm and propelled him to the surface. Apollo was there. He grabbed Frank's shoulders as he gasped for breath. Apollo tried to pull him into the boat, but Frank shook his hands off and hung from the gunwale. The tigers brushed against his legs. He lowered his face to the water to see them. They swirled around him for a few seconds more, then drifted downward together. He strained his eyes to watch them as long as possible. They disappeared, not like sharks, but like ghosts.

Frank raised his head and motioned to Apollo, who pulled him into the boat.

"You okay?"

Frank nodded. "What just happened?"

"I don't know. I've never seen anything like it. It was like they wanted to play with you."

"It was like I was one of them."

"No. It was like you were fucking Poseidon the god of the sea. They were paying some kind of homage to you."

"That's fucking crazy."

"Well, you explain it. They could have taken you any time. They should have taken you. They made sure you made it to the surface."

"Got to be some other explanation."

"Some kind of powerful mojo, brother. Has to be an omen."

"I always said I couldn't be killed." Frank kicked off his fins and unzipped the wet suit. He leaned back and stared out across the empty ocean. It was incredible.

Apollo grabbed a cold beer from the cooler and used the bottle opener to pop off the cap. He passed it to Frank. "Here, drink this."

Frank took a long drink. He kept shaking his head. "They were twins. Did you see that? They were twins. That mark over their right eyes must be some kind of birthmark, right? Did you see it?"

"I saw. You were as good as dead. I thought you were lost for sure."

Frank stared at the label on the beer bottle. Imperial beer carried a black phoenix on a field of gold as its logo. He held it up for Apollo to see. "Talk about omens. This is a phoenix."

"Back from the dead."

"Unbelievable."

17

Frank stopped swimming. He rolled onto his back and stared at the black Texas sky above him. The stars were muted. He could make out the shapes of thick clouds moving. They slid past quickly like spectral fish in an ink-black sea. Frank turned over and swam to the side of the pool. He hung there for another minute while the memories of Apollo and the twins dispelled. He pulled himself onto the pool deck, wrapped a towel around his waist, and walked to his room.

Frank removed his wet boxers and dried himself. He looked in the mirror. He looked tired. Worn out. The fake scar seemed to stand out on his face. There was a knock on the door. Frank wrapped the towel around his waist again. He grabbed his long-sleeved shirt and put it on. The white fabric stuck to his still damp flesh, vaguely revealing the sleeve of tattoos on his left arm.

He didn't look out of the peephole in the door. It was the surest way to get shot. Hitters often knocked and place their gun against the door just below the peephole. When the peephole darkened by someone looking out, the shooter just pulled the trigger. Frank had latched the chain, which was almost useless in stopping an intruder. He walked to the door and took a position beside it.

"Yeah?"

"It's me," came Cherry's voice.

"What do you want?"

"Open the door. I need to talk with you."

Frank sighed. He slipped the chain and opened the door. Cherry tried to wedge past him into the room. He kept his arm across the doorway. He didn't say anything. She maneuvered to get past him, but Frank didn't budge. She looked at him as if waiting permission or a clue. She was carrying her large red purse. It was the reason he had decided to help her. Always choose red.

Frank didn't speak. He just stared at her.

Finally, she said, "Dorian. My real name is Dorian. But I hate it."

"Dorian what?"

"Dorian Holloway. I hate it because it's so lame. I tried different versions, Dori, and Doris, and Holler, but nothing worked, so I just decided to be Cherry."

The Dorian Greeks were the predecessors to the ancient Spartans. Doric style pillars were common throughout Sparta. They were renowned for their no-frills, solid function. Unlike later styles that were more ornate, Dorian columns spoke of strength and effortless power. It was another good omen.

"Dorian is a good name. You should be proud of it."

"I hate it. Please don't call me Dorian. It makes me sound like I'm eighty years old."

"I like the name."

"So can I come in?"

"Can I call you Dorian?"

She thought for a few seconds, nodded, "Deal."

Frank dropped his arm and let her pass. He scanned the hallway just in case. It was empty.

"Do you have a bottle? I can't fall asleep. I thought a drink might relax me."

"No."

"Really? I've never met a traveling businessman who didn't bring a bottle."

"Now you have. What do you want?"

"I saw you swimming and thought I would come over."

"Why?"

"You know, to talk and stuff."

"So? Talk."

She scanned the arm blocking the doorway, appraising him as she would any mark.

"I didn't know businessmen had tats like that."

"I wasn't always a businessman. What do you want, Dorian?"

She stood with her hands on her hips. She seemed angry. "You aren't making this easy."

"What do you want?"

"Can't we just chat for a few minutes?"

"No. What do you want?"

"Do you want to fuck?" she blurted out. "There I said it."

"If this is part of your scam…."

"It's not. You can have my cell if you're worried."

"I'm not worried."

"So do you?"

Frank pointed to his wedding band. "Didn't you notice this?"

"Yeah, but what has that got to do with anything? I told you, I got picked up by lots of married guys. They always wanted to fuck. And besides you don't give off a married vibe."

"Dorian, it's late and I'm tired."

"I know. I know it is, but, do you want to fuck me?"

"Dorian…."

"Well, do you?"

Frank smiled. "Yes, I do."

"Really? You're not teasing me? I mean, you act like you hate me."

"I think you're a very beautiful girl. A man would have to be a eunuch not to desire someone like you."

"Really?"

"Really."

She almost sprang into his arms. She was kissing him with a feverish passion. She tore his shirt open and saw the Spartans tattoo on his stomach.

"What is that?"

"College tattoo. I went to Michigan."

"You mean Michigan State? Michigan State is the Spartans. Michigan is like Wolverines or something."

"You're quick. Good. I like that. Yes, Michigan State."

"Is that where you got the scar too?"

"Hazing accident."

"It looks like a knife wound. How did you…"

"Dorian, do you want to fuck or talk?"

She hesitated a moment before kissing him again. "I want to fuck."

Frank pulled her close. Dorian sat back and pulled her shirt over her head. Her body was extremely thin. Her ribs stood out on her chest, accentuating her small breasts. Her nipples stood out firm and hard. She noticed his gaze.

"When I'm turned on my nipples get harder than most guys' dicks. You could cut glass with these babies."

"I like them."

She stripped off the rest of her clothes. She had a Medusa tattooed on her shoulder. Medusa's eyes burned red amid the tangle of green and blue serpents.

"Medusa?"

"She was beautiful and wicked."

"Just like you? Is that why you got it?"

She stared silent for a moment, she sighed. "Do you want to fuck or talk?"

"Fuck," said Frank and he tossed the towel aside.

Dorian laughed. "Well, hello big fella. Looks like somebody got turned to stone."

18

Kevin came to first. His shoulder hurt where his arm had been twisted behind his back. He stretched his shoulder and got to his feet. His head was throbbing. The cowboy trucker and the pipe man were moaning on the ground nearby. He checked the pipe man first. The right side of his face was swollen from the elbow strike. The bruise was the size of a saucer. His right arm hung at a strange angle. It was obviously broken. He helped the pipe man to sit up.

"What the fuck happened, Kevin?"

"What happened? We got our asses kicked, Thumper. That's what happened."

"Fucker broke my damn arm."

"Take it easy. We'll get you fixed up, Thumper. I thought you had him with the pipe."

"I did too. Fucker was fast. Never seen nobody so damn fast."

"And lucky."

"How long we been out, Kevin?"

"Fuck if I know."

Kevin went over and checked on the cowboy trucker. He was still unconscious. He slapped him lightly on the cheeks until his eyes popped open. There was terror in them. They ran wild until they locked on Kevin and settled down. He started to speak, then grimaced and grabbed his jaw.

"He broke your jaw, Clay," Kevin said.

Clay winced as he lifted his left hand. Shards of plastic protruded from the broken hand.

"Looks like he fucked up your hand too. Come on, we'll head to the nearest hospital and get you patched up."

Clay mumbled something about payback as he limped after Kevin toward their car. When they reached the car they all froze. They saw the flat tires. This wasn't good. They had no wheels.

"What do we do now, Kevin?" Thumper asked.

Kevin stared at the car for several seconds controlling his boiling rage.

"This was a piece of shit anyway. We'll consolidate what we need in one bag."

Kevin opened the trunk and took out a duffel bag. It was old and worn. He unzipped it and dumped the contents into the trunk. He laid the duffel bag on top on the car. "Get what you got to have. Leave anything you don't need."

Thumper sat down on the pavement. "Fuck it. I feel like I'm going to puke or pass out again."

Kevin patted him on the shoulder. "Rest up, Thump. I'll grab you a change of clothes." Kevin rummaged through the trunk, emptied a battered suitcase, took some clothes, and tossed them into the duffel bag. He opened a small canvas bag and pulled out an old Navy Ka-Bar knife. It had the classic seven-inch carbon steel blade in a dull gray finish. The handle was leather-wrapped. There was also a smaller lock-back knife. He tossed them into the duffel bag. Clay pointed to what he wanted and Kevin added a few things of his own. They traveled light like all mobile criminals.

"Now give me your wallets and any money you got."

"What for?"

"Look, Thumper, the only way you guys are going to catch a ride to the hospital is in an ambulance. Cops will pop up. They don't need to be checking anybody's I.D. Clean out anything from you pockets that may get you busted."

"I got a joint."

"In the bag, dumb ass. And that includes anything you got stashed in a boot."

"What are you going to do?"

"Lone guy with a duffel bag. I'll hitch in."

"You could steal our shit."

"Yeah, I could. And you would be fucked. We run together a long time. You know me better than that."

"I guess so. Sorry. What's our story?"

"Bunch of beaners in a pick-um-up truck jumped you in the parking lot. That's all you remember. They all look alike. Old truck. Maybe white. Thumper, you pretend amnesia. Clay can't hardly talk so it should slow the cops. I'll meet you outside the emergency room after they finish patching you up."

"I'll help get Clay, inside. Get some good citizen to call 911."

"After the ambulance leaves, I'll follow. If I'm not there when you get out, wait for me."

"I can't believe one guy did this to us."

"One guy and that bitch, Cherry. She had the drop on him, but put the gun down," Kevin said.

"No way. That bitch is straight up gangster," Thumper argued. "She would have shot him stone cold dead. Must be some other reason she didn't shoot."

"I saw what I saw. I told her to burn him. The cunt put the piece down, then he choked me out."

"Unreal. Cherry. Cherry. Cherry."

"If I ever find that bitch I'll carve her tight ass up but good."

"I like to tap that ass before you do," Thumper said. "Always wanted a piece of that."

"You never said."

"You seemed to have staked a claim on that mine. We knew she was off limits."

"DP her," Clay mumbled.

Kevin shook his head. "Won't be none of that. Unless you want to fuck her after I kill her."

"Sounds good to me," Clay mumbled and managed to signal thumbs up with his good hand.

"You're sick," Thumper said. "I get seconds."

Kevin laughed. They might be fools, but they were his fools.

19

Frank had planned to sleep a couple of hours to recharge and then complete the drive to Fort Worth. He awoke and looked at his watch. It was nine thirty. He spun toward Dorian. She was gone. He jumped to his feet and checked where he had left the keys to the Mercedes. They were gone. Fuck.

"Bitch," he said aloud.

She had taken the car. He pulled on his clothes and dug the GPS tracker out of his bag. She might still be in range, he thought. Maybe he could catch her before she got too far away. He activated the GPS. The screen glowed lime green. It showed the Mercedes just outside. Frank looked out the curtained window. The car was parked where he had left it. He spun around and checked the room. He went to the bathroom. She had showered before she left. He could see the wet towels dropped on the floor. How had he slept through that? Had she drugged him? He doubted it. He was wide-awake now. Any drug would still be in his system. Yet, she was gone. Her red purse was gone. It didn't make sense. Then he saw the note on the mirror.

She had written it in cherry-red lipstick.

"Gone 2 breakfast. Don't leave without me."

Frank figured she took the keys because she counted on him abandoning her. They'd already had sex. What else did she have to bargain with? Frank got his stuff and slipped the GPS into his pocket. He took the car's remote, went outside, and put his bag and clothes in the trunk. He considered just heading on to Fort Worth. It wouldn't be right. Maybe she had left word at the front desk. Frank was headed that way when he saw the International House of Pancakes. He jogged across the road to the restaurant.

Inside he scanned the room. Dorian waved at him across the crowd. A waitress was talking to her. Dorian said something to the woman who laughed and hurried off.

Frank pulled out a chair and sat down.

"Finally up, sleepy head?"

"You must have been very quiet."

"I have a lot of experience slipping out of beds without waking anyone."

The waitress returned with a mug of hot coffee and set it in front of Frank.

"I ordered it for you. It's pretty good."

Frank sipped it, "Not bad. Thanks."

Dorian cut her pancakes and took a bite. "You should try these chocolate chip pancakes. They are to die for."

"Could I have the car keys back, please?"

Dorian pulled the keys from her pocket and passed them to Frank.

"I wasn't sure you would wait for me and I was starved."

"I might not have. It was the right move."

"I could have taken the car if I had wanted to."

"I know. I appreciate your discretion."

"What good would a hot set of wheels have done me? I would much rather hang with a hot dude for a few days."

"Sounds like a plan."

The waitress returned and placed a stack of chocolate chip pancakes in front of him.

"I didn't order this."

"I did. Try them," Dorian said.

"I don't eat sweets."

"Why not? Are you a diabetic? Are you a sugar hater or something? Live a little. Life is a short run at best. My motto is to enjoy what you can while you can."

"I'm more of the will power type." Frank cut a small piece and tried it. The pancakes were very good. The chocolate chips added a delightful flavor.

Dorian said, "I believe you. Still, sounds kind of boring."

"I'm kind of boring."

Dorian snorted and almost choked on her pancake.

"You too funny. Do you know that? No guy that fights like you, or fucks as good, is boring. That was some wild shit."

"I'm glad you approve," he said.

"I do. I can't wait for round two."

"I'll make a note."

"Can I ask you something?"

"Sure."

"Who's Helen? Is she your wife?"

"No. Where did you hear that name?"

"Last night when I was cuddled up with you, you called me Helen."

Frank didn't lie. "She was a woman I was in love with once."

Dorian nodded as if it all made perfect sense. "She dead?"

"Probably. I really don't know. I haven't seen her in years."

Dorian reached out and touched his hand.

"I could be Helen for you. Just tell me what you like."

Frank smiled at her sincerity. "Just be you. That's enough for now."

"Just saying. I'm good at role playing," Dorian said and looked up at him. "It would make me happy to make you happy."

Frank laughed. "You don't sound like a hardened criminal."

"I'm trying to go straight."

"Finish up your pancakes. We need to hit the road."

"What's the hurry? A few hours won't make any difference."

Frank found himself smiling. She was right. And the pancakes were exceptional.

20

Agents Redding and Harris sat in their car outside the house. Redding had gotten the search warrant just as he had promised. He reached inside the breast pocket of his coat and removed a crumpled cigarette pack. He tapped out a cigarette. He fished around in his pocket for a lighter and lit up. Redding took a deep draw, held it, and blew it out the window. He watched the house through the haze of blue smoke.

"Excuse me, sir. I thought the department banned smoking in company vehicles."

Redding turned an icy stare at Harris. "Bite me, rookie."

He took another deep drag and blew it out the car window.

Harris didn't respond directly. After another minute he said, "What are we waiting for? I thought you were in a rush to get inside."

"Local cops. It keeps the neighbors away and is good for our relationship with the locals. Everyone wants to work with the FBI. We are the rock stars of law enforcement. Here they come now."

A black and white prowl car eased to the curb behind them. Redding and Harris got out.

"Morning, gentlemen," Redding said. "Sorry to have to get you out here so early."

He showed them his identification wallet.

Two uniformed officers got out. They were young, with close-cut hair and the air of military service about them.

"That's our job, sir. Is the perp home?"

"I don't think so. We got a warrant so we're going in. Once we clear the place you secure the perimeter."

"Yes, sir."

"One of you take the front door. The other comes with us around back. Have your weapon out. This is a known violent felon. I don't want anyone getting hurt. Especially me."

The police officers removed their firearms. The second officer followed Redding and Harris around back. The yard was quiet. A raven perched on the top of the wooden fence separating the house from its neighbor. It cawed its annoyance at their intrusion. Redding didn't like that. He knew all about the Spartans and their omens. The more he hunted them the more superstitious he had become.

Redding approached the door. He stubbed his cigarette out against the side of the house and let it fall to the ground. He used a toe to crush the remaining embers. Redding and Harris drew their pistols. Redding checked each man's eyes to be sure they were focused. They were. He rapped on the door.

"FBI! Open up."

No response. He rapped again, harder.

"FBI! Open up! We have a warrant!"

No response. Redding jiggled the door handle to be sure it wasn't unlocked. He nodded at the police officer. The officer smiled, drew back his foot and kicked the lock in. They stepped into the empty house.

"Don't touch anything. This guy is famous for his booby traps."

Harris stiffened. The policeman smiled. Had to be former military, Redding thought. They moved with practiced deliberation. They paused occasionally to shout out that they were police serving a warrant. The house was silent as a trap. When they were sure no one was there, the policeman was dismissed to secure the back door. Redding and Harris returned to check out the rooms.

The house was particularly neat. The kitchen was scrubbed clean. The dishes had all been washed and put away. The dishtowels hung in two precise sets of folds on a rack. There was a small-unused soap dispenser beside the sink.

The dinning room appeared unused. The living room had a large sofa and one chair. They were well worn. There was an old coffee table. It was bare. There were no magazines. The television was a fifty-two-inch flat screen, an indulgence. Harris noticed the PlayStation 3 attached to it and a stack of video games.

"How hold is this guy?"

"His name is Keith Masnick. He's fifty seven years old."

"Isn't that a little old to be playing video games?"

"Just don't touch anything until I check it out."

The master bedroom was minimally furnished as well. There was a dresser, nightstand, and double bed. The bed was well made. The ends were tucked in with military precision. The closet contained half dozen shirts that could have been purchased from Goodwill. They were all pressed. A small iron and ironing board rested in the back.

The bathroom was spotless. The bare minimum of products: liquid soap, shampoo, toothbrush, toothpaste, disposable razor, shaving cream. There were no exfoliates, or skin softeners or hair conditioners. There was no sign of a feminine presence.

There was a second bathroom in the hallway, but it was empty. There wasn't even any toilet paper.

The second bedroom had been turned into an office. There was a computer desk from Costco. The monitor was an older model. It probably weighed forty pounds. The printer was an old HP 940 series, but the tray had a good stack of paper resting inside. The tower sat on a ledge under the desk.

Harris reached to turn on the computer. Redding grabbed his wrist.

"Don't."

"I was just going to check to see what was left open."

"The wires from the monitor to the tower aren't connected."

Redding kneeled down and looked behind the tower. There was no back. The tower was hollow. Inside a wire led from the 'on' button to a clear glass container filled with a gel-like material. Redding got back to his feet. "It's booby trapped."

"Shit."

"Is that a Bureau approved term, agent Harris?"

"I apologize. It startled me. I could have set it off. How did you know?"

"Like I told you, Masnick was one of the founders of the Spartans. He was one of the Gods, as they called the most elite among them. They called him Prometheus because he brought fire. He was incredible with explosives. He could rig anything, anywhere. This was a smart-ass joke he left for me. Just to let me know who he is. He knew I would find it. It's very amateurish. It's beneath him. He wanted me to find it. Like leaving a business card. Let's check out the basement again. Might be a hidden workshop down there."

They went down the stairs slowly. Even with the overhead light it was dimly lit. The stairs were narrow and old. The basement smelled of mold and earth. There was nothing there except an old lawnmower and an empty gas can. There were no hidden rooms.

"The house is a blind. It has been for a long time. Masnick may come here from time to time, but he doesn't live here anymore. We're too late. He's in the wind."

They started up the stairs. Redding tapped out another cigarette and lit it. He smoked as he climbed.

"Any ideas where he might have gone?" Harris asked.

"A couple. But they're long shots. This isn't good."

"Can I ask you something, Redding?"

"Shoot."

"How did you turn him? What could he have done so bad that these animals would have killed him for it?"

Redding smiled at the memory. He hesitated, but his ego made him tell it.

"Masnick had a brother who was a sheriff. It was when the Spartans were first starting to gain real power. The brother was squeezing them pretty hard. He was a hard-ass sheriff in every sense of the term. Word I heard was Cyrus decided to eliminate the brother."

"And Masnick warned him."

"You want me to tell it or not?"

"Sorry."

"Cyrus could have just had it done. Apollo, that was the name of this crazy black guy they had. They claimed he was a sniper in the SEALs, but we could never verify it one way or the other. Apollo could have popped this guy from a mile out. Or Kane or The Jake could have just bulldozed their way in and taken the sheriff out, but he wanted a show of loyalty from Masnick. He wanted Masnick to do his brother."

"My god. Is that when he came to you?"

Redding gave Harris the bad eye.

"Sorry."

"You should be. No. Masnick did his brother as told. But it weighed heavy on him. It tore him apart inside. I mean, they were brothers. Masnick found a shrink and started going for therapy to deal with it. He told the psychiatrist everything. He unburdened a soul filled with guilt."

"That was pretty risky. What if the shrink violated his oath and spilled the beans?"

"The Spartans had a motto. I think it was originally Blackbeard the pirate's saying, but it goes; 'Two can keep a secret as easy as one, as long as one of them is dead.'"

"What…?"

"Masnick had been in therapy about three months when he had a break- thorough and started feeling better. He figured he had had enough therapy. He planted a small device in the doctor's car one day after work. The doctor cranked his car and was blown away."

"What happened to the records? Did you find them in his office?"

"No. Masnick may be a psychopath, but he's no fool. He blew up the doctor's office. He blew up the doctor's home. He blew up his vacation home."

"My god. What happened to the psychiatrist's family?"

"Masnick purposely chose a psychiatrist that was unmarried. He knew from the start he was going to kill him eventually."

"So how did you get control of him?"

"The doctor had something going on with his secretary. Her name was Trisha Ware. She was a hot little brunette. She was very petite and wore these cute glasses. The doctor asked her to hold a duplicate set of files on Masnick. After the doc's death, she freaked out. She finally decided to bring them to the Bureau.

I was the AIC. They brought her to me. I think the doc knew he was in deep water from the start."

"Why didn't you prosecute Masnick for the things in the files?"

"There were legal issues, and in the big picture he was a small fish. We wanted to bring the entire organization down, and now we had an in. We weren't going to risk it. The Director met with the U.S. Attorney General and decided how to work Masnick. They gave him full immunity. I was the only one he would talk to."

"Impressive. That was a nice feather in your cap."

"Yes, it was." Redding stepped into the bathroom and dropped the butt into the toilet. He flushed it and turned to the mirror to straighten his tie. He froze.

"You smell that?"

"What? The cigarette smoke?"

"No. Blood."

Redding scanned the room. His eye stopped on the open bathroom door. "Harris, get in here."

Harris stepped inside the bathroom. Redding eased the door closed. On the back of the door was a series of glyphs written in blood beneath a large lambda. Dried red tears of blood trickled from the symbols.

"What does it mean?"

"It's ancient Greek."

"You can read ancient Greek?"

"No. But I know what the Spartans use to write in ancient Greek. I can read that. The Lambda is the Spartan's sign. The message below it is simple, it says Fear the Spartans."

"Whose blood is it? Masnick's?"

"We got his DNA from before. We'll know for certain after the techs check it out, but my bet is that it's his. This is a warning for others. I think Masnick is dead. The Spartans are rebuilding."

21

Bruce Burns sat at his desk. A cold cup of Starbucks coffee rested on the table before him. The Russian giant stood by the office door as silent as an ice-tipped mountain. Dimitri passed the time flipping between television stations. He didn't stay on any channel for more than five seconds.

Dimitri's cell buzzed in his coat. He took the phone out and spoke Russian. He nodded his head, smiled. He closed the cell and spoke to Bruce.

"Still no call, Mr. Burns? What could be the problem?"

"I told you, I don't know. The product should have been here by now."

"Yes, it should have. The Greek has set a penalty for late delivery."

"Sure. Just tell me how much. I'll pay whatever you want. I just want my wife back."

"And you shall have her."

The giant growled something and Dimitri laughed.

"What?"

"He says the Greek must like you. Otherwise he would have killed your wife to teach you a lesson."

Frank reached Fort Worth without incident. Dorian rode with her face pressed to the window like a child marveling at everything that passed by. Frank drove to a small boutique hotel that DC had listed in the file, The Ashton. It was on the main street. The Ashton only had thirty-nine rooms. It had a gym, business center, spa, pool, and restaurant. They let the valet take the car and went inside.

A U.S. flag and a Texas flag flanked the ornate entrance. People were sitting in the lobby reading newspapers and talking on cell phones. An older couple passed them going to the Grille, the little hotel restaurant. Frank approached the desk.

"I need a room. I'm Mr. Nomin. I called ahead."

"Very good, sir. We have several suites available. How long will you be with us?"

"Let's start at five nights."

He slid some paperwork over for Frank to fill out. "Just fill this out. And how will you be paying?"

"Cash," Frank said and pulled out a stack of hundreds.

"Very good."

Frank filled out the registration form and paused near the end.

"I don't remember the license."

"Don't worry about it. We'll take care of it for you. Here are your keys."

Frank took the two room keys and led Dorian to their room on the second floor. It was very nice. There were a lot of little touches to justify the high cost. Double pedestal sinks in the bathroom, large flat screen television, floor to ceiling windows, and a deep, claw-footed Jacuzzi tub.

"This is awesome," Dorian said falling down on the king-sized bed. She rolled onto the down pillows and hugged them to her chest.

"Glad you like it. I don't want to be too boring."

Dorian giggled and jumped off the bed. "I need to get some clothes and things if we're going to be staying here. I need to fit in with everyone else."

"First, I'm going to wash the road dust off me, then we can go shopping. And you're right, I need you looking nice if you're going to help me with my business."

Frank hung his coat across the back of one of the chairs. He kicked off his shoes. "I'll make it quick."

Dorian started to remove her top. She paused before letting it fall to the floor. "Would you like some company? I could wash your back."

"Sounds good."

Kevin paced outside the emergency room. His shoulder still ached where the man had twisted it. He smoked and waited. Thumper, the pipe man, was sitting on a nearby granite bench. His broken right arm had been set and placed inside a plaster cast. A dark blue sling supported it across his chest. His head ached and he still felt dizzy. The docs thought he might have a concussion. They were waiting for Clay. Clay was still in surgery. A local oral surgeon had been brought in to wire his broken jaw shut. He had lost two teeth. They had put a cast on his left hand and wrist where Frank had broken it.

The police officer stopped on his way out of the waiting room. The hospital was required to notify the police in the case of violent injuries. The officer looked at them through the periphery of his vision. He did not speak. They had given him their statements about their assault. It was all lies. The policeman knew it. They knew he knew. Everyone played their parts. He would file his paperwork and all would be forgotten. It was the game.

The policeman moved off. They had no identification on them, because they alleged their wallets had been stolen. The policeman didn't believe that either. He would call in the information he had. He knew everything, but their physical descriptions would be false. They were predators that had run into something worse than themselves. They would disappear to lick their wounds and plan their revenge. He couldn't care less.

Clay came outside. His face was black and blue. Kevin handed him his cigarette. Clay took a deep drag. He tried to pass it back to Kevin who shook him off. He drew another cigarette from the pack in his pocket and lit it.

"What the fuck really happened back there?" Thumper asked. "The more I think about it the more impossible it seems."

Clay added something through wired teeth that no one understood.

"That guy made a fool of us," Kevin snarled. "What else you need to figure out?"

"No shit. But he was only one guy. Why didn't Cherry pop him if it went down like you said?"

"Next time it will be different," Kevin said. "Next time we'll be ready."

"Fuck next time. I see that son of a bitch again, I'm running the other way."

"I want that car," Kevin said.

"Fuck that car. He could be anywhere. We'll never find him again."

Kevin looked off into the sun-brightened street. "Karma. Things have a way of turning out. That bitch, Cherry, sold us out. I owe her. She'll get hers too."

Thumper laughed. "She's like the damn car, Kevin. Long gone."

Kevin turned around. He ignored the comment. "We need to get a car. Get back on the road. Score some cash."

"No problem. Just pick one out and Clay will boost it like always. Then what? Where to next?"

"I don't know. Might as well go home for a spell. We're close. I got some connections there might be able to put us into some coin. Deal a little dope. Get back on our feet."

"Where's the main stem, Kevin?"

"Fort Worth."

22

Frank called the lamp store from his hotel room. The secretary had said Mr. Burns was in conference and unavailable. She offered, in her kindest voice that she did not know when he would be available, but would be glad to take a message. Frank declined. He had taken Dorian to a department store and bought her some new clothes. She seemed excited and left her old outfit in the garbage can at the store.

He drove to the lamp store. Burns' place was called The International House of Lights. It was a presumptive name. He wondered if they sold pancakes. It didn't strike Frank as much of a business, but it could be a good front for smuggling. The outside sign proclaimed deep discounts on unique international designs. They parked on the side street.

A female jogger passed in front of them. She wore a smart-looking lime green tracksuit. She had ear buds in place and was lost to the music in her head. Frank didn't like headphones. They muffled unseen approach. They distracted the wearer from their surroundings as they were intended to do. They identified her to predators as prey. She jogged down the street unconcerned.

"I need to see if the owner is really in. I couldn't get a meeting with him over the phone. So just do as I say, all right?"

"Sure, no problem. I can be very convincing."

"Just take your time. Look around for me."

"Are you sure you aren't casing the place to knock it off later? I mean it's cool if you're in the life. We can work together."

"Sorry, I'm legit."

"Are you sure? I can spot a criminal. You act like someone seriously bent."

"I love pretty criminals. So trusting. Now get going."

Dorian leaned over and kissed Frank. "Anything for you."

She headed across the street. The lamp store was a stand-alone building. It was the size of a small warehouse. The front had a façade of modern columns and white aluminum siding. It was still a warehouse. A chain link fence circled the back of the business where deliveries were made. He could see an old broken-down panel truck with the hood up. There was a blue tarp draped over the front. He couldn't see the rest. Frank watched Dorian until she disappeared inside. Now was the wait. Frank was good at waiting.

His mind drifted once more to the twins and the other Burns he had known, this one in prison.

When Frank went to prison he was initially sent to segregation. It was standard treatment for anyone with gang affiliations. After six months he was moved to Gen Pop. Frank's first cellmate was a sixty-two-year-old forger named Levi "Doc" Caldwell. He was a good cellmate. He was quiet and kept to himself. His age discouraged the rape gangs. His skills as a forger protected him from some of the random violence. Cons were quick to try to learn his secrets. Doc was friendly and open, but Frank knew he always held something back. It was the smart play. They got along well. When Doc was paroled Frank got a new celly.

The new guy was a twenty-year-old surf punk from Huntington Beach, California. His name was Bruce Burns. He said his nickname was Fire Starter. He said it was because he burned up the waves. Or because it was a knock-off of his last name. Or because he moved heavyweight ganja and got the weed fires started. Or because he was so hot he set the girls on fire. Frank figured he might have been a pyro. Frank did not like the Fire Starter. He was loud and cocky. He told stories so full of shit that you turned brown just listening to them. Frank knew the kid was going to have trouble. He was young with long blonde hair and a slight build. The predators were watching him the minute he got off the bus to be processed. A fish was a fish.

Burns was doing twelve months on a five-year beef. The other forty-eight months had been dismissed. Burns had been caught with a tractor-trailer loaded with bales of marijuana. A missed weigh station ended his ride. The prosecutor had pressed for trafficking charges, but Burns had a good lawyer. The lawyer argued for something called constructive possession, claiming Burns didn't know what he was hauling since the back was padlocked. The judge wasn't sure about his guilt, thus the sentence.

By then Frank was a short timer. He reasoned there was no reason to get involved with the kid. Whatever protection he could offer would expire when Frank was paroled. Better to let the kid go his own way. Find his own path to survival. That all changed before lunch call.

Burns was yammering on about some hot surf trip he had been on in Indonesia. The glassy swells. The huge barrels. The beautiful women. Frank liked the concept of surfing. Frank liked anything that got you in the ocean. But he wasn't a surfer. He wasn't built for it. He was big and heavy with a high center of gravity. Surfing was a sport best learned when you were a kid and then perfected as you aged. Frank was lying on his top bunk staring at the ceiling. Burns had pulled down the top of his prison scrubs because of the heat. They got the call for lunch and lined up. That was when Frank saw the tattoo on the kid's right arm. It covered the length, as a full sleeve. The detail was perfect. Even the scars or birthmarks were exact. It was the twins. It was the two tiger sharks that Frank had seen in Costa Rica.

"Nice tats," Frank said.

Burns looked at his arm and smiled. "Great story with this one, man. Unbelievable. I met the twins in Indo with this dude named Collin Walker. He was a full-on shredder. Should have been a pro. We were surfing a locals-only spot. Started catching some flak from them. Then the twins showed up and chased the locals out. The twins seemed to be trying to play with us so we stayed. It was totally awesome. Once in a lifetime shit. Had to get the tats after that."

They lined up and went single file to the cafeteria. Frank was still puzzling what it meant. Indonesia was a long way from Costa Rica. Burns took a seat at the end of a long empty table. Two black cons sat at the other end watching him with angry eyes. He was new to prison. He didn't understand about property. The table was the territory of the Black Muslims. He smiled at them. They made no movement. Slowly, the table filled with other Black Muslims.

The white inmates watched and waited. The kid was about to get a beating. A pair of black men took spaces on either side of Burns. The largest one smiled at him and took an apple off his tray. He took a bite and kept smiling.

"You looking for a daddy?"

"I don't know what you mean."

"You come to my table, you must be looking for a man what take care of you. That what you want? Be my prison bitch, white boy?"

"No, man. I was just looking for a place to sit."

"Don't seem that way. Seem like you lookin' fo' someone take care of you."

Frank did not see that he had any choice. Omens were omens. He approached the table and stood to the side of the largest convict. The man turned slowly toward him. The smile slipped away.

"You want something, motherfucker?"

"You're in my seat."

"This don't concern you."

"He's my cellmate. It concerns me."

"Then we got a problem."

The man stood and stepped to within inches of Frank's face. His brow was furrowed. He leaned in closer.

Frank spoke in a whisper only the man could hear. "We can do this one of two ways. The kid meant no disrespect. He's new. Let us walk. Let me take him to find another seat."

"And da other way?"

"I kill you where you stand. And you die shitting your pants in front of your punk ass friends."

The convict seemed unimpressed with the threat. But Frank saw him weighing the options. He knew who Frank Kane was. He knew what he was capable of doing. It wasn't a bluff. He wasn't sure Frank could do it. He wasn't sure he couldn't. The black convict tossed the partially eaten apple back onto Bruce Burns' tray.

"Take yo' bitch and get off my table or I will fuck you up. You hear me, motherfucker?"

Frank made no expression. He nodded at Burns. "Come on, let's sit somewhere else."

Burns got up slowly. He was pale and a little shaky. Frank led him over to a table of white convicts. They made space for them.

"Thanks, man. I didn't know."

"Not a problem. Now tell me again about how you met the twins."

Burns perked up. He loved telling a good story.

Dorian entered the lamp store. She wandered the aisles checking out the merchandise. There was a wide assortment of lamps and shades. Every style. Every color ever imagined. Some lamps were bizarre. The weirder the lamp, the higher the cost. There was a good assortment of shoppers. Saleswomen moved around assisting them.

She saw where the back of the warehouse was blocked off for inventory. The doors were open and she saw endless rows of lamps and shades.

Burns' office was on an upper level. It was a small office. There was a single door. There were three windows along the front of the office. It allowed Burns to look down, but shoppers could not see in. The wide metal stairway was closed off with a chain. The sign on the chain read PRIVATE in red letters.

Dorian walked to the front of the store. A pair of pretty young salesgirls stood waiting at the checkout counter. Dorian approached the youngest.

"Would it be possible for me to speak to Mr. Burns?"

"In what regards?"

"I am the chairwoman for a group raising money for the Fort Worth food bank. Mr. Burns and I talked last week and he promised a sizeable donation. But I haven't been able to get in touch with him."

"I'm so sorry."

"Is he here?"

The girl looked up at the office. "He's here, but we've been told he is not available to see anyone. He's meeting with some foreign investors and doesn't want to be disturbed."

"Oh. Isn't there anyway I could see him? Even for a few minutes?"

"I'm sorry. He was very explicit."

"I guess I could see him at home. It's just so inconvenient. How long have these investors been tying him up?"

"They came in yesterday. I think they're Russians. They look kind of scary."

"What do you mean?"

The girl waved her in closer. "One of them is a giant. The other one looks like a used car salesman. He thinks he's slick. They don't look like businessmen to me. I wouldn't trust them."

Dorian laughed. "Well, I hope it goes well for him."

"Do you want me to tell him you came by? Do you have a card?"

"Don't bother him. I'll come back tomorrow. Maybe he won't be so busy. I appreciate your help."

"Have a nice day."

"You too."

Dorian left by the front door. She looked around the parking area, as criminals tend to do. She walked to the car and fell into the passenger seat. Frank backed the car out to the road. At the loading dock behind the building he saw a giant of a man looking at the Mercedes.

"Let me tell you what I found out," Dorian enthused.

Frank studied the mountain of a man who continued staring at the car. "Later. Let's go get lunch."

Frank pulled away slowly. No need to look suspicious.

23

The Applebee's restaurant was swamped. Jenny had a big table; a father, a mother and five kids. It was madness and she loved it. She liked the excitement. She liked the chaos. She liked the feeling of things almost being out of control. She would never tell anyone. She would moan and complain like the other waitresses. That was expected. She looked over at Caron and smiled. Caron liked it too, she could tell.

"Can I get you folks some dessert? The chocolate volcano brownie is incredible."

"What do you think?" the father asked.

"I don't know. I've been trying to lose a little weight lately," the mother said. She looked like she needed to lose a hundred pounds to get down to being called fat.

"They're really huge. One would be enough for the table," Jenny said.

"We want dessert. We want dessert. We want dessert," the five kids chanted in unison.

Jenny reminded herself that she never wanted to have kids. Maybe a small dog.

"I would like a bite of something sweet. But just a bite," the mother said.

"We want dessert. We want dessert. We want dessert," the kids chanted.

Jenny smiled. "It looks like you're overruled. Do you want me to put that order in for you?"

"Yes. One bite of chocolate won't hurt her," the father said. "She can start her diet tomorrow. And I wouldn't mind a little myself."

He looked like someone not used to resisting temptations of the palate.

"We want dessert. We want dessert. We want dessert," the kids continued.

Maybe even a dog was too much trouble, Jenny thought. Maybe a fish. How long did they live anyway?

The mother motioned her closer. Jenny bent down. The woman whispered in her ear.

"There are so many of us I don't know if one will be enough for the kids. You better bring two."

"I think you're right. Good choice."

Jenny turned her order in. She grabbed the tea pitcher and was heading back to the floor when she saw Caron talking to a table of three boys. They all wore football letter jackets from Ragsdale, a local high school. They gave off a weird vibe. They were laughing and talking to Caron and the biggest one kept patting her side. It gave Jenny the creeps. She would have to ask Caron who they were the first chance she got.

Caron flirted with the boys at the table. It went with the job. The three football players were Zack the quarterback, Morgan who played center and Brian who was the team manager. Zack was handsome with thick black hair and an athlete's swagger. His dentist-created perfect white smile made it clear that it was good to be him. Morgan was a huge man-child. He weighed three hundred and twenty pounds. A lot of him was fat, but it took huge muscles to support that much weight. Like Zack, he was a gifted athlete at his position. Morgan wasn't dumb, but he played like he was. It was what was expected of big linemen. The last was Brian. He was a freshman. He was team manager. He was thin and eager and nervous. He was thrilled that Zack and Morgan allowed him to hang out with them. They were older and way cooler. It didn't matter that he paid when they went out to dinner. It didn't matter if they had him steal booze from his dad's liquor cabinet. It didn't matter if he always had to drive. It didn't even matter that they were mean to him sometimes. Those were small prices to pay to be allowed to hang out with them. Even doing some of their homework wasn't bad. Brian was smart. School was easy for him. It was an honor to be asked to hang out with them. People noticed. Girls noticed. Brian really wanted girls to notice.

"That is some nice ass," Zack said as Caron went to wait on another table.

"I'd like to ratty tat tat that ass," Morgan added.

"You and me both."

Zack held up his hand and got a high five from Morgan. He held it a second for Brian, but Brian was too slow to catch on. When Brian went to slap the hand was already coming down. He slapped the hand clumsily. Brian forced a smile.

"What about you, Brian? I bet you would like some of that," Morgan asked.

"She's very pretty."

"Pretty? Fuck pretty. She's hot. You can tell. She knows stuff. I bet she fucks like a she-devil."

"Rip your dick right off," Zack said.

Morgan laughed and Brian joined in.

"I wonder who she is," Morgan said.

"Her name tag says Caron, with a C," Brian supplied.

"Not her fucking name, numb nuts. Who she is? Where she goes to school? Where she lives? Has she got a boyfriend? Does she like to give head? She spit or swallow? *That* who she is."

"Oh. I could probably find that stuff out for you guys."

"Really? How?" Zack asked.

"Facebook and stuff. I know lots of kids at other schools."

"You'd do that for us?"

"Sure, if you want. I'd be glad to."

"Cool. We'll get the low down on Caron with a C and come back tomorrow night. I think she has the hots for the big man," Zack said.

"Fuck you," Morgan growled.

"No, fuck *you*. I saw the way she looked at you. And I saw you touching her hip. I bet she goes to the back and masturbates after we leave."

"Fuck you, Zack."

"You have a very limited vocabulary. Oh, wait. You're a fucking lineman. That means you are one IQ point above retard."

"You're the one with your hands on my ass every day, faggot."

"You know you love it. I know you're just begging for a good ass-fisting."

"Fuck you. You are such a faggot."

"Hey, Brain get the bill and let's roll. And leave her a good tip for us. We don't want to look like cheapskates."

Brian looked the bill over. He figured out twenty per cent and started to leave it as a tip, but Zack might ask him how much he left. He decided on twenty-five percent. That was much better. She would remember that. Zack and Morgan pulled on their letter jackets and paused for a second in case anyone was looking. They wanted to give plenty of time to check out the two stud football players. Zack slapped Brian on the shoulder. It was a little hard. He motioned with his head and they turned to go.

Morgan watched Caron pouring ice tea at another table. Her ass looked like two apples in her tight skirt. He wanted her and he was pretty sure she wanted him too. She turned back toward their table and saw Morgan watching her. She smiled and did a little wave. Morgan smiled and waved back. Oh, yeah, she wanted him bad. Real bad.

Caron watched the three boys leave. Inside she was laughing. They were trying so hard to act grown up. In her head she renamed them the rapist, the retard and the dork. They flirted hard with her. They would be back. She bet they left a good tip. She was good at manipulating men. It was a gift.

24

Frank drove until he spotted a little bistro off the main road. There was a small parking area beside the restaurant and he pulled in. The lot was pretty full and there were a number of other expensive looking cars parked there. The Mercedes would blend right in.

He got out and stood by the car looking the place over. Dorian waited to see if he would come around and open her door. It took Frank two seconds to figure out what she was waiting for. He walked to her side and opened the door. Dorian popped out of her seat like a Jack in the Box. She was giggling. She got up on her tiptoes and kissed him on the cheek. Women, thought Frank, were different.

The bistro had a Mediterranean feel to it. The dark wood and brick looked Italian. There were stained glass windows with images of rolling hills and vineyards. The sign had a small bunch of grapes carved into the lower corner. The final clue was the name. It was called, originally enough, The Italian Bistro. It was a small place, but had an outside sitting area off to the side for smokers. They went inside and got a table. They ordered salads with chicken strips and sipped water. The bistro had added pine nuts, cranberries, and Mandarin orange slices to the salads to jazz them up. It worked. It was a nice contrast of textures and tastes.

Dorian told Frank everything she saw in the lamp store. He listened without comment. He could picture it. He would go back and see if he could see Burns. He would be better able to evaluate the situation if he had a chance to read his body language. What was obvious was that the Russians were still there and not giving Burns much space.

Dorian looked at him expectantly.

"What?"

"What now? What's our play?"

"You are such a pretty little criminal. *My* play is, I am going back to see if I can get Mr. Burns to buy these designer lamps. If I do, my company will make a big profit. I will earn a huge commission. Mr. Burns will resell the lamps and he will make a big profit. Everybody will be happy."

"Who are the Russians?"

"I don't know. I don't care. It's got nothing to do with me unless they are planning on buying his business."

"Are you going to drop me at the hotel or do you want me to go with?"

"I'll drop you off. It might look suspicious if someone see us together again."

"If you'll give me a little money, I can cruise the shops downtown while I wait. Girls love to shop."

"How much do you want?'

"I want a million bucks," she said with a straight face. She paused for effect like a good comedian then added, "but I would settle for fifty."

Frank peeled off a Grant and passed it to her.

"Done."

"I should have asked for a hundred."

Frank smiled. He was getting good at smiling, he thought. It might even be something he started doing without trying if he wasn't careful.

"Yes, you should have."

Dorian leaned over and kissed him. "Thank you."

Frank paid and they went outside for the car. Two young couples were just coming in. They were having a spirited conversation over something called the Tea Party and how it was evil and full of racists. One of the boys said they were all Neanderthals. The girl with him was full of passion and agreeing with every word. The other young man added his two cents about neo-Nazis. The other girl looked completely bored. She wore a tired fake smile. The first boy wasn't watching his step and stumbled over a broken piece of concrete. His body lurched toward Frank. Frank shifted slightly and took a half step to the side, avoiding the collision. Frank took another half step to be back beside Dorian. It was instinctual. It was effortless. It was very fast. The boy caught his balance and righted himself. He never realized how close he had come to falling into Frank. Dorian only caught a glimpse of movement.

Frank walked to the car and used the remote to unlock the doors. He walked around to the passenger side and opened the door. Dorian slipped inside.

"Just like a princess in a fairy tale," she said.

"What am I, the moat monster?"

"No. You're the knight is shining armor."

Frank laughed. She was crazy, but he liked her. He kept his smile all the way to his side of the car. His eyes caught on the gold Porsche 911 parked two spots away. He had read about the new turbo Porsche 911. Five hundred horse. Zero to sixty in just over three seconds. A direct fuel injected rear engine. The rear wing was supposed to pop up into place at seventy-five miles and hour to increase the down force. Nice chariot, he thought. Somebody wasn't hurting in this economy.

The man sitting alone at the outside table of the bistro was sipping a dessert wine as he tinkered on his Apple G4 laptop. A half eaten pastizzi rested on a small white plate. He looked like a younger, blonder Kevin Costner. He wore black

Gargoyle sunglasses with amber tinted lenses. He was well-dressed in an expensive linen jacket and a gray Italian silk shirt. He wore a Rolex Submariner on his left wrist and a thick gold bracelet on his right. The bracelet had the name David inscribed on the face. The man's name was David Carpenter, although his birth certificate identified him as Jeff Foster. He never used that name. A cigarette resting in the ashtray trailed a thin sliver of smoke. The ashtray was full. He took up the cigarette and took another puff.

He saw the two couples barely miss the big man and his daughter. It caught his eye. The man had avoided the contact without anyone realizing there had almost been a collision. The big man had flowed around it like a stream of water slipping around a rock. He didn't recognize the man immediately. He looked strangely familiar. The clothes, the glasses, the suit, they were all distractions. The man focused on what was real. The speed was real. The reflexes were real. He knew the cat-like movements as sure as a mother recognized her child's face. It was Frank Kane. But Frank Kane was dead.

David Carpenter showed no reaction. He had trained his face to not reveal his thoughts. He was one of the Spartans' founders. Cyrus had renamed him Helios after the sun god. Some lay-people confused Helios with Apollo. They were wrong. Helios was said to drive the sun across the sky each day pulled by four flaming horses. Helios saw everything. Helios knew everything. Homer, the blind poet, had written in the Odyssey that it was Helios that had seen Aphrodite's infidelity and reported it to her husband who trapped the lovers in an enchanted net. Carpenter had a similar function for the Spartans. He gathered intelligence. He gathered the powerful to him and used their influence to protect the Spartans.

He watched Frank pull away in a nice black Mercedes. He noted the license number. What was Frank doing in Fort Worth? The clothes and car were part of his disguise. Who was the girl? She was definitely not his daughter. Was she part of it or only a recent conquest? Part of it, he reasoned. She would have to be a part of whatever Frank was doing or she wouldn't be with him. Frank Kane worked alone. Maybe Frank was using her as part of his disguise. Wouldn't put it past him. Frank Kane was a very clever man.

Carpenter typed in the license number of the Mercedes. A top end disguise meant Frank had to be staying some place expensive. Expensive hotels were sticklers for rules after 9/11. With a few clicks of his fingers he found that Frank was staying at the Ashton Hotel under the name Frank Nomin. That Frank, always the clever one with names.

Carpenter signaled the waitress. He finished his wine and gave her cash for his lunch. He closed his laptop, got up and left by the little outside wrought-iron gate. He walked leisurely to the Porsche. He eased into the seat and put on his seat belt. The control panel lit up like a plane's cockpit. He adjusted his rear view mirror as he backed out of his parking space.

It was chance that had brought him to that table at that moment. He had just been passing through on his way west. Carpenter knew it was an omen. There was no other explanation. The gods had brought them together for a purpose. Why, he didn't know. In time he would. He would have to make arrangements to stay over for a few days. He figured he would keep an eye on Frank and see what was what.

Carpenter remembered Frank telling him about a Greek from Miletus named Thales. He was the first philosopher and the first scientist. He was revered by the Greeks and later the Romans who designated him as one of the Seven Wise Men of the world. His discoveries acted as a guide for Euclid's work. He developed the theory that in the ever-changing world there was an unchanging substratum. It was the elemental building block of the universe. It was the core of all things. In a moment of ego Frank had told him that Thales said that the unchanging element was water. "All is water," Thales said. Frank had really liked that even if it wasn't true. Frank Kane did not change. Carpenter knew he could not. He was as pure a creature as he had ever met. Frank's business would be easy to figure out, he thought. Just wait for the bodies to hit the floor. When Frank Kane was around there were always bodies.

25

Frank parked the Mercedes and went inside the lamp store. There were only two other people still shopping inside. Both were older women. Both ignored him. He approached the checkout desk. There was only one girl working. He smiled. She was tall and coltishly thin. She had to be five nine. She had long brown hair with blonde highlights, and high cheekbones. Her mouth turned up at the corners giving her the appearance of a slight smile. She was very pretty. He liked her face. He was sure he wasn't the first man to notice how attractive she was. She was wearing a peach colored sundress. He removed one of his business cards from his jacket and passed it to the girl. Her nametag identified her as P.K.

"How can I help you Mr. Nomin?"

"I'm here to see Mr. Burns. You can call me Frank."

"I'm so sorry, Frank. Mr. Burns is in meetings all day and can't be disturbed."

"Really?"

"Really."

Frank smiled again. "You see, Mr. Burns called me, I've driven a long way at his request."

"Perhaps tomorrow would be better. If you could check back...."

"Tomorrow would not be better for me. I'm in town for today only. Mr. Burns expressed an interest in acquiring some Frederick Cooper designer lamps. Ordinarily we do not work with independent dealers, but we made an exception in this case. It's a sizeable number of lamps."

"I see. I didn't know."

"Now you do. Take my card to Mr. Burns. Tell him Frank is here as he requested. Let's see if we can do business or not."

"I know he loves Frederick Cooper's pieces. We carry a good selection. Wait here a moment, please."

"Thank you."

The checkout girl took the card and hurried up to the office. She was obviously nervous. She knew she wasn't supposed to disturb him. She knocked lightly on the door. She could hear stirring inside. Voices were low.

"Yes? What is it?"

"It's P.K., Mr. Burns. There's a man here to see you. He says he came a long way to meet with you."

The door opened slightly. "Man? What man?"

P.K. smiled, handed him the card.

Burns stared at it. "I don't know anyone named Nomin."

"This gentleman says it's urgent he speak to you about some Frederick Cooper lamps he has. He said to tell you Frank was here. He said you called him."

Burns started nodding to himself as he sorted it out. Then he knew. He knew who Frank was. He stepped outside the office and looked down at Frank. The man was dressed like a businessman, but he was a killer. Bruce could feel the danger radiating off him like heat. It was too late for a negotiator. Burns forced a weak smile. He shook his head and handed the business card back to PK. There was nothing Frank could do for him now.

"I'm sorry he's come such a long way, P.K. I can't meet with him today."

"He said he was only in town for the one day or I wouldn't have bothered you."

"It's alright, P.K. I just can't do it. He'll understand. Tell him I'm sorry."

Burns turned and went back into the office. P.K. hurried down the stairs. She handed Frank's card back to him.

"I'm so sorry. Mr. Burns says he can't meet with you today."

Frank slipped the card back into his pocket. "That's unfortunate."

P.K. stared back up at Burns' office. She turned back toward Frank with a new smile on her lips.

"Are you sure you can't stay another day, Frank? Fort Worth is a very nice city. There's a lot to see and do."

"I don't think it's possible. I have other obligations."

"If there's anything I could do to change your mind," P.K. said with an alluring smile.

Her teeth were perfect and white. Her eyes crinkled when she smiled.

"No. Unfortunately, this deal requires Mr. Burns' approval."

"When are you leaving town?"

"I'm not sure. Probably early tomorrow."

"If you would like some company for dinner, I get off work at six."

"That is a very tempting offer, but I am afraid I would be poor company."

"Maybe I could cheer you up."

Frank's smile was genuine. "I believe you could. What does P.K. stand for?"

"Take me to dinner and I'll tell you."

Frank shook his head slightly. "I wish I could. I really do. I just have too much work to get done before I leave."

P.K. gave a little shrug. "Tomorrow you will wish you had taken me up on my offer."

"I'm sure I will. I'm regretting it even now."

Frank turned and left. Must be the suit he thought. Even a one-eyed gorilla like him looked pretty damn good in an Armani suit. Or it could be the smiling thing. He was getting real good at that. He would have to check in the mirror to see if it looked better. It would have been nice to see Dorian's face if he brought P.K. back to their room. See who was shocked then. Hell, Dorian would have probably suggested a three-way. She was unflappable. Women. And people said the ocean was mysterious.

As Frank reached the exit door Dimitri came in. He brushed past Frank with only a sideways glance. Frank scanned him with a glance and continued outside. There were definitely two Russians. He would have to make a move soon.

Burns sat back down behind his desk. There was a tap on the door and Dimitri came into the office.

"Who was that man?" Dimitri asked.

"Salesman. I sent him away."

"Not our merchandise?"

"No, I had hoped it was when P.K. came to get me."

Dimitri smiled his ferret smile. "P.K., she is the pretty girl downstairs?"

"Yes."

"If we are forced to wait too much longer, you will force me to introduce myself to her."

"Leave her alone. She's just a kid."

"She could have her uses. It might help me pass the time while we wait."

"I said to leave her alone."

"Or what, Mr. Burns? What will you do? Would you risk your wife for this girl's honor?"

Burns glared at Dimitri, then looked away. "No. There's just no point in involving anyone else. It only gets more complicated."

Dimitri nodded. "You are right, Mr. Burns. And you are sure this man was not bringing our merchandise?"

"The delivery guys are from El Salvador. Did that old guy look like he was from El Salvador to you?"

"Temper. Temper, Mr. Burns. He did not move like an old man. There was something about him I found unsettling."

"I wouldn't know. I didn't talk to him."

The giant said something in Russian and Dimitri nodded in response.

"I take it you did not hear anything yet about our merchandise?"

"No. Not a thing. But it will get here, just give it a little more time."

"I am afraid we are running out of that luxury, Mr. Burns. I told you interest payments were coming due."

"I know. I know. What do you want me to do about it?"

Dimitri spoke Russian to the other man. The giant nodded. Dimitri smiled.

"You have nothing you can do, I am afraid. You tell me so many times. Others must bear this burden. Others must pay this cost."

Dimitri spoke again in Russian. The giant grabbed Burns and lifted him to his feet. He locked a huge arm around his neck from behind. Burns clawed at the arm. His eyes bulged and his heart pounded. The giant eased the pressure off just enough to let Burns draw in a tiny sip of air.

"Stay calm. This is for your own protection. You must not cry out. I have brought you something."

Dimitri removed a handkerchief from his pocket. He unfolded it slowly on the table like unwrapping a present. Inside was a woman's left ring finger. The delicate nail was painted a pale pink that stood out against the bloodless white finger. The finger was wearing a wedding band and a large diamond engagement ring. Burns stared at the ring for a moment before he recognized it. He tried to scream, but the giant had cut his air off again. He struggled, jerking his body around to break free. The giant held him effortlessly in his viselike grip.

"Yes, Mr. Burns. This is your wife's finger. It is very sad. She was crying when I left. She was begging for you to help her. She is very afraid."

Burns continued to struggle until he went limp. The giant dropped him back into his chair.

"You brought this on yourself, Mr. Burns. You made me do this terrible thing. The Greek warned you."

Burns started to weep. Dimitri walked around the desk and patted him on the shoulder.

"This gives me no pleasure, Mr. Burns. Believe me. But it must be done. You must realize we are serious men. This is a serious violation of our contract. There are costs being incurred by your lateness in delivery."

"I can't do anything. Don't you understand? I can't do anything."

"That is unfortunate. The interest is compounding."

Burns looked up. "What do you mean?"

Dimitri leaned in close. "Tomorrow I take her hand. The next day her arm. After that, who can say?"

Burns slumped down on the desk sobbing. Dimitri spoke to the giant in Russian. The giant answered same. Dimitri laughed.

26

Kevin, Thumper and Clay moved slowly though the bar's packed parking lot. It was a busy place. They wanted something old, but not worn out. Earlier when the subject of jacking a car came up, the Saturn with only two hubcaps came to mind. If it was so easy for Clay to boost a car, why were they driving such a ratty one in the first place? It needed to be invisible. Boring in color and shape. Near the back of the lot they found what they were looking for. An Impala. Clay used a slip bar to slide behind the window and pop the lock. He was busy lying across the seat working on the wires when the cowboy showed up.

The man was about twenty, in tight straight leg blue jeans, and a starched white shirt with a big straw cowboy hat. He wore a large belt buckle that proclaimed him the winner of last year's calf roping competition.

"Hey, buddy, just what the fuck are you doing in my car?"

Clay didn't bother to look up. He kept working. It was hard to hot wire a car with only one good hand.

"I'm talking to you, asshole."

Kevin appeared from the shadows, smiled, and held his left hand up. The palm was out to show it was empty. "I think you are mistaken, friend. This is my car. You must have had too much to drink."

The cowboy was confused. It was late. He had been drinking. A lot. He looked around to orient himself. He wanted to be sure it was his car. When he turned back around toward Kevin, Kevin had the Ka-Bar knife in his right hand. He stepped up quickly and drove the big knife up under the cowboy's rib cage. The cowboy gasped and slumped forward. Thumper caught him from behind. Kevin ripped the blade free. Thumper guided the cowboy over to the area between the wall and the next parked car. He sat him down gently. The cowboy was still trying to force air into his lungs. He held his hands against the knife wound. It was a fatal wound. The blood seeped out between his fingers. The cowboy was going into shock at the loss of blood. He fell back onto the asphalt of the parking lot. He stared off into the night sky. No one knew his last thoughts as he died.

Thumper went through his pockets and took the cash from his wallet. He found a cheap black plastic comb and put it into his own front shirt pocket. Kevin took his hat. He snugged it down onto his head. He wriggled it around to get it to feel right.

"You want his belt buckle?" Thumper asked.

"No. You can have it."

Thumper undid the belt and pulled it loose from his waist. There was blood on it. He wiped the blood off on the cowboy's white shirt. He slipped it through his own jean loops. It fit pretty well. Thumper smiled.

The car came to life beside them. Clay slid into the driver's seat.

"Let's roll," Kevin said, wiping the bloody blade on the cowboy's pants.

Thumper got into the back seat. Kevin fell into the passenger seat. He adjusted the hat in the mirror to see how it looked. Not bad. He liked it.

"Dumb shit kicker," Thumper said. "He should have just walked away. He didn't have to get himself killed."

"Sucks to be him," Kevin added. "I didn't have any other choice. Maybe if Clay could boost a car a little faster, the boy would still be alive."

Clay looked over at Kevin.

"Fuck you," he mumbled and backed them out into the night.

"I can't wait to get to Fort Worth," Kevin said. "I got a boy there who will hook us up."

"What's his name?" Thumper asked.

"Chavo."

"He ain't white is he?"

"What the fuck does that mean? He's a spic, but he's dialed in. Ain't a white dude. That's some racist bullshit, Thumper. You know that? Racist bullshit."

"I'm just saying."

"Fuck you. You got a better plan, then let's hear it. If not, shut the fuck up."

Clay smiled as he drove. Sometimes not being able to speak was a blessing.

27

Dorian sat on the sofa in the room sipping a glass of dark wine. She heard the key card in the door and turned. The door opened and Frank stepped into the room. Without thinking she ran to him and threw he arms around him. Frank hugged her back.

"What was that for?" he asked.

"You came back. I wasn't sure you would."

"I said I would."

"Men lie."

"That's true. We do. Now let me go."

Dorian released Frank and went back to the sofa. She sipped her wine. "Come sit down and tell me how it went."

"Not good. I'll have to figure something out." Frank took a seat across from her. He smiled.

"What?" she asked.

"I was just enjoying how pretty you are."

Dorian turned to her profile, and giggled. "Do you know who I look like?"

"Who?"

"Lindsay Lohan. My eyes and nose are just like hers. Everybody says so."

Frank nodded, "Oh, yeah. I can see that."

"Really. That's what I'm told all the time."

"I believe you."

Dorian stared at him for a moment and laughed. "You don't know who Lindsay Lohan is, do you?"

"Not a clue. Probably a singer."

"Well, she does sing, but she's a famous actress. And she designs clothes."

"I don't get to the movies much."

"She's everywhere. In all the magazines and on TV and in the newspapers. You really never heard of her?"

"Sorry. But if you think you look like Linda Logan, I'm sure you do."

"You are so weird. I can't believe you don't know who she is. I mean, I actually try to look like her with my makeup and hair and stuff."

"Why?"

"Why what?"

"Why do you want to look like her? Why don't you want to look like Dorian Holloway?"

"Because she's a movie star and Dorian Holloway is a loser."

"I don't think so."

"You wouldn't understand."

"Because I'm ugly."

"You're not ugly."

"You're just such a man. You don't care how you look."

"It doesn't define who I am. It shouldn't define you either."

Dorian took a deep drink of wine. "You're so strange. Are you sure you're legit?"

"Yes, and thanks."

Frank got off the sofa and walked to the window. He looked out, then turned and walked across the room. He spun again and went back to the window. Frank continued pacing the room until Dorian sighed loudly.

"Walking won't make anything happen any faster."

"It can't hurt."

"It's getting on my nerves. Sit down and have a glass of wine. We'll figure out our next move."

Frank wasn't worried. He knew what was coming. He would have to take the hard way. People would be hurt. The thought did not excite him or fill him with dread. It was merely a fact. What concerned him about violence was two-fold. The greater the violence the more attention it drew from law enforcement agencies. Which made it harder to cover up. You had to be careful and lucky. But it couldn't be helped. The second reason was Frank's own demons. He liked to picture them locked in a dungeon behind a thick, iron-studded door. They were chained in a central keep surrounded by high stone walls and a deep moat. He knew that once he let them out they were hard to force back inside their cell. Frank did not want to be that man any longer.

Frank sat down on the sofa beside her. The flat screen TV was on some show about home decorating. Frank ignored it. Dorian poured him a glass of wine. Frank sipped it. Not bad. The Spartans had drunk red wine with water.

"How is it?"

"Fine."

"You drink a lot of wine?"

"No. Why?"

"I see you as more of a beer man. Or straight liquor. It seems more manly than wine."

"You're right. I don't drink much wine, but this is okay."

Dorian took a sip. "I could get used to this."

"What are your plans after *this?*"

"My plan is to make you fall in love with me so you take me with you."

"Not a good plan. Any fall-back?"

"Not really. I guess I'll have to get a job."

"No more life of crime?"

"Not much future in it. Sooner or later everyone gets busted. Better to quit while I'm ahead. I got to get into the real world sooner or later."

"I like that plan. If you could be anything, what would it be?"

"For real?"

"For real."

"Hair. I would do hair. I've always been good at it. I did all my friends' hair growing up. I have a real feel for the way hair should look. I guess I would open a little shop and do hair."

"That's a good plan."

"It's only a plan. I don't have the formal training or the money to open a shop. But I could probably rent a chair in a shop and build a clientele. It would take time, but it's worth a try."

"It's definitely worth a try. Where would you set up shop?"

"Probably go home to Ohio. What about you? What's your fall-back on the lamps?"

"I guess I'll have to go back tomorrow and force a meeting. I need to move those lamps or I won't make my quota. I don't make my quota they might fire me."

Dorian took another drink of wine and clicked the TV off.

"Since we only have a few days left together I have an idea."

"What would that be?"

"I think we need to take this bottle and run a hot bath. The tub is huge. It'll easily fit two people. Then we order some room service. We should make the best of our time."

Frank laughed. "I like the way you think."

Dorian slid over to Frank and kissed him. Their kisses grew more passionate. She stood up and removed her clothes. Frank stood and she started to strip him as well. Suddenly she pulled away.

"What's the matter?"

"I almost forgot. I got you something when I was out."

"Condoms?"

"No, nasty. It's way better."

Dorian hurried over to a bag on the counter. She fished around inside and found what she was looking for. She hid it behind her back.

"Close your eyes."

Frank complied. He knew better than to argue with her. He could hear her moving closer to him.

"Now open them."

Frank opened his eyes. She was holding a cigar in her small hands.

"Surprise."

Frank took the cigar. He smelled its rich aroma. He rolled it in his fingers. It was a Montecristo white label. It was a very fine cigar. He smiled at her.

"Thank you. I'll save it for later. That was very sweet."

"Yes, it was. It was your money anyway."

"It was still very thoughtful."

She settled into his lap.

"I hope you like it."

"I do."

"You can show me how much in the tub."

The sound of Frank's cell phone ringing broke the mood.

"Don't answer it."

"I have to. It could be the office."

"Or your wife."

"Or my wife. Go start the water. I'll be just a minute."

Dorian grabbed the bottle and her glass and sauntered toward the bathroom. She turned at the door and stuck her tongue out at Frank. When the door closed behind her Frank opened the phone.

"This is Frank."

"Yeah, man. It's DC."

"What's up? Anything new on Elliot's brother?" Frank asked.

"No. That's not why I called."

"Has something happened to the girls?"

"No. They're fine. I'm on my way over there now to check on them."

"Then what?"

"You know that little girl? The one you told me you see some mornings when you're running?"

"Yeah, Rosa. What about her?"

"She got shot. There was some kind of drive-by shootout. She opened her door and caught one in her arm. Her uncle went to grab her and he got hit too."

"Are they going to be all right?"

"Don't know yet. They took them both to the hospital."

"Did the police show?"

"They showed, but by then the gangbangers were all gone. They cops went home. It's not the type of neighborhood the cops keep an eye on."

"Fuck the police."

"I figured you would want to know. I'll update you when I learn something new. Anything you want me to tell Elliot?"

"No. I saw his brother. He's got some Russian watchdogs with him. I'll make a move tomorrow. Tell Elliot to be patient. Look after Jenny and Caron for me."

"No worries there, Frank. I'm looking after 'em."

Frank said, "I'll call you tomorrow." He closed the cell phone. He would deal with the MS-13 thugs when he got home. There was nothing he could do about it now. Frank picked up his wine glass and walked into the bathroom. He liked the idea of maximizing his time with Dorian.

28

DC parked on the street in front of Frank's house. The girls' yellow Volkswagen was parked in the driveway. He hurried in. He was nervous. He knocked on the door. Caron opened it.

"DC, come in."

She hugged him as he came through the door. Her hug lingered a second or two longer than it should have. He could feel her breasts pushing against him through his thin cotton t-shirt. They headed for the kitchen. Jenny met them in the hallway. She gave DC a kiss on the cheek. He held up two bottles of wine.

"Just like I promised."

"You are *so* sweet," Jenny said.

"I told you he would come through."

"Did you rent a movie?" DC asked.

"Yeah. We got one on the way home from work. It's a comedy. The new one by Will Ferrell."

"I could use a comedy."

"Why? What happened?"

DC told them about the shooting.

"That's horrible. I hope she's going to be all right."

"Me, too. She's so young."

"Frank wanted me to double check on you girls just because of that kind of stuff. It's dangerous out there. You be extra careful while he's gone. Lock the doors and windows. And don't let anybody you don't know in. If there is any trouble, call me. Anytime."

"We will," Caron said.

"I have a baseball bat in the umbrella stand by the front door just in case."

"We could always let DC stay here to protect us," Caron said.

"I think that would be more dangerous," Jenny said, "for us."

"And me," DC said. "Frank would kill me."

They all laughed.

"Come on. I'll get some glasses. Caron you put the movie on."

DC and Caron went into the living room. Caron put the DVD in the player and turned it on. She turned the lights down. DC was sitting on the sofa. Caron snuggled up beside him. DC was slightly alarmed. He felt drawn to Caron the way men were always drawn to attractive women. He had felt the first stirrings of that when he had met her in Atlanta. Nothing had ever come of it. Nothing ever should.

Jenny walked in carrying three glasses and a wine bottle opener. She passed the corkscrew to DC who attacked the bottle seriously. He finessed the cork out and Jenny passed him the first glass. DC poured each of their glasses in turn. Jenny gave Caron a strange look and then snuggled close to DC's other side. They all clinked glasses.

"To best friends," Jenny said.

"To best friends," DC parroted.

"To better than best friends," Caron said.

They all took a drink.

"That's not half bad," Caron said.

"I like it too," Jenny said.

DC smiled, "The lady at the wine shop said it was a blend. She said it was all the rage."

"Its kind of mild. I like that. Sometimes reds are so dry and harsh."

"Yeah," Caron added, "and sometimes whites are too fruity."

"All I know is it gets you buzzed. That's good enough for me. Now shut up both of you, the movie's starting. I've been wanting to see this."

Ignoring the ambient bar noise around him, Special Agent Richard Redding swirled his single-malt Scotch in front of him. He stared at the amber fluid and tried to work his way through what was happening. Things were shaking loose. People were on the move. Something big was going on and he couldn't get out in front of it. The FBI didn't tend to prevent crimes. They solved them. They were relentless. They brought in state-of-the-art forensic experts to look at hair, blood spatter, fingerprints, DNA, fiber, paint chips, insect larva, every damn thing, even plant growth profiles. Their thoroughness solved crimes. They interviewed everybody. They amassed incredible amounts of information. They traced and retraced until the evidence led them to the conclusion.

One of Redding's gifts as an agent was to be able to see a pattern and predict its next step so he could be waiting. About this, he didn't have a clue. That wasn't entirely true. He had a lot of pieces. He just couldn't connect them in a way to make sense. Frank Kane returning for retribution. Keith Masnick disappearing. The old Spartan warning written in blood in the bathroom. Was it significant that it was in the bathroom? Was someone cleaning house? Is that what it was supposed to mean? Why on the back of the door instead of the living room wall? There were a lot of variables. Hell, some of it might not even make any sense anyway. And what about Special Agent Ed Harris? There was something off there. He might have another agenda. Redding was pretty certain he did. He would have to watch him too.

Redding took a drink of his single malt Scotch. He liked the burn. It would all come out. Sooner or later he would understand, and then he would get in front of it. It would work out. Absently, he let his hand touch the Glock on his hip. He would keep his weapon close. Redding knew he couldn't trust anyone. He never had.

A woman came over and stood to his side. She was in her late thirties, a good twenty years younger than Redding. She had dark hair and a risqué neckline on her dress. Her large breasts winked out at him. She wore a string of pearls. He thought she was very pretty. Redding smiled.

"Do you mind if I have a seat?"

Redding pulled his badge wallet from his pocket and opened it for her so she could see he was FBI. "You sure you want to sit here?"

The woman smiled. "You're a cop?"

"Yep."

"Do you have handcuffs?" she asked. A thin smile played across her face.

"Yep."

"I think you could be fun. Even if you are a cop."

"I'm on duty."

"If you're drinking it must be good duty. You shouldn't drink alone."

Redding laughed. "You do my old heart good."

She pulled the chair out beside him.

"So you don't mind if I sit?"

Redding looked at his Scotch again.

"Hit the bricks. I don't know who sent you, but tell them I'm not a rookie anymore."

The woman looked shocked.

"No one sent me. I just saw you across the bar and thought you looked lonely."

"Lady, no one ever saw me across a bar and thought I looked lonely. Now go on. You tried. It didn't work. Now beat it."

"You got me wrong. I was only...."

"Give it up. It isn't working tonight. Try me again later."

The woman turned and walked away.

Redding took another sip of the Scotch. She was too hot for him. Anyone could have sent her. He didn't know why. What was the purpose? It was probably a good sign that things were on the move. He would keep his eyes open. He took another sip of the scotch. He savored the burn all the way down his throat.

29

At just after one a.m. Frank got out of bed. He put his regular clothes on with a sport coat. He left the room without waking Dorian. He slipped downstairs and had his car brought around. If the valet was surprised at his late night trip he made no sign.

Frank drove across town to where Burns' house was. It was in an expensive neighborhood. Large old oak trees acted as neatly spaced sentinels along the narrow street. The house was a large Victorian-style home with a huge attached garage. The front yard was treeless. A short row of rosebushes decorated the front of the house. They were in bloom. A sprinkler system chinked out its thin lariats of water. Chinka. Chinka. Chinka. The dry grass lapped up the day's ration of water.

The big house was silent. No lights were on. A sign, warning of a home security system, was in the front yard in the center of the grass. The sign threatened an armed response. Frank cruised past twice, then parked two houses down on the other side of the street facing the house.

He watched the house. Apollo had taught him the sniper's gift for patience and silence. He didn't know what he was watching for. He just sat there unmoving. The house felt locked down. He could go in now. Take care of the Russians. Talk with Burns. There would be casualties. His demons growled and moaned. They wanted release.

Frank thought about the girls back home. He hoped they were okay. He thought about Rosa and her Uncle Carlos. He thought about Dorian. She could go either way. Nothing moved in the dark house. The water sprinklers stopped. In the silence Frank thought about Burns and his wife. He would try the easy way for one more day. Try to finesse something. The demons protested. Frank was resolute. He would give it another day.

Frank restarted the Mercedes and pulled back into the night. He kept the lights off until he was out of sight of the house. If he were quiet he might get back without waking Dorian and her hundred questions about where he had been.

The Russian giant stood in the blackness and watched. He saw the Mercedes pass. He saw it pass a second time. He watched it park and turn off its lights. It was the same one he had seen earlier at the lamp store. The giant watched, still as a statue. It was movement that gave you away. He had learned that in Bosnia. The giant could feel the comforting weight of the big pistol under his arm. There would be plenty of time to draw the weapon if it was needed. He did not flinch.

After a very long time the Mercedes started again. He watched it pull away with its lights off. He didn't doubt for a second that someone was coming to help Burns. He smiled. It wouldn't matter.

30

When Frank awoke he found Dorian already awake with her head resting across his chest. She smiled and sat up. She stared at him. She seemed suddenly serious. Something was wrong.

"What is it?"

"Your scar is gone."

Frank ran a hand over where the scar had been on his cheek. The skin had returned to its original position. The heat, water, and time must have dissolved it.

"I must be a good healer."

"Scars don't heal."

Frank didn't answer.

"The gray in your hair is also a dye. It's starting to fade. I told you I was good with hair and makeup. I can tell. Your hair isn't really turning gray."

Frank didn't answer.

"Why are you disguising yourself?"

"Never sleep with a criminal. You guys are too suspicious. Look, it's simple. I need to look a little older so these business stiffs take me seriously. The scar was just an idea to make my eye a little more noticeable to them."

"Are you really blind in one eye?"

Frank mimed crossing an x over his heart. "Cross my heart."

"How did it happen?"

"I caught a glimpse of myself naked once."

"I mean it. How did you lose it?"

"You are awfully nosy. The truth isn't as exciting as the scar makes it look. I was mowing the lawn and a little rock hit me in the eye. And yeah, I know you are supposed to wear protective goggles and I didn't. Who does? Happy now?"

Frank knew the only way to sell the eye was to make the lie about something else. Something insignificant. Maybe male pride would work. She was very observant.

"And your glasses. The lenses are clear. I checked. Why do you wear them?"

Frank forced a sigh. He hoped it sounded exasperated.

"I'm trying to look smarter. Glasses make you look smart. Don't you know that? Clients see me and they think big old dumb ex-jock. The glasses make me look like I might know a thing or two."

"I don't get you. The tats, the scars, the disguise, the way you fight, and the way you fuck. It all says criminal to me. I tell you it doesn't matter if you are a crook. Yet you keep swearing you do straight work for a living."

"I do. Listen, I'll be straight with you," Frank lied. "I had a rough past. I lucked into this job. I did good. I got promoted. This sale is my big break. If I pull it off, my job is locked in. If I don't, they really might fire me. They're making cuts in a few weeks. I have to pull this off."

Dorian didn't speak right away. She continued to stare at him. She didn't look angry or accusatory. She actually looked a little sad.

"Something else?"

"Who is Helen, really? Is she your wife?"

"No. I told you."

"Do you still love her?"

"Not any more. Our time is past."

"Last night, afterwards…you were asleep and whispered, 'I love you Helen'. It was sweet and sad at the same time."

"If you say so."

"Do you want her back?"

"No. It's not even possible. I think she died a long time ago."

The emotion of the statement was reflected in his voice. Dorian read it.

"I'm sorry. I thought you might have been lying about her."

"I'm being honest. Things happen. People move on. I'm sorry if I called you her name. I didn't mean to. I'm sorry."

Dorian lie down and snuggled against him once more. "You can call me Helen if you want to."

"I don't want to."

"Maybe I could still be your new Helen?"

"My wife wouldn't appreciate that."

"You're not married."

Frank didn't confirm or deny it. "What makes you think that?"

"When we were in the tub your ring had slipped up on your finger."

"So?"

"There wasn't a tan line under it. A lot of married men take their rings off when they're on the prowl and you can spot the white band where it used to be. You don't have one. It takes months of it being off to tan back in."

"I don't always wear it anymore."

"Why?"

"I'm divorced. We're trying to reconcile."

"Why did you get divorced?"

"I cheated and got caught. I got a thing for pretty little criminals." Frank pulled her up and kissed her. "Enough questions."

31

Kevin came back to the car. He was all smiles.

"We're in. It took a little while to hook with Chavo. But once I did, he was good to go. We got a history from inside. He controls a lot of shit around here."

"All right," Thumper said, "Time to make a little money. Is it coke?"

"Yeah, as long as you stay away from dealing crack the cops won't bother you."

"How many times we goin' to step on it before we try to move it?" Thumper asked.

"Normally, I would say twice, but I figure we double that, we make a little leeway. Start squirreling some money."

"That sounds about right."

"Dopers got nobody to complain to anyway. Let's get to town and get the stuff we need."

"How about a little taste first when we get the stuff?"

"Fuck you, Thumper. I know you. You'll snort up all the product. When we start mixing it, I'll trim a little off for us. Not much. But a little of the pure."

"Now you're talking."

"We can't fuck this up. Chavo is a serious dude. He's SNM, Syndicato Nuevo Mexico. They play hard. He'll cut our nuts off."

"Fuck him. He's a spic."

"I'll tell him you said that when he's cutting your nuts off. Now let's go. We do good, he gives us more to move."

"We could always double him and take his stash. Then it's nothing but profit."

"Are you a fucking retard, Thumper? We ice him now, that's the end of the coke pipeline. We don't know who else he's working with. SNM could come after us. I don't want no SNM gangbangers hunting us. Those dudes are totally crazy. Anyway, it's too early to go cowboy. This time we play the long game. When the time is right, we go on our own."

"Whatever you say. You're the boss."

"That's right. Whatever I say, asshole."

32

Frank was wearing a lightweight navy blazer and nice chino slacks. He even had his dress shoes on. Dorian was dressed more casually. She wore a pretty yellow dress with black daisies decorating one side. The material gave the illusion of weightlessness, like gossamer. She looked gorgeous in it. The valet brought their car around. She waited while Frank opened the door on the Mercedes.

"I'm not wearing panties," she whispered.

"Thanks, that's the thought I want to have distracting me when I meet with Burns."

"Just thought you might want to know what's waiting for you when we get back to the hotel. It might make you conclude your business a tiny bit faster."

"It will. I need to focus on what's important, not just business."

Frank held the door, but Dorian didn't get inside. "Can I drive?" she asked.

"No."

"Please. I've never driven one before."

"No."

"I'll do something special for you back in the room. You'll like it."

Women were a mystery. Frank put his palms against his eyes and rubbed them. To have a conversation with a woman was to lose the conversation. He let his hands fall. He smiled.

"Ok. But be careful. No speeding. And don't run anybody down."

"I promise."

"You do have a driver's license, right?"

"Yes. And it's current."

"Just checking."

Dorian slide behind the wheel. She ran a light-fingered hand over the steering wheel. She looked the controls over. She adjusted the seat and the mirrors. And then she smiled. It was a child's birthday morning smile when she first saw the cake and candles. She beamed.

It made Frank happy.

"Thank you."

"Not a problem. Where to first? My meeting isn't until this afternoon."

"I need to pick up a few things. And I need to get some more wine. That was good."

"I might learn to actually like wine," he said.

"Yes, I might civilize you yet." Dorian paused and reached out and touched his arm. She looked at him with a serious expression. "Sorry I'm so nosy. You have the right to do whatever you want. You don't owe me any explanations."

"Forget about it. Let's head down Main Street. I'll tell you when to stop."

Dorian pulled away from the awning and out to the street. Traffic was light but she was completely focused on driving. She drove while constantly scanning the street and her mirrors. Frank liked that she wasn't playing around.

"This is great. The car is so quiet and the ride is so smooth."

"Glad you like it."

"I do."

"You look good behind the wheel. Like you belong there."

"Thanks. I'm glad we met."

Frank laughed. "It was a most unusual meeting, Dorian. But I'm glad too. Pull over here."

Dorian pulled the car over into a space on the street. "What now?"

"I've got some things I need to buy at the grocery store. Why don't you check out some of those shops? Women are suppose to love shoes and purses."

"We do."

"Then get to it, girl."

They got out of the car. Dorian stood on her tiptoes and kissed him on the cheek.

"This is so much fun. I never had money before."

"Keep it under a hundred," Frank said and handed her a bill.

"Can I have a little more? I've always wanted some real Tony Lama cowboy boots. I think cowboy boots with a dress looks sexy cool."

"Whatever speaks to you."

Frank gave her another two hundred and watched her swish into the shoe boutique. He walked into the grocery store two doors down. He needed some things for his plans and to cover his tracks. He checked the GPS in his pocket to be sure the Mercedes was still parked and unmoving. Dorian had the car keys. He liked her. He even trusted her to a certain extent. He knew he had been stupid to leave the keys with her. That couldn't be helped now. Any movement and he would be on it.

The grocery store was small, but he knew it would have everything he needed. He got a bottle of what he hoped was good wine, two heads of garden lettuce, three large squirt bottles of mustard, a big jug of vinegar, a box of black, heavy-duty garbage bags, some paper towels, a large bottle of Clorox, a pack of disposable lighters, and some bread and milk to make it look legit. He came outside and went to the car. He saw Dorian was still inside the shoe store trying on cowboy boots. It figured.

Using the remote, Frank put the grocery bags in the back of the car. He was going to go inside the shoe store when he saw the ice cream store across the street. Frank knew he was getting soft. The sign over the store read Cathy's Ice Cream. It had a painting of a small blonde girl with blue eyes. She had a huge smile and large perfect teeth. Obviously, she didn't eat a lot of ice cream or she brushed regularly.

Frank went inside. It was a small shop. There were only three tables. It was primarily take-out. You buy the ice cream. You hit the streets. It was probably a big hit with tourists. There was a lone man behind the counter. Even Spartans could indulge, he rationalized.

David Carpenter sat in his blue Honda Civic. He had parked the Porsche 911 turbo and rented a less conspicuous car. After driving a high performance vehicle the Civic felt like a blue turtle. He lit another cigarette and smoke quietly. He had parked in front of the Ashton and waited for Frank and the girl. They did not disappoint. He saw the Mercedes being brought around. Surprisingly, the girl drove. Odd to say the least. Carpenter did not try to figure out what Frank was doing. He merely observed. He had no preconceived ideas to mislead him, only time to learn. It was interesting to watch the most deadly man he knew, shop. And then, against all probability, Frank Kane went for ice cream.

33

Redding stood in his kitchen drinking a cup of coffee and working on a cigarette. It was his third cup and fourth cigarette. His land line rang. He stubbed the cigarette out in the sink and answered.

"Special Agent Redding."

"It's me, Harris."

"Yeah, what you got for me?"

"I just got off the phone with headquarters. The hard copies are gone."

"What do you mean gone? It would take a couple of trucks to haul all of it."

"Three trucks, according to the manifest."

"You have to sign it in and out. Someone has it. Someone is responsible for it."

"No, sir. The material was removed by a sealed order two years ago."

"On whose authority?"

"They're checking. The paperwork was perfect, but the signature is a phony."

"You got to be kidding me?"

"I wish I were."

"What about the DNA? Did we get a match on the writing in the bathroom?"

"More bad news. It's gone too. We got nothing."

"How do you delete DNA?"

"They say a virus corrupted the records."

"All of them?"

"Appears so."

"We still got fingerprints on file? Tell me we still have fingerprint records."

"That data base seems mostly intact where we've been able to check it. The prints on the principals have been reclassified beyond our reach."

"We are the FBI. Who reclassified them?"

"It was NSA. We contacted them and were informed they consider the founders of the Spartans to be domestic terrorists and not our jurisdiction."

"Fuck me. Is there a go-around?"

"I contacted my father to see if he can help. He has a lot of power. He said he would see what he could do."

"Can the techs rebuild any of the prints from our original files?"

"I requested that. They didn't sound hopeful."

"Shit. We got anything we can use?"

"I think we've hit a dead end. We have nothing."

"Not so fast, rookie. I have copies of most of the murder books and information I collected before I turned it in. A lot of the material is in the public domain, newspapers, magazines, stuff like that. The material I got isn't. It was from my own investigations with the Bureau."

"Is it someplace secure?"

"Very."

"Can you get it?"

"There's a lot of stuff. It will take me a day to access it."

"It is a start. What are you doing now?"

"I am following a lead about Masnick. Meet me later this afternoon at the office."

"Yes, sir. Do you mind telling me the nature of your lead?"

"Yeah, I do."

Redding hung up the telephone and stared out the window. He lit another cigarette and thought about the pretty woman from the night before. Damn, she was hot, he thought. He should have tried to fuck her. She probably wouldn't have gone that far, but he should have at least tried. He might have gotten lucky.

Harris hung up the telephone and punched in another number. He waited for four rings. The other party did not identify themselves when they answered. It was the same voice that had answered his previous calls.

"This is Special Agent Harris. Redding has copies of most of the information on the Spartans from when he was the AIC."

"We were afraid of that probability. Redding is old school. It's imperative that we acquire that information. We need to know what exactly he has in his private files. And then destroy it."

"I realize that. I should have the material in the next twenty-four hours."

"Don't spook him."

"I don't appreciate your tone. I know what I'm doing."

"We're aware of that or you wouldn't be in this position. Does he trust you?"

"I think so."

The other person paused.

"Then he is an idiot."

"That's apparent. Whatever abilities he once possessed are long gone. He's getting old and careless. I'll contact you once I have the documents."

The phone went dead. Harris wasn't worried about Redding. He was old and cynical and burned-out. He would manipulate him into thinking what he was doing was by his own choice. By the time he realized there was a noose around his neck it would be too late to do anything about it. Harris smiled. He hoped at some point Redding would realize he had placed the noose himself. Harris smiled. It was moving faster now.

34

Clay drove to the address that Chavo had given Kevin. It was a run-down section on the outskirts of Fort Worth. The houses were small, close together, and tired. The yards were overgrown. Rusted cars dotted many of the yards. Sofas and chairs had been dragged out to front porches. Mongrel dogs patrolled the streets in skittish packs looking for food. Everywhere the gringos looked, they met suspicious stares.

Small groups of Latinos strolled the streets laughing and drinking forty-ounce cans of beer. No one seemed to be going anywhere specific. They too turned to stare at the gringos.

Clay found the house nestled between more houses that looked just like it in-cluding the black iron bars on the windows. Chavo said to look for the wooden Indian. And there it was, an old cigar store Indian. It marked the entrance to the house. The SNM symbol had been painted on it. There were bullet holes in the wooden Indian, attesting to a hard life in the barrio. Clay pulled to the curb.

Three Latinos stood smoking a joint in the front yard. They were covered in tattoos that identified them as officers in SNM. They each wore white wife beater T-shirts. It was an easy way to show off their gang colors. Two more Latinos sat in chairs on the front porch. They stood when Clay stopped.

"I don't like this," Thumper said.

Kevin didn't like it either. In for a penny, in for a pound.

The gangbangers moved as a group toward the car. Two were openly carrying weapons jammed into the front of their pants. Kevin figured the others were armed as well. Kevin got out of the car. Thumper did too. Clay stayed behind the wheel. He stared straight ahead, kept the engine running.

"You lost, gringo?" someone called.

Kevin held up his hands, palms outward to show he was unarmed.

"Just here to see the man. Chavo knows I was coming. I don't want no trouble."

"You got that right," another voice added.

A thin Latino with a pistol looked to be in charge. He approached the car. His hand was on the butt of his pistol.

"You got business with Chavo?"

"I do indeed. He inside?"

"What's your name, gringo?"

"Kevin. Chavo's expecting me."

"You carrying?"

"No"

"How about the one arm?"

"No."

"I guess he's unarmed," the pistolero said emphasizing the last word to a round of laughter from his crew.

"That's right. He's one-armed," Kevin said getting in on the laugh.

The pistolero nodded.

"Okay. Come with me, gringo."

Kevin and Thumper started toward the house. The five men moved in. The pistolero drew his weapon.

"Got to pat you down."

"I understand," Kevin said. "I got a knife in my boot, but no guns."

The pistolero lifted Kevin's pant leg and pulled the Ka-Bar from the boot.

"This all you got?"

Kevin nodded. Thumper nodded.

The pistolero held it up for everyone to see. He shook his head, seemingly embarrassed for the gringos.

"Shit. Keep it."

He handed the knife back to Kevin who put it into his boot again. The pistolero turned and the two gringos followed him into the house. The inside was a wreck of old furniture and empty beer cans. The house reeked of marijuana. There was a giant TV screen in the main room hooked to an array of video game machines. Two young Latinos were fighting space aliens on the big screen. They didn't even look up. The pistolero led them into a back bedroom.

It was a stash room. Drug paraphernalia filled the tables. There were small plastic Ziploc baggies, weighing machines, and rubber bands. A second table had a money counting machine, and bundles of old money were stacked beside it. On the floor were kilo size bags of white powder. Chavo sat working the money machine.

"Chavo," the pistolero said, "I got some gringos here to see you, man."

Chavo turned. His head was shaved clean. An array of gang tats decorated his arms and neck. His arms were huge. He wore a Desert Eagle in a shoulder holster over a baggy shirt. His jeans were new. Kevin didn't recognize the designer, but knew they were expensive. He wore unlaced Timberlands. He turned toward Kevin. He smiled. He spread his arms wide for a hug.

"What, you got no love for me?"

Kevin embraced him in a fierce hug.

"Long time no see, Chavo."

"Just got out of the joint. How long you been out?"

"Coupla three years."

Chavo laughed, "Now you ready to do a little man's work?"

"You got that right. I need to score some serious coin."

"You called at a good time, man. I'm expanding my business. I got a big load in and I need to move the weight. You up for that?"

"You know me, Chavo. I'm up for anything you got. Still moving coke?"

"Nah. That shit is yesterday. I got a straight line on some kick ass Mexican Brown. Primo product."

"Heroin? We talking heroin?'

"You got a problem with riding the horse?"

Kevin hesitated. "Nah. It's all good. Just thought you were into the coke, that's all."

"More money in the horse, man," Chavo said and punched him in the shoulder. "We got the city locked up. No competition."

"Sounds good. What can I do?"

"You got cash or you want to work commission?"

"I'm tapped out. Have to be commission."

"That's cool. Unless you can't pay later. Then I got to ice you. You understand?"

"It's just business. I know. Get me a starter pack and let me see what I can move for you. Where do you want me?"

"Downtown. No one's doing shit down there. Cops won't hassle no white dude. Should be clear sailing. Try some of the bars. The hotels. You know how to work the shit."

"Can do."

"You got protection?"

"The gringo has a knife," the pistolero offered.

"Just a knife?" Chavo asked.

"Why don't you loan me one of your nines? I'll take really good care of 'em."

The pistolero said something in Spanish and Chavo laughed. The pistolero laughed too. Chavo started shaking his head.

"Can't do it, man. Tell you what. You make me some money, I'll cut you a good deal on one. Straight family price."

Kevin was seething. He hid it with a smile. It was a good thing he didn't speak Spanish or he would have to cut some motherfucker's throat.

"No problem, Chavo. Just thought I would ask."

The pistolero spoke some more Spanish and Chavo laughed again. He turned back to the table and passed a large Ziploc bag to Kevin. Inside, already sorted by weight, were small bags of heroin. Kevin looked at the bag and shook the contents.

"You take good care of my little pony, Kevin. We're friends from the joint, but business is business. Don't make me sorry I trusted you."

"You won't be sorry," Kevin said.

Chavo and the pistolero started speaking in Spanish again and Kevin turned and walked out. Thumper followed him. They passed through the knot of gang members to the car. Clay was still sitting rigidly behind the wheel. His knuckles were white. Kevin and Thumper got into the car. As Clay pulled away, Thumper looked over his shoulder. The Latinos were all laughing.

"That friend of yours... Chavo."

"Yeah, what about him?"

"He's an asshole even for a spic."

"You figured that out all by yourself."

Thumper didn't answer. He just watched the house fade behind them. Chavo wasn't the only asshole, he thought.

35

Frank noticed the picture of the pretty blonde woman in a frame behind the counter. It was probably Cathy grown up. There was also a small picture of a baby. It was a boy, judging by the blue blanket. A happy family picture. Frank didn't know much about ice cream. He rarely ate it. There were at least fifty different flavors. Most he had never heard of. He decided to play it safe. Just get a chocolate cone and a vanilla cone. She could pick. Everyone liked chocolate or vanilla.

The ice cream man looked up from his work.

"May I help you?"

"Let me have two cones. A double scoop of vanilla and a double scoop of chocolate."

The man lifted an ice cream scoop out of the hot water it rested in and pulled two cake cones from a dispenser.

"Cake cone be all right?"

"Fine."

He worked the scoop into the big tubs of ice cream. He packed the ice cream deep inside the cones. There was something familiar about the way he moved. Frank couldn't put his finger on it. The ice cream man rang up the charge. He was smiling as he talked to Frank. It was inane shopkeeper's talk. But Frank didn't hear the words. He was staring at the man's face. He knew that face.

Frank passed him a twenty. The ice cream man punched the keys on the register and counted out Frank's change. Who was he? Where did he know him from? And then, he knew.

Dennis Torney. Encouraged to disappear seven years ago before he could be a grand jury witness against the Spartans.

Dennis extended the money to Frank and, looking into those blue eyes, froze…. "It's you!"

Frank smiled. It was not unpleasant. He really had been practicing smiling.

"I thought I recognized your voice, but those eyes. I'll never forget those eyes."

Frank didn't answer.

"Oh, shit. You told me if I ever saw you again, you would kill me. Is that why you're here? Are you going to kill me? It's not fair. I kept my word. I never told anyone."

"I'm not here to kill you," Frank said.

"Then why are you here?"

Frank looked around the ice cream shop. "You're married now. Have a baby?

Dennis nodded.

"I just wanted to let you know that it's over."

"Over?"

"You're safe. No one is looking for you anymore. You can do whatever you want. Live wherever you want. See your sister."

Dennis seemed stunned. "Really?"

"The Spartans are done."

"Thank you," Torney said

Frank took the money and stuffed it into his front pocket. "It's the least I could do. You're a good man, Dennis Torney. You deserve a good life."

Frank walked outside into the bright sunshine. He saw Dorian come out of the shoe store. She was carrying a bag. The new cowboy boots were on her feet. She was floating with happiness. From his peripheral vision he saw Kevin step into her path. He read the fear on her face. She turned and bumped into Thumper who had moved up on her from behind.

"As I live and breathe. If it isn't Cherry Red."

Dorian stifled her reaction. She didn't look surprised at all. She was very good.

"It's about time you showed up. I got your car."

"I see. Where's the big man?"

"He got us a hotel room after the set-up went bad. He went to take a leak and I slipped out with his wheels. It was straight up Plan B."

"Then why didn't you call us?"

"My phone died. I drove back to the diner, but you were gone. There were cops there so I turned around and followed the route he was on. I figured you guys would catch up sooner or later."

Clay pulled up in the white Impala. Dorian smiled and waved at him.

"It could be the truth," Thumper said.

"Fuck could be," Dorian said. "It is. I wouldn't lie to you guys. You're my friends."

"Let's go for a ride, Cherry. You stole it so you got the keys right?"

Dorian pulled the keys from her purse. She dangled them in front of Kevin, who smiled.

"You drive," Kevin said and took her purse.

Dorian got in the driver's seat. Kevin took the seat beside her. Thumper sat behind.

"Where to?" she asked.

Frank dropped the ice creams into the garbage can outside. He watched Dorian drive away. A cold voice in his head said to let her go. He didn't have to have the car. There was nothing in it that could be traced to him. He could figure how to replace whatever he needed in the car. Dorian had done good. She hadn't ratted him out. This was on her. It wasn't his business. Change hotels and he would be invisible again. She knew about the lamp store, but so what? They weren't after him. They wanted the car and the girl. Hell, she could probably talk her way out of it anyway.

Then Frank smiled. She had stood instead of kneeled. Spartans didn't leave warriors behind. He pulled the GPS tracker from his pocket. He flipped it on. The screen loaded instantly. The white dot moving north was Dorian. He looked up and down the street. A line of Yellow Rose Cabs sat parked down the street. He had only walked half a dozen steps in their direction when a driver noticed him. Frank waved him over.

He jumped in as soon as the cab stopped. It looked like it was going to have to be the hard way. He was going to have to bust some heads. The demons in his soul gibbered and squealed with delight. Red time.

"Where to?"

"Head north."

36

"Keep heading north," Kevin said. "We need some privacy and I know a good spot. Turn right here."

Dorian followed Kevin's directions. She appeared calm. Kevin dumped out her purse's contents into his lap. Rummaging, he asked, "Where's my gun?"

"The big guy took it from me. He tossed it out the window when we were driving."

"If we had the piece, I would be tempted to go back to your new boyfriend's hotel and kill that motherfucker."

"He's not my boyfriend. He's a square. He's a trick. I thought you would be thrilled."

Kevin laughed. He stroked her cheek with the blade of the Ka Bar. "Cherry, Cherry, Cherry. You are such a good liar. I never know what to believe."

"And you are such a dumb ass if you think I am stupid enough to cross you."

"She's got a point."

"Shut the fuck up, Thumper. I do the thinking, you do the heavy lifting. That's what you're good at."

Thumper sulked in the back seat.

"Don't worry, Thumper baby," Dorian purred in her sexiest voice. "We'll work this out and it will be just like old times. I might even give you a special treat for trying to stand up for me like that."

Kevin laughed. "Turn left. And quit pulling his dick. Thumper, what's in those bags back there?"

Thumper poked around inside them for a few seconds. "Household shit and some food."

"No beer?"

"No. There's some wine."

"Fuck that," Kevin said. "I ain't no fag."

Kevin ejected the CDs from the player. He looked them over. "What is this shit? He can drive a car like this but he has to burn copies of CDs? What a loser." He tossed the three CDs into the back at Thumper.

Thumper knocked them out of his lap into the floorboard. "I don't want that shit."

Kevin laughed. "Pussy."

The cab driver tried to start a conversation a few times until it was clear Frank didn't want a new best friend. It was obvious that Frank wasn't going to tell him a destination either. So he shut up and followed Frank's commands. Tourists were weird, he thought. As he drove, he dreamed of long-legged cowgirls and cool glasses of beer.

Dorian was easy to follow. The GPS tracker worked perfectly. He was able to stay a good half mile behind her. There weren't a lot of options for him. It would depend on where they took her. He would get her back. That part he was sure of.

Dorian drove on out of town. She didn't like this. Kevin was taking her some-place specific. That was bad.

"Take Harvey Road," Kevin said. "It's just up ahead. It leads to an old pump-ing station. At least it used to. It's on the right. Take it."

"You've been there before?"

"Yeah. I'm from Fort Worth. Didn't I tell you that? That's why I found you. Just bad luck on your part."

Dorian sighed like a parent might with a slow-witted child.

"I knew you were from Fort Worth, Kevin. You told me a half dozen times. That's why I came here. Where else would I go? I don't know who to sell a hot car to."

"I never told you I'm from Fort Worth."

"Think about it, Kevin. Why else would I be here?"

"Bad luck, like I said."

"Don't be stupid. You don't really believe that I could go anywhere in the country and I just happen to pick your hometown?"

"You're good, Cherry. You always were. That's the road up ahead."

Dorian turned down the dirt service road. There were weeds growing be-tween the well-worn tire tracks. She stopped in front of a chain blocking the road.

"Now what?"

"Thumper, see what you can do."

Thumper got out. He walked over to the chain. It was old and rusted. It had been set with bolts. There was no lock. It wasn't meant to be opened anytime soon. He tugged on the chain. It held fast. Thumper checked both sides. The wood where they were fastened too was worn, but solid as well. He kicked at one and felt it give. It wasn't set very deep in the ground. Government workers, he thought. He kicked it again, harder, and it moved more. A few more kicks and he was able to wrench it free. He dragged it across the track. Thumper got back in. Dorian turned up the dirt road. Clay followed in the Impala eating their dust.

Frank saw the car stop. He saw the white Impala park behind it, waiting. He had the taxi driver slow down. As the cab rolled innocently past, he saw Thumper kicking the post. As the taxi continued on, the map showed a service station up ahead. "Pull in here," he said.

He paid the driver and gave him a fair tip. Too small and he might remember the cheapskate. Too big and he might remember the big spender. Frank watched the taxi leave. A blue Honda Civic cruised past and then the road was empty.

He didn't enter the convenience store. They often had camera surveillance. If the cops were looking at a crime scene they might come here and check out the tape. No reason to make it too easy for them. He started back down the road at a slow jog. He reached the service road. The GPS tracker showed it was only a quarter mile to some building it didn't identify.

Normally, Frank would have been cautious and approached slowly. He didn't expect there to be any security along the road. This was a kill site. That's why they had come. They would all be inside. Frank ran up the road. It probably wouldn't take them long.

David Carpenter had watched as the girl was snatched. He followed Frank's taxi. He saw Frank paying the taxi and drove by without varying his speed. He didn't look at Frank. Once he was out of sight he found a place to turn around. He came back slowly. If Frank were still there he would pull into the gas station and get some gas. A reasonable explanation for turning around if Frank noticed. Frank wasn't there. Carpenter caught a glimpse of him jogging up the road. It, whatever it was, would show up in the newspapers in the next few days. Maybe the body count and reporting would tell him what the hell Frank was doing.

Dorian parked. Kevin tried to open the glove box.

"How do you open this thing?"

"How should I know? It's not like it's my car."

Kevin punched random buttons on the number lock. It didn't open.

"What's he got in here that has that kind of lock?"

"Who knows?"

"We can pry it open later," Thumper said.

"I don't want anyone fucking up this ride. We'll figure out a way to bypass it later. Now that we got this baby, we got all the time in the world."

""Pop the trunk, let's see what's back there."

They all got out. Dorian had her arms crossed like she was angry. It was the best pose she could manage. A good bluff was her only chance. She couldn't outfight them. She couldn't out run them. Maybe she could con them.

Clay met them at the trunk.

"Cherrby," he mumbled as a way of greeting.

"Clay. Damn. He messed you up, baby. Are you all right?"

Clay nodded. But his eyes said he was still in a lot of pain.

Kevin tried to pull the case out, but it wouldn't come. "What the fuck?" he said, jerking harder. It ripped free from the Velcro. He ran his hands over the edges, tried to open it.

"Figures," he said, tossing the case to Thumper

"Bring it inside and we'll bust it open. Maybe the jerk was a diamond salesman."

"That would be sweet," Thumper said. "With that and the smack we would be set."

"You got smack? Awesome," Dorian said. "We can have a party."

Kevin smiled. "Yeah. A real party," he said as he pulled a tool bag and length of rope from the trunk. "Let's go," and pushed Dorian in front of him toward the door of the pumping station. It was a small brick building. The outside was covered with gang graffiti. The door was busted off its hinges and propped against the frame. Some of the windowpanes were broken, but most were intact. Spider webs trussed the corners. They went inside. There was an old metal table and two broken chairs. The floor was covered with debris. There were broken bottles and syringes. The electrical equipment was gone. The circuit breaker boxes were empty. There were huge metal pipes curling up from the floor on one side, and an old monitoring system box on the wall.

Dorian used her sleeve to wipe off the table. Thumper dropped the case on it. Clay scurried over to have a look. Time was running out for Dorian and she knew it. She walked up to Thumper and ran her hand over his chest. His face lit up with a big smile.

"How about a welcome back kiss?" she asked.

"Hell, yeah."

Before Thumper could get his kiss Kevin shoved him back. "Damn, Cherry, you are relentless." He handed the rope to Thumper. "Tie her pretty ass to those pipes."

"What the fuck, Kevin? What are you doing?" Dorian asked.

"Yeah, man, Cherry's cool. The team is back together. Everything's fine," Thumper said.

"Put your dick up and think about it for a second. She's playing you. Now tie her up."

Thumper did as he was told. He gently moved her back against the pipe. He started tying her hands to the pipes, spreading her arms.

"Come on, Thump, you know me. I wouldn't cross you. We're friends. You know that."

"I know, but Kevin says tie you, I got to tie you. Sorry, Cherry."

"Kevin isn't your daddy. You don't have to do everything he says. Let me loose and we'll get out of here. We can start a new crew."

Thumper smiled. "I would like that, Cherry, but I got to do what Kevin says. He looks after me."

"I could look after you. I can take care of you in ways Kevin can't. I could make you feel so good."

"I'm sorry, Cherry. I really am."

Kevin walked up to Dorian. "You're a clever girl. Maybe even more clever than me. It's hard to know what to believe, Cherry."

"Kevin, you know you got this wrong. We've been through too much for this to make any sense."

"I know. That's what is so weird. It doesn't make any sense."

"Why now? It's crazy," Dorian pleaded.

"You didn't pop him when you could have."

"I was shaking like a leaf. I was afraid I might hit you instead."

"Could be true. But you did tell the fucking gorilla he could tear my head off."

"That was part of the con. It was the only way we had a chance to get you your car. Think about it. If I don't shoot him, what have I got to play him with except me? You know the drill. Tease him. Please him. Squeeze him."

Kevin nodded. "It all sounds right."

"Cut me loose. You can trust me, Kev."

"Cherry, you are a mystery. The one thing I do know is I can't trust any of these fucks and I sure as hell can't trust you."

Kevin placed his knife against her face and watched her reaction.

"Come on, Kev. Be smart."

"You're so damn pretty. After I'm done no one will ever think you look like Lindsay Lohan again."

Kevin slipped the knife down the front of her dress and cut it down the middle. The fabric parted, showing her new bra and lacy white panties.

"Kevin. Come on."

"Only way I can be sure is to peel that pretty skin off you. The truth will be hiding among your screams."

"Kevin. You don't want to cut me up. You know that, baby. Look at me. There are a lot more fun things you could do with this body than slice it up. Let me show you that you can trust me."

Kevin placed the tip of the knife under her bra and popped the clasp. The bra parted. He used the blade to pull the bra back from her breasts. The nipples were hard. Kevin looked up at her and smiled. "I'm going to miss you, Cherry Red. Yes, indeed."

37

Frank reached the parking area without being seen. The trunk of the Mercedes was still open. The contents were gone. He opened the passenger side door. He punched in the glove box code and the front opened. He took the gun out. He opened it to be sure it was loaded. He took a deep breath and set his demons free. He felt the surge of adrenaline like a living beast racing through his blood. His hearing became more acute. His vision became sharper. His muscles quivered with new strength. He thought he heard his demons howling in ecstasy at their release. Then Frank realized he was hearing Dorian scream. He stood up and glanced into the back seat. He saw the CDs lying on the floor of the car. I. M. P. Frank had an epiphany. I'm P. I'm Poseidon. It was a perfect omen. He turned toward the building.

Clay didn't bother with the combination lock. There were what, a gazillion possibilities? He had a screwdriver out and was trying to pry the case open. He couldn't find an edge, but he didn't relent.

Thumper had turned away from Dorian. He didn't want to see what Kevin was doing. He took the baggie of heroin from his pocket and used the tip of his knife to lift some out of one of the small shooter's bags. Everyone was busy. They wouldn't notice and he needed something. He snorted it and felt the rush. Even if Kevin was going to kill her, why couldn't they have had some fun with her first? She looked so hot, he thought. Thumper smiled. He was getting an erection.

The Spartan maxim said, "Life is balanced on the tip of a spear." Frank liked it. He thought he understood it. It wasn't obtuse and weird like the prophecies from Delphi. It meant life was precariously balanced. It meant certain actions could tip it in either direction. You didn't live forever. He even rationalized that it meant that the safest path was straight ahead. The Marines called themselves "The tip of the spear." He marched in the front door. He held the pistol low along his side.

He took in the scene. Clay was the weakest threat physically, but he was working on the case with the C-4. It was the most lethal variable in the room. Clay turned at the sound of Frank's footsteps. Frank held the LCR in one hand and shot him twice in the head.

Dorian was tied up to some big pipes. Her clothes were cut away and she was bleeding. Kevin held a knife out in front of him. He spun as Frank approached him. He drew the knife back, but Frank grabbed his wrist with his free hand.

Frank shoved the gun into his stomach and turned Kevin's body away from Dorian. He pulled the trigger twice. He felt the life leave Kevin even as he released him. He raised the gun and pointed it at Thumper.

Thumper dropped the heroin, but didn't move. He was frozen.

"Drop the knife," Frank said.

Thumper stared at his hand, almost surprised to see the knife there. He dropped the knife.

"Kick it this way."

Thumper did. Dorian was crying.

"You came back for me. You came back for me. Why did you do that? You big dumb knucklehead. You were clear. Why did you come back?"

Frank smiled. He took the handkerchief from his pocket and picked up Kevin's Ka-Bar knife in his left hand. It was a long heavy blade. Kevin was dead, but he still made light gasping sounds. Frank ignored him. He walked over to Thumper. He held the gun out, pointed at Thumper's head.

"Raise your hands."

Thumper did as he was told. The broken arm gave him the appearance of trying to salute.

"Hey, man. I didn't do nothing to her. You ask her, she'll tell you. We're friends."

"Not much of a friend," Frank said.

Frank was not a knife man. It was a tool. He stabbed Thumper three times in the abdomen in less than a second. Thumper's hands dropped to protect himself. His eyes were wide in shock and pain. Frank stabbed him three times more in the neck as he fell. Frank stood over him and watched him bleed out. It took twelve seconds. The whole time Dorian didn't speak. When Thumper was dead, Frank wiped the handle of the gun. He placed it in Thumper's big left hand. He closed the fist around it and then let the finger fall open. The gun fell to the dirty floor. He took Kevin's knife and put it back in Kevin's hand. He walked over to Clay. He was dead beside the table. His brains covered everything. The case of C-4 was still unopened. Finally, Frank turned to Dorian. She had been cut twice. They weren't deep. They weren't meant to be. It was torture. He lifted her chin with his hand. She was sobbing.

"Why did you come back for me? No one has ever come back for me."

"You're too valuable to lose," he said as he untied her. "Why didn't you rat me out?'

"No reason to. It wouldn't have made any difference to them. If I thought it would have, I would have done it in a second."

"No, you wouldn't have. It was very brave. Thanks."

When the rope came untied she slumped into his arms. He held her for a few seconds before she pushed back. "I'm getting blood all over you."

"Not the first time. Here," he said and took off his coat and put it around her. "Cover up. I can't take you anywhere looking like that."

Dorian slipped her arms into the coat and forced a smile. "I think I might throw up," she said.

"Not in here. Too much forensic evidence in vomit. Come on outside."

Dorian moved slowly toward the door. Frank picked up the tool kit and the metal case. He dropped the rope and the tools into the tool kit. They went outside. Dorian bent over at the waist with her hands on her knees. She breathed deep breaths. She didn't vomit. She got some of her color back. She followed Frank to the car.

Frank put the stuff back in the trunk and helped get Dorian belted into the passenger's seat. Frank stood for a second to be sure he hadn't forgotten anything inside. When he was sure, he got in the driver's seat and cranked the car. Dorian leaned over and kissed his cheek.

"Thank you."

"Not a problem," he said as he backed out. "I'm a little disappointed. I thought you said you weren't wearing any panties?"

Dorian actually laughed. "Men are so nasty."

At the end of the road he propped the post back into its hole and stamped the dirt around it to make it appear sturdier than it was. He had left a good scene. Drug deal gone bad. Everyone dead. Murder weapons on the scene. It played pretty straight. A top forensics team might figure there were other players that were gone, but there wasn't any evidence to point them toward Frank or Dorian. A thorough investigation would take time and money and he doubted Fort Worth law would want to waste valuable financial assets on this trash. Another senseless murder. They were good to go, but he had to take care of the Russians today. He couldn't put it off any longer. This was a sign. Things could spin out of control. When he got back into the car Dorian was staring straight ahead lost in her thoughts.

Frank took Dorian back to the hotel. No one paid her a second look. Once they were in the room, he undressed her, which took all of five seconds, and put her in a warm shower to clean up. When she was done he helped dry her off. The adrenaline rush was gone and her body was shutting down. He got a T-shirt on her and helped her into bed. He put the bottle of wine he bought on the table.

"Stay with me."

"I can't. I have business I need to take care of."

"What you did back there. You saved my life. Weren't you afraid?"

"That? That wasn't scary. It happened so fast. There wasn't time to be scared."

"That didn't scare you? I can't imagine what does."

Frank pondered her question for a few seconds before answering. "Monkeys. Monkeys scare me. The little skinny ones. They're so fast and they have those little bitty hands."

Dorian laughed. When she stopped she said, "I don't believe you."

Frank didn't answer. He watched as fatigue crept over her.

"I'm so tired," she said. "I just need to close my eyes for a couple of minutes."

"Just rest for awhile, Dorian. Don't leave the hotel. You get hungry, eat downstairs in the restaurant. Or call room service."

"Are you coming back?"

"Yes."

Dorian smiled and snuggled down into the bed. "I believe you."

Frank got the Mercedes. He checked his notes and drove to Burns' lamp store. As he drove he remembered what had happened to the other Bruce Burns in prison.

38

Frank was due to be released from prison in the next few weeks. Prison had been easy time for him. There had been very few incidents. Things were different for his cellmate. Burns didn't have the reputation or skills that Frank had. Frank's protection had ensured Burns' safety. Now Frank was leaving. Burns had six more months to go. He held no illusions what those six months would be like if Burns couldn't stand up for himself. Despite what cons always preached, that "if you carried yourself like a man you were treated like a man," or that bullshit about, "if you give respect you get respect," the truth was, it was a jungle. There were predators and there were prey. Burns would be challenged within a day of Frank's parole. Some would be drawn to his youth, or his long hair, or as a way to get at Frank. But most would be drawn to his vulnerability. Burns was a stand-up guy. Frank liked him. They had gotten to be friends. It bothered Frank. Burns was more philosophical about it.

"There's nothing you can do about it so don't worry."

"I do."

"Lots of guys make it through here. I'll be all right. I got the luck, brother. You know that." He pulled up his sleeve. "Remember the twins."

"I remember."

"Hell, even without them I'm protected. And I'm not all that bad with my hands. You taught me some shit. I'll do okay."

Frank smiled. Burns had heart. In a straight up man-to-man fight he could probably hold his own. But this was prison. Fights weren't fair. Fights weren't one-on-one. If they came, they would come in a group. It took Frank most of a day to come up with a plan. He called Evan Hamrick, his attorney, and arranged for a meeting.

They met the next day in one of the conference rooms. There were three of them.

"You are good to go, Frank. The parole board has approved your release."

"Thanks, Evan. I didn't know who else to call."

"Always glad to do anything I can for you, Frank. You know that."

"Is this the detective?"

"Frank Kane, this is Tim Smith."

The two men shook hands. Frank could tell that Tim was a hard man. He had that look. His hand was a rock with five fingers on it.

"Good to meet you."

"You too."

"Tim worked for the FBI for ten years, then NSA until he retired. He has a security firm, but also does some freelance detective work for special cases."

"Am I a special case?"

"As special as they get."

"Can we talk in here? Is the room clean, Evan?"

"By federal law they can't record our conversations in here. It's as sterile as we can get."

"Great. I have some important things to say to Mr. Smith."

"I'll wait outside with the guard."

Evan knocked on the door and was let outside.

"I have limited time so I will be blunt. Here's what I need from you."

It only took Tim Smith forty-eight hours to accomplish the task. It was simple.

Bruce Burns was red-eyed and weary. He didn't know what to do. They had mutilated his wife. There was nothing he could do about it. He was powerless. He held his head in his hands. He wished he could cry or even that they would just kill him and be done with it. The giant stood silent as a golem behind him to his right. Dimitri sat in one of the office chairs with his feet propped up on the desk. His eyes were half closed.

Dimitri's cell phone buzzed. He popped it open. He talked in Russian He smiled and looked at Burns. He covered the cell against his chest.

"The Greek wants to be certain you have received no calls."

"No. I've been here all day. You jerks have been with me the whole time."

"What do you think went wrong?"

"How the hell should I know? Maybe it got hijacked or they're rotting in a Mexican jail."

"But you think you would have heard if this were true?'

Burns sighed. "Yeah, I do."

Dimitiri spoke again in Russian on the cell phone. He nodded to whatever was being said. He closed the phone.

"It seems it is time for a second interest payment."

Burns lunged to his feet. The giant slammed him back into his chair. Burns struggled to get to his feet again. The giant held him down.

"Please, don't. She hasn't done anything. It's not her fault."

"Interest is a penalty. And a penalty must be exacted," Dimitri said.

Burn stuck his arm out. "Then do me. Take my finger. Leave her alone."

"Mr. Burns, we are beyond the finger stage. The interest is compounded. The penalty is a hand."

Burn looked around panicked. He looked pale, but he screwed his courage up before he spoke.

"My hand. Take my hand. If you got to have a fucking hand, take mine, you cocksuckers."

Dimitri smiled and spoke to the giant. The giant smiled.

"It is a noble gesture, Mr. Burns. We, as soldiers, are impressed with it. However, there are certain risks associated with collecting the penalty. We cannot at this juncture afford to lose you. I am sorry, but your wife will have to pay the penalty for your poor business dealings. The Greek was very specific."

Burns slumped down across the desk. He started crying. He had thought he was out of tears. He sobbed in huge ragged breaths. The giant laughed.

Frank took the Mercedes and drove to Bruce Burns' house first on the off chance he was there. It would be easier at his house than place of business. If it had to be the hard way it was better to be as isolated as possible. The house was impressive in the daylight. Frank estimated it had to be close to five thousand square feet. It was three stories tall with an attached three-car garage. Frank liked that. Threes were lucky numbers for the Spartans. It was a good omen. He considered slipping inside and waiting for Burns to return home from the lamp store, but that would eliminate any possibility of finessing this. He decided to try the lamp store and bull his way in. Even with the Russians there, they would be hesitant to do anything drastic. He knew they wouldn't call the cops. He would try to jam them up enough to get them to talk. Maybe he could negotiate this straight. He laughed at the thought. Elliot wouldn't have asked him to go if he thought it was going to play out straight. One last try for the easy way. One last try for the new Frank. His demons whined their discontent.

Frank called DC as he drove.

"Today's the day. I'm going to take care of things. Anything new on your end?"

"No. Still no word. Elliot's worried."

"Anything on the shooting?"

"I haven't heard, but I'll check. All the medical charts are electronic now. I think I can access the doctor's notes since they transcribe everything on computer. It'll take me a little to crack the hospital password, but I'll see what's up."

"Thanks. The girls doing all right?"

"Yeah. I'm keeping an eye on them. We've been chilling out at night watching DVDs."

"They hit you up for booze or dope yet?"

"No. Just Coke and popcorn."

"Right," Frank said sarcastically. He knew DC was lying. It was all right. The girls weren't children. They had been through more than most adults. He just liked to nudge DC a little, let him know he wasn't stupid.

"Let me know if you need anything else."

"I will."

Agent Harris met with Agent Redding at the field office.

"Did you find your copies?"

Redding smiled. "I know where they are, but I didn't get them yet. I'm working another angle."

"What angle? We're at a dead end?"

"They teaching you pups anything at the Academy? You ever hear about contingencies?"

"I know what the word means. What does it have to do with the Spartans?"

"I think the key is to find Masnick. He'll know what's happening."

"How do we do that? He's in the wind. You said so yourself."

"Come with me and I'll show you."

"Have you got a line on him?"

Redding laughed. "If you can call a cunt hair a line. They say you can pull a battleship with one."

"I don't understand."

"I'm talking about Sandy Jones. She was his girlfriend. Masnick told me once they were soul mates. I think we should talk with her. We might learn something."

"Do you think you can find her?"

"I know exactly where she is."

"And you're sure she'll be there. She might have run with Masnick."

"If she's still alive, she'll be there."

"How can you be so sure?"

"I may be getting old, but I still got some tricks. You want to find out about the Spartans, this is where it starts."

Redding got up from his desk. He took his gun from the drawer and put it back into his holster. He stared at Harris.

"You coming with me, Harris, or have you got somewhere else you need to be?"

"I'm with you."

Redding smiled and headed down the hall, Harris following. Redding liked that Harris didn't know everything like he thought he did. There was something going on with Harris that Redding didn't understand. Harris was making a play of some type. Could be for anyone, he figured. Might be I.A. Might be the old guard Spartans that disappeared after the fall. Might be someone in the Bureau with a different set of goals altogether. He would keep an eye on him.

39

It was early, but the sign outside the lamp store said closed. The lights inside were still on. The parking lot out front was empty. Frank parked at the side of the building near the door. He walked to the door and took a last look around. He turned the knob. It was unlocked. He opened the door and went inside. The trap closed.

Burns sat on the bottom stair that led up to his office. He looked terrible. For a brief moment Frank thought he had gotten lucky. Then Dimitri closed the door behind him. The giant he had seen earlier stepped into view from an aisle to Burns' left. Frank scanned them quickly. The big one was really big and the skinny one moved like someone who knew they were fast. Frank smiled to disarm them.

"Mr. Burns, I am glad you are still here. I stopped by one last time on my way out of town. I came by earlier to discuss a shipment of rare Frederick Cooper lamps I have available."

Burns stared at him without speaking. Frank continued as if he were unaware of his situation.

"Perhaps I could have a few minutes with you alone in your office?"

Burns seemed unmoving. His mouth opened to speak, but nothing came out.

Dimitri said, "You are not here about lamps, I think."

"Of course I am. Why else would I come?"

The giant pointed a thick finger at Frank and then at his own eyes. In slow English he said. "I see you."

"What are you talking about? If this isn't a good time I might be able to come back tomorrow morning. I have a schedule to keep."

Dimitri spoke Russian to the giant. The giant smiled.

"Did you bring the merchandise?"

"What merchandise? The lamps?"

Dimitri laughed and asked Burns, "Is this your driver? Does he have our product?"

Burns seemed to shake off his haze. "No, he's not my driver. He's just some salesman. He's got nothing to do with any of this."

"You are positive?"

"Yes, I'm positive. I'm sorry, sir. You've picked a bad time for me. I'm not interested in any lamps. Thank you just the same."

Dimitri clapped his hands. "Bravo. Bravo. Very nice. If he does not have the merchandise, then he is here to rescue you."

"I don't know what you guys are talking about, but if I am bothering you, I can just leave."

Dimitri ran a thin-fingered hand through his greasy black hair. The smile never left his face. "I am afraid this is not an option."

The giant pointed again at his own eyes and then at Frank. He repeated his earlier sentence. "I see you."

Dimitri removed his coat and draped it over a chair. He was wearing a custom rig over his short knit shirt. It held a long knife. Frank knew instantly that he was a professional.

"Listen, you're right. I am not a lamp salesman. I am here to negotiate the return of Burns' wife. I can help make a deal."

Dimitri continued to smile. He licked his lips like he was hungry. "The time for talk is over."

"Tell me what you require and I will make it happen," Frank said.

"You cannot provide that which we seek. We are not here to negotiate and you are in no position in any case."

"We can work this out."

The two Russians talked and Dimitri laughed.

"Your presence here is not wholly unwelcome. You will serve as an example for Mr. Burns to cease his obvious delaying tactics," Dimitri said.

The giant produced a Russian MP-446 semiautomatic pistol. It was a big black gun called the Viking. The Viking was a military handgun. It carried a magazine capacity of 17 rounds of 9mm parabellums. The Viking was famous for its use of durable materials. It had a polymer frame that would not rust under any conditions. It was the pistol equivalent of the AK-47. He pointed it at Frank.

"Remove your jacket," Dimitri said.

Frank looked at the gun. He did as he was told. He started to wrap it around his arm.

"Toss the jacket away if you do not mind?"

Frank tossed the jacket. The giant slipped his pistol back into its shoulder holster. The giant crossed his arms over his massive chest. He looked like a man waiting for a play to begin. He looked happy.

Dimitri spoke to Burns. "Pay attention. Let this help you become motivated."

40

Dimitri drew the long knife. It was one piece of polished stainless steel. The blade was just over four inches in length. The handle was another four inches covered in a light handgrip. There was a thumb notch to provide better control. The blade was thin and sharpened on each side. It appeared elegant in his hand.

Frank looked at Dimitri's bare arms. They were free of any visible scars. Either he was very new or very, very fast with a blade. Frank watched as Dimitri wove the blade back and forth in front of him. He used an eastern European style with the blade down almost along the wrist. The Southeast Asian style with the blade out front would make what Frank had planned that much harder. Dimitri was smiling. Frank tried to look scared. It wasn't hard. He was.

Spanish Johnny had worked with Frank on how to defend against a knife fighter. Professionals didn't go in for the kill. They bled you. Slowly. They dragged it out until you couldn't lift your arms anymore. It was, after all, a dance to them. Spanish Johnny had told Frank about a technique that he could try. It was dangerous. You had to be fast and Frank was fast. You had to lure the knife man in. You had to tempt him.

Frank spread his arms and stepped back. The two points that Frank remembered most from Spanish Johnny's lessons were that knife fighters always fought to the death. That was the point. The weapon was too intimate. You did not cut and flee. You could not shoot your adversary with a pistol and try to escape or disable them. The knife was a killing tool. It was not a fight. It was life and death. The second point resounded in his head. Spanish Johnny said, "When you fight a knife man, always realize you are going to get cut."

Dimitri stepped forward weaving with the knife. He slashed and Frank jumped back. Dimitri smiled. He darted in. Frank jumped back again. He cut at Frank's arms, but Frank was able to keep them just out of reach. Frank waited. He knew it would come. He spread his hands wider. Exposing his chest. Inviting Dimitri in.

Dimitri cut at Frank's right leg. Frank danced away.

Dimitri's attack was like a cobra's, a darting out and back. Frank jumped back, but not as far as before. He bumped into the checkout desk and stopped. Dimitri moved in, carving the blade in a lethal figure eight through the air. He slashed with the blade cutting for Frank's chest. He was confident. The outcome was inevitable.

Frank tried to twist his body away from the blade. He was a hair too slow. The blade cut through the front of his shirt. Frank stepped to the side. Dimitri smiled and moved in quickly. He wanted blood.

This time, as the blade licked out, Frank stepped forward. It was unheard of. No man moved toward the blade. Frank just caught the wrist above the knife hand with his opposite hand. Frank jerked Dimitri toward him and across his body. With Frank's strength and the momentum of the lunge, Dimitri couldn't resist. Dimitri tried to regain his balance, but by then Frank had stepped closer and locked a massive hand around his chin. He ripped backward, breaking Dimitri's neck. Dimitri fell to the floor in a twitching heap. The knife fell from his spasming fingers only inches from Frank's foot.

Frank knew if he could reach the knife, his odds would go up against the giant. He glanced toward the giant hoping the death of his compatriot had paralyzed him. It hadn't. The big black gun was in his bigger hand. The giant was smiling. He pointed toward the knife with the gun and then mimicked kicking it away. Frank understood. He kicked the knife away.

The giant pointed the Viking at Frank. Frank didn't flinch. There was nothing he could do. He was too far away. As fast as Frank was, he would never reach him before a large bullet slammed into him. The giant seemed to be trying to say something.

Finally, he said, "Bonh."

The giant nodded, confirming the word to himself.

"Bonh, dah. Bonh. Warrior."

Frank didn't answer. He nodded at the compliment.

The giant thought for another few seconds before saying another Russian word. Frank couldn't even come close to pronouncing it. The giant stood thinking, and then said, "Fast."

Frank smiled. He nodded again.

The giant slipped his gun back into its holster. He made his huge hands into fists and motioned Frank over. He raised his hands like a brawler. Frank took a second to look at the cut on his chest. It was minor. The blade had cut through the outside shirt and the red nylon shirt beneath but had barely nicked his skin. He moved forward on the balls of his feet.

They moved around the center of the room. Frank's motto for fighting was unchanged from when he was a teenager. Hit first. Hit fast. Hit often. Frank threw a pair of range finding left jabs. The giant made a late move to avoid them. Frank moved to his left and stung the giant with a hard left jab. The giant's nose exploded in a spray of blood. Once more Frank caught him with the jab, and the giant threw a huge looping right. If it had landed it would have knocked a building down. Frank ducked under it and threw a right cross that just missed.

Frank feigned a left to the body and the giant's hands dropped, exposing his chin. That was what Frank was looking for. The giant came forward and threw a pair of slow hooks. Frank dodged them without effort. Time to set him up for the knockout. Frank moved to his right and then back to his left. The giant was not light on his feet, and the change in direction made his movements even more awkward. Frank moved in and feinted toward the body once more. The hands dropped involuntarily and Frank unleashed his right, the power shot. He was stepping into it so his shoulder turned just as his hips and legs released their power into the punch. The giant's eyes seemed to sparkle. That was when Frank knew he had been had.

It all seemed to process in tenths of a second. The huge head and square jaw. The iron cables of neck muscle that ran upward to the head. The huge lumps of shoulder muscle. The thick scarred eyebrows. The small chipped teeth. It was a face meant to take a punch. It had taken punches before. The giant was offering his chin, just like Frank had lured Dimitri with his chest.

The giant moved forward into the punch. Taking the blow before the full power could be unleashed at the end of the punch. Even as he struck the massive head was rolling to the side, slipping more of the punch's power. Still there was a lot of power in Frank's right. The giant stumbled slightly, but struck back with a left that Frank never saw coming. It struck him above the ear and things went bright. Fireworks exploded behind Frank's eyes. The giant followed with a hard right to the body that tore something. Pain burst like flames in his ribs. The world swam drunkenly.

Frank fell to his knees. The giant moved forward closing the distance. Except now he moved quickly like one of the dancing hippos in the Disney films. Frank slipped another right and the left hook that followed. He was still trying to keep distance and clear his head when the giant caught him with another hook to the body. Frank turned and blocked with his arm, but the blow still tore him off his feet and hurled him back into a stack of lamps.

Frank was stunned. He never thought anyone that big would be able to move so fast. He saw the giant's grinning face as he closed in to finish the job.

41

Caron and Jenny got to work early. The parking lot was already filling with cars. They had a double shift. It would be a long night, but they should make good money. They sat in the car for a few minutes before going inside.

"Listen, Caron, this weekend we need to sit down and figure out what we're going to do about next year and college."

"Wherever we go, we go together, right?"

"Right. But where? We've already got the acceptances. We've just got to make a final decision."

"Frank said money wasn't an issue. We can go wherever we want to as long as it's in state."

"But where do you want to go? We got into our top three choices."

"Where do you want to go, Jenny?"

"I'm not sure. I'm mixed up. There are things I like about all of them. It's hard to make a decision."

"I've been trying to think about it logically. You know, not let it be all tied up with my emotions."

"What kind of emotions? You mean like more freedom or something?"

"That and other stuff. I mean we want a good school where we will get a good education…."

"But? I hear a but."

"But we also want a good place to play. I want a school with a good rep for partying too. And a good ratio of boys to girls. Stuff like that too."

"So does that mean Chapel Hill, UNCG, and Wilmington are in or out?"

"In, all definitely in. They're still my top three choices. How about you?"

"Part of me wants to stay close to home, but part of me wants to try it out on my own. You know?"

"I know. I know. It's scary and exciting at the same time."

"Yeah. I just don't want to mess up. I want to eventually go to law school and where we go to undergraduate school counts."

"Don't worry about it, Jenny. How can we mess up? They're all good schools. It'll work out no matter where we go."

"I hope you're right."

"I know I'm right."

"UNC Wilmington would be cool because it's near the ocean. I really like the idea of being at school near the ocean."

"Yeah, surfer guys are super hot, but the ratio of girls to guys is something like five to one."

"What about UNCG. It's close by."

"I don't know. It's maybe too close. I was thinking a little more distance. What about Chapel Hill? I think it's my top choice."

"Chapel Hill is cool. I've always been a Tar Heel fan."

"Me too."

"So it's number one. We'll talk about it more this weekend and make the final decision so we can tell Frank when he comes home."

"Sounds like a plan. Now let's make some tips so we don't have to work all the time at college."

Redding drove without talking. Harris sat beside him sulking. Redding knew Harris resented the slow way he divulged information.

"We've been driving for an hour. Can you at least tell me where we're going?"

Redding turned slightly in his seat. "I'm sorry. I was thinking. What did you want to know?"

"Where are we going?

"I told you to meet with Sandy Jones, the girlfriend."

"I understand that, but where is she?"

"Oh, I'm sorry. I thought I told you. She's in Winter Park."

"So that's where we're headed?"

"Yes. She's our next best lead. We need to pursue it while there's time."

"I don't understand. You were confident earlier that she would be there."

"She will be. It just occurred to me that if she does know something, she might be at risk."

"From Masnick?"

"Or someone who doesn't want us to find him. It isn't cut and dried. If I know where she is, so do other people."

"Shouldn't we alert the local authorities?"

"To what end?"

"To protect her."

"It's complicated. If the Spartans are reorganizing, they'll already have law enforcement personnel on the payroll. If we alert them to our destination they may be ineffective, they may help us, they may alert others who will terminate Ms. Jones. I think it's better that we arrive unannounced as quickly as possible."

"I see your point."

"I'm glad you do. The turn is just ahead."

42

Frank fell to the floor. He tried to get to his feet, but the synapses were firing a little slow. He couldn't get his body to respond. Time stopped for Frank. He was suddenly back in a boxing gym he visited in south Boston.

The Spartans had been expanding and Frank had gone there with a few other Spartans to work out. It was a bare, worn, red brick building. There was no air conditioner. There were no plush locker rooms or high tech saunas. The gym radiated the raw primitive feel that all good gyms did. There were no women in attractive exercise outfits. There were no aerobics or yoga glasses. There were only lessons in boxing. Given by serious men to serious men. Frank liked the place immediately.

Behind one of the three boxing rings, mounted on a bare wall was a poem written by James "Gentleman Jim" Corbett, the former heavyweight champion of the world. Frank only knew of Corbett from the Errol Flynn movie of the same name. He had liked the old black and white film. Ward Bond had played John L. Sullivan, the heavyweight champion Corbett had to beat. When Frank read the poem it stayed with him. The words came back to him now as he tried to get to his feet in the lamp store. It was called, *One More Round.*

When your feet are so tired that you have to shuffle back to the center of the ring, fight one more round.

When your arms are so tired that you can hardly lift your hands to come on guard, fight one more round.

When your nose is bleeding and your eyes are black and you're so tired that you wish your opponent would crack you one on the jaw and put you to sleep—don't quit. Fight one more round!

The words scrolled through Frank's mind as clear as if he were reading them from the wall for the first time. He regained his feet. He would fight one more round.

The giant looked puzzled, but smiled and charged. Frank threw a quick combination. Left jab; right cross; left hook; right cross. The blows lacked knockout power, yet they stunned the giant, stopping him in his tracks. Frank moved out of range of a counter strike. Over the giant's shoulder he saw Burns. His face was grim. He was holding a lamp like a baseball bat.

Burns struck the giant across the back of his head. The giant was surprised and stopped his approach. Burns smashed the lamp again as the giant turned. The lamp shattered into a mist of dust. Blood trickled from the giant's head. The giant struck Burns across the face with a backhand blow. Burns stumbled. The giant grabbed the front of Burns' shirt and pulled him up. The huge right fist drew back.

Frank responded with some of the old quickness. He grabbed a lamp cord and leapt onto the giant's back. He threw the cord over the horse-thick neck and pulled backward trying to choke the giant. The giant lost all interest in Burns. His hands flew to the cord. Frank leaned back drawing the cord deeper into the giant's steel-corded neck. The giant's short powerful arms couldn't reach Frank. His only hope was to dislodge the cord before his oxygen was cut off. Frank pulled harder, wedging a knee into the broad back. The muscles in Frank's arms stood out as he strained against the giant's thick neck muscles.

The giant realized he couldn't shake Frank off and he couldn't loosen the lamp cord. He stumbled to one knee. His right hand reached for the gun in his holster. It was the right move. There was nothing Frank could do to stop him and maintain pressure with the lamp cord. Frank did his own calculations. The giant had to draw the gun and fire over his right shoulder. The giant's huge arms would limit the field of fire to a narrow arc. The giant would be firing blind. Frank could feel the giant weakening. He made his choice. He staked his life on the giant failing.

Thick fingers grasped the butt of the gun. Burns lunged forward and tried to pull the giant's hand away. He slowed it, but the giant was too strong. He could not stop him. The gun slipped free from the holster. Burns held onto the thick wrist and bit into the hand. The gun fell free. The giant made a swipe of his hand at Burns, but missed. The hand reached feebly for the dropped gun.

It was over. The giant's eyes bulged. He struggled a final time before slumping forward. Frank did not relax the pressure of the cord until he was sure the giant was dead. When he was certain, he released the cord and fell across the giant's back, gasping for breath of his own.

Burns stood staring at the two fallen men.

"The Russians, they're both dead."

"As dead as they can get," Frank said as he pushed himself up to his feet.

"You. . .you killed them."

"That's what I do. They had their chance, but they didn't take it. Their loss. I couldn't have done it without your help."

"I think I feel sick."

"Man up, Bruce. You did what you had to do."

Burns stared at him in disbelief at his casualness. Awareness seemed to finally dawn on him.

"You really are Frank Kane aren't you?"

Frank nodded.

"I'm sorry I took so long. I was trying to figure another way to play this." He took the giant's gun and slipped it into the back of his pants.

"Thank God you came. I was afraid Elliott had decided not to send you. Then, after your visit, I was afraid it was too late. I hated myself for sending you away."

"Your brother's a good man. You can count on him. And I don't quit a job."

Burns seemed to actually hear the words. He stood silent while he thought about them, then a weak smile came.

"Yes, he is. I've always been able to count on him."

Frank took the two spare magazines off the giant's shoulder holster. He checked to be sure they were 9mm rounds. He patted the giant's pockets down. There was no passport or other I.D. There were sixty-one dollars and some change. Frank stuck it in his pocket. He checked the labels of the clothes. They had been cut out. He pulled his shoes off and checked his socks. Sometimes men hide things in their socks that a frisk wouldn't uncover. There was only lint.

He walked to Dimitri, the knife man. His sides ached from the giant's blows and his head throbbed. There would be time for that later. Dimitri's clothes had no labels and no information. Frank found the knife and replaced it in the under-arm rig. He didn't need a knife like that for what he needed to do. Dimitri's socks were also empty. There was a cell phone in one of his pockets. Frank checked the call screen. Dimitri had talked to someone an hour ago. Frank turned the cell phone off and put it in his pocket. Dimitri had thirty-seven dollars and some foreign bills that could have been Russian, but looked like monopoly money to Frank. When finished, he took out his handkerchief and wiped down their shoes where he had touched them. No labels were a bad sign. It meant they didn't want to be identified.

"Do you have some rolls of plastic?"

"In the back for shipping. Why?"

"We need to get these guys rolled up. Helps control evidence transfer. Show me where you got it."

Burns led Frank to the storage area in the back. There were large rolls of bubble wrap. Frank carried the largest roll back to the bodies. They rolled Dimitri up easily. The giant was more difficult. Frank felt like the tragic Greek figure Sisyphus who pushed the boulder up the hill for eternity. They managed to get the giant wrapped up. But just barely.

"All right, now tell me what's up so I can figure out what I need to do."

Burns sighed and sat down on the steps that led to his office.

"I'll tell it as straight as I can."

"I appreciate that. I know it's tempting to spin it one way or another."

"I run a straight business in Fort Worth. It brings in a lot of money. It also gives me the means to smuggle weapons up from South and Central America. I have a route nailed down. Bribes are in place. Manifests look legit for lamps. MS13 provides the security. They bring the shipment across the border and I unload the contraband."

"What kind of weapons?"

"Mostly semiautomatics and AK-47s. There are always black market weapons available down there. My primary contact arranges the purchases. I handle the transport."

"Does he know your transport routes?"

"No. I don't trust him that much."

"Good."

"Anyway, if I didn't have a specific buyer I moved the weapons through the Greek."

"The Greek?"

"I don't know his real name. Everyone just calls him the Greek. He has a bunch of businesses here; carpet cleaning, restaurants, and lawn care. He's very diversified. He also moves lots of guns to the gangs."

"So what happened this time?"

"The Greek came to me about a month ago with a good proposition. He had weapons ready in Colombia. I was to arrange shipping by land to Forth Worth. He was paying forty thousand above the usual costs."

"Sounds a little too good to be true. There's always free cheese in a rat trap."

"There wasn't a down side. If the shipment made it, I got paid. If not, I wasn't out anything."

"So what went sideways?"

"The merchandise was surface to air missiles. Three of 'em."

"Shit."

"Exactly. No one needs SAMs except terrorists. I guarantee if some raghead shoots down a plane the FBI will be able to trace the launcher back to me. I would prefer not to spend the rest of my life getting fucked in some secret black bag prison we run in Afghanistan or Iraq."

"What did you do?"

"I called the Greek. He was always a good guy. I couldn't believe he would be mixed up with something like this. I told him no way would I do the deal. He agreed with me, but seemed very distant. The next day the Russians showed up and took Judy."

"What do they want?"

"Their shipment. They've starting cutting off my wife's fingers to motivate me. I told them I couldn't contact the driver and he couldn't contact me until he showed up. That was part of the security."

"Is that true?"

"No. But otherwise they would have killed me."

"When do you expect the shipment?"

"I thought you had it figured out. They're already here."

"Where are they?"

"Out back in the white panel truck. The one with the hood up and the tarp over the front."

"I thought it was a broken down vehicle."

"You're supposed to."

"And the missiles are in the back?"

"Yeah."

"Why didn't you give them the missiles when they started getting rough?"

"It wouldn't have done any good. Once they had them there was no reason for them not to kill my wife and me. I had to hold on and wait for you. And then it all just seemed so hopeless…."

"That's enough for now. How often do they call in to the Greek?"

"Not very often. Once a day or so. At least that I hear."

"We need to get out of here. And we need to take the SAMs with us. Help me lug these sacks of meat out to the truck. You get the skinny one. I'll bring King Kong."

They dragged the bodies into the back of the white truck. Frank tossed the tarp aside and closed the hood.

"You drive to your house in the truck. I'll follow you in my car.

"Why don't we take my car?"

"They may have put a tracker on your car. Plus, if they can't raise the dead guys they'll come here first. If they see your car, they'll waste time looking for you. And I have tools in my car that I'll need."

Burns didn't argue. He got into the truck and headed for home.

43

The drive was uneventful. No one tried to stop them. Burns' garage door rolled up. Frank pulled into the garage and the door closed as Burns got out.

"We're just going to leave them?" he said, nodding toward the truck.

"They won't start stinking anytime soon even in this heat. Have you got a small screwdriver? The batteries in my electric one are dead."

Burns found him one. Frank tossed his coat inside the Benz. He got down on his back under the car and went to work with the screwdriver. He removed a container that had been screwed into place beneath the car. It had been painted to match the underside of the Mercedes. It was nearly invisible to casual inspection.

The ancient Spartans were considered the finest warriors in Greece. Their laws dictated simply that they conquered in battle or died. They approached the preparation for war with the seriousness it deserved. The Spartans called their standard battle kit a panoplia. It consisted of greaves to protect the front of the lower legs, as well as a formed leather cuirass covered with a thin layer of bronze to protect the front of the chest. The Spartan cuirass did not cover the back of the hoplite. The Spartans regarded such added weight as unnecessary. There was no need to protect a warrior's back since he would never flee in combat.

The panoplia also included a helmet of bronze, often topped with a thick plume of red horsehair. This crest was worn both in honor of horses, which the Spartans held in high esteem, and to add extra height to the warrior, although Spartans were the tallest of all the Greeks. There was also a large round shield of hammered bronze. The shield was sometimes decorated with a family symbol, but most commonly it bore only the Greek Lambda, an inverted V, to signify Lacedaemonia their homeland.

Each hoplite warrior carried a nine-foot long spear with a broad iron blade. The "long shadow" spear, as it was known throughout Greece, was the principal weapon of a hoplite warrior. It was the same spear that had broken thousands of Greeks and Persians in over six hundred years of merciless combat. Spartans also carried a short sword on their left side called a Lakonia. The Spartan Lakonia was shorter than most Greek swords. The leaf-shaped blade measured only about eighteen inches in length. The Spartans claimed the length was because they "liked to get in close." Many soldiers also wore a parazonium, a utility knife, which could serve as a weapon of last resort. This, along with their long red battle cloak, made up the warriors' battle clothes. Legend tells that the red cloak was so that no enemy would ever see a Spartan's blood. British researchers recently concluded that the color red was associated with both ferocity and dominance, words often used to describe the Spartan war machine.

Frank Kane's panoplia was different, but no less lethal in purpose. He called it his killing suit.

Frank placed the container on the hood of the car and carefully unpacked it. He spread each item carefully. He took off his black Polo shirt, still marveling that the knife had only cut the material and left him with the tiniest scratch, virtually unharmed. Beneath his shirt he wore a dark red nylon muscle shirt. The sleeveless design drew attention to his massively muscled arms and the tattoos and ritual scars that decorated them. Frank kicked his boots off.

He put the bulletproof vest on first. It was heavy, weighing nearly twenty pounds. He fastened it with three broad strips of Velcro secured across the front. He pulled thick kneepads on over his khaki pants. He stepped into a large nondescript gray coverall and pulled it over his pants and the vest. The coverall was thick and had deep modified pockets in the front and rear. Frank zipped it up to just beneath his chin. He put his boots back on and covered them with hospital type paper shoe covers. He noticed the giant's dried blood still splashed across his hands and wiped them on the legs of the coveralls.

There was a large lock-back knife in the kit. The blade was just over three inches long. It was utilitarian, but unremarkable in any way. He slipped the knife into his left rear pocket. Frank was ambidextrous, but preferred keeping his edged weapons on his left hand side.

There was a SIG Sauer P226 in the kit as well. It gleamed with a fine patina of oil. It was the same pistol used by Ranger teams and the British SAS. The SIG P226 had contrasting night sights. The rear was green, the front Tritium red. Frank liked red. Frank wiped the pistol with the cloth it had been wrapped in. He broke it down and reassembled it within seconds. It always paid to be sure your weapons worked. The SIG P226 was produced in .357 and .40 caliber, but this one was a 9mm. There were four clips containing fifteen rounds of super-hot NATO ammunition. The bullets were specially made to fragment on entry. If you couldn't get the job done with sixty rounds of these, you couldn't get it done. Frank slapped a magazine into place and racked a round into the chamber. He slipped the other clips of ammunition into his other pockets.

There was a high quality machined noise suppressor in the kit. Frank screwed it into place. It was long and narrow in diameter. Made from stainless steel and a high tech alloy, it was very lightweight. The best part was that the suppressor only minimally affected the pistol's accuracy. He had used similar "silencers" before and appreciated that precision. He unscrewed it. This went into the other front pocket with the gun.

Frank always favored the soft leather shooting gloves made by GripSwell because they contained slight padding in the palm that offered some dampening to
recoil. He had probably fifty pairs at home. There were no GripSwells in the
black box. Instead there were two distinctly different pairs of gloves. One was
dark blue, nylon. They were thin and fit very well. They were liner gloves. The
second pair was ordinary leather work gloves. The two pairs ensured that if you
had to dump the work gloves at the scene you would leave no DNA behind. And
if you dropped the others outside they'd carry no gunshot residue that could tie
you to the scene. It was just another layer of protection that a good attorney could
exploit for you. Last was a black nylon balaclava. When pulled down it covered
the entire head with only an opening for the eyes.

Frank moved around getting used to the weight of the vest and the fit of the
coveralls. He smiled. This was who he was. This was what he had done for the
Spartans. He solved problems. He found compromise with men who would not
compromise. He bargained with men who did not bargain. He negotiated with
men who could not be negotiated with. He heard the far off boom of thunder.
Rain would be coming soon. It was a good omen. Apollo always liked the rain.

"What's the plan?" Burns asked.

"The plan? The plan is I kill everyone and let the gods sort it out."

"The Greek has a wife and a new baby boy."

"How old is the kid?"

"One or maybe two."

"That shouldn't be a problem."

"What about his wife?"

"If she's mixed up in this, she's a liability."

"What if she's not?"

"Then she won't be home."

"I don't feel right about this. She is a sweet girl. I can't believe Dasha is involved. She can't be."

"Do you want to save your wife?"

"Yes, but…."

"Do you want to save your wife? Yes or no? If I don't do something now they
will cut her to pieces and then do the same to you."

"All right. All right."

"Now, there are some things I need you to do for me."

"Name 'em."

"First, tell me about the Greek's house. You've been inside before, right?"

"Yeah, a few times. We were business associates more than friends."

"That's clear. A friend wouldn't screw you up like this."

"What do you want to know?"

"How many floors? What's the layout? Where are the bedrooms? Anything you can remember."

"It's two stories. There are five bedrooms, all upstairs. That includes the master suite. The master is the last bedroom on the right after going up the stairs. The downstairs is typical, but big. There's a media room and workout room. The usual stuff, dining room, living room."

"Where's the kitchen?"

"At the back on the first floor. Why?"

"When we go in it will be early enough for people to be up. Late at night people, even thugs, like to hang in front of the TV or in the kitchen."

"Got it."

"What about an office or a study?"

"Ground floor. It's off to the left if you go in the front door."

"Is there a basement?"

"I think so, but I don't know what's down there."

"Get a piece of paper and draw me a diagram. Label what you can."

Burns turned to go into the house. He stopped and hesitated like he was going to say something, then went inside. In a minute he returned with pen and paper and sat down to sketch out the Greek's house. Frank noticed he had very neat penmanship. Frank wrote like a doctor. He tended to print so there was a chance that what he wrote could be deciphered. When Burns finished he handed the drawing to Frank.

"That's nice work, man."

"Thanks."

"What kind of security does the Greek have?"

"I know he's got a system. I saw the keypad on the wall by the front door. There's another keypad in the kitchen near the back door."

"The Greek will not want to trip the security system. He doesn't want the cops showing up at his house. He probably has it turned off. With all this muscle he doesn't need it."

"There's a tall fence around the property. It's electrified. The front gate has an intercom system. You have to call the house to have them open it for you to drive up."

"How tall is the fence?"

"About six feet I guess."

"It won't be a problem. Anything else?"

"He's got a Doberman. It was in the backyard last time I was there. I don't know if it's guard-dog-trained or not."

"I have a way with dogs. How many guys did you see with the Greek the last time?"

"I didn't see him after things went bad."

"That's okay. It doesn't really matter. I'm going anyway."

Frank worked the action on the Sig. It was smooth. He felt confident. If he was fast, and lucky, it should work. The Spartans said that life balanced on the tip of a spear. Now he thought maybe they meant whoever held the spear determined if you lived or died. That made better sense, he thought. Frank felt like he held the spear.

"After this is over, you'll be on the clock. Someone will know you worked with the Greek. Someone will come looking."

"Like the cops?'

"No, the cops won't care. I'll make sure nothing leads them back to you. But the Greek has family. Cousins, brothers, uncles, friends. Someone will know the plan. They'll want to settle up. Your brother says you're smart. You got an off shore account somewhere?"

"Turks and Caicos. One of the last places the U.S. can't take a look."

"Good. I'd say you got about two weeks before someone thinks it's safe to come after you. So you need to be long gone by then. Tomorrow call your attorney. You have an attorney to handle your business affairs?"

"Yes."

"Tell him your wife is sick and you're moving to Oregon or some place out West. Tell him you're closing your business and he'll handle the matter. Call a realtor. Sell your house fully furnished. Liquidate your lamp business. Transfer the money through your attorney to the Turks and Caicos."

"Do you think all of this is necessary?"

"I'm not done. Sell all your cars if they're in your name and buy a new one in your wife's maiden name. Your brother is thinking about opening a bike franchise in Pennsylvania. Call him and set it up. You can run it through your wife's maiden name again."

"I still don't think this is necessary. If the Greek is dead...."

"You may be right, but is it worth the risk? People spending this kind of money and time are serious players. They'll want payback. I know I would. You're an easy target so you have to disappear. You should have things in motion within forty-eight hours. Then you pack what you can and get out. You can do the rest by phone with your attorney acting as your agent."

"I will. I know you're right. I can't thank you enough."

"There's one more thing. It's something I need from you."

"Anything."

"You have to make me a promise."

"What kind of promise?"

"You go straight. No more gun running or anything illegal."

"Why?"

"Part of the deal. Helps me pay off a debt."

Burns stared at him like he was looking at a space alien. He thought about it for thirty seconds before he finally answered. "You have my word."

"That's all I need. It's enough between men. Now we got to kill some time before I visit the Greek. This house isn't a safe place. It's the second place they'll look, but we don't have any other good choices."

"So do we stay or do we go?"

"Stay. Sometimes a bad choice is the only one you have left."

Burns seemed to be struggling with something he wanted to say, but couldn't. Finally, he said, "Why are you doing this? You don't even know me. Why risk your life to help me?"

Frank stared at Burns. "Honor. Your brother asked me to help. I said I would. This is what I do. Now I need a stepladder."

44

Jenny's cell phone chirped in her pocket. She let it ring as she placed the food on the tables. She smiled like a good waitress always did.

"Is that everything or is there something else I can get you?"

The family smiled back at her. The dad nodded as he shoveled in another fork full of food. The mother smiled at her husband and turned to Jenny.

"No, this should be all."

"I'll check back in a few minutes in case there's anything else. Is everyone good on drinks?"

All heads bobbed the affirmative. Jenny gave them her high-wattage smile and left. Once in the kitchen she pulled the cell phone out. The phone screen told her she had missed a call from DC. She pushed the call back button. DC picked up on the first ring.

"Jenny, girl, what's up?"

"You tell me, DC."

"I got us a flick for tonight. It's a classic. You'll love it."

"God help me. What is it?"

"*Bullitt.*"

"Is that the flick with DMX?"

"No, it stars Steve McQueen."

"Who?"

"Steve McQueen. You've heard of him, right?"

"No. What has he been in?"

"*The Great Escape,* where he jumps that bike over the fence."

"Is this a biker movie?"

"No. I mean he rode a bike in real life, but he wasn't a biker. He was the model of cool."

"Uh huh. What else was he in?"

"*The Getaway. Junior Boner. The Thomas Crown Affair. Wanted Dead or Alive*, that was TV. And *The Magnificent Seven,* I know you've heard of that."

"Is that a porno?"

"No. I swear. Frank would kill me if I brought a porno for you girls to watch."

"So you're saying you have got some porno, you just don't want to bring it."

"Yeah. I mean no. Let's start over."

Jenny laughed. DC was very sweet and innocent in some ways. "I was just kidding. I've seen *The Magnificent Seven.* Steve McQueen was the good-looking guy. And yes, he was pretty cool. That should be fine."

"Who you talking to?" Caron asked.

"DC."

"Let me have the phone."

Jenny passed her phone to Caron.

"DC you coming by tonight?"

"Yeah. I got a flick for us to watch."

"It's a porno," Jenny shouted.

"Cool," Caron said.

"It's not a porno. It's a Steve McQueen movie."

"Who? Is he related to Queen Latifa?"

"Forget it."

"Hey, you going to bring some weed with you?"

"I don't know. Frank might not appreciate it."

"Come on, DC. It would be so sweet. And we've been good."

"Maybe. Look, I got to go. I'll come by after you get off work."

"Bye."

"Bye."

Caron passed the phone back to Jenny. "He's bringing weed."

"No way."

"Way."

"We better leave the windows open tomorrow so Frank doesn't figure it out."

"I got some Febreze, we can use that too."

"Good idea."

A server stuck her head into the kitchen. "Caron there's a new table asking for you."

"Who is it?"

"A couple of football studs and their geeky friend."

Caron smiled. She liked football players, so predictable.

45

Agents Redding and Harris arrived at the Jeb Bush Hospital for Mental Illness. The guard at the gate buzzed them inside. They parked and went up to the main door.

"This is why you said she would still be here."

"Sorry. It was a joke. She's confined here whether she likes it or not."

"I get it. Why is she here? Is she nuts like Masnick?"

"In a way, yes. In other ways she's brilliant. She was a scientist. A noted chemical engineer. She published extensively. She lectured internationally. She was an expert in accelerants. She still is."

"As in things that make small fires big?"

"The same. She was working with different compound carrying systems. She was trying to discover new chemical triggering systems. She was trying to discover unique systems of ignition or acceleration. The military was very interested in her work. She received numerous grants for her studies. Until the accident."

"What accident?"

"I'll explain after you see her."

They took the elevator to the second floor.

A nurse at the desk eyed them with suspicion, "It's after visiting hours."

Redding flashed his badge wallet. "FBI business."

"Who are you here to see?"

"Sandy Jones. I know where her room is. Is she awake?"

The nurse shrugged. Redding and Harris went down the hall. Their shoes made a strange hollow sound as they walked. Harris loved the power of those three letters the farther you got away from Washington, D.C.

Sandy was in a semi-private room, but she didn't have a roommate at the time. The room was government issue. Almost no furniture. Each bed had a nightstand and a single chair. There was one small stand-alone closet. A single television on a stand for both occupants. A thin white curtain that separated the two beds. The beds were hospital grade, adjustable and old.

They approached the bed. Sandy was lying on her side on the pillow. The lights were low and the television off. The stark white sheet was pulled up beneath her chin. She had short brown hair that had been cut like a man's without any real style. The skin of her face was smooth. Asleep, without a care, she was beautiful.

"Should we wake her?" Harris asked.

"Of course we should. Sandy. Sandy, wake up you've got visitors."

The right eye fluttered behind the closed lid, then slowly opened. She turned in the bed toward them. For the first time Harris could see the other side of her face. The skin was red and leathery where it had been burned. The left eye was gone. The left half of her lips were burned away, exposing her teeth in a death's head grin. Harris could see the burn scars travel all the way down her neck and disappear under the white sheet. The burned flesh against the whiteness of the sheet and pillow almost made Harris retch. Redding appeared not to notice.

"Good evening, Sandy."

Sandy smiled a death rictus. "Good evening, Agent Redding."

"This is Agent Harris."

Harris nodded toward her but did not speak. He tried not to look at her.

"I think your new friend is shocked by my appearance. If I had known he was coming I could have put on lipstick." She laughed. It was a crazed cackle from a horror movie.

"He's a big boy. I think he can handle it."

"What do you want, Redding?"

"You know, Sandy. What do I always want to talk about?"

"Spartans. Spartans and Prometheus, the Fire Walker."

"That's right. I want to talk about Prometheus."

Her eye seemed to light up with excitement. She struggled to sit up in the bed. "Can I have a cigarette?"

Redding reached into his pocket for his pack. He shook one loose and tamped it on the back of his hand to pack the tobacco.

Harris leaned in close and whispered. "It's a no-smoking facility. She's not allowed to smoke."

Redding ignored him, offered the cigarette to Sandy. Her arms came up from beneath the sheet. The left arm was burned to the same leathery red. The hand was gone halfway up the wrist. The right arm had an array of small burns, but was mostly unburned. The right was distorted. Only two fingers remained, the thumb and the index finger. The others had been burned away. Charred flesh rose up the wrist on the inside to the middle of the forearm. Sandy leaned forward and delicately took the cigarette from Redding.

Harris looked down at the lower half of the bed, wondering what damage had been done below. He could tell from the outline of the sheets that her legs were gone beneath her knees. Harris tried not to vomit as he felt his stomach heave. He looked up at Sandy, who smiled grotesquely.

She held the cigarette to the right side of her lips. Redding got his lighter out and lit it for her. She took a deep drag and held it. Redding put the lighter back in his pocket. Sandy blew a cloud of blue smoke at the ceiling.

"Thank you," she said.

"You're welcome," Redding replied.

"Ask your questions. I will answer them if I choose to."

"As always. Tell me what you will."

Sandy took another draw on the cigarette. She held the smoke for a long time.

"We've heard that the Spartans are reforming."

"How could a creature like Sparta not try to rebuild? Their time was glorious. Who can blame them for wishing to return once more?"

"It's logical that they should try to rebuild. Yet until now they haven't."

"A serpent without a head cannot live."

Redding smiled. "After your accident, the Spartans regarded you as one of their oracles, like the Delphic oracles of old. What words have you heard? What omens do you see?"

Sandy stared at the glowing tip of the cigarette. She marveled at its bright heat. She gazed at the glow with a love that mothers reserve for their children. She smiled her demon's smile.

"There have been signs. There have been whispers."

"Can you tell me what you've heard?"

She looked at him. "Only that death's angel is coming."

Redding looked into her eye and held it.

"We hear that Frank Kane has risen from the grave."

Her color blanched slightly.

"He's a monster."

"We hear he's exacting retribution on Sparta's enemies."

Sandy's eye seemed to glaze over and she stared off into space. "If Kane comes for you, then you're already dead. He cannot be stopped. The ferry has docked. All aboard."

"Is he coming for you, Sandy?"

Her vision seemed to return.

"Why would he come for me? I'm no threat. I was always a friend to Sparta. There's no ill will between us. I sought only to serve, as did he."

"And Prometheus?"

"What of him?"

"He's disappeared. He may be dead. We don't know."

"The Fire Walker lives. He is everywhere. You will not find him if he does not wish it."

"Is Kane looking for him?"

Once more there was a slight blanching of her face. She seemed to tremble.

"Kane seeks whom Kane seeks. Even the Fire Walker cannot hide from the Angel of Death. If Kane seeks him, then he is dead."

"Is that why Prometheus has gone into hiding? Is he afraid?"

Sandy laughed her crazed laugh again. "The Fire Walker fears nothing. He is a god. What does a god fear?"

"He may be in danger. We can protect him."

"You can do nothing if Kane comes for him. The Fire Walker will meet death when it is his time. Even gods die. He knows this. The ancient warriors of Sparta said, 'to be a man you must enter fire.' That is where the Fire Walker lives, in the flames. In the midst of the flame's heart. When you see him he is always bathed in the flames."

"Where's Prometheus?"

"I can't say."

"Does he still come to see you?"

She smoked for a moment, but did not answer.

"Does he still love you?"

"We are the same. We are twins. He will always love me. I will always love him."

"Won't you help me?"

"Do you know the legend of the Hydra?"

"I think so. The beast that, when Hercules cut off one of its heads, two more grew from the neck?"

"Yes. Do you know what finally destroyed it? Fire. The hottest kiss. Hercules burned the stumps before they could re-grow."

"So you're saying the Spartans are like the Hydra and re-growing?"

"Only fire consumes completely. It is pure and elemental. All life is beholden to its power."

"What are you saying, Sandy? I don't understand. I'm just a dumb old cop. Help me understand."

Sandy looked again at the tip of the cigarette. She blew on it until it glowed. Redding watched her place the tip against her arm. She shivered in pain. Redding slapped the cigarette away. He stomped it out on the floor. The wound oozed and bubbled with fluid. Sandy laughed.

"Are you crazy?" Redding yelled.

Sandy smiled. "I am tired of the pain. I am ready to die. Fire is a fitting death for a handmaiden of the flames."

"Is that what Prometheus talks about when he comes? About your death?"

"Death and fire. Is there anything else?"

"Life."

"I have been dead for a long time. It is only the pain that holds me here. But he has promised."

"Who? Who has promised? Prometheus? What has he promised?"

"To take me with him?" Sandy started laughing.

A large black nurse came in.

"I smelled smoke. Somebody smoking in here. This is a no smoking facility. I better not catch anybody smoking. FBI or not I will throw your butt out."

"No one's smoking in here." Redding said.

"I can smell it."

Redding flashed his credentials. He held them inches from her face.

"If you are smart, you didn't smell anything. If you're not, I'll have you brought to the Bureau's attention first thing tomorrow."

The nurse turned and left without a word. Sandy kept laughing. Harris tugged on Redding's arm.

"Let's get out of here."

"Sandy, is there anything I can do for you before I go?"

Her laughing stopped. She stared at him like she was seeing a stranger. Her eye was glazed. She started humming a tune that Redding did not recognize. He waited another moment.

"We're leaving. I'll be back later. You rest. We're the only hope Prometheus has. Help us help him."

Redding gently pulled the sheet back up over her arms. He straightened her pillow and she laid her head back down. With reverence he closed the door behind them as they left her room.

Harris spoke as soon as they were outside. "What happened to her?"

"She was burned making a firebomb for Masnick."

"Why didn't you tell me before?"

"I thought it would be a good for you. A little shock by proxy."

"It wasn't fair."

"Grow the fuck up. You're an FBI agent now. Start acting like one."

"I don't appreciate being spoken to like that."

"Then kiss my ass. Grow up or ask to get reassigned. This is man's work."

They walked in silence toward the front desk. Redding stopped. He leaned across the countertop until he caught the night duty nurse's eye.

"Yes, sir."

"Does Sandy Jones have a visitors log?"

The nurse at the desk looked through her paperwork. She shook her head from side to side. "No. We don't keep logs on every patient here."

"Do you know if she's had any visitors lately?"

"I haven't seen anybody, but Nashira works the day shift. You can ask her. She might know about that."

"Can you call her? It is important." Redding flashed his credentials again. "Very important FBI business."

"Sure." The nurse picked up the landline and called.

"Nashira, an FBI guy wants to talk to you," she said, passing the handset to Redding.

"Nashira, this is Special Agent Richard Redding of the FBI. The lady who called you can vouch for my credentials if that's necessary."

Redding waited for the reply.

"How can I help?"

"You have a patient, Sandy Jones. "

"Yes, room 307."

"Has she had any visitors recently?"

"Poor woman don't have no visitors. Ever."

"None. I am specifically thinking about a white man about fifty. He has dark brown hair. He had a beard the last time I saw him."

"No. Come to think of it she did have a visitor last week. But it was a woman. I saw her leaving."

"And no one since?"

"Not that I seen. But I got a lot of rooms to look after. Someone could have come and gone and I might never have seen them."

"All right. Thanks for your help." Redding passed the telephone back to the night duty nurse who hung it up. "Thank you, ma'am." He turned and continued out of the building. Harris followed.

"Do you mind filling me in on the details of her accident?" Harris asked.

"Not much to tell. She got burned making an explosive for Masnick. She should have died. She's tough. She never connected it to Masnick. Denied every-thing. But over the years she's given me tidbits that paid off."

"Well, she didn't give us any tidbits tonight. It was a waste of time."

"Was it? Let's see. We learned Masnick is alive. We know she's afraid of Frank Kane. She thinks the Spartans are reforming which means that's what Mas-nick believes. We know she still loves him."

"Then why hasn't he come to see her?"

Redding stopped walking and turned around in a complete three hundred and sixty degree circle.

"Wow. I almost missed it. Masnick has been here."

"But her only visitor was a woman."

"Don't you get it? The woman was Masnick. He shaved his beard and dressed like a woman. She said they were twins. It was a clue."

"That's a stretch."

"I'll tell you something else that's a stretch. Call the Bureau; have them check birth certificates on Sandy Jones. See if there is any overlap with what we still have on Keith Masnick. We know he had a brother, trace it through him if you have to. Maybe she was telling us the truth. Maybe he is her brother. Maybe they really are twins. That would explain his devotion to her and hers to him."

"You're kidding, right?"

"Make the call, now. If Masnick is still around he'll be back. We need to get a team on this ASAP."

Harris punched the numbers on his phone and waited. He asked Redding, "What was that stuff about walking in flames?"

Redding looked off into the night. He took out a cigarette and lit it. "Sandy said when she sees Masnick he's covered with flames. That's why she calls him the Fire Walker. He brings fire wherever he goes. I think it's an omen of how he will die."

46

Frank stared at the map that Burns had drawn for the thousandth time. He ran scenarios through his mind. He tried to calculate men and weapons and security and probabilities. He started to call the hotel. What was he going to tell Dorian anyway? He tapped the phone off. He checked his watch. One o'clock. They had gotten lucky. They had decided to stay at Burns' place despite the risk. No one called. The Russians hadn't shown. Frank stood and stretched.

"Time to go."

Burns nodded.

"I'll take the truck. I'm dressed for it. You drive the Benz. Don't go over the speed limit. I'll follow. Go straight to the Greek's house. Park half a block away where you can still see the house."

"Then what?"

"You wait. When it's clear, I'll flash the porch lights three times and open the gate. If the gate opens and I haven't flashed the lights, get out of there. If the lights flash twice and the gate opens, get out of there. Keep the window down. If you hear gunfire, get out of there. If I don't surprise them and it turns into a gun battle, I'm dead. Go to the police. They can help. It's your only chance to save your wife. You'll do time, but at least you'll both be alive."

"What if you get stopped on the way or the truck breaks down?"

"I'll deal with that when and if it happens. Something goes wrong, pull over and park within view."

"I'm pretty nervous about this," Burns said.

"Not unusual. If cops come while you're parked near the Greek's house, tell them you think your wife is sneaking around on you and you're waiting for her."

What if they don't believe me?"

"They'll believe. Every cop thinks his wife's cheating on him. They're suspicious by nature."

They drove slowly. Frank gave the Mercedes about eight car lengths. He put the Sig on the seat beside him. He hoped he wouldn't need it on the drive.

Caron approached the table. She was all smiles and swaying hips.

"Did you guys request me?"

"We sure did."

"That was awfully sweet. I waited on you boys before."

"We saw you the other night and Morgan thought you were hot," Zack said.

"Well, aren't we the bold one?"

"We play football. We have to be bold."

"Is that right? Where did you say you played?"

"Ragsdale. Morgan and I are All State. We got full ride scholarships to Chapel Hill."

"Wow. That's great. My best friend and I were just talking about going to Chapel Hill. We got accepted, but we didn't get any scholarships."

"That would be so cool. We'll probably see you on campus."

"Probably."

"Which one is your friend?"

Caron waved Jenny over. Jenny had a table that she had just served. She didn't have time for this. She gave Caron the bad eye, but Caron just waved her over again.

"Boys, this is my BFF, Jenny. We live together with her uncle."

"Hi," Jenny said.

"Hi, yourself. You're hot too. I'm Zack, the big boy here is Morgan and this is Brian," Zack said pointing to the others at the table. "I play quarterback, Morgan plays center and Brian's team manager. He looks after us."

"It's nice to meet you," Jenny said.

"Caron says you guys are thinking about going to Chapel Hill."

"Yeah, we are. We haven't made a final decision."

"It's number one for us, so far," Caron said.

"Where do you girls go to school?" Brian asked.

"Westchester Country Day School," Caron said.

"Wow. You must be rich."

"Right," Jenny said, "that's why we work at Applebee's."

"Hey, private school's expensive, zall I'm saying. Somebody's paying a lot of money."

"My uncle takes care of that. Look, I have to go. Good luck at Chapel Hill."

"We play Page on Friday. Come see us play."

"We'll try," Jenny said inching away.

"There's a big party afterward in Cedarwood. You can't miss it. You ought to come to that. It'll be off the hook."

"Thanks. I think we have to work. Maybe after we get off."

Zack smiled and sat back.

"Great, we'll see you there."

"You can count on it. We'll be there," Caron said. "Now let me get your order in. What do you three studs want to drink?"

DC pulled up the Cone Hospital web site. It didn't take long to bypass their firewall and gain access. He searched admission records for the little girl and her uncle. He didn't know their last names so he just ran a match between emergency room patients and admissions and got an overlay. They were right there, Carlos and Rosa Dominquez. It took thirty seconds to figure out who their doctor was, a hot shot from Emory named Gaines Hunter. He found Dr. Hunter's electronic notes and scrolled through them. DC didn't understand all the things about IVs and drugs but he did understand that Carlos had been struck twice. He would recover fully. The wounds were not life threatening. One was superficial and the second had struck no vital organs. He was to be dismissed after a few more tests confirmed that he was stable. DC knew he was a lucky man.

Dr. Hunter's prognosis for Rosa was not as good. She had lost her left arm below the elbow. She had lost a lot of blood and suffered massive trauma. She had died three times, but Dr. Hunter pulled her back each time. She would survive, but would require extensive physical and psychological rehabilitation to overcome the loss of her arm. He noted that there was a type of electronic prosthetic limb that was ideal for her case. He noted that it was highly experimental and extremely expensive. The custom fitted prosthetic was made by a company out of Tennessee, but due to her age the device would need to be replaced every two years as she grew. The initial cost for the prosthetic limb was forty-seven thousand dollars. Dr. Hunter made a recommendation to search for possible grants that might be able to fund it for her. He had listed the names of four organizations that he would contact for help.

DC felt a cold knot in his stomach. He felt bad for Rosa. He dreaded having to tell Frank.

47

Burns parked down from the Greek's house exactly as Frank told him. Frank pulled up behind him a few cars back. Frank studied the house from the road. The map was pretty accurate, he thought. There was a nice cover of trees along the side of the house. The neighboring houses were large with big lots full of gazebos and pergolas and water features and tiny islands of trees. Their yards were fenced, but there was space between the two fences for him to move safely. The neighboring houses were both dark. It was a workday tomorrow. He wondered if the neighbors even needed to work if they could afford houses like this. Frank smiled to himself. It was work that got you these houses. It was work that kept you in them.

Frank got out of the truck and walked around to the back. He opened the doors. It was strange cargo. Two bubble wrapped bodies and three huge metal cases carrying surface to air missiles and a ladder. Frank took the ladder and moved quickly off into the darkness. He moved with surprising speed and complete silence through the darkness like some huge misshapen cat. Frank went to the back of the property. There was a door in the metal gate. It was the lowest point on the fence. Frank didn't try the fence or the door. Burns had said it was electrified and there was a sign attesting to the fact. He opened the ladder and positioned it beside the gate. He climbed the ladder and balanced on the top for a moment and then he was over. He landed and sank down, hiding his profile.

Frank crept over behind the pool house. There was a sweet pork smell in the air. He quickly located the body. The throat had been cut. At first he was afraid it might be Burns' wife. It wasn't. It was the dog. The body had been dumped here to keep it out of sight. It was a big dog. It had been powerful with thick muscles. Frank felt a spark of rage. What had the dog done to deserve death? What kind of owner couldn't control his own dog? It didn't make sense. Apollo had told Frank once that things didn't always make sense because you didn't know all the facts. The more you knew the more you understood.

Frank screwed the noise suppressor onto the SIG Sauer. The swimming pool blocked him from a straight approach to the house, but the pool house was decent cover. There was a light on upstairs in the bathroom, or it could be a reflection from a hallway light. No shadows danced past. It seemed quiet. The downstairs was lit up. He would need to enter through the back door. His left hand touched the lock pick kit in his pocket. He would try to pick it quickly before they knew he was there. He heard an owl off in the night trees. He smiled. It was a good omen. It was an owl's call that had saved his and Helen's life a long time ago. It had been the final straw that had tipped the balance in their favor. Maybe the door would be unlocked?

He was just rising from his crouch when the back door opened. A tall man in a short sleeve shirt and black slacks stepped outside. He looked to be about thirty years old. He carried an AK-47. Frank froze. He knew it was usually motion that gave you away. The man scanned the backyard. He took three steps down onto the river stone deck. He leaned the AK-47 against a bush and unzipped his pants. Frank heard the splash of urine and the man's deep sigh of relief. Frank understood the pleasure of peeing outdoors. The man finished his business, did a little hop step and zipped up. He turned back toward the house and picked up the AK-47 casually by the barrel as he passed. As soon as his back was turned, Frank was moving.

The man opened the door and Frank was nearly to him. The man stepped inside and the door swung closed. Frank caught the handle just before it engaged. He opened the door and stepped into the kitchen behind the man. The man must have sensed him or heard the abnormally long delay in the door closing or maybe he felt the force of air Frank generated as he moved up behind him. In any case, the man started to turn. The rifle came up in his hands.

Frank placed the silenced pistol into his back and fired three times. He caught the man as he died and eased him to the floor. The Ak-47 was still gripped tightly in his fingers. Frank stepped over him and moved toward the living room. He turned toward the den and heard a voice with a heavy accent.

"Yuri, come. You have to see this."

Frank stepped into the room.

A man about the same age as the first was sitting on the sofa. His back was to Frank. The television was on. It was an old M*A*S*H episode. Frank put his first shot through the center of his head. The man seemed to freeze and then slumped over. There was a Glock on the end table.

Frank did a quick sweep of the downstairs rooms. They were empty. Could be Judy was being kept in the basement. For an instant he considered checking the basement. He played the scenario over in his head. Find Judy. Sneak her out. Pick the devil's pocket as DC liked to say. Get them out of town tonight.

Frank turned toward the stairway. He would check the bedrooms first. That was the easiest place for them to keep her. He heard the man upstairs before he turned the corner. The man said something in Russian. He started down the stairs. His big feet made a clomping sound. At the bottom of the steps Frank stepped out and shot him twice. The man crumpled where he was. Frank hurried to him. He took the gun from the man's hand. Frank placed his gloved hand over the man's mouth.

"How many are in the house?"

The man stared at him. He knew he was dying. His eyes were fierce. He didn't speak.

"Where are the others?"

The man held his gaze.

"Where's the hostage?"

The man's brow furrowed against the pain, but he did not speak. Frank knew he wasn't going to talk. He remembered what the Russian had said.

"Bonh. Warrior"

The man nodded. Proud. Strong. Frank respected that. He leaned back to avoid the splatter and shot him in the forehead.

Frank moved up the stairs. The first bedroom was empty. It was a mess. The sheets on the beds were in disarray. The room smelled of cigarettes. He checked the second bedroom. He turned on the light. A heavy-set Russian in a dingy white T-shirt sat up against the light. He was very hairy. Frank shot him three times. He released the magazine on the pistol. There were still six rounds left, but he felt it was time for a combat-reload. There was no way to be sure how many more there would be and it would be easier to reload now than in a firefight if it came to that.

The other bedrooms were used, but empty. There was no one in the child's room. The walls had a mural of Greece painted across them. The artist had been very good. It had a 3-D effect. There was Mount Olympus and the Acropolis. Rolling fields were dotted with vineyards. Ancient Greek men and women and children were painted in their daily pursuits of work and play. There were fishermen straining to pull in a net brimming with fish. There was even a Greek warrior in full battle gear. Frank thought he was probably a Spartan, but some of the details were wrong. He stared at the boy's room. It had to be an omen. Maybe the gods were telling him to go to Greece and see it for real, one time before he died. He had always planned to. Maybe it was something else. He turned off the light and left the boy's bedroom.

The master was the last bedroom. He opened the door and turned on the light. A man was sitting up in the bed. He was in his fifties. He was balding and a little overweight. He had a beard that was more gray than black. Frank swung the pistol up. His finger drew back on the trigger. Seeing that one of the man's hands was handcuffed to the bed. He stopped.

The man's black eyes seemed confused. And well they should be. Waking to a giant pointing a gun at your head was surely a shocking spectacle. Frank moved toward the bed.

The man's lip was bloody. He had a bruise on the side of his face. Frank jammed the gun against his head.

"How many are in the house?"

"Who are you?"

Frank prodded him with the gun again. "How many are in the house?"

"Four I think. I don't know for sure. There are usually four of them."

"Where do you have the hostage?"

"I don't have her anywhere. I'm a prisoner too."

Frank ignored him.

"Who's in the basement?"

"No one. I mean not that I know of."

Frank had seen men fake their own injuries before. But there hadn't been time. He checked the handcuff. It was solid.

"See, I told you. I'm a hostage."

Frank removed the pillows near the man to be sure there was no obvious key or weapon nearby. There wasn't.

"Maybe," was all Frank said.

Frank left the man secured to the bed. He went back downstairs. He did a thorough sweep of the house and the basement. There was no one else there. He took one of the Russian's guns and removed all the ammunition. He replaced the empty magazine. He removed the silencer and put his own pistol in his front pocket. He carried the empty gun in his hand. Time to find out the truth, he thought.

The man was still where he had left him. He was fully awake now. His eyes were clear. Frank sat down on the bed next to him. He placed the gun within easy reach of the man's un-handcuffed hand. He reached for the handcuff and tested the mechanism.

"You the Greek?"

"That is what I am called."

"You okay? I need to get something to pop the cuff. Sit tight."

Frank left the gun and walked into the bathroom. He stalled for thirty seconds. He wanted the Greek to have plenty of time. When he came back in the Greek was still handcuffed to the bed. The gun was untouched. Frank went to work on the handcuff with one of his lock pick tools and had it open in seconds. He turned his back on the Greek a last time. There was plenty of time to pick up the gun. The Greek didn't fall for it.

"Let's go downstairs. We need to talk."

"Who are you?"

"I'm the man with the gun."

The Greek got up, rubbing his wrist. Frank picked up the empty gun and motioned the Greek with it. "You first."

The Greek left the bedroom and went down the stairs. He stepped over the body without a word. In the television room he picked up the remote and turned the television off. He sat down in a leather chair near an empty bar.

Frank took a seat beside the dead man. He rolled the balaclava up on his head so his face was visible. The Greek tried not to look at the dead man. The Greek was starting to look a little shaky.

"Can I fix a drink? I've got some more liquor in the other room."

"No."

"Then what? What do you want?"

"Explain it. Keep it real simple."

The Greek leaned forward and began his tale.

48

Caron finally finished with the last table. Jenny was already done. She was in the back counting her tips. It had been a good night. Double shifts were hard, but they did pay well. Finally, the last young couple left. Caron came into the back and the busboy hurried over to clean the table.

"Almost done," Caron said with a grin.

"We still have to clean up. I hate to mop and vacuum."

"No shit."

"I'm glad we don't have to do it very often."

"Me too," Caron said.

"How did you do tonight?"

"Good. You?"

"I did good too."

"Not like the money we made in Atlanta."

"No, not even close. But the work is easier."

"You think making small talk and humping plates is easier than what we did?"

"It's easier on my soul."

"Well, yeah, if you're going to get all spiritual. I meant from a physical labor point."

"I like this better."

Caron smiled. "Me too, Jenny."

"What was up with those football guys?"

"I got a twenty-five dollar tip from them on a thirty-four dollar bill."

"That's creepy."

"I don't think so. They were kind of cute."

"They were assholes. The big one kept pawing you. They acted like because you waited on them that gave them the right to hit on you."

"It does. It's all business."

"So that stuff you were saying about going to their party was a lie? And hoping to run into them in Chapel Hill if we go, that was just bull too?"

"Of course. That's how you get the big tips."

"What happens when we don't show up?"

"Next time they come in we'll tell them we had to work. Or got sick. Or had a flat tire. It doesn't matter. Who cares? If they want to believe they will. If they don't F them."

"You are bad."

"No, I'm good with customers. So are you. People love Miss Jenny."

"Come on, lets get this over with so we can go home. I'm beat."

"Did you call DC?"

"No. I'll do it right before we leave."

"I hope he brings the herb."

"Do you really think he was telling the truth about that guy named Steve McQueen?"

"You are so gullible, Jenny. He was pulling our leg."

Special Agent Harris checked to make sure he was alone. He punched in the number on his cell phone. It was answered immediately.

"This is Harris," he said.

"Of course. What do you have to report?" It was a different voice, but he recognized it.

"I need to speak to him."

"He's not available. He's an extremely busy man. You can say anything to me you would say to him."

Harris was angry. He felt like they were diminishing his importance in this. He was a professional. He understood the stakes. He shoved his anger down. He had sacrificed a great deal to be in the position he was in.

"I may have discovered something useful. There's a woman in the mental hospital in Winter Park. Her name is Sandy Jones. She was a very close friend of Masnick. There's still a strong link between the two of them."

"Does she know where he is?"

"Hard to say. She knows something. A lot, I would guess. She makes hints. Redding is convinced she's the key."

"Then we must have her."

"My thoughts exactly. I'm supposed to be sending a team to watch over her. I sent the request to my answering machine. We have a small window, a few hours at best. You need to get someone up there. I'll have to make the call soon or Redding will find out."

"Will she be difficult?"

"She's a burn victim. Incapacitated."

"Will she give us what we need?"

"If you apply the right incentives I think she will. If the Bureau gets hold of her they'll shut her down. We'll never know what she knows."

"Thanks. Good work. I'll tell him you called." He hung up.

I'll tell him you called, thought Harris. The man treated him more and more like a servant. That would have to change. I'm the key to the successful resolution of this matter. They had better remember it. They had better appreciate it. Harris was tired of being an errand boy.

49

The Greek's story was simple. He told it slowly so he wouldn't forget the details, as if being able to speak them made them truer.

"A few months ago my wife's cousin came to see me. He wanted me to arrange transport for an important cargo that he had."

"The SAMs."

"Yes. I didn't know it was SAMs at the time. He promised me money. I told him I would do it for my wife as a favor, but I would need forty thousand dollars for my partner to cover his end. I had a partner, a good man who could handle it for me."

"Bruce Burns."

The Greek's face showed shock that Frank knew, but he continued. "Exactly. I don't know how he does the shipments and I don't want to know. We've done similar shipments. He's great at logistics. I told him that I had a product that needed to be shipped up from Colombia, South America. I told him the price and he agreed. It should have been easy money."

"What went wrong?"

"What went wrong? I'm not sure. I got a call from Bruce. He said he wasn't comfortable with the shipment. He said they were SAMs and we needed to talk."

"I was shocked. I mean I've moved a lot of different stuff, including weapons, but not something like this. Who needs something like that? It had to be some kind of error."

"What did you think you were shipping?"

"AK-47s. My wife's cousin said he had a connection in the Colombian military. It was supposed to be sixty brand new AKs."

"What kind of person needs sixty AK-47s?"

"He said he was hooked into the Russian mob. I've gotten them handguns before."

"But not this?"

"Of course not this. The risks are too big. They get used; they can be traced back to me sooner or later. And they would be."

"You got that right. Did you tell your wife's cousin?"

The Greek shook his head, amazed at his own stupidity. "Yes. I didn't think he could possibly have known about this. He has always seemed reasonable."

"How did he take it?"

"He seemed genuinely shocked. He said he would check back with his boss. It had to be a mistake. The next day he showed up with a bunch of Russian goons.

They beat me up and took my wife and son away."

"They did the same to Burns."

"By Poseidon's beard, they will pay for this."

Frank had never heard that expression before.

"What's that mean? What's Poseidon's beard?"

"Sorry. I grew up in Greece on Elafonissos. You've heard of it?"

Frank shook his head and the Greek continued.

"It is a small island off the coast of the Pelopennesus. I like to say I grew up off the coast of Sparta. Elafonissos is in Laknikos Bay, the bay of Laconia. We were fishermen. When the sea was very rough, or the nets became tangled, or the fish were hiding my father would say, 'By Poseidon's beard.' It was our local curse word. We used it for everything when we needed to swear."

"I didn't know there were any islands there."

"Oh, yes. There are only four hundred locals, but it has become a popular spot for vacationers now. There are several beautiful beaches for tourists to enjoy. It's only a short ferry ride from the mainland."

"But locals still fish?"

"Many have turned to tourism. They sell trinkets, and operate inns, but yes, many still fish."

Frank nodded. It was a good omen. Not as good as the Greek not going for the gun, but pretty damn good.

"All right. Your story could be true. Go open the gate on the driveway and flash the outside light three times for Burns."

"It's a signal?"

"Of course. Burns is parked down the street waiting."

The Greek did as he was told.

Frank kept his gloves on. He still might need to shoot the Greek, but the omens were good. Frank waited by the front door with the Greek for Burns. He heard the owl again.

Burns parked the Mercedes and jumped out. He ran toward the front door and stopped when he saw the Greek.

"Where's my wife?"

"I don't have her. Come, sit. I will tell you everything."

Burns looked to Frank for confirmation. Frank nodded. "Come on. I think he's on the level. It's Ockham's razor."

"What's this Ockham's razor?" the Greek asked. "He is a Muslim?"

"He's English," Frank said.

"Pluralitae non est ponenda sin necessitate," Burns said.

Frank smiled. He hadn't known Burns spoke Latin.

"The simplest solution is usually the correct one," Frank said.

Burns nodded. They went inside. They took seats in the kitchen, stepping around the dead body. Burns fought to remain calm.

50

The Greek began his tale again. Frank listened. It was an old cop trick. Have them get the story out quickly, then have them retell it. You listened for the changes the differences, the embellishments. It didn't so much matter what they said the first time; it was how the story changed over time. That was how you knew if someone was lying. If the Greek was lying it changed everything.

The Greek's story didn't change. Which might indicate that it was well rehearsed or it could mean the Greek had been trying to figure out how he ended up handcuffed to a bed with his wife and son taken hostage. Or it could just be the truth.

"They cut off Judy's finger to pressure me."

"Poseidon's beard," the Greek said.

"What are we going to do?" Burns asked.

"We have to find them," Frank said.

"Make a deal," Burns said.

"Yes. Give them the damn missiles if that is what they want. They are not worth the lives of our wives and children," the Greek said.

"No," Frank said.

"What are you talking about?" the Greek asked.

"We can't give them the missiles. Then there would be no reason for any of you to stay alive. This way we have leverage. We know what they want."

The Greek spat. "Leverage? For what? We are in no position to negotiate."

"You don't negotiate. I do. We will find them. We will take them out. I promise you."

The Greek turned to Burns. "Who is this man?"

"His name is Frank. He's a negotiator."

The Greek nodded at the dead man. "This is negotiating?"

"Yes," Frank said. "But it's your call. You want your families back? You want your lives back? If yes, then I'm in.

"You can't do what you have to? Then tell me now so I can be gone tonight."

Burns spoke first. "If it wasn't for Frank we would both still be hostages."

"I just can't see how one man…."

"Neither can I, but there aren't any other options. We call the cops, the Russians kill them. We run, they kill them. We try to cut a deal, they kill us all."

"By Poseidon's beard. I do not like this. But you are right. Very well. What are we to do?"

"Make some coffee. We're going to be up for a while. I need to check the bodies and the bedroom they were using."

"I could use a drink," Burns said.

"Me too," the Greek added.

"No booze," Frank said. "You need to stay sharp. Stick with coffee."

Both men frowned like chastised children and set about making coffee.

Frank checked the man on the sofa first. His clothes had no labels. His pocket held twenty dollars. Frank took the cash. He stacked up the gun and spare magazines on the large ornate table in the dining room. Next, he searched the man in the kitchen. He had a picture of a woman taped to his leg. A girl-friend or wife. Some special keepsake he had brought that he was not supposed to have. There was another Glock, but no spare magazines. Frank liked that. It could mean several things. He took the AK-47 and placed it on the table. The AK didn't have a spare banana clip either.

Frank went up to the stairway. He checked the dead Russian soldier. The man had more money, a hundred and twelve dollars. He had two spare maga-zines and a brand new Glock. He also had a cell phone. Frank took them all to the big table. There would be time for inspection later.

The man in the bedroom had a Glock on the nightstand beside him. There was no extra magazine. He had an array of prison tattoos that didn't mean any-thing to Frank, but probably explained a lot about who he was. He understood the concept of tattoos as codes. The Spartans, and every other gang, used them for identification. Frank didn't care what they meant. There was a second cell phone beside the bed resting on top of a twenty and a five. Frank gathered the stuff and took it to the table. Burns and the Greek were sitting in the kitchen talking quietly over their coffee. When they saw Frank, Burns called out, "We made you a cup."

"Thanks. Maybe later."

Frank went upstairs and found a linen closet full of clean sheets. He started with the Russian in the bed. He stripped him and rolled him into the sheet. The bullets had mushroomed inside the body like they were supposed to but there was still a lot of blood. He carried an armload of fresh sheets downstairs. He stripped and wrapped the other three men. No one spoke to him as he completed his grisly deeds.

"Burns, bring the truck up here."

Burns got up without speaking and left the table.

"First thing we need to do is get rid of these bodies. Any ideas?"

The Greek looked around to be sure Burns was gone. "Yes. I know a place near the Red River. There's a sinkhole."

"How long will it buy us?"

"I've used it before. Those bodies have not been found."

Frank nodded. It gave the Greek a little more depth in Frank's world. The Greek had been here before. "Can it handle six more?"

The Greek shrugged. "It is very deep and very isolated."

"Good."

They heard Burns pull up in the truck. They waited in silence. Burns came in and they all sat around the kitchen table.

"I need to figure this out. I have a few more questions for you two."

"Shoot," Burns said and grimaced at his word choice. "Sorry."

"How long have you been married?"

Burns answered first, "Twenty years."

"My first wife died," the Greek said. "Dasha and I have been married for a little over two years."

"How did you meet?"

"I own a Greek restaurant where I do the cooking. She came to work there."

"How did you start dating?"

"She was new to the U.S. She didn't know anyone. She was broke. I felt sorry for her so I tried to look after her."

"Plus," Burns added, "she's beautiful."

The Greek laughed. "She is very beautiful. In truth had she been fat or ugly maybe I would not have been so quick to help."

"Do you routinely date your staff?"

"No, no, almost never. It is not good business, but Dasha was different. There was something special about her. One thing seemed to naturally lead to the next."

"How old is she?"

The Greek jumped to his feet. "What are you asking? Are you trying to say my Dasha is involved in this?"

Frank barely responded. He looked up and then motioned for the Greek to sit. "I am saying how old is she? Remember it's her cousin who started this."

"Yes, but even he seemed surprised at the cargo and...."

Frank added a touch of ice to his request. "How fucking old is she?"

The Greek sighed and sat down. "Twenty-four. Now. She was twenty-one when we met."

"Tell me about her cousin."

"Like I told you. He is from Russia. Moscow, he said."

"In the Russian mob?"

"He is a lieutenant in the Russian mob. She told me. To warn me. She loves her cousin, but she is afraid of his associations. I deal with many criminals in many organizations. It made no difference to me. I can look after myself."

"What's this cousin's name?"

"His name is Vladimir. Everyone calls him Vlad. Like the Dracula character. He made a joke about it."

"You do business with Vlad before?"

"Yes. I did not meet him until the wedding. He asked me a favor. Said he had heard I was a man who could acquire certain things. We talked. He needed handguns. Twenty. I agreed and we made a deal."

"Did he pay you?"

"Yes. Up front. It made me trust him, I think."

"The next time?"

"The next time, it was AKs. I went through Burns and we made the arrangements. We made good money."

Burns nodded. "He seemed on the level."

"Then this shipment?"

"That is right," the Greek said.

Frank thought about it. It was classic. Lure them in. Establish the connection. Take your time. Don't seem to be in a hurry. A practice run with the AKs to make sure it would work, then the real deal. The Spartans had done the same thing many times.

"Do you think if I hadn't found out what was in the crates they would have just left us alone?" Burns asked.

"Probably. Might have killed you, but I doubt it. There was no need to. They had what they wanted and would have been gone. You would have thought everything was fine until the FBI kicked in your door and you woke up in some secret prison with your balls hooked to a car battery. Don't beat yourself up. Everything happens for a reason. You found out what the cargo was because you were supposed to."

Burns didn't look convinced. He stared at his cup of coffee.

"We have a child," the Greek said.

No one answered. Frank knew it meant nothing. It might just be another way to bind him to Dasha and her cousin. Might have been an accident. Might not even be his. It didn't matter.

"Have either of you talked with your wives since they were taken?"

Both men shook their heads.

"Your son?"

"He is only a year and a half old, but no."

"How are we going to find them?" Burns asked.

"First, we got forensic issues. You got blood splatter that we need to deal with. The simplest way is to burn your house."

The Greek gasped. "Not my house."

"It's your ass. The Feds come looking…they will find trace evidence. You can't clean it all up. There's just too much."

The Greek thought for a minute. "There is a better way. I have many businesses. I will call my brother. They replace carpets. I can have them here tomorrow morning. They can replace all the carpet. It will take them only a day or two."

"They will need to get rid of the mattress and box spring upstairs and the sofa."

"This sofa cost twenty-eight thousand dollars. It is an antique from Spain."

Frank didn't speak. He gave the Greek the thousand-yard stare.

"Very well. They can haul everything off at the same time."

"You trust your brother."

"With my life."

"You just have."

"When the Russians find out something is wrong, Vlad and his goons will come here. Make sure your brother comes with a bunch of guys he can trust. Have everybody dressed like workmen, in coveralls. Vlad doesn't want to involve the police. He won't start anything here. I'll make sure his focus is somewhere else."

"I will tell my brother of this Russian. He will have his own security in place."

Frank thought his plan to burn the house was better, but than again he didn't own a three-million-dollar home.

"Got another consideration," Frank said. "Do you have someplace you can lay low for a day, maybe two?"

"I have a large family. We can stay with one of them."

"No. No family. They might be able to trace you. Some place no one would know about, including your wife."

The Greek glared at Frank over the insinuation. "Yes. I have a warehouse. It cannot be traced to me. I store certain items there until I find buyers."

"Weapons house?"

"Yes."

"And no one knows where it is?"

"I am the only one. I consolidate my product there. There are cots and a microwave. It is not so bad."

"Write down the address for me."

"Don't you have a GPS?"

"Yes, but not here."

The Greek went into the kitchen and got a note pad and pen. He wrote it down for Frank. Frank read it and folded it into his pocket.

"Have another cup of Joe, gentlemen. I need to think."

Frank went back through the house. He gathered up the shell casings since he had the time. No reason to be sloppy. He had read there was new technology that might be able to trace fingerprints off the copper jackets. Technology was making it harder to be a criminal.

He went upstairs. He got a large pillowcase and brought it downstairs. He sat at the long table looking at the items he had collected. He thumbed through the magazines. He checked the Glocks. They were brand new. The serial numbers had been eaten off with acid. That was good. These guys were thorough. They had probably wiped their own trail clean, which would make it hard for the Feds to trace them back to the Greek or Burns. But they had limited resources. They had limited money. This operation was well planned, but they hadn't considered all the contingencies. It smelled like a military op. If Burns hadn't screwed the pooch it would have worked like a Swiss watch. When he did it was FUBAR. Now the Russians had to think on their feet.

"Guys come over here. Bring that pad and pen too."

The two men came over. They looked a little stunned. The adrenaline rush was burning off. Frank handed each man a loaded Glock and two spare magazines. The Greek checked the weapon and stuck it into the small of his back. Burns looked hesitant.

"What's this for?"

"Just in case. Do you know how to use it?"

"Yes. No. Sort of."

The Greek took the gun from him and ratcheted the slide back, chambering a round. He passed the gun back to Burns.

"Put it in your pocket. Something happens when we leave you just pull the trigger. When the slide locks back, it's empty. Press that button here and the empty magazine will fall out. Slap another one in and pull the slide back like I did. You're ready again."

Burns looked oddly at the gun. "All the guns I've moved, I've never held one before. I was always insulated."

"Times change," Frank said. "I'll take the other guns. We might need them."

"We won't. The warehouse is stockpiled with state of the art weapons," the Greek said.

"Can these be traced back to you?"

The Greek looked the AK-47 over.

"Could be mine, but they can't trace it to me. I'll dump it with the bodies and the other pistols if you want."

Frank stuffed the remaining weapons into the pillowcase. He kept the pocket money, photos and cell phones.

"Do it."

Frank punched up the cell phone numbers and wrote them down, including the one he'd taken from Dimitri. He scrolled through their call lists and made lists of calls made and missed. They were all prepaid cell phones. Tracing them would be harder, but DC sometimes could do magic. He entered his cell number and added I.D. He took the batteries out of two of the phones and passed each to a man.

"Take these with you. Put the batteries back in at two o'clock tomorrow. I will call you then. Don't answer any other calls except from my number. I programmed it in. Don't listen to any incoming messages. Lay low. If something goes bad, you get caught by the cops, you get shot. You call my cell and leave a message. But there won't be anything I can do."

"Why have the batteries out?" Burns asked.

"If these guys are terrorists, they may be on a government watch list. They may have a government contact helping them. Who knows? You can triangulate a cell phone's position if it's on. I doubt these guys are capable of that, but we don't want the Feds dropping by in the middle of this. You want to mess things up, just invite the Feds. After this is over we'll get rid of the phones."

"Come on," the Greek said. "Help me put these dogs in the truck. We have a long drive tonight."

"You want us to dump the bodies?" Burns asked. "I thought you would do that."

"I can't do it all. They have your wives. Your kid. You need to share the risk," Frank said.

Frank sat at the table and watched them load the bodies. He didn't offer to help. It was important to get them dirty. It was important to lock them in. He didn't speak again until they were done.

"I'll call you tomorrow at two. We'll get everyone back if you do what I tell you. Be careful. One last detail. What size shoes do you wear?"

"Ten," said Burns.

"Eleven," said the Greek. "Why?"

"It's not important. Two o'clock sharp."

Each man shook Frank's hand and they left. Six dead bodies. Three Surface to Air Missiles. It was a scene from a comic book, Frank thought. He opened his own cell phone and called DC.

198 JOHN F. SAUNDERS

51

Jenny and Caron were laughing hysterically at the Steve McQueen movie. It wasn't meant to be funny. It was a thriller, complete with fistfights and gunfights and mystery and probably the best car chase ever. What it did lack was humor. The marijuana made up for the script oversight.

DC had finally decided it would be all right to bring a joint, but just one. Then he wondered about how big a joint. What was proportional for three people? He couldn't bring a big Bob Marley spiff. But he couldn't bring a supermodel-thin joint either. If he was going to bring one, they all deserved to get a buzz. He finally decided on a fatty. Not too big. Not too small. Just right. Okay, he would bring one spare, just in case. He had decided they could smoke it after the movie. Then everyone could crash and get a good night's rest. His resolve lasted for all of five minutes. McQueen's movie suffered because of it.

DC's cell phone rang. It played *No Rest for the Wicked*, by Cage the Elephant. The girls giggled wildly. They were definitely Bogarting that joint.

"It's Frank's ring tone. Ssh, it's Frank. Ssh. I mean it."

The girls tried to get quiet, but started giggling again. DC answered the phone. "Hi Frank."

"What have you got to tell me?"

DC got up and walked out of the living room. "I checked on Rosa and her uncle Carlos like you asked. It's bad. She lost her left arm below the elbow. Major reconstruction. She almost died a couple of times."

"What about prosthetics?"

"The doc talks about it in his notes. He says there's one that would be good, but it's like fifty K and has to be replaced all the time until she's grown. Probably run close to four hundred thousand by the time's she grown and that doesn't count the physical therapy. The doc's going to look into grants and stuff. Try to get her one. He doesn't sound hopeful."

"The uncle?"

"He pulled through. Got clipped with a couple of rounds, but he's fine. They're discharging him today."

"Good. I got something else for you to do. You got a pen and paper?"

"Hold on. Yeah. Go ahead."

Frank read him the cell numbers. "Can you trace these? They're prepaids."

"I don't know any way to. I can check. I can find out where they were bought. Who bought them. How. You know, cash or charge. When do you need it?"

"Tomorrow is good. You with the girls?"

"Yeah. I am trying to turn them on to Steve McQueen. They never heard of him."

"Hard to believe. He was the coolest guy when I grew up."

"Dude, that's what I told them."

"Got to run. Give Elliott a message for me."

"Sure."

"Tell him his brother is safe. I'm working on the rest."

"How much longer do you think it will take?"

"I think I can wrap it up in the next couple of days."

"It'll be good to have you back home, big man."

"I know what you mean."

"Do you want to talk to the girls?"

"No, tell them I miss them and to take care of things while I'm gone."

"I will."

"Thanks. I'll call you tomorrow morning. See what you can do on the cell phones."

DC went back to the living room to find the first bottle of wine was almost empty. A tiny sip still rested in the bottom of the bottle. Caron was working on opening the second bottle. The first joint had been reduced to a tiny unsmokeable roach. They had smoked almost two thirds of the second one. Steve McQueen was chasing the bad guy across an airport runway, dodging planes. The movie was almost done too. Caron got the cork out and held it up to show her victory.

"I can't believe you ladies are so wasted."

They both looked guilty and then broke into more laughter. He told them what Frank had said and finished it with a, "so behave."

The girls looked at each other and started giggling again.

"Let me have the other bottle. I think you've had enough."

Caron hugged the open bottle to her chest. DC motioned for her to hand it to him. She giggled and took a deep drink, then passed the bottle to Jenny who did the same.

"Come on. I'm serious. Let me have the bottle."

Jenny passed it back to Caron who took another drink. Jenny was laughing. Caron passed the bottle back to her. She took a second large gulp.

DC put his hands on his hips like an angry dad. "I'm not kidding. You've had enough. Give me the bottle and I'll put it in the fridge for tomorrow. Come on."

The two girls looked at each other. Jenny nodded. Caron extended the wine bottle. DC took it in one hand and picked up the empty bottle and carried it to the kitchen. He tossed it into the garbage can. He wiggled the cork back into the other wine bottle and put it into the fridge. He went back and got their empty wine glasses. He rinsed them in the sink, then decided to go ahead and wash them by hand. He used some liquid soap and scrubbed them out before rinsing them again and putting them on a kitchen towel to dry. When he turned around Caron was behind him.

"What's up?"

"Sorry."

"About what?"

"About Bogarting the weed. And chugging the wine. And laughing at the movie."

"It's cool."

"No, we were bad. You were trying to be good to us. We were bad."

"Not a big deal. I'm glad you had fun."

She stepped closer. "Let me make it up to you."

DC started to say something when she moved against him. Her slim arms wrapped around his neck and pulled his mouth to hers. He hesitated, but her lips were so soft. Her skin felt so warm. She opened her mouth and her kiss became more passionate. Her tongue started to fence with his. He started to respond. Something stopped him. He pushed her gently away. Her eyes were dreamy and half closed.

"What?" Caron asked.

"I have to go. Frank's got some stuff for me to do."

DC saw Jenny standing in the kitchen entrance. She had a puzzled look on her face. He didn't know if she had seen the kiss or not. He felt panicky. He had to get out of there.

"Good night. I'll call you tomorrow."

DC grabbed his jacket from the sofa and headed outside. His head was swimming. What was going on? Shit. Frank would kill him. Not just figuratively, but literally kill him. Fuck, he thought. I am fucked. Fucked. Fucked. Fucked.

The nurse came into Sandy's room. She was carrying the large vase with a dozen red roses.

"Looks like somebody has they self a secret admirer."

Sandy smiled. "Would you read the card please? See who it is from."

"Sure honey. Let's see. It ain't signed."

"What does it say?"

"Funny. It says, 'The rains of winter bring renewal from pain.' What do that mean?"

Sandy smiled. "I don't know. I think it's beautiful. Would you place it near my bed please? So I can smell them."

"Sure thing, honey."

"Thank you, Vanessa. You've always been very kind to me."

"Glad to, baby girl. You sound like you fixin' to go somewhere."

Sandy smiled again. "How could I go anywhere?"

"Jest the way you say it make it sound like somethin' else is all."

"Don't worry. I'm fine. I'll see you in the morning before you go home."

"I'll stop by on my way out."

"I would appreciate that, Vanessa. May the gods grant you grace."

"Thank you. Now you get some rest, Miss Sandy."

"I will."

52

Frank took off his coverall. He wrapped the shoe covers, gloves and balaclava inside it. He tossed it all into the back seat of the Mercedes. It was close to three in the morning. He had a plan, but he had to get the upper hand for it to work. He couldn't pull it off if Burns and the Greek were nearby. Driving away, he picked up the Russian's prepaid cell phone. He looked at the last number it had received. They should have cleared the memory. That was a mistake. Maybe they weren't as smart as they thought they were.

He punched the number and waited. The phone rang somewhere out in the Universe. He waited some more. The voice that answered was angry. It had been asleep. He could hear it in the words. The words were foreign. Probably Russian. He let the person vent until he finally stopped.

"Is this Vlad?'

"Who is this?" the voice was nervous, wary.

"This is the third man."

"Third man? I do not understand."

"The guy you didn't know about. The other partner. The boss."

"There is no third man. You are lying. Who are you?"

"Suit yourself."

"I would have known about a third man."

"Is that what the women told you? Do you really think they know all about their husbands' business interests? How stupid would that be?"

"It does not matter who you say you are. The deal has been made and it will be adhered to. Further delays will result in more penalties. The Burns woman will lose her hand if you do not get me my merchandise."

"I have your merchandise."

"You do?"

The steel returned to Vlad's voice. "If you have my merchandise, then give it to me or the women will suffer. I will start with the Burns woman, but I will treat my cousin in the same way. Do not test my resolve in this. I am not a man to be treated lightly."

"Fuck you, you Russian cocksucker. You are not in control here. I am. I brought the shipment. I control it and I control you."

The Russian began to scream in Russian. Frank hung up the cell phone. He waited. It started to ring almost immediately. He answered. The Russian started screaming again and Frank hung up again. The wait was longer this time. Frank figured Vlad was trying to get himself under control. The phone rang. Frank answered.

Vlad said, "If you listen closely you can hear the Burns woman scream as we remove her hand and then the boy's hand."

Frank yawned. "Listen, you do what you have to do. Cut them up into little fucking pieces if you want to. They are nothing to me. They are not my wife or my child. However, I will require further cash compensation if they are damaged."

"You would let a child be maimed?"

"You would. Listen, this is business. Pure and simple. I have what you want. You have my money and the hostages. We work this out or we don't. Either way it's just business."

"Let me speak to Brunko to verify what you are saying."

"Which one is Brunko?"

"He is the one in charge."

"Brunko was a good soldier. Too bad I had to kill him."

"He is dead? I do not believe you."

"Believe what you want. So is Yuri, and some fucking carpet with glasses, Dimitri, a fucking giant, and some other Russian fuckers who got in my way."

"They are dead?"

"I do not play. Burns and the Greek are gone. I have them with my people."

"Your people?"

"My associates if you will. My gunmen. Now do you want to talk business or do you want to scream some more so I have to hang up?"

Vlad was silent for a time. Frank would have loved to have seen his face.

"I would very much like to do business. I have gone to a great deal of trouble. I need this matter resolved."

"And you have gone to a great deal of expense. The cost is still forty thousand as agreed before. I will allow you the finger of the woman as a goodwill gesture. The next one will cost you another ten thousand."

"You are too generous."

"What can I say? I'm a generous man."

"How do I know you have the merchandise?"

"Three Soviet made SA-7 GRAILs often called the Strela 2. Man portable, shoulder fired, low altitude, SAM system, containing a high explosive warhead and passive infrared homing guidance. That sound familiar, Vlad?"

Vlad paused. "How can I be sure you really have this merchandise? Perhaps you are only aware of what I have ordered. Maybe."

"You tell me."

"I will need specifics to validate your claim. I have the serial numbers from the weapons system. Read them to me to verify and then I will believe you."

"Tomorrow. I had my men move the SAMs to a safe location."

"Most troubling."

"Fuck you. You want 'em; you wait until tomorrow for the serial numbers. If not, I can find other buyers."

"Very well. What time?"

"Two fifteen. I'll call on this same line and we can set up the exchange."

"Fair enough. One thing more."

"What?"

"They were good men. How did they die?"

"Like soldiers. They asked no quarter. They got none. You want to turn this into payback? We can do that, but it will cost you in men and time. My guess is you're running out of both. I think it would be a foolish waste of resources."

"I agree. We had served together for a long time. I am glad they died well."

"I understand you have to check out that what I am telling you is true. Unanswered cell phones aren't verification. Just keep in mind that only civilians will be at the Greek's home and the lamp store. If they are harmed, I will take it as a personal insult and our deal is off."

"As you say. If they are civilian, they are off limits."

"Good. Now get some sleep. Tomorrow is going to be a long day, I promise you."

Frank hung up the phone. His heart was racing. He hoped it hadn't shown in his voice. The Russian would be up all night. Vlad would be organizing plans, checking security, verifying. He put the SIG and the silencer in the glove box. He drove back to the hotel. He was bone tired and his head still rang from the giant's blows.

53

Zack inched closer to the television screen. The porn he had brought to Brian's house showed a young girl having sex with three guys at the same time. It was smoking hot. When he looked at the girl he imagined it was that fox, Jenny. He bet she liked doing it. He wondered if he could get her to do all of them. Brian would have a stroke. It might be worth it just to see the look on his face.

"Do you think they'll come to the party?" Brian asked. The porno made him nervous. Asking a question gave him an excuse to look away. He hoped his mom and dad didn't wake up and catch them.

"I guarantee it," Zack said.

"That is pretty cool that they live together," Morgan said. "Do you think they ever do each other?"

"I wouldn't be surprised. You can tell by looking at Caron that she would be into that girl-on-girl scene."

"Really? How can you tell?" Brian asked.

Zack laughed. "I have experience at this stuff. I can just tell. Am I right Morgan or am I right?"

"You are definitely right. I would love to see the two of them go at it."

"More than you want to play with her?"

"Well, after I do her."

Morgan high-fived Zack. Brian was quicker this time and got his high five before Morgan dropped his hand.

"You still want me to try to Facebook them?" Brian asked.

"Nah. Not necessary. They're on the hook. They are hot to trot. I could see the steam rising off them at dinner."

"Okay, if you say so. I can't wait until tomorrow."

"What the hell was that?" Jenny shouted.

"What?"

"You know what. I saw you kissing DC."

"So?"

"So. He's supposed to be our friend, not your boyfriend. It could fuck everything up."

"Chill out. It was just a kiss. It was no big deal."

"It was."

Caron suddenly looked embarrassed. "I'm sorry. Okay. I was high and we were talking and he looked so adorable. I couldn't help it."

"Bullshit. You planned this. As soon as I went to the bathroom you ran in here so you could kiss him."

"No way."

"Way."

"Well maybe a little. I'm attracted to him."

Jenny sat down on the floor. "Shit. This could be bad."

Caron came and sat down beside her. She put her arm around Jenny's shoulder. "Come on, Jen. It's not that big a deal. I won't let it happen again. I promise.

"You swear? You just can't start dating DC. It would be too weird."

"I won't. Platonic from now on. No more kissing."

"No friends with benefits?"

"No friends with privileges." Caron mimicked making an X over her heart. "Cross my heart."

"Okay. I mean it. I think it would be too weird."

They got up from the floor and turned off the light. They started walking upstairs toward their bedroom.

"Haven't you ever thought about kissing him?" Caron asked.

"No."

"Really?'

"Really."

"Then you don't want to hear what it was like."

"No, I don't."

They turned out the lights downstairs and checked the locks on the door. Above they were walking upstairs. They walked into their bedroom. Jenny turned to Caron at the doorway.

"Well?"

"Well what?"

"How was it? I know you want to tell me."

Caron grinned. "It was awesome. He has the softest lips."

Jenny punched her in the arm. "You are so bad. You are going to get us in a world of trouble."

When Agent Redding walked into his house he could tell someone had been there. The place felt disturbed. He drew his weapon and moved slowly into the house. He swept each room. They were all empty. He went upstairs. There was a light in the bathroom. He opened the door slowly. A candle burned on the back of the toilet. He had not left a candle burning. He wasn't an idiot. He leaned in to blow it out and something caught his eye. On the top sheet of the toilet paper roll was a Spartan lambda. Redding pulled it out. There was more writing. He unrolled the sheets until the writing stopped. He sat down on the toilet and read the message.

"Tomorrow night. 11. Johnson Park. Carousel. Insects. Alone. Purity of fire. Prometheus."

Redding folded the message neatly, went into his study, and placed the note in his desk. It would be safer there; the desk had an electronic bug detector. Redding swept every inch of his house to be sure he was not being monitored. He went outside. He found the first bug in the door frame of the car on the passenger's side. Another bug was in the interior light fixture. They were standard Bureau issue. He thought it must be Harris. But it could be Prometheus trying to make him think it was Harris. Could even be a third party all together. The bugs were weak, voice-activated monitors. He swept the car and found the GPS tracker that was attached to his engine block. Redding did not like being watched or followed.

For a moment he wondered what Prometheus wanted to see him about. Redding wasn't afraid Prometheus was going to kill him. Hell, if Prometheus knew where he lived, he could have killed him at any time. Tomorrow would resolve a lot of issues. You could only change the things you could change. He would make sure he wore his vest tomorrow night. He wasn't an idiot. He needed a smoke.

54

Vlad took slow deep breaths trying to calm himself. Six men dead. Six professional soldiers dead. Six men committed to the cause. Men that had served with him. Men that he had known and trusted. Krumbak, the giant, was his brother. He would avenge him. He said a silent prayer that Allah would grant him this promise.

A third partner was not something he had expected. How many others were involved, he wondered. There had to be at least six to overpower his men without alerting the authorities. That meant, counting the new partner, the Greek, and Burns they had a minimum of nine men. More men than he had left. They might have more, but manpower was expensive to keep. He doubted it. Nine, he decided, that was his working assumption. Of course Burns was no threat and he doubted the Greek had ever fired one of the weapons he sold. Maybe the odds were better than he had first thought.

"Omar, take two men. Check out Burns' house and the lamp store, and then go to the Greek's house. Call me when you get to each place. Describe exactly what you see. Do you understand?"

Omar nodded. "Yes, sir. Do we engage?"

"No. Absolutely not. Just report what you see."

"If we are fired upon?"

"Retreat to a safe distance."

"These dogs killed our comrades. I don't like the idea of running from them."

"I do not care what you like, Omar. You are a professional. You will do as you are told. We will have our chance at payback, I promise you."

Omar was not happy. "Yes, sir," he said.

He was a soldier. He was used to taking orders he did not like. He would do as he was told. He had served with Vlad for a long time. Too long to refuse an order.

Vlad sent a man out to check the perimeter. The man, Peter, took one of the AK-47s.

It wouldn't do for him to lose sight of his objective because of his anger. Vlad went to the bedroom at the top of the stairs. The plan had seemed so foolproof. Even when Burns had balked at the cargo, Vlad had an operational contingency planned. It was in play within hours. But this mystery partner was something new. It made him uncomfortable. The mission success depended on him controlling as many factors as possible.

He opened the bedroom door. Judy Burns was asleep in the bed. She sat up as he entered. Her hands were tied to the headboard behind her. A large red stained bandage wrapped her left hand. She shrank back from his approach. Terror trimmed her voice.

"What is it? What's happened? Is it here?"

Vlad sat down beside her on the bed. She was a lovely woman. She was thin and athletic. She had pretty legs. She was terrified of him and he enjoyed her fear more than her beauty.

He smiled and then slapped her hard across the face. She screamed. Vlad sprang on her and grasped her around the neck. His strong fingers locked around her neck as he squeezed the life out of her. He increased the pressure. Her eyes bulged. She tried to shake his hands free. His grip held. Her face turned red. Vlad leaned in. "You whore. You lied to me."

Judy's eyes were wild. Her struggles weakened. Vlad released her.

Judy gasped for air. She took deep ragged gulps.

Vlad gently straightened her blouse that had been twisted as he strangled her.

"Take short shallow breaths, Mrs. Burns. It works better. You will recover faster."

Judy's breathing slowed from panicked gasping. She did as he suggested. Her lungs filled again. She relaxed a little.

"What are you talking about?" she gasped.

"I should kill you. You didn't tell me there was another partner. A third man."

"Third man? There isn't a third partner."

Vlad slapped her again. "Tell that to my men. Six of them are dead. The third man and his crew killed them."

"Impossible," she said.

Her teeth were red with her own blood. Vlad drew his arm back, but stopped. "You should have told me. You should have known."

"If there was a third partner, I would have known. Bruce told me everything."

"Yet, you did not know about the third man."

Judy thought for a minute. She tried to come up with some explanation. Vlad watched her struggle.

"Perhaps if I let my men take turns with you, your memory will return. They have been most insistent. It seems a shame to waste one so beautiful. Especially if she continues to lie to me."

"No. No, please. I don't know anything else. If I did I would have told you, I swear."

"Perhaps. I will give you a little time before I send the first one up."

Judy began to cry. Vlad laughed as he left the room. He knew that the threat of rape was a terror many American women held. It was a dark nightmare that seemed always lurking nearby. In his country it was a reality that most women lived with. It was brutality exercised by those in charge to break the masses. He had no pity for fears.

Vlad went to the set of rooms at the top of the second set of stairs. He opened the door on the first bedroom. An old crib sat in one corner with a sleeping child. He closed the door and went to the second bedroom. Dasha sat up in the bed.

"What is it?"

"A third man has arrived."

"What do you mean?"

He slapped her hard and her head jerked back. She regained her poise. Blood trickled from the corner of her mouth. Her eyes were on fire.

"You have been keeping secrets, whore. The Greek answers to someone else. This third man has killed six of my soldiers and freed the Greek and Burns."

"The Greek has no boss. He answers to no one."

Vlad slapped her again on the other side of her face.

Dasha laughed. "Is that the best you can do? You have grown weak like an old woman."

He grabbed her hair and twisted it in his hand. The laugh stayed on her face. Her teeth were red just like the Burns woman's. He pulled her close to him.

"Perhaps I will let my men rape you until you can remember."

She was still smiling as she grabbed a handful of his dark hair and spit into his face. "That might be fun, but you first," she said and pulled his mouth to hers.

Her kiss was fiery and he returned it with a passion of his own. Her fresh blood smeared their faces. His hands were everywhere on her body. Her fingers found the buckle to his pants and undid them. They raced to get their clothes off, then sprang at each other like wild animals. The sex was uncontrolled, bordering on rape. Dasha screamed as he bit her neck.

55

Frank unlocked the door to his room. He went in quietly. Dorian was sitting by the window staring out into the darkness. She looked surprised to see him.

"You came back," she said.

"I said I would."

Dorian ran to his arms. She pressed against him. He held her. She didn't speak for a long time. She just disappeared in his huge arms.

"I didn't think you would come back."

"I can tell. I'm not perfect by any stretch, but I don't break my word."

"Let's go to bed."

"Let me get a quick shower."

She let him ease away from her. Frank went into the bathroom and closed the door behind him. He removed his jacket and hung it on the door. He took off his shirt with the cut and tossed it into the garbage can. He removed the red nylon undershirt and tossed it as well. There was a huge bruise across his ribs. He pressed in at the center and felt a stab of pain. He wasn't sure if a rib was broken. It hurt like it was, but there wasn't much you could do about a broken rib or two anyway. He kicked off his shoes, dropped his trousers and got under a cold shower.

He had read that a cold shower was best for flushing toxins out of the bloodstream. Something about lactic acid or some shit. It had said something about constricting blood vessels and helping micro tears to heal quicker. The article had also claimed it reduced post exercise soreness. Frank knew he was going to be sore tomorrow. No doubt. Some athletes claimed the post workout cold shower cleared your mind. Frank didn't doubt the science, although he was not swayed to do or not do things just because scientists claimed it was true.

Frank took the cold shower to test his will. The shock of cold water was similar to being stabbed. The body froze. The mind froze. You couldn't react. Frank had found that frequent cold showers conditioned the body to respond differently to shock. Frank also believed it hardened his will. It somehow made him stronger.

The bathroom door opened. He glanced out of the shower. It was Dorian. She started removing her clothes. Frank turned the water to warm. She pulled the curtain back.

"Would you like some company?" She said it quietly, like a child.

"Yes, I would."

She stepped into the shower. She lifted the liquid soap and squirted it into her hand. She lathered Frank's back.

"Turn around," she said, "so I can get to the other side."

Frank turned and let the warm water wash the soap away. Dorian saw the bruise on his side. She saw the dried blood on the side of his head. She saw the red swollen ear. She didn't say anything about the wounds. She washed his chest.

"I am glad you came back."

Frank didn't answer.

"Did you get your business handled?'

"No. The lamp store was a bust. He didn't want to buy. I got one more good lead to follow up."

"How much longer are we going to be here?"

"I plan to wrap up my business in the next twenty-four."

She soaped his privates. Frank laughed. Dorian smiled.

"Let's do it the first time in the shower."

"The first time?"

"You're a big boy. I think you can handle two or three times in one night."

"I'm not that young anymore."

"Is that a challenge?" Dorian squeezed his erection.

Frank pulled her closer. He leaned down to kiss her. Before their lips met he said, "Yes, it is."

56

Vlad smoked quietly in bed. Dasha, her head across his chest, toyed with the hair around his left nipple.

"That was fun," she purred. "We should do it like that more often."

"I am afraid it would ruin your beauty."

"I think scars are beautiful."

He passed her the cigarette and she took a deep drag. She passed it back to him.

"So you think I am no longer beautiful?"

"You will always be beautiful to me, my wife."

Dasha pinched his nipple hard, and then released it. "Is the mission compromised? Can we go forward?"

"We have invested too much to turn back. This third man troubles me."

She kissed his nipple. "Have you come up with any ideas?"

Vlad kissed the top of her head. "Battles are won before they are fought. Planning is the most important element. I have a plan."

"Tell me."

"Do you know what a magician's force is?"

"No. I don't understand. This is a child's game, yes?"

"No. The magician lets you choose, but uses your choice to force you to pick what he wants you to. The magician tricks the person into believing they have chosen the card freely."

"I still do not understand."

"I will offer them the return of one of the hostages as a show of good faith. That hostage will then report back to me secretly."

Dasha laughed. "You are a devious man. And you think you can control them so that they choose me? This magician's force?"

"I do."

Dasha rolled over so that she was sitting on top of him.

"And my bruises will convince them I can be trusted."

Vlad smiled. "They will."

"And I have been raped. My body will say this to the Greek."

"Yes. Your injuries are real. Who can doubt them? Not even the third man."

"You are a wicked, wicked man."

He laughed. "You did not seem to mind when first we married."

"I do not mind now, my husband. That is what I love about you. Your wickedness. Your wickedness and this."

Dasha reached between his legs. He was erect and she guided him into her.

She rocked back and moaned. She looked into his face and smiled. She leaned down and kissed him gently. He brushed her blonde hair from her face.

"Hit me again," she said.

Vlad slapped her hard and her head jerked back in ecstasy. He slapped her again and she cried out. She spit into his face. He pulled her close and found her hungry mouth. The pain became confused with pleasure for her. He licked her slim, pale neck.

"Bite me again, my vampire lover. You know how I love it. Bite my neck hard."

Vlad kissed her throat. He sucked on the flesh and then bit until he tasted blood. Dasha moaned in ecstasy. He bit harder. She screamed.

"More. I want more," Dasha screamed.

Vlad's passion matched her own and for a time he was indeed Vlad Dracula.

57

Frank got out of bed. He stretched his aching muscles. His ribs ached. His hands were sore. His head throbbed. But by the gods he was still alive. *One More Round.* It was not that bad. It buoyed his spirits. If you were in pain, you were still alive. He picked up the hotel phone and ordered room service.

Dorian stretched in the bed. She felt sad, but wasn't sure why. Something was happening that she didn't understand. She watched Frank as silently as a cat. She got out of bed and put on one of the hotel robes.

The breakfast came and they ate in silence.

Frank brushed his teeth and used the bathroom. He dressed in khaki colored pants, the Oakley boots, and a light blue denim shirt. It was long sleeved. He wore a long-sleeved red nylon shirt underneath. It made him look younger somehow, like a construction site manager. He put on dark sunglasses.

"You should stay close to the hotel today."

"And do what?"

"Go to the spa. Catch some sun. Go for a swim. Pamper yourself a little bit. You've been through some hard times. You deserve a break."

"Eat here too?"

"I would feel better knowing you're safe."

"All right."

"I *will* come back. I'm not going to disappear."

"I believe you. You'll come back. But soon you'll be gone."

"Yes."

"Going back to the lamp store?"

"I might, but that lead has dried up. I have some other things to do. Burns turned me on to one of his suppliers who he thought might be interested."

She stood and stared at him. "Be careful."

Frank started to say something glib, but stopped himself. "I'll try."

Dorian walked over slowly to him. She wrapped her arms around him and held him. After a minute she let him go and walked into the bathroom. Frank picked up the phone book from the room and left. He needed addresses. He needed to go shopping. He needed to buy a cowboy hat. He needed to call DC.

Jenny went to take a shower, but Caron had beaten her to it. She decided to just shower in Frank's bathroom. No one was using it. It made perfect sense. She rationalized to herself that he had never said she couldn't. She carried her robe and a towel into his bathroom. She slipped the knife into the robe pocket. She didn't

216 JOHN F. SAUNDERS

want to take the chance that Caron would find it. And she never went anywhere now without it.

She took off her T-shirt and panties and stood in front of the mirror. She felt very wicked. Her senses seemed heightened. Her skin actually tingled. She eyed herself critically. She was pretty. Her breasts were small, but so what, at least they were the same size and pointed the same direction. Her stomach was flat. She had nice musculature to her arms and legs. Her face was pretty. She was no beauty, she argued, but she was pretty. She didn't like her hair. It was long and brown and boring. It looked like everybody else's hair. Maybe she should get it cut into a bob. Or she could do that Victoria Beckham thing with one side longer than the other. That would be cool. She could even color it. It needed to be jazzed up. She tried to mimic the hairstyles she thought about, but it was hard to tell. If it looked lame, that would be worse than what she had.

She stepped into Frank's shower. She looked for the soap. He didn't have many choices. Caron and Jenny had about four different shampoos, body lotions, gels, liquid soaps, conditioners, exfoliates, all things necessary for a female shower. Frank had a bar of white soap and a jug of some kind of discount shampoo. She doubted he even knew what brand it was. Men were so weird.

She shampooed her hair first so it would have a little longer to dry. The shampoo didn't smell too bad. The soap was a rough bar. It reminded her of the farm she had grown up on. It felt thick and rough in her hand. She started lathering up. She kind of liked the rough feel of it on her skin. She wondered if that was what Frank's hands would feel like on her skin. Strong and rough. She felt a thrill of excitement. For an instant she imagined him in the shower with her. She imagined his rough hands and hard muscles. The shame and embarrassment struck her immediately.

What was she thinking? That was so gross. He was way too old for her. He was like her uncle. It was sick. She looked around, afraid there was someone watching her. Afraid someone might have read her thoughts. She was alone. It must be the leftover traces from the marijuana she had smoked. Maybe it was spiked with something. That had to be it. Her and Frank? That was just not right.

She got out of the shower and wrapped her hair. She hurriedly dried and slipped on the robe. Her fingers found the knife in the pocket and closed on it. It centered her. Her heart slowed. She felt calm again. It didn't mean anything. Guys had those kind of unrelated sex thoughts all the time. Didn't mean she wanted to do anything. Not for real.

She wiped the shower out with her towel, careful to put everything back exactly as it had been. She hurried to her room to get dressed. She could hear Caron still in the shower.

58

Johanna hit a lob and Helen returned it with a powerful backhand. Johanna reached the shot as it was going off the court. She caught it with a passing forehand that just cleared the net. Helen stepped in and easily hit it to the other side of the court where it couldn't be returned. Johanna stopped where she was, panting.

"Game, set, match. I forgot how good you are."

"You're just out of practice. It won't be long until you're beating me as usual."

"It's sweet of you to say that. But I think we both know I'm not nearly as good as you are."

Helen took a small white towel and dabbed delicately at the moisture on her brow. Johanna picked up her own towel and wiped her arms and face. There was a small Igloo cooler on a nearby bench and both women took disposable white Dixie cups and got a drink of cool water. Johanna was smiling.

"That was fun."

"I had a great time. We must make this a regular thing."

"I agree. It was marvelous. I do love a good workout."

"So do I. Do you want to grab a bite of lunch before going home?"

"I really shouldn't. They'll be screaming at the gallery."

"But it's your gallery."

"True. Why not? What are you in the mood for?"

"Something spicy. There's a new Thai restaurant I've been dying to try."

"What's it called?"

"A Taste of Thai. Not very original, I know. But the food is supposed to be exceptional."

"Then Thai it is. I love that peanut sauce. You lead and I'll follow."

"I have to make one stop first, to pick up a prescription, if it's ready."

"I think we can squeeze that in, "Johanna said. "I really have had a great time, although my butt will be killing me tomorrow from all that tennis."

Helen laughed.

The two men in the white Honda Accord watched the tennis match through binoculars. The driver punched a number into his cell phone.

"Reed reporting in, sir. No contact was made. She played tennis with the same woman she had dinner with the other night."

Reed listened.

"No, sir. No one approached them and as far as we could tell they spoke to no one else except in greeting to the couple that was leaving the court when they arrived. Yes, sir."

Reed listened again.

"They're leaving now. I don't know if they're planning on going to lunch or not. We'll follow at a discreet distance."

Reed listened a final time.

"Yes, sir. The electronic device in her car is active. There's been no suspicious talk. She has the radio on now. Yes, sir."

Helen smiled as she drove down the highway. She knew they were following her. Cyrus was no fool. But neither was she. Watchers, electronic surveillance, maybe even videotaping, all very modern, very James Bond. She had her own way to get information. Sometimes old school was the best.

She picked up her purse and took out her cell phone. She pushed a button on the speed dial.

"Midtown Pharmacy, how can I help you?"

"Hi, is this Kim?'

"Yes, who is this?"

"It's me, Helen."

"Hi, Helen. How you doing?'

"Super. I need to pick up my birth control prescription. Is it ready?"

"Hold on."

The line went silent. "Yes, it's here waiting for you. When do you think you'll pick it up, or do you want the courier service to deliver it for you?"

"I'm going to lunch in your part of town, I'll swing by on the way and get it."

"That would be fine. Have a nice day."

"You too. Bye."

Helen turned the music up. It was an old AC/DC song, *Thunder Struck*. She sang along with the lyrics. Frank had told her that the ancient Spartans loved singing. She sang louder. After all, she was a Spartan.

59

Frank parked the Mercedes on the street. There seemed to be a lot of open spaces. He went into the store and browsed the racks for a cowboy hat. He found a black hat, but decided on the white version. Black was too cliché. He was, after all, trying to be good. The hat had a wide brim and an imitation rattlesnake skin hatband. It was made of woven straw. It looked and felt like a work hat. He paid cash and put it on. He pulled the brim low, hiding his face from cameras.

Once on the sidewalk he called DC.

"Frank," DC answered.

"What have you got?"

"Not much. The telephones were bought in Oregon. Sold to a Mr. and Mrs. Johnson. The address they gave is a fake. They paid cash. Only thing you might find useful is the number of phones."

"How many?"

"Six."

"That's good. We got three. So probably cuts his numbers down to half."

"Sorry I couldn't do more."

"I appreciate what you've done. Everything quiet at home?'

DC paused. "Fine. I don't think they appreciated Steve McQueen, but what can you do? Elliott said to tell you thanks."

"I'll be home soon. Tell the girls I miss them."

"Will do."

"How's Rosa?"

"Her condition is unchanged as of this morning. I'll keep an eye on it."

"Thanks."

"Later," DC said and hung up.

Frank heard something in DC's voice. He was evasive instead of open. The tone was off when he asked about the girls. He would deal with it when he got home. He had enough things to worry about.

Frank walked down the street to the hardware store. He bought two mechanic's blue painter's coveralls. He bought some paintbrushes to add to the illusion. He went back to his car and got out the Fort Worth phone book. He looked up the nearest Army Navy surplus store. He checked his GPS. It was nearby. He drove over.

The building was a dilapidated warehouse. Frank thought it might be a law that all Army Navy Surplus stores were in old run-down buildings. He didn't see any surveillance cameras outside. Which made sense. Who broke into an Army

Navy surplus store? And the people who bought stuff here tended to value privacy. They wouldn't like being taped. He got out of the car and pulled the brim down low.

Inside, a middle-aged woman greeted him. It surprised him. Usually these stores were run by ex-military types. The woman had short, auburn hair and was very attractive. She had an air of authority and dignity. Her low-cut top revealed part of a huge snake tattoo. The pattern on the snake's skin indicated it was a rattlesnake. The part he could see coiled over her right shoulder He wondered where the head of the snake was. He could see the imprint of a nipple ring on the breast closest to where the snake's head would be. She had a mischievous smile on. There was a half empty bottle of Wild Turkey bourbon on the counter to her right. A whiskey glass held about an ounce of the dark liquid. It was not her first drink of the day.

"Hi, hon. I'm Jan. Anything I can help you with?"

"Looking for boots. Got a hunting trip coming up."

"We got a fine line of military boots from traditional to Special Forces. They're in the back aisle near the wall."

"Thanks."

"Anything else you need for your trip, you let me know. We got a lot of outdoor camping gear too. We got the best snake bite kits in town."

"Thanks. I'll take a look."

"I think you already did. What you boys goin' to be hunting?"

"Lawyers and maybe some dentists."

Jan's laugh was a hoot. "Let me know if you need an old lady to ride shotgun. We got a surplus of those idiots around here and I wouldn't mind shootin' a few myself. Might even be a bounty on 'em."

Frank laughed. It was a forced laugh and he knew it, but he thought it worked anyway. Texans were used to people being private. He found the boots. They had a lot to choose from. He found some that had similar tread to his. They were described as a Special Forces boot used by the Rangers in Iraq and Afghanistan. He bought a pair for the Greek and for Burns.

Jan was sipping from the glass. She looked the boots over. His eyes were drawn back to the snake coiling around her chest.

"You want a taste…" she paused for effect… "of the kickin' chicken?"

"No, I'm good. Thanks."

"You are more than good. You are fine," she said and smiled. "Ben Franklin wanted the turkey as the national bird, not that damn scavenging eagle. He thought the turkey was more noble."

"Might have been right. Ben knew a lot of stuff. What do you think of the boots?"

"Good choice. Not too heavy, but they are sturdy."

"Thanks," Frank said. "How much do I owe you?"

"They're seventy-five apiece. I'll let you have them both for one twenty five with one stipulation."

"What's that?"

"You let me mount them heads you get hunting. I'd like to put one over my toilet."

"I'll do that."

"I wouldn't mind getting a little head," she said.

He gave her the money and she counted out his change. She didn't print a receipt and didn't offer him one. There was no bag.

"Thanks," Frank said taking the boots.

"Watch out for cougars out there. They're a menace around here. Got some would tear up a fine man like you."

Frank wasn't sure, but he might have blushed. He nodded and left. He carried the boots to his car and put them in the back seat. He realized he was a little turned on. He drove off. In his rear view mirror he could see she was watching him from the window. He saw her take another sip of the Wild Turkey as she turned away.

Frank drove in a random pattern around Fort Worth, down side roads looking for pay phones. He wrote down street addresses and phone numbers. He spent a couple of hours finding the best places. They needed to be obscure. They needed easy access and exit. He needed to be able to see the surrounding area without being seen. He was writing down the telephone number of the pay phone on the corner of Charles and Lee when he saw the car.

It was a classic Hispanic low rider, white with black accents and Mexican scrollwork. He put the pad back into his shirt pocket as the car slid to the curb in front of the Mercedes. Frank turned so his right side was facing them. He pulled the SIG from the back of his pants and held it against his leg. More carjackers. Or gangbangers. They might be opportunistic predators. Seeing the car pulled over and one white guy, it might have been too much to pass up. They could just be punks.

There were two of them. Both Hispanic. They got out on opposite sides of the car. The passenger moved a little away from the car. They were separating to make it harder for Frank to watch them. The driver moved directly toward Frank. The passenger drifted farther to Frank's right. The driver was wearing a white

T-shirt and old blue jeans. He had a black bandana on his head. The passenger was wearing tan chinos with stains on the legs. He had a black T-shirt, but no bandana. Frank didn't spot any consistent gang colors or tattoos. Maybe they were just thugs. That would be simpler. He sighed. The damn Mercedes was like a cursed jewel. It seemed to attract trouble.

The driver moved up closer to Frank. He was working on a hard stare. Frank could see the outline of the gun in the front of his pants. The passenger stopped. He wanted to stay in Frank's peripheral vision. The squeeze was a simple play. The driver would jam Frank up. The sideman would draw a weapon. Outflanked, Frank would pass over the keys and they would take the car. If he was unlucky, they might put a bullet in his head afterwards.

The driver stepped in closer. Frank held up his right hand in a stop motion. It was a great move. It ranged your distance for you without appearing to be a threat. If anything it invited the more aggressive person forward. As the driver stepped in Frank struck him across the face with the pistol. The driver spun and fell across the back of his low rider. Frank jammed the gun into the base of his skull pinning him there. He reached around and took the gun. It was a nice Smith and Wesson MP 40, the U.S. answer to the Glock. Dependable. Moderately priced. Very tough. He pointed the MP 40 at the second man. The man was paralyzed with his right hand halfway behind his back.

No one spoke. Frank was not in the mood to play. There was no advantage in killing them. Gunfire would bring people and cops. The Mercedes would be seen. He would have to dump it and he didn't want that.

"Do not move or I will kill you. Hands in front."

The man brought his arm around to the front.

"With your left hand remove your weapon. Two fingers."

The man struggled to reach the gun behind his back. He finally got it and brought it forward.

"Lay the weapon on the ground."

The man did.

"Now walk around the front of the car to this side. Is there anyone else in the car?"

The man shook his head no. Frank looked down; there was blood all over the back of the car. He must have hit the driver harder than he thought. He stepped back from the driver. He kept a gun on each man.

"Put your friend in the back and get out of here. I see you or this piece-of-shit-ride again I'll figure I was too easy on you. Then I will have to kill you."

The passenger inched forward and got hold of this friend's shoulder and pulled him away from Frank. Frank stepped out from between the cars. The passenger pushed his friend into the back seat and got into the front. He pulled out quickly. Probably thought Frank might shoot them in the back.

Fucking Mercedes was a trouble magnet. Maybe he should just dump it and open a gun store with all the guns he was collecting. He got back in the Mercedes, put the new iron in the glove box and continued driving. He watched his mirror to be sure the low rider wasn't shadowing him. It wasn't. He found the final spot near a Tex-Mex restaurant called Sugar's. The plan could work. He thought about going back to the hotel to check on Dorian. There didn't seem a point to it. He thought about calling DC, but again, he didn't have anything concrete to ask him. He just felt restless waiting for tonight.

He stopped at a restaurant and had a lunch of chicken and pasta. He ate a double order, watching the people, killing time. He thought about the twins and the other Bruce Burns he had known in prison. He wondered about his choices back then.

60

Carpenter was invisible in plain sight. He was sitting on a bench across the street. He wore yellow Madras shorts, calf-high white tube socks, new black Nike tennis shoes, and a dark blue Lacoste shirt topped off with a blue and silver Dallas Cowboys hat. He even wore a pair of too large cheap sunglasses. His outfit screamed, "I am a tourist." There were dozens dressed just like him. When Frank drove off he climbed into his rental car. He followed Frank on his rounds.

He had an odd mental image of one of those hamsters in their little wheels. He wondered if that was what was under the hood of his rental car. He missed the Porsche. He thought of it as his sun chariot. If it was, then each of the tires could represent one of the flaming steeds that pulled it, Pyruis, Aeos, Aethon, Phlegon. He couldn't wait to get out of this car. How did people stand it? There was no power. There was no nimble response to commands. There was no feeling of oneness.

He smoked and watched and waited. It was a dull ride. Frank was scouting locations for something. The two thugs had been a mild diversion. He had enjoyed that. Frank hadn't lost any of his speed. Too bad he hadn't killed them. That would have told him some things about Frank. Maybe sparing them did too. He would have to think about it. When Frank stopped for lunch, Carpenter went back to his hotel. He would leave tomorrow. The news wires would eventually tie it all together for him. Carpenter traded information like men traded drugs. It might not even matter. He had learned a lot. He knew Frank Kane was alive. That information was priceless. He thought he might slip by the lot where the hotel parked Frank's car and leave him a note, but thought better of it. If Frank knew someone had figured out where he was, he might move again. Better to keep it quiet.

Agent Redding didn't go in to work. He called in sick. He drank coffee and smoked cigarettes on his porch. He worked over in his mind various contingencies. They all led to one solution. He didn't like it. He put his gun on the table and broke it down. He took his time cleaning each piece. He loaded and reloaded his magazine and his two spares. Things could go bad very quickly tonight.

Harris called.

"They told me at the office that you were sick."

"Yeah. I took a day."

"You're not coming in at all?"

"No."

"What about the investigation?"

"It will have to wait twenty-four."

"Do you want me to come out?"

"No."

"We could brainstorm."

"No, thanks."

"Did you access your personal files yet?"

"No."

"Are you going to?"

"Not today. I'm sick. I'm just going to rest up."

"Do you want me to get them for you?"

"I don't think I do, Harris."

"I didn't mean it like that. Is there anything I can do for you?"

"Find out who deleted the computer records."

"The tech said it was high tech virus. Must have been placed as a Trojan horse."

"That figures. What was the trigger?"

"The techs think it was the word Spartan. It swept through all the files with that heading in them."

"What about the brother-sister angle on Sandy Jones and Masnick?"

"Still gathering the data. The higher-ups have been informed and they seem very interested in that angle."

"Anything on the blood in Masnick's house?"

"Without a DNA sample on file we can't match it. The techs think it might not be human. They think it's from a cat. They're checking it out."

"It would make sense on some level. Some of the Spartans were into crush videos in the day."

"What's a crush video?"

"Killing animals on video. Cruel stuff. But it's a sick world out there. Spartans made a ton of money on the stuff. It's still legal I think. Any leads on who took the files and physical evidence from storage?"

"No. It's a dead end so far. Someone definitely had major pull."

"Okay, thanks. Listen, I'll check back with you later today. Otherwise we'll see what tomorrow brings."

"Yes, sir."

"What are your plans?"

"I guess I'll catch up on paperwork. I don't know what else there is I can do."

"We'll talk later."

Harris hung up first. Redding followed suit. He didn't trust Harris anymore. He was playing at something and Redding thought he knew what it was.

Harris dialed the number and waited. It was answered on the second ring.

"Anything?"

"No. Redding claims he's too sick to come in to work."

"Do you believe him?"

"No. He's up to something."

"We've discussed the Sandy Jones situation at length. There's some concern that she could be a valuable asset. We've decided not to acquire her and move her to another location. It would raise too many questions. We have been assured that the Bureau will do nothing for the next few days. We would like you to return and continue her interrogation without Agent Redding's presence."

"Anything particular you want to know?"

"I'm texting a list of questions to your cell."

"So you think she may know something."

"It's disturbing that we did not know about Masnick or her until now. She may be crucial to our next move."

"I understand. You can count on me."

"I hope so. Call after you speak to her, and… Harris, use coercion if you feel it necessary. Carrot or stick, it doesn't matter. Only the results are important."

"I'm on it."

60

Vlad sat at the kitchen table with Omar. They smoked and drank black coffee like a thousand times before.

"Omar, we are friends a long time. I trust your judgment. Tell me what you are thinking."

"I am worried. The mission is compromised. We are moving blind."

"I agree. But what else can we do? We must have the missiles."

"I know. I do not like this new man."

"Not me either. But if we can get the launchers, the sacrifices of our comrades are not in vain."

"It is a soldier's life. It has always been so."

"Yes, it is. The mission can still succeed, even with less men."

"Two-man teams offer many problems."

"They do, but they are not insurmountable. The driver can act as the spotter and security."

"The coordination is the key."

"As it has always been. We must take out the three planes from three different cities at the same time before they get fully airborne. Their government will go into panic. Their economy is already on the verge of collapse. They will fear air travel. They will fear us. They will fall into chaos."

"And they will know why?"

"Yes. Their president claimed to support our cause for independence. When the Chechen Republic fell in 1999 the United States promised to restore our government. Yet they have done nothing to aid our cause. Our brothers fight in the North Caucasus without support or even acknowledgement by the world. The war is declared won by Russia and all eyes turn away from their atrocities that continue against our people."

"Akmed Zakayev has called for a stop to rebel actions. The war is over."

"Not for me. The world has forgotten us. Russia has forgotten us. Even our leaders have forgotten us. The Americans now sign treaties with Russia outlawing any dissent in Chechnya. We will make them see us again."

"We once fought for Russia."

"Yes, we did. How sad that once we even killed for a Russia that has betrayed us, my friend. Allah will see us victorious."

"Do you think Allah still hears our prayers?"

Vlad laughed and slapped his friend on the shoulder. "Of course he does, Omar. We are good Muslims. We follow his will. Remember the Chechen saying,

'Muhammad may have been an Arab, but Allah is surely Chechen.'"

Omar chuckled. He took a slow drag on his cigarette.

Vlad smiled, "It has been a long time since I heard that, but it is true. You are right as always. We must strike them hard so they will see us."

"The Americans will make our Russian masters see us again. Then we can regain our freedom. We have been invisible too long."

"This is our time, Vlad. I will do whatever you say. Allahu akbar."

"Allahu akbar."

Jenny and Caron were having lunch in the living room. Jenny had ordered pizza and the girls were pigging out with it and Coke Zero.

"Have you heard from DC?" Caron asked.

"No. You?"

"Not a word. I texted him, but he didn't answer."

"I called him to see if he was coming over. I left him a voice mail too, but no response."

"Maybe his phone is dead."

"Not likely. I think he's avoiding us."

"Because of the kiss?"

"I don't know. Maybe it weirded him out."

"Could be he's afraid Frank will find out he brought us wine and a little herb."

"We wouldn't tell. He knows that. It's not like we've never done anything before," Jenny said.

"What eighteen-year-old hasn't?"

"Exactly."

"We need to talk to him before Frank gets back. We don't want him blabbing it out and getting us in trouble."

"I don't want to get into any trouble with Frank. He's been good to us."

"He saved us," Caron added.

"Yes, he did. We got to respect that."

"I agree. From now on we fly straight until he gets back. No more partying."

"Deal. Try DC again. You must be a really bad kisser to have run him off with just one kiss."

Caron smiled. "I could try sexting him see if that gets a response. Send him some topless shots."

"I will kill you," Jenny said.

"I'm only kidding. Hey, we could send him some nudie shots of you. That would blow his mind. He wouldn't know what to think."

"I think he would think we wanted a three way."

"That would be too weird. I love you, Jenny, but I don't want to be naked with you and some guy."

"Thanks. I think something like that is a little out of my comfort zone too."

Caron took a bite of her pizza and, nodding her head, said, "But can you imagine his face if he came over and we were both naked? He would die.

"He would have a heart attack."

"Exactly. It would be awesome."

"You are sick."

"Thanks. It takes one to know one," she said and stuck her tongue out at Jenny.

"Wow."

"What."

"That's the tongue that scared DC. Now I can die having seen it all."

Caron flicked her tongue in the air like a snake. "He doesn't know what he's missing."

"I hope he never finds out."

"Miss Sandy, I'm done for today. Is there anything I can get you before I go?"

"No, Vanessa. I'm fine."

"Are you sure? I could get you a fresh pillowcase."

"No. This is fine."

"You want me to raise the bed up a little bit more in case you want to watch some television?"

"That would be nice. That way I can see out the window a little."

Vanessa raised the bed. "Is that good?"

"Perfect."

"You didn't touch your breakfast. If you don't start eating they going to stick a tube in you again and force you."

"I don't think it will come to that."

"You don't know these peoples. They all business."

"You are very sweet. There is one thing you could do for me if you don't mind."

"What's that, baby?"

"My roses are wilting. They need water. Could you water them before you go?"

"Sure thing."

Vanessa got the pitcher and went into the bathroom. She filled it with water and came back to the plants. She carefully filled the planter.

"You were right, Miss Sandy. Those flowers were plumb dry. They sucked that water up like nobody's business."

Sandy smiled. "Thank you so much. Now go on home."

"I got nowhere I have to be. If you would like I can sit and read to you for a spell."

"No. Just go," Sandy snapped.

"What's got into you? I was just trying to be nice."

"Get the fuck out of here. I don't need you to baby me. Get out," Sandy screamed. "Get out. Get out."

"What's the matter? What is it?"

"Leave me alone. Get out of here you stinking nigger bitch."

The words stung like a slap in the face.

"I don't need to stand here and listen to this."

"Then get the fuck out you goddamn nigger. And close the fucking door."

Vanessa turned and stormed from the room. She struggled to control her anger. She didn't deserve such treatment. She had thought Sandy was her friend. She had no call to say that. She had always treated her nice.

Thirty seconds later Sandy's room exploded in a ball of flame. The force of the explosion blew Vanessa off her feet even though she was thirty yards down the hall. Vanessa crawled up to her knees. Smoke and flames shot out of the room. The fire alarm claxon sounded. The overhead sprinkler system turned on, spraying everything with water. Vanessa's ears rang. She turned back toward the room. What happened? Gas line must have ruptured, she thought. What else could it be? She stumbled toward the room, but the heat forced her back. Far away she heard a voice screaming wildly. It was several seconds before she realized it was her own.

62

Frank recalled what he had done for Bruce Burns in prison. He remembered the long walk across the prison yard. He was headed toward the south weight pile. It was the home turf of the Norse Men. It was an Aryan Nation wannabe collection of criminals and killers and racists. They were small in number, but they made up for it by being utterly ruthless. Their leader was a skinny redneck who went by the name of Loki.

A large asphalt track circled the yard. Frank followed it, skirting the territories of the Southern Mexicans, the Northern Mexicans, the Black Muslims, and the various hodgepodge areas of the different gangs. They all watched him pass. They knew who he was. His destination was obvious. To see Loki he would have to pass through another set of twins.

The Norse Men watched his approach. Those that were lifting weights stopped. Those that were talking stopped. The members moved between him and Loki, who sat on a bench in the center. Frank slowed his walk as he approached them. A half dozen Norse Men blocked his path.

"I need to see Loki," Frank said.

The men in front didn't move or speak. A few, encouraged by their numbers, pressed in close to Frank. They tried to stare him down. He tolerated the disrespect. He waited. Slowly, the group opened and he was allowed to move in farther. Their ranks closed behind his back. He knew some of them had weapons. They could kill him if they wanted to. The men funneled him toward the back of the weight pile. He could see Loki sitting god-like, watching. Two huge men stood in front of Loki. The inner guard. These two men were his most trusted generals.

The two men stood before him. Their massive arms crossed in front of them. He saw the Viking tattoos. Runes. Swords. A broken Thor's hammer. The guard on the right had a wolf's head on his forearm. The guard on the left had a dragon with amber eyes.

Frank stopped. They did the ritual stare down. Frank waited. Loki spoke.

"Let him pass."

Frank stepped between the two men. They both frisked him thoroughly and roughly. When they were satisfied that Frank was unarmed they nodded to Loki. Loki nodded back. Frank straightened his clothes. The guards were careful to stand as close as possible to him as he passed, but they did not touch him again. It was a level of respect between supreme predators.

"Excuse me, Loki. Could I have a moment of your time?"

Loki was in his late fifties. He was bald with a shaven head. He wore a long set of chin whiskers. His skin was dried from years of smoking. He held a cigarette now and puffed at it almost delicately. Norse tattoos decorated both his arms. He seemed amused.

"And to what do I owe the honor of a visit from the great Frank Kane? Or should I call you Poseidon?"

"Frank would be fine. I see your own children are grown stronger. The Finris Wolf and the Mitgard Serpent are terrifying to behold."

"I see you know your Norse lore. I'm impressed. And thank you for your kind words; my sons strive to measure up to standards which you yourself have set."

Frank smiled. "I have an ask."

"I figured as much. Who would have thought Frank Kane would need me? I'm honored. What do you want?"

"My cell mate, Bruce Burns…."

"Long hair and shark tattoos."

"Yes. The same. I'm out on parole in a week. I need to have someone look after him. I came to you first."

Loki smiled. His teeth were yellow. He stroked his chin hair pretending to be thinking.

"I can see what you mean. Without you here to protect him, others will step in to take advantage of him. How much longer does he have?"

"Six months."

"Indeed. He would never last that long without protection. He would be on his knees by nightfall. He would be sold out to be used within a day. Hard days ahead for the young man."

"Yes."

"And you want us to protect him. To make it clear to the gangs, and pervs, and punks and animals that he is under our protection. This would be a great task, but we could handle it. You know my next question, Frank."

"What's in it for the Norse Men?"

"Exactly. What do you propose?"

"Keep it simple. Money."

Loki templed his hands in front of his face. The cigarette hung from the corner of his mouth.

"Not favors? Not future considerations? Not repayment on the outside? Just money?"

"Simple. Easy to verify. I don't think you want to trust me."

Loki laughed.

"You are too honest for your own good, but I have heard that about you. Very well, money it is. Six months protection is worth fifty thousand dollars. I will need it wire transferred into my outside account before you are paroled."

"Fine. But I think ten thousand would be a better price."

"Ten? Ten isn't worth my time. I could see my way to drop it to forty."

"Fifteen."

"You're being stingy. This is a friend's life we are talking about. Thirty-five is my best price."

"It seems we have agreed upon thirty."

"Then thirty it is. Have the money sent to my attorney, Josh Seibert, in Chicago. He is a partner in Osborne, Seibert and Peddrick. He will make sure I'm informed."

"I'll set it up."

Frank turned to leave. Loki spoke, as Frank had expected, a final taunt, a final chance to demonstrate his newfound power over Frank Kane. He couldn't help himself.

"How do you know you can trust me? And what can you do if you can't?" Loki chuckled.

Frank turned back toward him. "May I step in closer?"

Loki waved a signal to the guards. He motioned Frank in closer. Frank leaned in and whispered.

"Francis Riggs, nurse, wife, mother to Bobby Riggs. 3127 Northridge Road. Chicago. Three-bedroom house. Off white with blue trim. A large vegetable garden in the back…"

Loki fought to control his rage.

"How did you…? Do you dare threaten my family? I could have you killed with a snap of my fingers."

"True. But I have men in place. They would carry out my last orders if I fell."

"The Spartans are no more. You are the last of them."

"I still have a core of true believers. They will do as I have asked if anything happens to me."

"You will not harm my family or…"

"Not me, you, Loki. If you honor our agreement they will stay safe, but by the god if you do not, I will have them each raped and tortured until they are begging for death and then they will be nailed to the side of their homes."

Loki snarled. "I will hunt you for this."

"No, you will not. You will pretend we never had this conversation. You will pretend that you are a man of honor. You will pretend that your word has value.

You will tell all that will hear that Frank Kane came to you on his knees and begged a favor. You will gain power and prestige and money. All you have to do is honor your word. If you do not, then their deaths will be on your head and may they haunt you to your grave."

"You will die too."

"I would expect to. None of us lives forever, even gods."

Frank leaned back from Loki. He did not smile. His face was stone. Loki watched him. Loki extended his hand.

"We have an accord."

Frank shook his hand. "We do indeed."

The Norse guards parted. Frank passed through without incident. He had lied to Loki. He had no men in position. He had no core group of true believers. He did not make war on the families of his enemies. There was no honor in that. The money was real, but the threats were not. It was a ruse, a bluff. If it did not work, there was nothing he could do. He had done all he could to protect Bruce Burns. He never sought Bruce Burns out afterwards to see if it had worked.

63

Helen stopped at the drive-thru window of the pharmacy.

"Kim, how are you?"

"Fine. I got your prescription. You just need to sign. Are you paying cash or with the card?

"Card."

Kim passed the HIPA forms, and directions sheet to her through the metal slot. Helen took the paperwork and signed it without reading it. She passed them back inside with her credit card. Kim took the papers back and swiped the card. She put the prescription bag into the compartment with the receipt. Helen signed it. She tossed the bag onto the passenger seat.

"How was your game?"

Helen smiled that perfect smile. "I've played better, but it was fun. Do you play?"

"Oh, no. I tried in high school, but I stunk pretty bad."

"Sometime you can play with me. I can give you some tips. It would be fun."

"Thanks, but I wouldn't wish that on anyone. You have a nice day."

"You too."

Helen raised her window and cranked the music back up. The classic '70s rock and roll hid the sound of her hand reaching into the bag. She found the folded piece of paper and slipped it out. She slid it into her bra. She closed the prescription bag. She sang along intermittently as she drove to the Thai restaurant. She parked to the side and waited beside her car for Johanna. They went in together laughing about old times.

The first watcher showed two minutes later. Reed took a seat near the door and ordered a salad and iced tea. He was very good. He never made eye contact with the women. He sat facing away from them, but he could see their reflection in the window. He couldn't hear their conversation. No one approached them. He thought Cyrus was being paranoid.

Helen excused herself to go to the restroom. The small bathroom was empty. There were only two stalls. She entered the far one. She sat down on the toilet and locked the door behind her. Helen removed the note from her sports bra. It was damp with her perspiration. She unfolded the paper. The script was small and neat.

"The old connections are reestablished. Frank is a ghost. All ears are out. All eyes open. If anyone hears we will contact you. Sorry."

There was no need for the last word, but these women were friends, they wanted to help her if they could. She tore the note into tiny pieces and flushed it down the toilet. She left the stall and washed her hands. She returned to the table.

They finished their lunch and a final glass of wine. Johanna hugged her good-bye. Helen walked past the man at the table near the door without a second look.

He didn't escape Johanna's dark eyes. She caught his eye and smiled. He smiled back. He seemed like a nice man. If she weren't married she might sneak back after Helen was gone. She hadn't had a nooner with a stranger in a decade. She smiled at the thought. She felt younger than she had in years. It was good to be around Helen. She made you feel alive.

"She's turning onto the street now. We are breaking surveillance. No contacts."

Reed listened.

"No, sir. No calls either. She picked up the one prescription and then went to lunch. Yes, sir. Call us if you need us tomorrow."

Helen entered the house. Cyrus was watching the news on television. The man in the sunglasses was sitting on the sofa across from him. They both turned as she entered.

"Another good day, darling?"

"Yes. It was a lot of fun. I really like Johanna."

She tossed the prescription bag onto the counter. She gave Cyrus her best smile. The man in the sunglasses smiled at her. She despised him. He was evil. Yet, something in her was drawn to him. He had something that women found irresistible. She ignored him. She held her cordial smile. She walked to Cyrus and gave him a kiss on the cheek.

"I need a shower. I'll be right back."

When she had gone upstairs the man in the sunglasses rose and went to the prescription bag. He opened it and poured the contents out. He went through each piece before replacing it in the bag and closing the top.

"You are more paranoid than I am."

"Possibly. I have a lot at stake."

"As do we all. Any more word from our contacts?"

"Strange things, brother."

"In what way?"

"You remember Keith Masnick's girlfriend?"

"No."

"Her name was Sandy Jones."

"Was?"

"She died yesterday under what the authorities describe as suspicious circumstances."

"What circumstances?"

"She was bedridden since one of Masnick's firebombs went off. She had third degree burns over most of her body. Anyway, her room was consumed in a fireball."

"Prometheus?"

"Apparently. He disappeared before the purge. We all assumed he was dead. Our contacts in law enforcement had no idea if he was or wasn't. It appears he is very much alive. It was a statement explosion. It consumed the room entirely, but didn't spread beyond."

"What's he trying to tell us? Do you think he's working with Kane?"

"I have no idea. He was never the same after he had to kill his brother. It changed him."

"We are his family. To be a god you must break all ties to your previous family. He was weak. Did we not have anyone watching him?"

"We did. They all disappeared. We have several high level contacts within the Bureau. Our number one says the Bureau has been secretly keeping tabs on Masnick for years. He has just learned that Masnick was listed as a closed C.I. No one knew except the Director and the U.S. Attorney General. Our contact says he can find no evidence that Masnick ever gave them any real intel. He cut some kind of immunity deal. Now he's vanished. The house he was listed as using is abandoned and booby trapped."

"Why wasn't I informed before now?"

"I don't know. I assume they didn't think he was much of a threat if he was on the run."

"But if he's working with Kane it's a different story entirely."

"It could be a very dangerous union. With his abilities and Kane's vengeful nature it could go very bad very fast."

"Send some men to look around."

"Already have. Maybe we should check in on the others who survived that night, see what they're up to."

"We have to do it quietly. Don't draw any attention. If they're working with Kane we'll know soon enough anyway."

"What do you mean?"

"There's an old saying, 'We shall know their passing by the bodies in their wake.' They won't try hiding it. If Kane is coming for us, he will want us to know."

The man in the sunglasses nodded and got to his feet. He left by the front door without another word.

Helen came into the room a few minutes later.

"Is he gone?"

"Yes. He had business."

"He gives me the creeps."

Cyrus smiled. "I am aware of that."

"Does he have to come here? Can't you meet him somewhere else?"

"I could, but this makes him feel important. That's crucial to him. I must feed his ego when I can."

"Do you trust him?"

"Of course not. But he's useful at this time. When he isn't, I'll have him removed."

"Good," Helen said. "I don't like the way he looks at me."

Cyrus laughed. "All men look at you that way, my darling. They all desire you. It's your gift. You are irresistible."

He kissed her on the cheek. She sighed.

"I'm going to take the Super Glide out for a ride. It's been a long time since I was on a bike. Come ride with me?"

Helen was surprised. They never rode anymore. The thought lifted her spirits.

"Whatever you like. Let me put on some jeans and boots. And promise to wear a helmet."

"Anything to make you happy. I'll be out front."

Helen changed and met Cyrus in the driveway. He was dressed in blue jeans, boots, and an old worn leather jacket. He was wearing a black Harley-Davidson half helmet. Helen wore the Gucci. The thin black leather was as soft as her skin. It cost just under five thousand dollars. Her motorcycle boots were Chanel and lined with lambswool. She carried her three quarter fiberglass helmet with its full-face shield in one hand.

She climbed behind Cyrus and wrapped her long arms around his waist. She rested her boots on the pegs above the shorty exhaust. Cyrus revved the engine and clunked the bike into the first of its six gears. In a second they were gone.

On the back of the big bike, she didn't worry about anything. She gave herself to the feeling of flying. The road was a blur. The future was only a micro second away.

64

Frank called Burns on the Russian cell phone at exactly two o'clock. No one answered. Could be bad. Could be nothing. Could mean anything. He waited five minutes and redialed the number. Burns picked up on the first ring.

"Sorry," he said. "I couldn't find the answer button."

"Not a problem. Everything cool there?'

"Yeah. The warehouse is stocked."

"You trust the Greek again?"

"I think he's on the level."

"Okay."

"You coming over?"

"Yeah, give me the address again."

Burns did.

"What's it near?"

"Do you have a GPS?"

"No. And the next person who asks me that, I will shoot."

"It's outside of town. Take Highway 377 toward Wheatland, then take the Eagle Mountain turnoff. It's off a dirt road on the left. The road is called Cactus Creek. There's nothing else on the road. You should see the warehouse on your left."

"Got it. One more thing. Have the Greek uncrate the launchers. I need the model numbers or serial numbers or whatever they have."

"Can I ask why?"

"No. Take the battery out of your phone until I get there. I'm about twenty or thirty minutes out."

"I will. I'll make sure the Greek does too."

"And no outside calls. Turn off your personal cell phones."

"Consider it done."

Harris answered the cell phone.

"We heard about the explosion."

Harris didn't answer.

"Who do you think is responsible?'

"I have no idea."

"Really? What's your best guess? Redding or Masnick or the Spartans?"

"I don't know. It would only be a guess at this time. What do you want me to do?"

"We've discussed it. The consensus here is that since Redding is the only one involved that we can locate. You should stick close to him."

"Redding isn't coming in today. He claims to be sick."

"We have eyes on him. If he rolls out we'll contact you. Be ready."

"Of course."

"Harris, I do not like your tone. Do not underestimate Redding. He's very dangerous."

"Yes, sir," Harris said and disconnected.

He wasn't worried about Redding. Redding was old and slow and nowhere near as smart as he was. Harris considered the possibility that he might have to take Redding out. He wondered for an instant if he could actually shoot him. He decided he could. He sometimes wished he could just shoot the whole damn bunch of them and be done with everything.

65

Frank found the warehouse. He liked to think he was good at directions. All men liked to think that. The warehouse was at the end of a short dirt road. The building was run-down looking from the outside. He pulled the Mercedes up to a high, padlocked fence topped with razor wire. He honked the horn twice and Burns appeared at the warehouse door. He ran out and unlocked the gate, then relocked it behind Frank. Frank parked and got out. He got the clothes and boots from the backseat.

"What's in the bag?" Burns asked.

Frank didn't answer. A plan was starting to come together in his mind. He let it work in his subconscious. The inside of the warehouse was spartan. There was a wide-open storage area and a small internal office. The Greek was in the office watching cable television. Outside the office were three military style cots. Frank went to the office. There was a desk with a computer tower and a nineteen-inch flat screen monitor. A television stand supported a thirty-two-inch television tuned to the local news. There was a small office-size refrigerator in one corner. There was a small card table that housed a coffee pot that was hot, and assorted packets of sweeteners, creamers, and condiments. A stack of Styrofoam cups. No sink, but Frank noticed a door off to the side that probably housed the bathroom. That was probably the only sink and the only water source for the warehouse. He dropped the bag in front of the desk.

Frank took a seat on the edge of the desk in front of the monitor.

"Let's talk."

"Alright," the Greek said.

"You call your cousin?"

"Yes. They went out this morning. They said there were men parked nearby watching, but they didn't approach them. They're installing the new carpet."

"Is that the only call?"

"Yes. Well, I called work to tell them I wouldn't be in. Oh, and Burns called his office and told them the same thing."

Frank nodded. He crossed his huge arms in front of him. "Which part of no other calls didn't you understand?"

"There didn't seem to be any risk in calling…."

"It is simple. You want your families back; you do what I tell you when I tell you. You don't get to ask why."

"This isn't the army. This isn't war."

"Yes, it is. This is my army. Those Russians are former military, they think this is war."

"That's different."

"Look, you want my help, you do what I tell you. You don't question it. You don't whine about it. You just do it. When I was a kid a contractor came to our house one time to renovate a bathroom. I asked him how long the job would take. I told him I would come every day after school and help. He thought for a minute and told me it would take six weeks if I helped and four if I didn't. You get what I'm telling you?"

"Yeah. We don't know shit and you don't have time to teach us."

"More or less."

"I got it," Burns said. "Doesn't mean I like it."

"You don't have to," Frank said. "Burns, let's me and you take a walk."

They walked around the warehouse and Frank said, "You remember our deal?"

"Yeah."

"It still holds. When I get Judy back to you, you get out of the crime business and get out of town."

Burns objected, "But it's not the Greek. We don't have to go."

"Yes, you do. It not being the Greek doesn't make it any safer."

"Once we take care of these guys, who do we have to be afraid of?"

"This is bigger than the Greek. This is international terrorism. They'll send others when these guys don't accomplish their mission. It may take weeks or months, but they will send someone to find you. You have to make it hard for them."

"Are you going to tell the Greek?"

"We will have a conversation before I leave."

"Do you have a plan?"

"I told you, I always have a plan."

Frank went back to office. The Greek was drinking coffee and watching the news.

"You got those numbers for me?"

The Greek handed him a piece of paper with three lists of numbers.

"Good. I'm going to call Vlad. You both stay quiet and let me handle this."

Frank put the battery back in the phone and called Vlad. Vlad picked up as soon as it rang.

"Vlad."

"Yes. You are late."

Frank hung up and waited two minutes and then redialed. Vlad answered on the first ring.

"You ready?"

"I have been thinking, Mister third man. Perhaps you are not who you claim to be."

"You are wearing me out. So who the fuck am I, Vlad?"

"Perhaps there is another simpler explanation. The hostages claim no knowledge of you. So I think, who can you be? It occurs to me that you might be FBI, or ATF, or CIA. You might have my two associates in jail. Perhaps that is where my men are now. You could be setting a trap for me."

Frank sighed. "I have been accused of a lot of shit, but this is the first time I have ever been accused of being a Fed. Let me ask you a question."

"What?"

"Do you think your men would have allowed themselves to be captured?"

Vlad was silent. "You are right. They would have fought to the last man. Still, you could have killed them and still be FBI."

Frank hung up the phone again. He waited. Vlad had to want the deal. He had to need it to overcome his caution. Vlad was right. Frank could be anybody. The phone rang. Frank answered.

"Speak."

"You are a difficult man."

"Look, I don't have time to sit around jerking you off. You want to do business, then let's do business. You want to waste time, waste your own. Pull out now and you got nothing to worry about."

"My product."

"It's not your product. It's three Surface to Air Missiles. Go find some more and come back later. I'll just keep these babies as my share for the inconvenience."

"What of the hostages?"

"Look, you pull the plug on the deal, the hostages are as good as dead. I know that. Do what you got to do. It will force me to liquidate their counterparts here. I will have to get new partners, but that won't be too hard. Partners are not hard to find."

"So, you will let me kill them?"

"Listen, they're nothing to me one way or the other. I'm a businessman. I am here to do business. You are making this way too complicated. Work a deal or hang the fuck up. I have other matters to attend to."

Vlad thought about it. "Very well. I do not believe the FBI would let hostages die."

"I don't know if that's true or not."

"It is. Give me the serial numbers."

Frank read them off to Vlad who checked them against his own manifest.

When he was finally satisfied he spoke again.

"How do you wish to do this?

"I'm new at this so let's keep it simple."

"May I make a suggestion?"

"Sure."

"We set a public place. You park a vehicle with the missiles. We arrive with the hostages and the money. We make the exchange."

Frank laughed. "I said I was new at this. Not that I was an idiot. Here's how we do it. What kind of vehicle do you have?"

"I have several cars. Why?"

"Do you have a big SUV?"

"I have a Suburban."

"Perfect. How well do you know Fort Worth?"

"Well enough."

"Fuck well enough. Does your car have a GPS?"

"No."

"Go buy one. How far are you away from Fort Worth?"

"I don't know what you mean? I am in Fort Worth."

"Look, we both know you aren't in the city. It takes your men too long when they go out to meet with you. How far, time-wise, from the center of the city?"

"I don't know exactly."

"Best guess?"

"Thirty minutes."

"Fine. I will call you on this number at eleven o'clock tonight. I will give you the address of a pay phone. You will send one man in the Suburban. What color is it?"

"Black."

"It figures. You will place a piece of duct tape over the bottom half of the left front headlight so my men can spot your car. Your man wears a hat. Do you have a cowboy hat?"

"No. I don't think so. Maybe. I will check."

"Fine. I will call the pay phone fifty minutes after I call you. Your man answers, I give him a new address. I will bounce him all over. I'll run him down Exchange Street to the Stockyards and then up to the Cultural district past the Kimbell. We keep this up until I am satisfied he is alone. You send someone to tail him and the deal is off. I have a sniper. He will take your guy out as a penalty."

"Then I will kill the hostages."

"We've been over this. Kill them if you have to. I don't really care. If the deal goes south, then it just does."

"Continue, please."

"We won't be at every site, but we will be at some. At the final checkpoint we will have taped instructions underneath the phone where to go for the pickup. We will meet him there and transport him blindfolded to our location. We will sweep your car for bugs. If we find one, your man dies. If we spot a tail or think we spot a tail, your man dies. Your man comes armed, he dies. Are you starting to see a pattern with this thing yet? Have I left anything out?"

"You will send all the missiles?"

"No, of course not. I will send two as a show of good faith. You have your man bring half the money. Make sure he has a cell to contact you. When he has inspected the weapons he will call to confirm. Afterward we will keep his cell and take him back to a safe location with the missiles. He brings them to you. If everything is good, the next time he brings the hostages and the other half of the money."

"It is not a perfect plan. There are many variables."

"Life is hard and then you die. Deal with it."

"Oh, I shall. I appreciate your generosity with the exchange. As a show of good faith on my part I will allow one of the hostages to be returned to you at the delivery. Choose one."

Frank had both expected and dreaded this.

"You want to send someone, send the kid."

Vlad paused. "The child will be difficult. Without his mother he may be un-cooperative and draw attention to our exchange. I will send one of the women instead. Choose one."

Frank smiled. "No. You keep them both. We'll get them all at the end anyway. And it's only another day."

"You do not want one of the hostages returned?"

"Like I said. They don't mean anything to me one way or the other. I get one girl back, the other guy is pissed it's not his wife. It's not worth the headaches."

"One is better than none."

Frank knew than that the Greek's wife was dirty. Even the worst hostage knew intel that would be valuable. How many men. How well armed. How tired. How professional. She would house untold amounts of information that she didn't even know she had. The reverse was also true. A mole planted in their midst now would be devastating.

"You keep them safe for me."

"Very well. The women would like to speak to their husbands to let them know they are alive and safe. Would this be possible?"

"No. I trust you to look after them. Burns and the Greek got no say in this. Nothing good can come out of stirring them up."

"Very well. Half the money tonight."

"Half tomorrow night. What's the driver's name?"

"I will send Omar."

"Fine. Same driver both nights. Same rules. I'll use different run-around spots in case you get creative."

"You are a hard man."

"Don't forget it." Frank shut the phone down. He checked the call log on the phone. Vlad had tried to call him three times earlier.

"Why didn't you let him send one of wives back?" Burns shouted.

"If they want it, whatever the it is, it isn't good for us. They might plant a bug."

"I have device to check for that," the Greek said.

"Maybe something else. The thing is, you can't trust this guy at all. I need both of you guys tonight. One of you gets his wife back early he might fall off. I can't afford that."

"Why are you dragging it out to another night? Can't we just do the exchange tonight and be done with it?"

"No. I want him planning for a double-cross tomorrow night. He'll try to ambush us tomorrow after he gets the first load. Take the batteries out of your cells. He may try to have your wives call to break you down."

Frank opened the top drawer on the desk.

"Put them in here. We need to go over my plan."

66

Frank laid it out for them as simply as he could. When he finished he turned to the Greek. "Now what kind of weapons have you got for us? More Glocks and old AKs? You said you had something better."

"I do, my friends. Come with me."

The Greek led them to a pile of plain wooden crates covered with an old blue tarp. He pulled it back. It was labeled U.S. NAVY in heavy black stencil. He picked up a pry bar and inserted it under the edge of the crate. He popped the top. It had been opened before. Inside was a metal container. He pulled it out. The Greek flipped the metal latches and opened the top. Inside, packed in cushioning material cutouts, was an array of weapons.

"We jacked a truck at a rest area near San Diego and hit the motherlode. This is all state of the art Special Forces gear," the Greek said.

"Spec Ops. Navy Seals?" Frank asked.

"Exactly," the Greek said.

Frank smiled. It was a good omen. Apollo would approve. Frank lifted out one of the automatic rifles.

The Greek explained, "This is the M4A1 SOPMOD. It has thermal sighting and night vision. It comes with a suppressor that silences and suppresses the muzzle flash. It's real hard-hitting. It fires a 5.56mm NATO round. Fast runs at about three thousand feet per second. It's good against body armor and bulletproof vests."

"I thought there was a problem with the 5.56 not being lethal enough in Iraq. It didn't have knock-down power," Frank said

"They upgraded the ammo. It carries a heavier load now so it mushrooms immediately on penetration," the Greek said.

Frank looked the gun over. Saw the switch for semi and full auto. He knew its reputation for accuracy, asked, "How many rounds to a magazine?"

"Thirty."

Frank sighted down the barrel. The gun was light, only about six and a half pounds. He flipped through the different screens on the sight. "We got ammo for these?"

The Greek lifted the wooden top off a smaller wooden crate. There were four metal cans inside. "We have three crates of the 5.56mm and one of the .45 caliber for the handguns."

"Let's see the handguns."

The Greek took out a pistol. A .45 cal. semiautomatic in the 1911 style.

Frank looked the gun over. He ejected the twelve plus one mag. It was heavy, close to four pounds. Maybe more than four, he thought. "Who makes this?" he asked.

The Greek answered, "Heckler & Koch. The MK23 pistol comes with a KAC sound suppressor."

"This is some lethal shit," he said, looking through the rest of the package. He noticed something odd. A tomahawk. He took one out, made a few practice swipes.

"Who's that for, the skinny guy from Last of the Mohicans?" Burns asked.

"It's not your daddy's tomahawk. These are state of the art tactical tomahawks, forged from a single piece of steel so the head can't fly off. The SEALs use them instead of knives. Better for close combat and better at breaching. The handle is electrically insulated. The long spike is designed for serious damage. The head even has an extra cutting surface on the beard. This is a bad mutha."

Frank passed it to Burns who stared at it dumbfounded.

"You did good, Greek. This stuff will up our chances ten-fold," Frank said.

"You haven't seen the best thing yet. Come over here."

"If you have night vision goggles, I might kiss you."

The Greek laughed. "We won't need night vision. The scopes will do that for us. But this, this is truly amazing. It was in the same shipment. There was only one box."

They went to an open crate. The Greek pulled out a sweater vest in some type of futuristic woven nylon. The Greek passed them each one. They were light and very flexible. Frank sniffed it. There was a strange chemical smell, a little like a new shower curtain.

"Do you know what this is?"

Frank eyed it suspiciously. "Is it a bulletproof vest?"

"Yes. This is new space age stuff. It's called 'The Dragon's Skin.'"

"How do you know all this?" Burns asked.

"It's on the inside of the vest. Along the back. See?" the Greek said pointing to the words and the logo of the dragon. "I did some checking online. This stuff doesn't exist. But if it did, rumors say it's made from the same chemicals spiders use to construct their webs. It's supposed to be one hundred times stronger than steel and very flexible."

"But does it work?"

"My guess is the SEAL team this stuff was meant for was going to field test it. I shot it with a .45, a .9mm and an AK-47. Even the AK 762 copper jacket didn't puncture it."

"I'm impressed," Frank said, slipping the vest over his head. It weighed a little less than nothing and conformed well to his broad shoulders and chest.

"It has a special feature I discovered," the Greek continued. "It conforms to your body. Your body heats the fibers and it melds into the shape of your build. Poseidon's beard, with enough of these an army would be unstoppable."

"This is unbelievable. What are you going to do with this stuff?" Burns asked.

"I can sell off the pistols easily. If I strip off the special sights I can move the rifles. But to tell you the truth they scare me. There are lots of guns on the market, but nothing like this. The authorities would spare no expense in finding me. I should probably dump it all in the river."

"That's part of the deal," Frank said. "I already talked with Burns about it. There's a price for getting your family back."

"Name it. What's the price? How much money?"

"No money. Just your word. You get out of the crime business. No more gun sales. No more fencing stolen goods, or baking drugs, or whatever you're doing on the side."

"Just stop? It's taken me my whole life to build these associations."

"Just like that. Retire. You've been lucky. Live off your legit businesses."

"You ask a lot."

"I am giving you a lot. Without me you would still be chained to that bed waiting for a bullet."

The Greek thought about it for about thirty seconds before he sighed and nodded. "Very well. When this is over. I will send the word. It has been a good run. Perhaps it is time."

"One more thing. I think you should leave Fort Worth. The Russians will have friends that will come looking for you."

"This is my home. I will not leave."

"You're a big boy. You choose. I just needed to warn you of what's coming. You stay ready. One day they will come."

"I will, as you say, stay ready. But I will not leave my home."

"Fine. But no more crime. That's my price. Do I have your word?"

"You are a strange man, Frank. But you have my word," and they shook hands.

"Good enough. Now try on the clothes I brought. If something doesn't fit, I still have time to replace it."

The two men laughed as they tried on the coveralls and boots. They joked about painting and plumbing. When they were changed Frank explained the rest of his plan. They both nodded.

Frank left the men to their thoughts and called DC.

"What do you need, Frank?"

"I need you on standby tonight."

"You got it."

"Are you going to check on the girls?"

"I don't have to."

"It's okay, just bring your laptop."

"You got it."

"Anything new on the crack house?"

"Cops drove around. They're still in business as far as I can tell. Couple of Mexican types working the corners."

"I'll call when I need you."

"Be careful," DC added, but Frank had already hung up.

67

Vlad slammed his hand down on the table.

"Bastard," he snarled.

"What?" Omar asked.

"He doesn't want a hostage. They mean nothing to him."

"Then let us kill them now."

"No. He wants them tomorrow with the last missile. We must keep them alive until then."

"What do you want me to do?"

Vlad explained the exchange plan. Omar nodded without expression.

Vlad smiled. "This will work to our advantage, my friend. Tonight we will follow his rules. That will make him less suspicious tomorrow."

"What do you have in mind?"

"He is expecting tomorrow for the hostages to be in the car…"

"And Dasha could have a gun…"

"No. Too risky. When she is safely returned to her family she can find out who this third man is. We will have the missiles. We can return for revenge. You be careful tonight, this is a dangerous man."

Omar laughed. "So am I. I would like to ask a favor, one soldier to another, since I must take on this dangerous task."

"Anything, Omar."

"Let me have the Burns woman."

"With you it is always the sex. You think too much with your little head I think."

"True. So can I have her?"

Vlad slapped him on the back. "Of course, Omar. Go. Enjoy yourself. No one will miss a slice off a loaf that has already been cut."

"And the others?"

"Let them earn a taste of her as you have. Rewards are for those who earn them. This is not Russia."

Omar laughed. He pulled the hand-held stun gun from his pocket. He fired it twice to see the dance of blue sparks. Vlad eyed him suspiciously.

"Do not harm her."

Omar fired the stun gun again. "Do not worry, Vlad. This barely leaves a mark."

Santos scanned the streets for cars slowing down. Business had returned to normal. And business was good. The cops had snooped around for a day and MS13 had abandoned the crack house. Now the cops were gone. They had more to worry about than some crack house in a poor working-class neighborhood. Yeah, he had heard that some little bitch got shot, but hey, that wasn't their fault. The fuckin' Latin Kings shouldn't have tried to roll their spot. Had to defend your turf. Had to, no options on that shit. Shit happens in the crossfire. They don't like it? Then fuckin' move. Fuck 'em. They wasn't MS13. They weren't nothin'. Santos was a businessman. Yes, he was. He touched the gun in the back of his pants. Best not fuck with Santos. Latin Kings wouldn't be back no time soon. Locals didn't like them, so what. Locals couldn't do shit. Cops couldn't do shit. Everyone knew you don't fuck with MS13. A car slowed. It was a yellow mustang. It needed paint. Santos approached the car. The car stopped and the window came down. It was a white dude. Lot of white dudes doin' the shit now. Business was growin'.

It wouldn't be long until MS-13 was running the whole town. No one could stop them. No one even dared try anymore. It was so damn easy.

68

Frank sat alone in the warehouse. He had put his old vest and the Sig back under the Mercedes in the false bottom. He was carefully checking the MK23. It was a fine handgun. The KAC suppressor was a thing of beauty in his hands as he screwed it into place. The weight of the gun made it feel powerful and lethal. The Greek walked up to him.

"May I sit?"

"Sure. What's on your mind?"

"I know you think my wife has something to do with this."

Frank didn't answer.

"I know in my heart she is innocent. I want your promise that you will not harm her."

Frank stared at him. "I don't know if I can do that. Guarantees are hard to come by when bullets start flying."

"Promise me. If she has helped them, I will do her myself. It is my honor that needs to be restored."

Frank looked into his hard old face. "How will you know?"

"By Poseidon's beard I will know."

Frank stared at him, thinking. "Very well. You have my word. I will not harm her. Your wife is your responsibility."

The Greek sighed. "Thank you."

Frank didn't know what more he could say, so he added, "What is your son's name?"

The Greek's face lit up. "His name is Aristodemus. We call him Ari. It is a family name. Have you heard it before?"

"No," Frank lied. "Does it mean something special?"

The Greek smiled again and spit on the floor. "It symbolizes many things. Resurrection. Honor. Bravery. Loyalty. One of our great ancestors bore the name."

"I hope your son bears the name well."

"As all fathers hope. He is wild and strong as a boy child should be. The rest we shall see in time."

Frank nodded. He knew the name. Aristodemus had been a Spartan warrior at Thermopylae. He had been stricken with an illness and had temporarily lost his vision. Leonidas, the Spartan king, had sent him from the field of battle before the Persians had encircled and destroyed the Spartan forces. After the battle, when his sight had been restored, he returned to Sparta with a message from Leonidas. Yet he was greeted as a coward. No Spartan would speak to him. No one would offer to light his fire or share food with him. He was shunned for not dying on the battlefield like a warrior should. Yet, when the Spartan-led Greek army eventually destroyed Xerxes' army at Platea, Aristodemus had accompanied the army. He was singled out after the battle for extreme bravery and disregard for his own life in the service of Sparta. He received no official honors from Sparta, but his honor was restored. What other warrior could claim to have fought at the two most famous battles for Sparta?

It was a good name for a boy, Frank thought. It was a good omen.

Frank wished Bobby Ziglar or The Jake was with him. If they were here, the mission would be easy. They were as unstoppable as he was. Or better yet, to have Apollo and his sniper rifle. Frank sighed. Apollo was dead. He had seen his body blown all to hell in Costa Rica. He didn't know what had happened to The Jake. The last he heard, Bobby Z was doing a nickel stretch for gun running. He was tough. He could do five years standing on his head. You had to play the cards you were dealt. The Greek was a hard man. He would do what he needed to. Frank wasn't so sure about Burns. He was key to Frank's plan. If he couldn't do his part, the mission would fall apart. A lot of people Frank was supposed to protect would die. He hoped Burns had the steel.

69

Zack was drunk. He had thrown for three hundred and ten yards. They had beat cross-town rival Page, 28 to 3. It was such a bad beating it should have been against the law. The party was pumping at full volume. He spotted Morgan across the crowded living room. Big, dumb redneck had protected his ass in the pocket all night. It was hard to believe that fat fuck could move as quick as he could. He was a regular Fred fucking Flintstone. Zack had seen Fred on an old cartoon bowling for the Water Buffalo Lodge. They had called him "twinkle toes." Now every time he thought about Morgan he pictured Fred "twinkle toes" Flintstone. He laughed to himself. Morgan spotted him and came over. He fist-bumped him.

"Awesome game, man."

"We were awesome. There are some assholes bleeding over at Page where we fucked them."

Morgan laughed. "We put the hurt on them. Bunch of pussies."

"Maybe next year they can play in their dresses?"

"They'll remember this ass-kicking for a long time."

"That they will. I got some coke. You want to do a couple of lines?"

"Hell, yeah."

Zack pulled a small glass vial and a cut down McDonalds straw from his jacket pocket.

"Keep this on the down low. Take it to the bathroom and don't tell anyone."

"No problem. I'll be right back."

Zack grabbed his beefy arm. "Bring some back."

Morgan laughed. "I will. Just a boost, that's all."

Zack laughed too. Morgan was all right. He looked around the party. Everyone was having a good time. There were close to two hundred people there. Guys were hooking up. Girls were letting loose. The football team was reaping the rewards of a great season.

He was looking for the little waitress, Jenny. There was something about her he couldn't put his finger on. She seemed innocent and sweet part of the time, but there was also something about her that hinted she was dangerous. He liked that. There was something about her tight little body that he couldn't get out of his head. He bet she was a wildcat. What did they call it in English class? Dichotomy? Yeah, that sounded right. Dichotomy, joined opposites, like an angel and a devil. Like something cut in half. He smiled. That was what he wanted to do. He wanted to split her. She said she would come to the party, but he hadn't seen her.

A pretty blonde girl came up to him. Her name was Lisa. She was a flag girl or something. She was lean and tight. They had hooked up a few times, but not tonight. Tonight he wanted Jenny.

"Hi, Zack. Great game."

Zack kept looking around. "Thanks."

"You played great."

"Thanks."

Where the fuck was Jenny and her friend Caron who had the eye on Morgan? She should be here. Maybe they were working.

Lisa realized he was looking for someone. "Talk to you later," Lisa said and drifted away.

Zack ignored her. If all he wanted was pussy, he could have his pick. He wanted Jenny. Fucking cock tease. She was playing hard to get. That was her game. Cunt. He didn't care. She wasn't all that hot anyway.

Morgan lumbered up. He slipped the vial of coke back to Zack. Zack shook some out onto the web of his hand and snorted it.

Morgan tried to block him from the other people's view. He was protecting him as always. "Chill out, Zack. You don't want to blow your scholarship. Put that shit away. I'm supposed to be the dumb one, not you."

Zack slipped it into his pocket.

"Fuck 'em."

"Yeah. Who?"

"Everyone. All these lame fucks."

"Yeah, fuck 'em. Let's get some beer."

Morgan ushered Zack into the kitchen. He opened the refrigerator and pulled out a couple of Bud Lights. He popped the top of one and pushed it at Zack. Zack took it and took a drink. Morgan opened his own. More students passed by laughing and talking. Zack didn't hear them. He was in his dark place, as he called it. He wanted what he wanted. He had always been a great athlete. He had always been given special treatment. He deserved special treatment. Everyone should recognize it.

"Dude, you okay?"

Zack smiled. "Yeah, I'm just pissed those girls didn't show up. That girl Caron was super hot for you. I was sure she would be here."

Morgan glanced around as if for the first time he realized she wasn't. "Yeah, bummer. Must not have been that into me after all."

Zack gave him a punch to the shoulder. "No, she was into you. I could tell. Hell, she left wet spots when she walked away."

Morgan laughed. "Her loss."

"Not so fast, dude. Maybe she forgot or got hung up at work."

"I guess. She could still show up."

"Now, is that what coach taught us? I don't think so. If the other team doesn't want to do what you want them to, then you have to make them."

"Huh?"

"Let's find that punk, Brian. Get his ass to drive us to Applebee's and see if they're there."

"I don't know. I mean who cares? There are a lot of hot girls here."

"Not as hot as Caron. You know you want that shit. You know you've been wondering what it would feel like to bang that ass."

Morgan grinned. "I might have thought about it a time or two."

"See. Come on. Let's see if we can make this happen."

"You sure? You'd just ditch the party? You'd do that for me?"

"Of course. Hell, there's so many people here already somebody will call the cops sooner or later. It's probably better we aren't here drinking when the cops show up. We don't need to get busted for underage drinking."

"Good idea. Let me grab some beers for the road."

"Cool. Then help me find that pussy Brian. That bitch will do whatever we ask him to."

70

Agent Redding took his pistol out of the holster for the hundredth time. He unloaded and reloaded the magazine. He racked the slide arming the weapon. He took a drink of scotch. He savored the familiar smoky burn. He still had a couple of hours to kill until the meet. He smiled. He wondered if tonight he would die. It was possible. He had been an agent for a long time. He had cheated death a few times. He checked his watch. It was almost time to go.

Redding smiled. He wasn't afraid. He still had a few tricks up his sleeve. He took another sip of the scotch. They underestimated him because he was getting older. That could prove costly for them. At the very least he would like to know what was really going on before he died. That wasn't asking too much. That was only fair. Redding believed in fair. He based his life on it.

Jenny was watching television when Caron came in. It was a show called Gangland. The History Channel. This episode was about the Hells Angels in Montreal. She changed the channel to the Cartoon Network.

"What you doing?"

"Chillin'. Watching the tube. No word from DC?"

"No. Anything from Frank?"

"No. DC said he was wrapping things up, so he could show anytime."

"He likes to be mysterious."

Jenny smiled. "It's probably for our own good. Fewer questions, fewer lies."

"I heard that. I'm going to get a glass of wine. You want one?"

"Sure."

Caron went into the kitchen and got the half empty bottle of wine DC had left. She got two glasses and carried them into the living room. She stopped beside Jenny and passed her one of the empty glasses. She lifted the bottle to pour and stopped. She smiled.

"You know what would be cool?"

"What?"

"Let's put on our bathing suits and drink it in the hot tub."

"That sounds like a great idea. I got that speaker set I can hook up to my iPod."

"Cool. I hate to waste a night off work."

"But if you get all drunk and try to kiss me like you did DC, I will punch you out."

Caron flicked her tongue in the air. "You know you want this. Everybody wants some of this action."

"Is it okay if I vomit now? You are sick."

"Yes, and tired. Now get changed."

The two girls ran upstairs and changed into their bikinis. They started down the stairs when Jenny stopped.

"I forgot my iPod. I'll meet you down there. Do you want your robe?"

"Yeah, bring it. Thanks. I'll grab some towels."

Jenny darted back into their room. She put on her robe and tied the waist. She grabbed Caron's pink robe. She got her iPod and the little speaker it could dock with. She looked around to be sure Caron wasn't coming back upstairs. She picked her jeans up off the floor and slipped the switchblade into one of the pockets of the robe. She skipped down the stairs. She felt like a bad ass.

She met Caron on the screened-in porch. She hooked up the iPod and turned it on. Taylor Swift was singing about some boy belonging to her. Both girls giggled. Jenny checked to see that the screen door was latched. She hung her robe over the small table that sat on the porch near the four wooden chairs. Caron had already laid two big towels on the table.

They got in the water laughing and singing to the music. Caron filled her glass and then poured her own. She set the bottle beside the hot tub in easy reach.

"To best friends," Caron said.

They clinked glasses and took a drink.

"I'm sorry I got so freaked out about you and DC."

"It's okay. It was stupid. I'm an idiot."

"No. I'm serious. If you guys have a connection, that's cool. It's just that we all seemed like a team. You know?"

"I know. I was a stupid slut and I apologize. I wouldn't do anything to wreck what we have here. Sisters before misters."

"Listen, if you really like DC, you should tell him. I thought about it. I think I can be okay with it, if that's what you want."

"No. Forget it. He's older. What would he want with some kid anyway? Let's just pretend it never happened."

Jenny touched glasses again. "If you say so. I never saw anything."

Caron giggled. "What would be the point of being BFFs if you don't keep secrets?"

"So true."

They each took another drink. Pink started singing about a broken heart and something about being so nasty. The girls leaned back in the soothing hot water. The steam rose around them.

Jenny closed her eyes. Life was good, she thought. Her mind seemed to drift.

She had a sudden image of Frank in the hot tub with her. It startled her. She shook it away and looked at Caron. Almost expecting her to have read her thoughts. But Caron's eyes were closed. She was smiling. Jenny made a promise to herself to start dating more. This was getting too freaky. She glanced once more at Caron to be sure she hadn't read her mind. She eased back into the water. This time instead of Frank it was that hunk from Twilight, Taylor Lautner. Now that was a fantasy, Jenny thought. She never understood why girls always preferred vampires. They were pale and skinny and she bet they smelled funny. And who thought drinking blood was sexy. It was so gross. Lautner was built like a man. He was hot.

The sultry voice of the British singer, Kate Nash, came over the speaker. Both girls set up at the same time and sang along with the song….

"Why are you being a dickhead for?
 Stop being a dickhead.
Why are you being a dickhead?
You're just fucking up the situation."
The girls smiled as they sang. Every girl knew someone who was a dickhead.

Vlad answered the phone on the first ring. He couldn't keep the excitement from his voice. He knew they were close. "Yes."
"You ready?"
"Yes."
"You do this right, tomorrow we finish our business."
"I will do this right."
"Good. Here is the first address." Frank gave it to him.
"So it begins."
"One more thing."
"What?"
"Do you have a hat?"
"Why? Is this important?"
"Have your man wear a hat. A cowboy hat would still be best."
"I don't have a cowboy hat. There are baseball type caps here. Will that do?"
"Fine. It will give me another point of visual recognition. What color?"
"Black."
"Have him wear it. He's got fifty minutes until the call. Should give him plenty of time. My sniper spots anybody without a black ball cap on, he has orders to take him out. I make that clear enough for you?"

"Yes. He will wear it."

Frank hung up. He pulled the batteries out of the cell phone.

The Greek and Burns were watching him.

"He's on the way. Burns, give me a ride to the drop site."

Burns got his keys. "You got the scanner?"

The Greek passed it to him. "It will pick up any RF signal. It is very good."

Frank slipped it into his front pocket. He pulled his coat on. He removed the suppressor and slipped the MK23 into the small of his back. The Greek opened the doors to the warehouse and let them drive out.

In the car, Frank turned to Burns. "Stay frosty. This will all work out. You'll have your wife and your life back in a few hours."

"God, I hope so."

"You have to trust me on this. It can get messy. I will make sure you and Judy get clear of this."

"What about the Greek and his family?"

"I'll do what I can, but they aren't my concern. I came here for you."

They drove the rest of the way in silence, each thinking about the night ahead.

71

Zack was sitting in the front seat of the white Honda Accord. They were parked in the lot outside Applebee's. He was feeling good. The perfect football game, mixed with some beer and a little coke, who could ask for more? Except of course, to lay that little waitress, Jenny, and he was working on that.

Brian came back to the car and got in.

"Well?" Morgan asked.

"She's not working tonight. Neither of them are."

"Fuck," Morgan snarled and punched the back of the seat.

Coke always made him angry.

"Hey, this is my mom's car," Brian said.

"Fuck you," Morgan snarled. "And fuck your mom. Those bitches lied to us. They said they were working tonight."

Zack just smiled floating along on his super buzz. He looked over at Brian and did a hit of coke.

"What?" Brian asked.

Zack smiled at Brian. "You've got a secret," Zack said.

What do you mean?"

"You know where they live." Zack said. "I can tell, Brian. Am I right?"

Brian grinned. "I was saving it. I did a Google search yesterday anyway. I got their home address. It's not far from here."

Morgan sat up in the back seat. "All right." He started drumming his hands on the front seat. "Let's roll."

Brian hesitated. "You guys sure this is a good idea? I mean, we could get in trouble."

Zack patted him on the shoulder. "Don't worry about it, buddy. They'll be glad to see us. You saw that last night, right?"

"Yeah. They were flirting pretty hard."

"See? I think they'll want to party. Who wouldn't?"

"But if they don't, then we split, right?" Brian asked.

"Of course. If they aren't interested, we aren't going to push it."

"But if these girls really like to party, I don't see why you can't get some action too."

"You mean it?"

"We're friends, Brian. Of course I mean it. I'll look after you. If you don't mind seconds."

"Wow," Brian said.

Morgan fist-bumped Zack again. "This is going to be great. Caron is going to flip when she sees us."

"Yes, she will," Zack said.

Brian pulled the car out of the parking lot. He had butterflies in his stomach. He might finally get laid tonight. He knew he had been right to hang out with Zack and Morgan. Tomorrow everyone would be talking. Everyone would be envious.

72

Omar pulled to the curb and parked the Suburban. He had been bounced around to five phones. He had seen more of Fort Worth than he ever wanted to see. If they were watching, he couldn't tell. If he was being followed, they were experts. Twice he thought he had spotted a tail, but it had always turned off at the next light. He was glad they had used the GPS. He would never have found the addresses using a map. The pay telephone rang. He answered it again.

"Omar, is that you?"

"Yes. It is Omar. How much more?"

"Almost there."

Omar felt under the phone for the directions to the last stop. There was nothing there. He shook his head. It seemed ridiculous.

"No map. Another stop then?"

"No. Put your hands on the hood of the car. Spread your legs wide. I will approach from your left. If you turn to see, I will shoot you. Do you understand?"

Omar nodded.

"I asked if you understood."

"Yes," Omar said.

"Now hang up the telephone and get into position."

In the background before the caller hung up he heard him say, "Keep the scope on him. If he moves an inch…." and the line died.

Omar walked to the Suburban. He spread his legs and placed his hands on the hood. He remained motionless. He knew the sniper had him in his scope. He felt the chill all soldiers felt about snipers. He listened for the approach of the man. He never heard a sound. Suddenly, he felt a gun press into the juncture of his neck and head.

"Are you armed?"

"No. In my right outside pocket is a stun gun."

"I said no weapons."

"It was only to protect the money if someone tried to take it at one of these checkpoints."

Frank fished the stun gun out and looked it over. They had changed a lot since he had used one. This one was only about four inches tall and two inches wide. It was gray with a wrist strap. The cover of the stun gun said 1.2 million volts. That should be pretty strong. The red led light was lit. The stun gun was charged. Frank laid it on the hood beside Omar.

Frank's experienced hand roamed over Omar's body. The hand searched

Omar's genitals. Omar didn't flinch. He had probably been searched many times. Frank wanted him to know that he was a professional. It would make him feel safer.

"Hands behind your back."

Omar did as he was told. Frank secured his hands with a zip tie.

"Don't be alarmed. I am going to hood you."

Omar nodded. Frank removed his cap and slipped a black pillowcase over Omar's head.

"Step back from the car. Let me lead you. I'm going to put you in the back seat. Lower your head. When you get situated, lay down."

Frank pushed Omar's head down, guiding him into the car. Omar stretched out on the back seat. Frank took the cell phone out of Omar's coat pocket. He removed the battery and dropped it on the hood of the car. Frank closed the door. Frank took out the scanner. He swept Omar first. He was clean. Then he swept Omar's cell phone and the stun gun. Both were good places to hide a tracking device. Each had its own power source. They were both clean. Frank put them both in his pocket.

Next Frank swept the car. He moved methodically over the entire car. He found no trace of a tracking device. He popped the back gate of the car and scanned the inside. This was not the time to be in a hurry. He put the scanner back into his pocket. He looked around. The street was still deserted. He went around, got in the front seat, and pulled the door closed. He pretended to open his cell phone. He knew Omar would be listening to any information he could catch.

"We're secure. Bring the other cars up and follow us. Wait outside."

Frank smiled. That sounded pretty good. He drove toward the warehouse. Omar did not speak. That was fine with Frank.

The Greek opened the warehouse overhead door and Frank pulled the car inside.

"Everybody else outside," Frank said. "You two stay."

The Greek went and opened and closed a door. Then returned. Frank helped Omar out of the back seat. He gave the Greek the scanner.

"Recheck the car."

The Greek went to work. Frank led Omar over to where the SAMs were. They were called Strelas and this type had seen action all over the world. He removed Omar's hood. Omar looked around. Frank cut the zip ties on his wrists.

Omar rubbed his wrists and knelt before the missiles. He checked the three olive green launch tubes. Each contained its own thermal battery. He held one up and looked through the iron sights. Once the laser painted the target, the red light would buzz and turn green. Omar knew an experienced man could acquire and fire at a target in less than eight seconds. Once the rocket was away it would follow its target until detonation.

He had used the Strela 2 before. He knew the Strela's specifics. He knew that it had a four-mile strike range. Planes at altitudes over twenty thousand feet were out of its range, but planes just taking off were easy targets. Omar checked each tube carefully to be sure they were operational. He checked the rockets. He was surprised. There were five rockets instead of three. He examined each of the fifteen-kilogram rockets. They all appeared workable.

"There are supposed to be three only rockets."

"What can I tell you?" Frank said. He had the MK23 out with the silencer screwed into place. "Guess they sent you a couple of spares as a bonus."

Omar nodded. When he finished his examinations he stood.

"Satisfied?"

"Yes. The money is in the case."

"Bring it to me."

Burns brought it over.

"Open it."

Burns opened it.

"Scan it again."

The Greek scanned the stacks of money. The scanner was silent.

"Just as we promised. Half the money. Twenty thousand dollars."

"Check the money."

Burns broke open the stacks and rifled through the money. He used a marker to check that the money wasn't counterfeit. Burns gave the nod to Frank.

"Greek, help Omar load two tubes and two missiles."

"Yes, sir."

The Greek put the top on each of the crates. He and Omar carried them back to the Suburban and slid them into the back. They weren't heavy, only unwieldy. Omar slammed the back of the Suburban. He returned to where Frank stood.

Frank raised the pistol. "That's close enough, Omar."

Frank handed Omar's phone and battery over. "Keep it short. English only. No Russian."

Omar dialed the number. Vlad answered immediately.

"Omar. Do they have the product?"

"Yes, Captain. It is all here."

Vlad heard their code word, captain. It meant Omar was not speaking under threat. If he used the term again it meant the deal was safe.

"Are you satisfied with the product?"

"Yes, Captain. Everything is fine. There are even two extra rockets." The excitement was evident in Omar's voice.

"What?" Vlad was stunned.

"It is true. There are five rockets. All are operational."

Vlad thought of the possibilities. They had planned to coordinate the three attacks, but if there were extra rockets? Each tube could be used up to five times before they expired. The options were endless. He could wait a month until things were quiet again and target air traffic again. It would be a powerful message of the weakness of the West. American business would grind to a halt. The world would speak of nothing except Chechnya.

"Very good, Omar."

Frank motioned for the phone. Omar passed it to him.

"We good?"

"Yes. You are a man of your word."

"Tomorrow night, same plan, different stops. Omar does the delivery. Both women, the kid, and the rest of my money for the other launcher and the last three rockets. Understand?"

"I understand. What is the cost of the other two missiles?"

"Zip. Zero. They weren't in our deal. I know you can't afford them so I'm giving them to you to say back off. After this goes down I don't want any blowback from you or your people. Our contract is fulfilled. Our contact is over. You stay away from your cousin."

"I understand. I will do as you ask. I thank you for this. You will never hear of me again after tomorrow."

"I am going to take Omar's phone. I don't want him tempted to call you on the way back. My men will drive him around for an hour or so to disorient him, and then we'll set him free with the SAMs. I'll call you tomorrow night same time. You try anything tricky. You break our rules. You will never see the rest of your product."

"You are a businessman. I can respect that. We can work together."

"Whoop-de-fucking do. I am honored. Just be ready tomorrow night. Any tricks and Omar takes a bullet."

"We will be ready."

Vlad thought about how he would enjoy killing this third man very slowly for what he had done. But that was a dish best served cold.

"May I speak with Omar once more?"

"Keep it brief."

Frank passed the phone back to Omar.

"You have done well. Do as he says and come back safely. We are almost done."

"Yes, Captain. Almost."

Vlad ended the call and Omar closed his phone. He handed it back to Frank. Frank popped out the battery and put it in his pocket again.

"Burns, cuff him."

Omar put his hands in front of him.

Frank laughed out loud. "Behind your back."

Omar put them behind his back. Burns put a zip cuff on his wrists and pulled it tight. Omar saw the sadness in his eyes. The West was pathetic, he thought. He wondered if this man could smell his woman on Omar. Omar smiled at his secret. She had tried to fight him, but with the stun gun her struggles were useless. She had been good fun. She would remember her time with Omar. Perhaps Vlad would allow him another taste before they released her.

The leader put the hood back over his head and guided him to the back seat again. Omar didn't resist and squirmed quietly on the seat trying to find a comfortable spot. He felt the barrel of a gun prod him. He didn't flinch. He was not afraid. They couldn't afford to kill him. It was a poor bluff. He was the driver for tomorrow. He had learned much. He was eager to tell Vlad what he had discovered. Omar's brain registered a distant popping sound. He died without a sound.

73

Frank wiped the gun barrel on Omar's shirt. He leaned back out of the car.
"Shit," Burns said.

"Poseidon's beard," the Greek added.

"Disable the missiles and launcher tubes as we discussed. No matter what happens these fuckers aren't getting their hands on SAMs. Then load everything into the back of the Suburban. Cover this fucker with a tarp."

Frank got out his cell phone and called DC. "You ready?"

"Yeah."

Frank walked to the car and read him the license number. He moved to the driver's seat as he waited.

"Sorry, big man. It comes back as a Honda Pilot from Oregon. Same place they got the cells."

"Try this." Frank read him the VIN number from the dashboard.

DC did whatever DC did. After a minute he said. "Negative. Suburban stolen out of Austin. That's too far."

Frank thought for a few seconds. "Tell me how to work his GPS to find home."

DC explained it. Frank worked the buttons. The route popped out clearly on the screen. Frank smiled.

"Can you back-trace the address for me? See what kind of neighborhood. Stuff like that."

"Frank, I can do better than that. Welcome to the twentieth century. You got access to a computer?"

Frank called to the Greek. "Your computer work?"

"Of course. Otherwise it would be no good to me. It's booted up if you need it."

"Password?"

"No. Just type what you need."

"I got a computer, DC. What next?"

"Easy, go to Google Earth. Type in the address and it will give you a satellite picture. It's not instant, but it is accurate. I got the house pulled up on mine right now. Try it."

Frank felt stupid. He didn't like feeling stupid. He followed DC's instructions and the house appeared on the screen. It was at the end of a dirt road. There were no nearby neighbors. The land around seemed barren and undeveloped. The house was three stories tall with a four-car garage and a large parking area in front of the house. It had a large covered front porch. There were balconies with sliding glass doors on the upper two floors. The house looked expensive. It was a good base of operations, isolated and secure. Frank was sure the people who lived there were dead. It was the only way the Russians could be sure they wouldn't cause problems.

Frank studied the satellite photo. There was a small hill along the east side of the property. It would offer a good vantage point. He could see where the long gravel driveway began and then curved back toward the house. Frank had to guess at the number of Russians left. If he had been planning this he would have organized three teams of four men. He would have a shooter, a spotter, a driver in the getaway vehicle, and a man for security. That meant at least twelve Russians. Three would have to have been trained with the Strela to be able to hit their targets. It took practice. Vlad had used six men to control Burns and the Greek. So it would be likely that he would not use more than half his force for that. So there were probably between a minimum of six and a maximum of ten men. Ten men would be a lot of bodies in the house. Of course they were soldiers, so they were used to bunkhouses and hardships. Still, Frank thought, eight was a better probability, fewer if they were lucky. Deduct Omar and the Russians were down to seven. Frank studied the photo for where he would put sentries. There were two obvious places. A third man could patrol the area around the house. He revised his plan of assault. There was only one way to find out.

"DC, you still there?"

"I'm here."

"Thanks, this is very helpful. But kind of disturbing that this is available on-line to anyone that wants it."

"They say the government spy satellites can read a newspaper over your shoulder…in your own house."

Frank didn't answer.

"Okay," DC said, "the 'in the house' part was supposed to be a joke."

"I figured. You going to check on the girls for me?"

"If you want me to, I will. I had planned to just stay here in case you really needed me."

"You've done enough. Forget the girls if you want the night off."

"I am kind of bushed."

"Hey, DC, thanks, man. I mean it. You came through big time."

DC smiled at the rare compliment. "Glad to be able to help, big man. Take it slow."

Frank cut his cell off. He went back into the main room of the warehouse.

Burns and the Greek were loading the SAMs into the back of the Suburban. They had been disabled, their electronics smashed. They covered the cases with a tarp. Both men were wearing their dark blue coveralls,their new boots, and gloves.

"We good to go?"

"Ready," the Greek said.

"Gloves the entire time," Frank said. "You can't afford to leave a single print."

Both men held up their hands to show they were wearing powderless blue Nitril gloves.

"Burns, you drive Omar's Suburban. I'll follow in the Mercedes. Greek, you follow me in your Suburban. Good spacing, but keep eye contact with the vehicle in front."

Both men nodded.

"Got your weapons? Each man takes an M4 and four magazines."

"Do we need so much ammo?" Burns asked.

"When you run out of ammunition, you are out of the fight. Better to have too much than not enough."

"Makes sense."

"Burns, take one of the silenced pistols too. Load only one magazine."

Burns went to do what Frank asked. Frank loaded his own M4 into the front seat of the Mercedes. He dropped the extra magazines on the front passenger's seat. He put the MK 23 and a spare clip for it into the glove box and closed it. He stepped into his coveralls and zipped them to his waist. He tied the arms around the waist. He started to get in, then paused. He went back to the SEAL armaments and took one of the special hatchets. He liked the feel of it. He tossed it onto the seat with the ammo. He covered it all with his jacket.

Burns and the Greek were standing beside their cars waiting.

"Listen up. There's a turnoff about half a mile from the house. Burns, pull over there. We'll park and I'll do a quick recon before we approach."

Both men nodded and got into their cars. The Greek opened the door with a remote and they drove out. It was about forty-five minutes away. They took the highway and headed north.

74

Agent Redding got in his car and pulled out. The park was about fifteen minutes away. Normally he would get to a rendezvous early. A couple of hours had always been the norm, but since someone was following him he thought it would be best if they didn't have time to bring in anybody else or set something up. Redding trusted his own instincts. He shifted the Glock in its holster where it was starting to dig into his hip.

He lit a cigarette and rolled the window down. He knew why a cig was a dying man's last request. They tasted so damn good.

Agent Harris watched Redding pull away from his house. It was odd behavior for a man who was supposedly too sick to work. He knew Redding had been lying. This just confirmed it. The transponder beeped in the seat beside him. He let Redding get out of sight before he cut on his lights and followed him. No reason to make Redding jumpy. The transponder was working perfectly. He would follow him from just out of sight. Harris removed his weapon and placed on the seat beside him for easy access. He didn't know what he was running into, but he was going to be ready for anything.

Brian parked across the street from Jenny and Caron's house. There was only one car in the driveway, a Volkswagon Beetle. It was yellow and the back window was covered with stickers: Roxy, girl bands, peace stickers.

"Park here," Zack said. "I'll go see what's up. If they're cool, I'll wave you guys over."

Morgan opened another beer and drank half of it in one gulp. "Hurry up. I'm getting wood just thinking about Caron's big lips."

"Which ones?" Zack asked and laughed.

Morgan laughed too. Brian didn't get it, but laughed anyway.

Zack got out and walked across the street to the house. He looked around. The street was quiet. He walked to the front door and rang the bell. He was nervous and excited. Nothing happened so he rang it again and waited.

Jenny and Caron heard the doorbell from the hot tub.

"Fuck," said Caron.

"Who do you think it is? Frank has a key."

"Must be DC. He decided to forgive us."

"Good. I'll let him in. You get dried off."

Caron giggled. "The sight of me in a bikini might be more than he can handle.

He might have to have me right then."

"What happened to all that just friends stuff?"

"I didn't finish. I would have to tell him, no. We are only friends. We can never be more than that."

"That's better," Jenny said. She pulled her robe on and went back inside the house. She was still drying her hair when she reached the front door. She opened it without checking the keyhole.

Zack smiled. It was a perfect smile. "Surprise." He noticed she was wet and added, "I get you out of the shower?"

Jenny was surprised. She hadn't expected to see the football player from the restaurant. "What are you doing here, Zack?"

"Wow, you remember my name. I'm flattered."

"Duh, it's only been a day. I'm not retarded. So what are you doing here?"

"We just won our big game against Page and I thought you might want to come celebrate with us. Come to a party or something."

"How did you find where I live?"

"It was easy. Brian got it off Google. You can find anything there."

"That's kind of stalker creepy."

"I'm sorry. I didn't mean to be. I just thought we had some kind of connection going the other night. I wanted to see you again. I apologize. I didn't mean to make you uncomfortable."

He was handsome, Jenny thought. She was a little flattered. "That's kind of sweet."

"I can be very sweet. Why don't you invite us in and we can party a little?"

"Us?"

"Brian and Morgan. They're waiting in the car. What do you say? I'll be good. I promise."

"I don't know. I could get in trouble."

He flashed his killer smile again. "Give me a chance."

Jenny was tempted. He was very handsome. An image of Frank flashed in her mind. He would kill her. She straightened up a little more.

"I can't. My uncle is gone. He would kill me."

"Come on. I just want to get to know you. I know you felt the spark too."

"I can't. I'm sorry. Call me. We'll go out."

Zack's tone changed so quickly it was like a switch had been flipped. "You are fucking kidding me."

Jenny fought to act like she hadn't noticed. "No. You can't come in. It's late. I was going to bed."

"You would rather go to bed than spend time with me? What kind of cock tease are you?"

Jenny stayed cool. "I'm sorry if you think I was leading you on. Call me tomorrow."

Zack put his hand on the door. "I say we come in and party. You'll have fun. You know you want to."

Jenny saw the red glaze to his eyes. He was on something. She smiled. "Okay, Zack. You are a hard man to say no to. Tell your friends to come over. But just for a little while."

"Now you're talking, babe."

Zack turned and waved to the car and instantly Jenny slammed the door and locked it. She set the deadbolt and put the chain on the door. Zack spun as the door closed. He knew he had been tricked.

Zack pounded on the door. "You fucking bitch. No one slams a door in my face. You cunt."

Brain and Morgan were outside the car. They stopped when they saw the door slam.

"This is bullshit. You fucking whore. You fucking cunt whore," Zack screamed and beat on the door.

When Jenny didn't reopen the door, he turned and stormed across the street back to the car.

"What's going on?" Morgan asked, a fresh beer in his beefy hand.

"Fucking cunt. She shut the fucking door in my face. She tricked me."

"What do you mean?" Brian said.

"She said we were welcome to come party. When I turned around to signal you guys she shut the door. The stinking whore."

"Damn," Brian said. "I was really hoping."

"Man," Morgan said. "I was looking forward to some of that puss. Well, fuck it. Let's go back to the party."

"It wasn't Caron. It was just Jenny. Little miss goody two shoes. For all we know Caron still wants to party with the man."

Morgan finished his beer. Zack shook out some more cocaine and did a bump. He shook out some more and offered it to Morgan who snorted it up. He motioned to Brian who shook his head no. Zack stood staring back at the house.

"Come on," Brian said as he opened the driver's door. "We better go."

"What are you talking about?" Zack snapped.

"If we aren't going to get laid, we might as well go back to the party like Morgan said."

"Fuck that. We are getting laid right here."

"They locked the door. If we go back, they'll call the cops. You guys can't risk that. You'll lose your scholarships."

Zack stood staring. His rage growing. He smiled. He went to his dark place. "I got an idea."

"What?" Morgan asked.

"Jenny was all wet when she came to the door. I thought she had been in the shower, but now that I think about it she smelled a little like chlorine. You get it?"

Morgan and Brian looked at each other, totally confused.

"She wasn't in the shower. She was out back in a swimming pool or hot tub. That's why she took so long getting to the door."

"How does that change anything?" Brian asked.

"Well, dumb ass, if they're outside, they can't call the cops. We just slip around back and ask again."

"I don't know," Brian said.

"Pussy. Sometimes women want to be pursued. They say no until you get them to say yes. Don't you know anything?"

"You think Caron's back there too?" Morgan asked.

"I'm sure of it. Come on. You remember the way she flirted with you. She wants you."

Morgan grinned and nodded to the erotic images in his head.

"They might turn us in to the cops later," Brian said.

"Then it's just their word against ours. We can say they invited us back to go skinny dipping."

"Yeah," Morgan added. "They said they liked it rough."

"Now you're getting it. You know once you put that big thing in Caron she's going to love it."

Morgan squeezed his cock through his pants. "You got that right, bro. She can't say no if her mouth is full."

"Let's go get our celebration fuck."

Brian looked nervous. "This is crazy. We're going to get into a lot of trouble."

Zack grabbed his shirt and slammed him against the car. "You want to hang with the big dogs, you have to get off the porch."

"I don't want to go to jail."

Zack released him. He brushed his rumpled shirt out. "Okay. You may be right. I'll tell you what. You stay here and keep a lookout. Somebody shows up, you call me so we can get the hell out."

Brian started nodding. "I can do that for you."

"Good man. You got our back, right?"

"Right."

"Cool. That's what friends do. You ready big Morgan?"

"All set."

"Brian, if Jenny gets hot enough, I may call you to come over and get a slice. You still up for that?"

"Sure," Brian said, but he didn't sound enthusiastic.

Morgan and Zack started across the street at a jog. Brian watched them go. He knew this wasn't going to end well. He didn't know what to do. He felt scared and sick. He walked behind his mother's Honda and threw up in somebody's yard.

75

Frank checked his watch. They were on schedule. He watched Burns' tail-lights up ahead. He was proud that Burns was driving the speed limit. Stress tended to pump up the adrenaline and a heavy foot usually resulted from it. He checked his rear view mirror. He could see the Greek's headlights.

The county sheriff's car met Burns in Omar's Suburban. He noticed the half burning left headlight. He wondered if the driver knew it. He slowed his car down and did a quick u-turn. He turned on his light bar. Best plan was to pull him over and let him know. He could get it fixed tomorrow.

Burns saw the flashing lights. He didn't know what to do. There was no other traffic. The sheriff was definitely coming for him. He put on his turn signal and slowed down. He knew Frank would know what to do. He pulled to the side of the road and stopped.

Frank didn't know what to do. Something about Burns' driving had attracted the cop's attention. He was closing fast. Frank knew that when the sheriff approached Burns' car he would see the tarp in the back seat. He would immediately call for backup. Frank knew he could kill the man, but he didn't want to. He had nothing against police officers. They were just working stiffs like everybody else. Trying to make a living doing a dangerous job. He respected their dedication to a job that was growing more dangerous all the time and paid poorly to boot. He had to do something.

The sheriff's deputy was already out of his car and was walking toward the Suburban. Frank turned on his high beams. He flipped on his emergency flashers and started blowing the horn. He was glad to see it wasn't a highway patrolman. They were tough. They rode alone like old-timey Western lawmen. They were suspicious from years on the road. He was also glad it wasn't a female officer. They had gotten where they were by being better than the men who tried to stop them. A lot of them had chips on their shoulders. They too were very suspicious. The sheriff's deputy was older. Frank guessed in his fifties. He was a little paunchy. His hair was gray. He moved with the rolling gait of a man who tried to manage his weight.

The deputy turned as Frank stopped the car in a spray of dust. Policemen were trained to never position themselves in front of a vehicle where they could be hit. They would stand to the right front of a car to keep out of the line of fire. They would approach the driver's door only to a certain distance. They did not want to be in a position where they could be struck by an opening door.

The officer walked back toward the Mercedes. Frank needed to draw him closer for his plan to work. He reached into his jacket pocket and grabbed the stun gun.

Frank opened his car door and started to step out. He stumbled into the door and croaked, "Help me. My heart."

It was the only thing Frank could think of. A fifty-year-old overweight man would understand the risk of heart attacks. Stumbling near the door would disguise Frank's size. The Mercedes should soothe some of the deputy's inherent fear. Frank hit the ground. He moaned and put a hand to his chest. The deputy hurried to help him. He knelt quickly beside Frank's body.

The deputy sheriff heard the snap of electricity more than felt the charge running through his body. He fell and tried to regain his knees. He heard the snap again and everything went black.

When he came to, Hubert Ellisor was in the back of his cruiser. His hands were zip cuffed behind him. His legs had been wrapped with duct tape. His eyes were taped closed. He felt the cold barrel of a gun against his neck.

A voice said, "Lay still." The voice shouted into the distance. "Ensign, return to your vehicle. Officer, we have special authorization. Mission parameters authorize collateral damage when deemed appropriate for mission success. I do not wish to kill you. Do you understand?"

"Yes."

"Are you stable? Do you have any heart issues?"

"I take blood pressure meds, but I feel okay. Had bypass two years back."

"Roger that. Does your vehicle have a lo-jack device?"

"No."

The handgun poked him hard.

"Wait. Yes, it does. I don't know where it is or how to disable it."

"Roger. When was the last roll call?"

"Less than an hour ago."

"How long until it's repeated?"

"Two hours."

"Your personal radio has been disabled. Did you call in the stop of the vehicle?"

"Yes."

"What are the codes for off air?"

"I got a cheat sheet on the side of the car's computer. The access codes, and response codes are on it."

"Thank you."

He heard the person enter the front seat and begin typing on the computer.

The voice again to someone in the distance.

"Lieutenant, exit the convoy and follow me on my six. We will rendezvous back here."

The cruiser turned around. They drove for probably ten minutes before he felt them leave the main road. A few minutes later the car stopped.

The man returned to the back seat.

"I've removed you to a safe place. When they are unable to reach you on the radio they will send out a car to find you. The lo jack should bring them to you. I apologize for our rough handling. It's a matter of national security, I assure you. I'm going to tape your mouth so you can't call out. Is there anything else I can do for you?"

"Yeah. Could you turn me a little more on my side? I got a bad knee and this position is killing it."

"Roger."

"Thanks," he said.

"I've opened a window to keep the heat down."

"Thanks."

The man taped his mouth shut, being careful not to cover his nose. "Can you breathe all right?"

Ellisor nodded.

"Roger that."

He heard the man exit the cruiser. The last thing he heard was a second vehicle stopping.

"We need to hurry, lieutenant. ETA is compromised."

The car pulled away. The deputy tried to relax. He knew they would find him. He would just have to be patient. He tried to breathe slowly.

76

Agent Redding parked in the small lot. He took out his FBI-issue night vision binoculars and surveyed the park below. There was a man passed out on the ground near the carousel. There were two women drinking from a bottle in a bag. There was no one else. He left his car and went down to the park. A bench directly under a streetlight had been painted red. Fucking Spartans, he thought. He approached the red bench. There was a folder on it.

He picked it up. The cover read Agent Redding: Open. He did. The first page was a picture of him taken through his front window. It was taken that day. In the picture Agent Redding was smoking. The second page was another picture it was his partner, Agent Harris, parked in a cul-de-sac near his house. The heading said, TODAY. The next page said, Sit Down.

Redding looked around. No one seemed interested in him at all. The passed out man could be a plant. Could be anyone. While he watched, the two women laughed. One was blonde, the other brunette. They leaned in and kissed each other.

Redding sat down. He heard a click. Nothing happened. He flipped to the next page. It read: Keep sitting. You have activated an explosive device. If you attempt to rise it will go off. Continue reading the file. All will become obvious.

Redding's heart hammered in his chest. He concentrated on trying to breathe slowly. He hoped it would slow his heart rate. Redding checked his watch. It was 11:15. He started back on the file. The file contained pictures of Agent Harris and his father, the senator. They also contained pictures of Agent Harris and Cyrus. There were pictures of the Senator with Cyrus. There were pictures of the Assistant Director of the FBI with Cyrus. There were copies of telephone transcripts that might or might not be fakes. There were copies of deposits made in Agent Harris' or his father's name or the AD's name. Again they could all be fakes. The file purported to document Harris' and his father's extensive involvement with Cyrus. There were pages of information that Redding didn't understand. There was another page of pictures. The last page simply said, Stay seated. He will come.

Redding folded the file closed and leaned back on the bench. It was time to wait. He closed his eyes. It was starting to make sense at least.

Harris watched the scene from his own car with his own government-issue binoculars. He didn't understand what was going on. Redding was sitting on a bench. He seemed to be sleeping. There was some kind of file in his lap. There was a homeless man asleep and a couple of old lesbian hookers down near the restroom. No one else. He watched and waited. Finally, he left his car and went down to see.

77

Frank, Burns and the Greek parked where Frank had told them to park. He got out and approached the Greek's car. Burns was already outside.

"Do we still have time?"

Frank nodded. "We still got a window."

"Did you kill him?" Burns asked.

"No," Frank said. "There was no need to kill him. He was just doing his job."

"Good," Burns said.

"What do you want us to do?" the Greek asked.

"Stay here. I'm going to check out the house. See if there are sentries stationed outside. I will come back. Wait. Don't do anything. Don't go anywhere."

Both men nodded. Frank pulled his coveralls up and zipped them. He put the spare magazines into his outside pockets. He tucked the tomahawk into the back of the belt he had fastened around his waist. He pulled his balaclava down. He didn't want to risk a night reflection off his skin. He used the night vision and thermal scope to sweep the terrain ahead of him. He moved off into the scrub brush.

Frank was huge, but he moved without a sound. Each step was perfectly balanced. Each movement slow. Apollo called it noise discipline. He would move a few steps and sweep the area before him. The sound of thunder hid what little noise he made. The storm had been threatening for days, but not a drop of rain yet.

Frank had studied the terrain on Google. He knew where he needed to go. It was the best spot for a sentry. There was a second spot that was also excellent. Frank moved another hundred yards. He swung the M4 up. He could feel the sentry. He spotted his thermal signature on the ridge ahead. He watched the man. He was smoking a cigarette. He appeared to be focused on the driveway.

Poor training or laziness, Frank didn't know which. There was a slight breeze brought on by the approaching storm. Frank raised the M4. It was a simple shot, but he hesitated. There were too many unknowns. If he missed. If the man moved. If there was someone close enough to see or hear him fall. He shouldered the rifle and crept forward. He could see the glow of the cigarette in the twilight. When the cigarette died, the man lit another one.

The rain started. It was only a drizzle. The air felt wet and heavy. It hinted at the storm brewing. Frank moved forward until he was twenty feet away. The sentry was huddled near a large bush. He was trying to shield his cigarette from the rain. Frank swept the area with the night vision scope. No one was there. He slipped the weapon over his shoulder on its sling. He rose and took long quick strides toward the seated man. He covered the distance in under a second and a half. The man never saw him. The man never heard him. Frank raised the toma-hawk and drove the spike straight down into the top of the sentry's skull. The man shook and twitched for a few seconds. He made no sound. The cigarette smoldered on the ground at his feet. Frank stepped on the tip, crushing it. He scoped the surrounding countryside. There were two large SUVs and a smaller Lexus parked in the driveway. He scanned the house. He could see people moving inside, but they were unclear. He watched the area behind the house. He saw a man hurrying in to the back of the house, probably trying to stay out of the rain.

Frank eased back over the ridge and then when he felt it was safe he jogged back to where Burns and the Greek were waiting.

"What did you see?" the Greek asked.

"They're inside waiting for Omar."

"Any sentries?"

"No," Frank lied. "They must all be inside."

He looked at Burns. "You ready?"

"I think so."

"Think so won't cut it. You got to man up if you want to get your wife back in one piece. You good to go?"

Burns nodded. "Good to go."

"Just like we talked. Pull the hat low over your face. Park away from the front door. There's a spot just past the Lexus. As soon as you get the car stopped, slump forward over the steering wheel."

"What if no one comes to the door?"

"They will. They have to. They think you're Omar. You might have been shot. Just stay down until someone opens the car door on your side."

Frank glanced to the passenger side doors. They were locked.

"Keep your door unlocked. They won't be looking into the back seat. If they do they'll only be glancing back there. When your door is opened, shoot whoever is standing there."

"What if they send more than one?"

"They won't. They're all military men. They are disciplined. Most will mass on the front porch. It doesn't change anything. You got thirteen bullets. You just point and shoot until no more bullets come out. Drop the pistol. Grab your M4 off the front seat. You will have a few seconds before the others figure out what is happening. Get around to the front of the car. Get behind a wheel. Put as much metal between you and them as you can. They got nothing that can punch through an engine block and a wheel. You'll be safe. Don't panic. They will return fire."

"And you and the Greek will catch them in a crossfire, right?"

"Right. Like we talked about. Then we get the hostages out."

"And I don't go inside?"

"No. You stay out front. Shoot anyone that comes out the front door. Only bad guys will try to go out the front."

"Got it. I can do this."

"I know you can. We're going to get into position. Check your watch. In five minutes you drive up to the house. Not too fast. Not too slow. Keep your head down. They will see the headlights and recognize the car. Just wait for the car's door to be opened and fling lead."

Burns stuck out his hand. Frank shook it.

The Greek shook it as well.

"Good luck."

"You too."

The Greek followed Frank into the scrub.

78

Zack could hear that bitch Kelly Clarkson singing. Fucking whiner, he thought. He would give five bucks to slap that frown off her fat face. She just needed a good fucking. That would put her right. Morgan was close on his heels. There was no swimming pool. There was a big hot tub on a screened-in porch. Even better.

"Hey, ladies," Zack called as he reached the door. "Come out and play."

Jenny gasped. She knew this was not going to end well. She looked and saw the door was locked. It gave them time.

Zack grabbed the handle and tried to open the door. The latch held.

Caron hurried over and picked up the baseball bat. "Get the fuck out of here!" she screamed.

"Now is that any way to act?" Zack said. "Aren't you going to invite us in?"

"No. Now get out of here before we call the cops."

"You are so rude. Didn't your mommas teach you how to act?"

"She's right, Zack. Go now and we won't tell anyone about this," Jenny said.

Zack smiled. "You say that now, but I don't think you really want us gone. You're just playing hard to get. Morgan, get this door open for me."

Morgan jerked hard on the door handle, but it held. He laughed and punched a hand through the screen. He grabbed the doorframe and wrenched it backwards. The frame broke. Zack and Morgan hurried inside. They split up and approached the two girls.

"You sure are pretty," Morgan said looking at Caron.

"Get away from me," Caron warned, brandishing her bat.

"Come on. Give me a kiss. I know you like me."

"One more step and I'll knock your head in."

Morgan smiled. He grabbed the table in front of him and tossed it aside. He reached her before she could swing and ripped the bat from her hands. He tossed it back toward the door. He pulled her into his arms and started trying to kiss her. Caron spit into his face and Morgan slapped her hard. Her legs buckled. He was so strong. He lifted her up and pushed her back against the side of the hot tub.

Zack grabbed the front of Jenny's robe and pulled her toward him. Jenny slapped him hard across the face. Zack's eyes flared and he slammed her back against the side of the house twice. Sparks exploded behind her eyes. Jenny's knees felt weak. She tried to clear her head.

"Don't ever raise your hand to me, bitch. Do you understand?"

Jenny shook her head to clear it. Zack slipped his hands around her waist and pulled her close.

"I am going to fuck you so good, you will never want another man."

"Stop. Let me go. This has gone far enough."

Zack grinned and turned toward Morgan. "Big M, has this gone far enough?" Morgan laughed.

"I don't think we have got started good yet," Morgan said. He pulled Caron's bikini top up and tried to kiss her breasts. She beat on his shoulders, but he didn't seem to notice.

Zack laughed. "That looks like fun, Jenny. Let's go inside where we can have a little more privacy."

"Don't. Please," Jenny begged.

Zack slapped her. He held his finger in her face. "Never tell me no. Never. Morgan, I'm taking this bitch inside for playtime. You solid?"

Morgan spun Caron around and shoved her against the hot tub. He unbuckled his pants. "Go ahead, bro. I'm doing this little chick right here. I wait any longer I'll cum in my pants."

Caron started crying. Morgan pulled her bikini bottom down, but it rolled back up, so Morgan tore the strings on the side. He tossed her bikini bottom toward the door. Zack laughed. He grabbed Jenny by her hair.

"Now get inside, bitch. This can hurt or it can feel real good. It's your choice."

79

Harris walked down to where Redding was sitting.

"What are you doing, Agent Redding?"

Redding didn't open his eyes.

"Agent Redding, what are you doing here?"

Redding opened one eye and then the other. "Harris. I can't say I am surprised to see you."

"I asked you a question, Agent Redding."

"I'm supposed to meet Masnick here tonight."

"Is he here?" Harris asked looking around.

"Not yet. Did you bug my car?"

"No."

Redding removed a cigarette. There was only one left in the pack. He tucked the pack back into his jacket. He lit the cigarette and blew a smoke ring. Harris watched him. "Sit down, Harris. We have a lot to talk about."

"What's in the file?"

Redding glanced at the file. "Incriminating stuff. Claims you and your father, the esteemed United States senator, are in league with Cyrus. Says your dad was cozy with the Spartans for a very long time. Bribery. Collusion. General bad behavior."

"Hand it over."

Redding passed it to him. "Here you go. Check out pages two and three."

Harris flipped through the pages. He read the headline. "You're sitting on a bomb?"

"It would appear so."

Harris pulled his gun. "Remove your weapon, Agent Redding. Left hand. Two fingers."

Redding shook his head and did it.

"Toss it away."

Redding did.

"Who else knows about this?"

"Masnick. He left it for me in the park when he rigged the bomb, I expect."

"Are there other copies?"

"I would expect so. Masnick is very thorough. So it's true?"

Harris thrust the gun toward Redding, "More or less. Dad was working for the Spartans. Cyrus wanted all the files and evidence the FBI had destroyed. Dad made it happen. His top aide is very good."

"That's a long-range plan. You go into the Bureau as part of it from the start?"

"Cyrus sees the big picture. Pieces were put into place."

"But he didn't know about Masnick, did he?"

"No. That was a shocker. They'll find him soon enough. He can't just disappear."

"He's pretty good at it."

"Cyrus is concerned that there may be other information in your personal files that he needs to see."

"It's a fool's quest. I got nothing he needs to be afraid of."

"Where are your files?"

"I can hardly show you now, can I?"

"I will shoot you where you sit."

"What if I fall over? What then? We both go boom."

"It might be a fake. There might not even be a bomb."

"True. Can you risk it?"

Harris looked around. He didn't know what he should do. He took out his cell and called his father. The phone rang unanswered. He was spooked. The phone was always answered. If his dad didn't take it, the aide did; they were inseparable.

"Listen, Harris, I'm not a threat to you or your father or the Spartans. I got nothing. You want my records? You can have them. The file is a warning. It's Masnick's way of saying back off. Stop looking for him or he will bring you down. Let it go. That's all the proof he has right there in that file. He's making his case. I know him. Let it drop and he goes away. Tell Cyrus to let it drop. He's safe wherever he is."

Harris raised the pistol.

"You really want to do this? You really want to murder an agent of the FBI? Do you have any idea the kind of heat that will generate? What about the witnesses? They're pretty close. I guess you can do them too. What are a few more bodies? But that will interest the Bureau even more. They will look into this. Someone smarter than me may figure it out."

"You might be wrong. You've already shown yourself to be a liar."

"What if I am? You can always find me again if I don't get blown to shreds. I'm not going anywhere."

Harris looked at the two women. Their bottle was empty. The brunette tossed it into the woods. The blonde started kissing her again. The homeless man lay still in the shadows.

"Go home," Redding said. "Take the file. Talk to your dad and Cyrus. See what they think you should do. There's no step back once you pull that trigger."

Harris nodded to the voice of reason. "Okay. I'll take your advice. Don't make me sorry I let you live."

Redding smoked the rest of his cigarette. "I'll give you ten minutes to clear out before I call the bomb squad."

"How do you explain this?" Harris asked.

"Mostly the truth. I got a note to meet Masnick. He didn't show. Sat on a bomb. Called for backup."

"No file? No me? No discussion about the contents of the file?"

"Of course not. Who would I tell that would believe me without proof? Your dad is too powerful to throw unfounded allegations at. The same for the AD. You're safe. Go home. Figure it out."

Harris turned and quickly walked from the parking lot. Redding watched him reach his car and climb inside. In moments he was gone. The two women walked toward the bench.

"Have a seat, Prometheus," Redding said.

The blonde smiled. "That obvious?"

"Yeah."

"Deborah. Go run that little errand. I'll see you at the car."

The brunette kissed Masnick again. She was the lady from the bar. She was still hot.

"You make it difficult to talk with you in private."

"Sorry about that," Redding said. "I didn't know it was you."

Masnick sat down. "That was a nice little speech you gave Agent Harris."

"Thanks."

"Did you believe it?"

"No. Harris wanted to. Maybe he had to believe it. He's dirty. Running out of options. He needed to think he could control this."

Masnick laughed. "He never figured out you were dirty too."

Redding grimaced and got out his last cigarette. Masnick lit it for him.

"Our relationship has benefited you, Agent Redding."

"Yes, it has. Without your money my sister couldn't have gotten the cancer treatment she needed. She didn't have any insurance. She was up against it."

"Yet you violated your oath and the law by taking money from me."

"I did. I don't regret it."

"Even when your sister only lasted another year?"

"Even so. It gave here a chance she wouldn't have had. Family first."

"Very noble. And never anything for yourself."

"I didn't need anything else from you, Prometheus."

"In exchange for the money, you allowed me to help guide the FBI investigation away from my interests. You gave me information that compromised your cases."

"I know all that. What's the point in rehashing it? You got immunity."

"I've kept your involvement with me secret as I had promised. But that has to end now. Cyrus knows I've betrayed the Spartans. He will be looking for me. I have to disappear."

"I can't say I hate to see our relationship end."

Masnick shrugged. "No reason to keep my secrets anymore."

"Where did Deborah go?"

"She's dropping a second copy of the file off in your car. It will support your story better during the investigation."

"Where's the kid's father?"

Masnick pointed toward the homeless man.

"Fewer people to contradict your story. The aide is at their house."

"That was nice of you."

"Yes, it was. I value neatness."

"The homeless outfit was a nice touch."

"I'm glad you liked it. I felt it gave an ironic slant to the scene."

"It does. When will I get the file that incriminates me?"

"Do not fret, Agent Redding. I'll keep it safe for you. Continue to protect me and I will continue to protect it."

"They will look for you after this."

"They can't find me. I'm not afraid of them."

"So I'm a safeguard in case I am in position to help."

"More or less. Your discretion is something I always appreciated, Agent Redding. Perhaps this time you will get the promotion they overlooked the last time. The Assistant Director's job appears to be opening up."

Masnick pulled a cell phone from inside his dress. He punched in a number. He looked at Redding.

"Do you want to do the honors?"

Redding shook his head.

Masnick pressed the send button. There was a second's pause before they heard the explosion off in the distance.

"Harris?"

Masnick nodded. "Had to be done. He was too volatile. This was becoming too personal for him."

Redding nodded. "Is there really a bomb under this bench?"

Masnick smiled.

"Yes. I wasn't sure how reasonable you would be. I needed to get your attention."

"You could still trigger it remotely."

"Of course. But why would I wish you dead, Agent Redding?"

"Because you are a paranoid sociopath?"

"Think about that while you wait."

"Can I ask you something, Prometheus?"

"What?"

"Are the Spartans really reforming?"

Masnick looked off into the distance. "Some elements never disappeared."

"Cyrus?"

"He is the king of the gods. How could he ever die?"

"And his queen."

Masnick laughed. "I hear only rumors. Who is to say? She was almost too beautiful to be taken from this Earth. If she is alive she is with him."

"And Frank Kane?"

Redding saw Masnick tremble. "He is a true believer. He has slept for a long, time, but people whisper he is waking again. They say he is seeking those who betrayed the Spartans. I am not sure if I believe them."

"Does he know who made the deals? Who doomed his brothers?"

"I don't know. But Cyrus is afraid."

"Should he be? Kane is only one man."

Masnick smiled. "Frank Kane is not a man. He is a force of nature. If he believes Cyrus betrayed him, he will seek him out."

"And kill him?"

"Yes. Of course."

"And you? You betrayed the Spartans as well."

Masnick smiled and shrugged. "Yes, and me too."

"Where is Frank Kane? How can I find him?"

Masnick smiled. "You know the old saying. Speak the devil's name and he shall appear."

"And Sandy, why kill her now?"

"She had suffered so long. I had to leave. She needed to be freed."

"I understand. It was a mercy."

Masnick stood. "I still have friends. I still have connections. Do not look for me. I don't ever wish to see you again. Agent Redding. If I do it will not be pleasant for you."

Redding smiled. "A final request of the Fire Walker."

Masnick turned. "What is it?"

"Can you spare me another cig before you go? I'm out."

Masnick laughed. He wiggled his dress down where it had ridden up on his hips and walked away. Over his shoulder he shouted, "I don't smoke. It's bad for your health."

80

Frank and the Greek took up flanking spots to the east of the house. Frank remembered an ancient quote. "The arrow does not regret its flight." A Japanese Samurai wrote it, but Frank liked to think it applied equally to the Spartans. You made your plan. You found your target and you moved ahead. There was no place for regret or second-guessing. There was a moment when you could no longer turn back. That moment was now.

Frank turned to the Greek.

"Don't panic. Control your fire rate. Keep it on semiautomatic. Once the firefight starts, I will break off and go inside on the second floor. I will find the hostages."

"Remember, you promised not to hurt my wife."

"I remember. Anyone comes out the back of the house or the front, take them down. When it's over I'll bring the hostages to that balcony on the second floor," Frank said and pointed.

"That's where you're going in?"

"Yes. Anyone, anywhere else is an enemy."

"I am ready."

He heard the Suburban approaching. He raised the M4 to his shoulder. Frank smiled. It was good to be going to war with men again. He still wished he had Bobby Z or The Jake with him. He felt a moment's regret for Apollo. In some way he thought he had failed his friend. If he had been quicker or better or smarter, Apollo would not be dead now. The Suburban pulled into the parking lot and parked where Frank had told Burns to park.

Russians appeared on the porch. They hollered at the Suburban in Russian. Shouted Omar's name. They looked from one to another. A tall man in the center motioned for one of the men to check the car. He lifted a small walkie-talkie and pressed a button.

In the darkness where the dead sentry was, Frank thought he heard the click of the call.

The tall man was calling again. A Russian reached the passenger's side door and tried it. He beat on the window. The man hurried around to the driver's side.

The tall man shouted something in Russian. The man at the car turned back toward the porch. He put one hand on the door handle and drew his pistol with the other. He slowly opened the door.

81

DC parked in front of Frank's house. He felt bad. He had let Frank down. He had let the girls down. He had been a pussy all day avoiding their calls and text messages. They all needed to sit down and talk. He got out of his car and spotted a teenager parked across the street watching him. The kid started toward him as he got out of his car, then turned around and headed toward a parked car on the other side of the street. DC followed him.

"Hey, kid, what you doing?"

Brian said, "Nothing. Who are you? What are you doing here?"

"My friends live in that house."

The kid couldn't hide his shock. "You need to get out of here," Brian said.

"What are you talking about?"

"Listen, man. My friends are over there partying with those girls right now. They went around back. They'll be pissed if you ruin it for them."

"Who cares if they get pissed?"

"They're big deal football players. That got scholarships and everything. They don't like people messing with them."

"Tough. If you know what's good for you, you'll get out of here before the cops show up."

Brian looked around confused. "Cops? Why would the cops be coming? You didn't call them. You didn't have time."

DC ran to the nearest parked car and jumped on it. Nothing happened. He ran to the next car and slammed into it. The car alarm went off. He jumped against the next car and a second car alarm went off. Lights came on in the houses nearby. DC ran across the road toward the back yard.

He saw the destroyed door and a huge punk on top of Caron. He had to be three hundred pounds. DC could see the fear on Caron's face. DC grabbed the baseball bat. "Let the girl go."

"Run along, dude. Or you might get hurt," Morgan said

"Let her go."

Morgan let Caron go. She slumped to the floor pulling up pieces of her torn bathing suit. He turned toward DC. "You think that scares me, you fucking pissant?"

"I'm not warning you again."

Morgan took a small step toward DC. DC raised the bat like he had in Little League as a kid.

"You got one shot with that toothpick. You can't take me out with one shot.

Then I'll get hold of you and break you in half."

"I'm not going to try to knock your dumb ass out. I'm going for one of those big fat knees. Blow one of those babies and let's see if you keep your precious football scholarship."

Zack came through the door, dragging Jenny by the arm. "What's with all those car alarms?" he asked. "And who the hell are you?" he said, spotting DC.

Zack's phone rang in his pocket. He let go of Jenny and pulled it out. There was a text message from Brian on the screen. It said: Cops are coming.

Before he could pocket the phone, Jenny grabbed a fist full of his dark hair. She jerked his head backward. He felt something against his neck. It didn't hurt, but he could feel a little pressure.

"Don't even breathe hard you motherfucker. This blade is right against your carotid artery. One move and I'll bleed you out."

Zack laughed. "Morgan, what's this whore got against my neck?"

"Bro, it's some kind of knife."

"Bullshit."

"Zack, your neck is already covered in blood. She ain't fooling."

DC hefted the bat. "What's it going to be? You make a run for it now, you might beat the cops. You stay and fight, then people will get hurt. Die maybe. People will go to jail."

Morgan looked scared. Sirens sounded in the distance.

"Come on man, let's roll. I can hear the cops."

Zack howled like an animal in pain.

"Don't listen to them, Zack," Jenny whispered in his ear. "Call my bluff. See if I'll do it. I'm just a little bitch. I probably don't have the nerve."

"All right, we're going," Zack said.

DC stepped to one side and Morgan ran out zipping his cargo shorts. Jenny let go of Zack's hair. He turned and looked at her. She held the knife easily in front of her. There was blood on the blade. Jenny smiled. Zack wiped his neck and saw his fingers come back red. He snarled at her and ran from the porch into the night.

Caron ran to DC. She wrapped her arms around him. She was crying. DC held her close. Jenny closed the knife and slipped it into her robe again. She felt good. The adrenaline rush was still strong. She felt powerful. Caron started kissing DC's cheeks and head. The kisses quickly moved to his mouth. DC returned them.

Caron kept saying, "You saved us. You saved us."

Caron took DC's hand and led him into the house. She pulled him upstairs toward her bedroom. DC resisted but then let her lead him upstairs where he wanted to go.

Jenny watched them go. She didn't care. Not really. She locked the door to the house and followed them upstairs. She went into Frank's room and crawled into his empty bed. She pulled the covers up around her neck and closed her eyes. She relived the look on Zack's face when she showed him the knife. She felt fantastic.

82

The door pulled open. The Russian said something Burns couldn't understand. The Russian spoke again. There was a note of anger in his voice. Burns turned slightly in the seat. He pointed the pistol and squeezed the trigger on the MK23.

The Russian fell away. Burns heard no sound from the gun in his hand. Everything was silence. When the gun stopped firing, he dropped the pistol and reached inside the Suburban for the M4. He stumbled out of the car as he pulled the weapon to him. He crab-walked to the front of the Suburban. Rain beat down at him in huge silent drops. Shards of glass sprayed him from the bullets hitting the windshield. He heard nothing. He stayed down. He breathed deeply as Frank had told him. Sound returned. It was loud and full of fury.

The tall Russian knew there was a problem. The sentry, Klein, was many things, but he was a soldier. He would not abandon his post. His mind ran the data. He knew something had gone wrong. When the Russian he sent to Omar fell, he realized he did not need to understand to respond. The two men on the porch with him raised their pistols and began firing at the one they thought was Omar. The tall man lunged back inside the doorway as Frank and the Greek opened fire.

The flanking fire from Frank and the Greek swept the porch. One Russian was cut in half. The second Russian fell from two rounds. One hit his leg, the other his shoulder. He fired wildly. He didn't know where the firing was coming from.

Frank tapped the Greek on his shoulder. He moved toward the side of the house where the electrical box was. The night scopes were an advantage. In a house without light they were absolutely lethal. Frank let the M4 hang from its strap and took out the tomahawk. He moved quickly toward his objective, the electrical cable. A Russian stepped around from the back of the house. He was carrying an AK-47. Frank didn't think. There wasn't time. He only responded. The tomahawk was like a knife in his hands. It was only a tool. Frank knew that Special Forces were well trained. They would have spent hundreds of hours mastering the nuances of tomahawk fighting. They would be taught how and where to strike. Frank's skill was his speed and strength.

Frank swung like a baseball player. The axe moved as it was constructed. The tapered head concentrated the force along the cutting edge. The blade caught the Russian beneath his chin and traveled through the thick neck muscles like they weren't there. There was only a hint of resistance as it sheared the spinal column. The force of the blow sent the head in one direction, the body fell in the opposite direction.

Frank turned away as the body fell. He stepped to the electrical cables running into the house. He buried the tomahawk into the thick wires. Sparks sputtered out and the house fell dark. Frank knew it would be a morale crusher. He didn't expect what he heard next from inside the house.

"Kill the hostages," Vlad shouted.

Frank moved back toward the little hill near the second floor balcony. He ran and leaped. His fingers caught the lower edge of the balcony. He pulled himself up and over the rail. He tried the handle on the sliding glass door. He looked down and saw the bar placed to keep the door from being forced open. Frank kicked the heavy glass with his big boot. The glass didn't break, but it fell backward out of the frame. Frank stepped into the bedroom.

There was a woman on the bed. She screamed as he entered. He had found one of the hostages. He hesitated for a moment as the bedroom door burst open. Frank turned as the Russian stepped into the room. He fired twice and hit Frank center mass with both bullets. Frank stumbled backward and fell. The Russian turned the pistol toward the outline of the woman and fired a single round.

Frank was surprised. Not just because he had been shot, although that was a shock. He was surprised the bulletproof vest had worked. Even with the Greek's assurances he had doubted its ability. His chest ached and feeling was gone in his legs. His body was struggling to reboot his system. He raised the M4 from where he was lying and sent a swath of bullets across the doorway. The Russian shouted and fell outside the door.

Frank got to his knees and then his feet. He moved to the bed. He put a hand on the woman. She was sobbing. His chest ached.

"Are you all right?"

"He tried to shoot me."

"Did he hit you?"

"No. I don't think so."

"He didn't. You would know. Trust me. Are you Judy Burns?"

"Yes."

"Bruce sent me." He trailed his hands up her arms. She was tied to the bed frame. Frank glanced at the doorway. He pulled the lock-back knife from his pocket and cut her free.

"Can you move?"

"Yes. I think so."

"Where are the other hostages?"

"I don't know. They keep us separate."

"Is Dasha working with the Russians?"

Judy started to answer, but didn't. She seemed to think about it. "I don't know."

Frank helped Judy to her feet. "Hold onto the back of my belt."

Judy did. They moved out into the hallway. Frank checked through the rifle-scope. It was clear. Frank cleared the bedrooms and bathroom on the second floor. There was no one there. He moved cautiously toward the stair leading up-ward. He turned at the bottom and moved to the first step. A red image appeared at the head of the stairs. Frank fired five times. The Russian fell away. Frank did a combat reload. Just like with the pistol, it was better to have a full magazine than chance running out of ammunition.

The upstairs was quiet. Frank stepped over the body of the Russian. He swept the rooms. Bathroom? Clear. He checked the master bedroom. Clear. The last room was a small library. He opened the door. There was a crib in the corner. A small child was standing in the crib. Frank handed the child to Judy.

"Hold on tight, we're going out now."

Judy held the child in one arm and onto Frank's belt with the other. They moved back to the stairs. Frank heard gunfire from outside punching into the house. He moved to the stairs. The lights in the house began to glow weakly. The house's emergency generator set on a timer. It was trying to come on and relight the house. Frank hurried down the stairs. They went into the room he had found Judy in. Frank closed the door behind him. He led them onto the balcony. He scoped the darkness and saw the Greek running toward them.

He stopped below the balcony. Frank took the child from Judy and lowered her down to the Greek. Next he took the child and lowered the child as far as possible. He dropped him the last few feet into his father's waiting arms.

"Poseidon's beard. Where is Dasha? Where is my wife?"

"I'm going back to look for her. Stay out here with Judy. Tell Burns I'm going to the first floor and to hold his fire."

"Yah," the Greek said.

Or at least it sounded like Yah. The tone said 'fuck you.'

Frank went back inside. The lights were back to half-light but growing brighter. He never knew lights could be anything but on or off. Never too old to learn something new, he thought.

Frank didn't bother to re-clear the rooms. It was a risk. They could have come up the stairs when he was outside. It was a justifiable risk. It would take a brave man to come up those stairs in the dark against a heavily armed enemy. The smart play would be to run or find a defensive position within the house.

Frank moved down the stairs. He saw a body sprawled near the doorway. It was the Russian from the porch. The front of the house looked like Swiss cheese. Another body was twisted in death behind the front window. Frank did the math. Eight dead. No more than a couple left. The lights came up.

Frank stepped onto the first floor. He swept the rooms he could see. He listened without moving. He heard Vlad.

"I will kill her. Do you hear me? I will kill her."

Frank moved toward the sound slowly inspecting the rooms he passed for a trap. He found no one alive.

"Let us make a truce," Vlad shouted.

They were in the back of the house. Frank moved toward the voice. Vlad was standing in the middle of a man's large study. The walls were covered in dark wood. There were thick Persian rugs on the floor. The chairs were all aged leather. There was another door to Vlad's right, but it was closed. Vlad held Dasha as a shield. Her arms were pinioned behind her back. A gun was against her head. Vlad saw Frank.

Vlad pressed the barrel of his pistol harder against Dasha's temple.

"The third man. At last we meet. Let us make a deal."

Frank raised his weapon. It was an easy shot. "What do you have that I could possibly want?"

"Money." Vlad indicated a duffel bag on the desk. "It is all there, another twenty thousand."

"And I let you walk?"

"Yes. Once I am clear, I will release the hostage."

Frank looked at Dasha. Her face was bruised. Her lips were cut. There were bite marks all over her thin neck. Blood had dried in trickles from wounds on her throat. That was some sick shit, Frank thought. Her clothes were torn. She looked like a hostage. But there was something in her red-rimmed eyes.

"I would hate to disappoint the Greek. He does want his wife back. Might be easier to shoot you now."

Vlad smiled. "So it would seem. But we are at an impasse. All other paths lead to her death as well."

The other door opened slowly. The Greek stood there. His M4 rifle was held at his waist. The barrel was pointing at Vlad and Dasha.

"Vlad wants to deal. We let him walk, he releases your wife."

The Greek did not speak.

Vlad knew this was the tipping point of the spear. The Greek would decide his fate. He ground the barrel harder against Dasha's temple. She whimpered slightly at the pain.

"I will kill her. I swear it. It will be on you."

The Greek did not speak.

"Please," Dasha begged. "Do as he asks. Do not let him kill me."

The Greek did not speak. He opened his mouth, but no words came out.

Dasha pleaded, "My love. Do this for me. Give me a chance at life. So we can be together."

Frank didn't like the way her arm was turned behind her back. He watched her for even the slightest movement.

"Please, my husband. Tell the others to let my cousin pass."

The Greek stared, still not speaking.

"Do it for our child. Do it for our love. Please, I beg you. I do not wish to die. I love you."

"By Poseidon's beard," the Greek said and pulled the trigger. The bullets punched into Vlad and Dasha. Their bodies twisted and spun in a macabre dance. The Greek had set his M4 to full auto and he emptied the entire magazine.

Frank saw the gun fly from Vlad's fist. He saw Dasha's small hand drop the gun she had kept hidden behind her back. Their bodies ended twisted on top of each other. The Greek dropped his rifle and walked over to her body. He pushed Vlad's body away. He knelt beside his wife's body. He gently brushed Dasha's hair from her face.

"How did you know?" Frank asked.

"The marks on her neck. She liked to be bitten there during lovemaking. I knew then they were lovers."

The Greek knelt there lost in his own thoughts. Frank raised his M4. It would simplify everything. One quick pull. One less loose end. One less witness. The Greek must have sensed Frank's thoughts. He did not turn when he spoke.

"I am sorry for what I have caused. See that someone from my family takes care of the boy. Aristodemus is innocent."

Frank lowered the rifle. "A boy needs a father."

The Greek did not turn around. "Thank you."

Frank went upstairs and took a sheet from the linen closet. He brought it back down to the Greek. Together they gently wrapped Dasha in the cloth. Frank helped him lift her slim body and followed him outside. The rain had stopped. Bruce and Judy Burns were standing there hugging. Ari was between them They were both soaking wet. When they saw the Greek they put his son down. Aristodemus ran to him with his arms out. The Greek laid his wife's body on the ground and hugged his child.

"Are we done here?" the Greek asked.

"Almost. Bring the cars up."

The Greek handed his son to Judy.

"I am sorry," he said. "I truly am."

She started crying.

When the two men were gone, Frank spoke to her. "Things are going to be different for you now. Bruce knows what he has to do."

"He told me."

"It's time to see what is important in life. You don't often get a second chance."

"We know. I don't know how to thank you."

"Everything happens for a reason. Thank me with the way you live your lives."

Judy nodded. "We will. I promise."

Frank said, "That's all I ask."

The car lights approached.

"What are you going to do with your wife?" Frank asked the Greek.

"She is still my wife and the mother of my child. I will bury her in my yard and cover it with a building. She deserves better than to be left in a hole without honor."

Burns opened the back of the Suburban and he helped the Greek place her body inside.

"Last part. Leave your coveralls and boots on the hood of my car. Same for your gloves. I'll take care of them for you. And leave your weapons too. All of it. Vests and ammo too."

The men didn't ask questions. They did what they had been told. The Greek took his child in his arms and got into the back seat. Judy got into the front seat. Bruce approached Frank.

"I hope to see you again sometime."

"You can count on it. Be careful."

"I will," Burns answered.

He got into the Suburban and drove away.

83

Frank returned to the house searching for any link to the Greek or Burns. Vlad had used the study as his command center. Maps and flight schedules were stacked on the desk. There were pre-taped DVDs ready to be sent to news organizations after the attack. The envelopes were already addressed. There were documents in what Frank guessed was Russian. There was a ledger with figures in neat columns. There were two checkbooks in different names. Nothing tied it to Burns or the Greek. He inspected the cash and its bag for a tracker. He found none. He carried it out to his car.

Frank gathered anything from the house he felt was an obvious link. He took the bed linens from the rooms the women had been in. He packed the towels from those bathrooms. He took the restraints he found in Judy's room. He bundled any female clothing he found. He took the female toiletries from the upstairs bathroom Dasha had used with Vlad. He took it all outside and put it into four of the large black garbage bags.

Frank searched all the Russians' bodies. He found nothing that was incriminating. He pocketed their money and put their few personal items into separate garbage bags. He took the batteries out of the cell phones and stomped their screens to pieces. He put those into other bags. He left the Russians' weapons. He dropped the SEAL weapons randomly around the house. He discarded the unused magazines nearby. Let them figure it out. He left all the doors to the house open and went to his car.

Back outside it was starting to drizzle again. He took off his coveralls and added them to the pile of clothing. He put it into a couple of black garbage bags. He went to his back seat and got out the groceries he had bought before. The lettuce was mushy. He tore it into bunches and added it to the clothes. He emptied the large squirt bottles of mustard into the foul mix. The sour smell was strong. He poured the vinegar and Clorox inside as well. If anyone chanced to look inside the smell alone should stop him or her from continuing. It also would help contaminate the DNA. Frank didn't take off his boots. He liked his boots. They were broken in just right. He would clean them himself so there would be no evidence. He kept the high tech vest as well. It had saved his life. It might do it again. He put them into the trunk of the Mercedes. There were holes in his plan. There was conflicting evidence. It was the best he could do for the people who would do the looking. He never doubted anyone would look.

This was a hard-on for homeland security. They would stumble all over themselves to take credit. Each division, from ATF to FBI to CIA to NSA, would all think the other agencies were involved and covering up.

The rain would help. Time was the best friend he had. Frank wondered what had happened to the people who had lived here. He figured they were probably in a shallow grave out back somewhere. He hoped it had been quick for them. Frank got into the Mercedes. He was tempted to head home, but he had made a promise. He drove to Fort Worth for the last time. Along the way he stopped at a closed diner and dumped the garbage bags in their dumpster.

Dorian was waiting up for him. When Frank came in she rose and came into his arms. He held her close, neither of them speaking.

"I am glad you're all right."

"Me too," Frank added.

"Let's go to bed."

"Let me catch a shower first."

"You don't have to for me."

"I do for me. I stink."

Frank let her go and went into the bathroom. He locked the door behind him. He took off his clothes and turned on the shower. He used some liquid soap to scrub the soles of his boots. He did a fine job and then dried the boots with a towel made of organic Egyptian cotton. Fuck the Egyptians, Frank thought. He took a shower in cold water. He turned it off and he could hear that the storm had returned in full force.

He was tired and sore and felt alive. Dorian was waiting for him in the king sized bed. She pulled the covers back for him. Frank slipped inside. They made love slowly like it was the last time they would ever make love. It was. They both knew it.

They woke and had room service. It was very solemn. Dorian spoke first.

"Can I go with you?"

"No."

"I won't be any trouble. I swear."

"I just can't take you. I'm sorry."

Dorian fought back tears. "You know we're good together."

"Yes, we are. But it's not enough."

"Yes, it is."

"It is not safe for us to be together. I do have something for you."

Frank got the duffel bag. He carried it over to where she sat. He opened the bag. She could see the stacks of money.

"There's over forty thousand dollars there."

"So? What do you want me to do with it?"

"Go where you want to live. Open the hair and beauty salon you said you wanted."

"I don't want your money. I want to go with you."

"Start your life over. Be the woman you are inside. You don't have to live like this anymore. It's a second chance."

"I could do that with you."

"No. You need a do-over. You can't do that with me. You know I'm right."

Dorian stood up and kissed him. She pressed her head against his huge chest.

"I will miss you, Frank. If that's your real name."

"It is."

"But if I call that number on your business card, I won't reach you, will I?"

"No."

"There is no such company is there?"

"Not that I know of."

"I will miss you."

"And I will miss you, Dorian. You know, the more I think about it, the more I think you do look like Lindsay Logan."

Dorian laughed.

"You are a knucklehead. I think I'll just try to look like myself for awhile."

Frank kissed the top of her head.

"Good plan."

84

It was still raining as Frank headed out on Highway 39 toward home. He thought about a lot of things. He thought about love and betrayal. He thought about people he had tried to help and those he had failed. The rain made him think about Apollo and the night he was killed in Costa Rica.

Frank had always prided himself on his stealth. Apollo had praised him on this rare trait in a big man. But Frank had never beaten the peacocks. He had tried to sneak out a dozen different times and they had always sounded the alarm. This night was different.

Frank rose about two o'clock. Pilar was still sleeping quietly in his bed. He watched her sleep. She was beautiful and dainty. He pulled on his board shorts and strapped a knife to his ankle. He liked to swim at night and since he had the experience with the twins he felt invincible. He crept downstairs and out the ornate front doors. The darkness was still. He moved down the gravel driveway toward the dock and boathouse. The peacocks were silent. Frank turned back toward the house. He saw the glow of a cigar on Apollo's balcony. Apollo seemed to never sleep. He waved at the figure on the balcony. The figure waved back.

Frank went down the path toward the boathouse. There was a light burning on the dock. Frank climbed down the ladder into the water. He didn't carry a dive light. He wanted to feel the ocean at night. He swam with gentle strokes out into the harbor. The cove was protected, but the open ocean was not. Once he was outside the rock walls he could feel the pull of the sea. He let it carry him. He treaded water easily, loving the smell and taste and feel of the ocean. He swam for over an hour before turning his strokes back toward the lights of shore.

He could see the light at the boathouse and headed for it. It was during the return swim that he had felt his first stirring of danger. His ego had blinded him to it. Why had he finally escaped the notice of the peacocks? Why tonight? He was always silent. He was always careful. Something was wrong. Something had happened to the peacocks for him to slip past them.

He approached the dock. He quietly climbed the ladder to the dock. Frank scanned the dock. It was empty. He listened. Nothing. Frank moved up onto the dock and slipped into the dark shadows. His senses were alert. His ears strained for a betraying sound. His eyes searched for the movement of a shadow. He even smelled deeply of the air for some hint of danger.

As he moved up the path toward the house he heard the squawk of a radio. It was in Spanish. A man stood facing away from him. He had a gun on his belt. One hand held a flashlight. The other hand held the radio. Frank's Spanish was rudimentary, but he knew the man was looking for him. He was frustrated and angry. The man turned the radio off and clipped it to his belt. He drew his pistol and scanned the surrounding area.

Drawing the gun was the last confirmation that Frank needed. He drew his knife and moved up to the man. He did not try to cut the man's throat or stab him. The best way for a silent kill was the area where the head joined the neck. Frank drove the long blade into the area up into the brain. The man died without a whimper. Frank sheathed the knife. He took the man's pistol. It was in excellent condition. He checked the magazine. Full load. The man had a second magazine in his pocket. Frank took it as well. He left the flashlight. Spartans liked the dark.

He reached the side of the house without seeing anyone else. It was there he found the peacocks. All dead. Poisoned. Frank moved to the front door. It was ajar. There was a bloody handprint on the doorframe. Frank could smell the gunpowder. He moved upstairs toward the bedrooms. One of the girls was dead on the stairwell. She had been shot in the back as she was running. He went to Apollo's room first. There was a dead man in the doorway. A machine pistol had torn him apart. The girls who had been with Apollo were both dead in the bed sheets. Apollo was slumped against the wall. His head had been blown away at close range. Probably a shotgun, Frank thought. The Navy SEAL signet ring stood out on his finger. Blood had streaked down like claw marks obscuring the tattoo on his shoulder. The SEAL insignia on his chest seemed to glow. The machine pistol was still clutched in Apollo's hand. They hadn't even bothered to take it. Frank stuck his pistol in his trunks. He checked the machine pistol. It was down to three rounds. He left it. He left Apollo and went to his own bedroom. The girl, Pilar, was dead. Her blood soaked the sheets where they had lain.

Frank knew the killers were still present. They would be trying to get into the safe. He was not afraid. They had killed one of the only real friends he had ever had. He knew what he was going to do. He crept down the stairs leaving a trail of seawater tracks. He felt like Poseidon.

He could hear the men talking. He followed the noise. They were all huddled around the huge safe trying to pry it open. No one was on guard. No one was watching their backs. There were five of them. Frank shot them all. He dropped the magazine and reloaded as he approached their bodies. He turned at a noise. The cook screamed as she charged him. She carried a large carving knife. He shot her in the forehead. He remembered Apollo's words: It is always a woman that betrays you. Frank approached her dead body and shot her twice more in the head.

Frank didn't know who had sent them. He didn't really care. He went back upstairs to his room. He dressed in travel clothes. He tied his long hair back into a pony tail. He packed a bag of his things. He went to Apollo's room and took his Navy SEAL signet ring. It would barely fit on his pinky, but Frank wore it anyway. He took the silver cigar cutter and lighter with Apollo's initials on them. He took a box of Castro's cigars. He covered his friend with a blanket.

Frank went back downstairs to the safe. He opened it using the combination. Apollo had no secrets from Frank. The safe was full of money bundled in neat stacks. Frank took thirty thousand dollars for bribes. He also took the two diplomatic passports. The safe also contained weapons and jewelry. Frank left all of that. He went to the garage and pulled one of the Toyota Landcruisers up to the front door. He took one of the ten-gallon gas cans that remote locations always had on hand and loaded it into the back of the Landcruiser. He tossed his stuff inside. He went back to the garage and took two more gas cans. He returned to the house and doused everything he could with gasoline. He left a trail out the front door.

He looked back. Apollo's compound in Costa Rica had been his refuge. Apollo had been his friend. Maybe Apollo was right. Maybe he had been able to sense the coming danger when Frank had not. Children of the gun. He lit a pack of matches and tossed them onto the gasoline. The fire raced into the house. There was a roar as it found more fuel.

Frank got in the SUV and drove away. He stopped at the gatehouse. He went inside. The young guard was dead in his booth. He hadn't even had a weapon. The gate was open. So Frank pulled out. He knew the roads vaguely. He knew he had to go north to reach Nicaragua. He couldn't risk being caught in Costa Rica. He had entered illegally. It would cause too many questions. It might make it too easy for his enemies to find him.

Once he was on the road he called Claudia Murphy.

"It's Frank. I have a problem."

To her credit she didn't sound alarmed. She didn't even sound sleepy. "What can I do?"

"Apollo is gone. I am driving toward Nicaragua. Can you get me out?"

"Nicaragua is not good for us. Too many U.S. government eyes. Can you make it to El Salvador? It's farther north?"

"I think so."

"Call me when you cross the border. There are farms there we can use to land a plane."

"Send Bullington."

"He's out of the country on a trip."

"Bring him back."

"Okay. I will. He's the only one crazy enough to go in there anyway."

"I'll need to see a familiar face to know it's not a set-up."

"You know you can trust me."

"Always have."

"Don't contact anyone until you're clear."

Frank crossed the border. It was amazing how similar his face was to a handful of Ben Franklins. He had stopped only to refuel and pushed across the country. He called Claudia and she sent Bullington in the plane to pick him up as she had promised. There had been a day of waiting in the jungle for the plane. But Frank was good at waiting. Apollo had taught him that sniper's trait. He smoked cigars in his friend's memory.

Bullington looked nervous as he got out of the plane. Hell, he always looked juiced on something. No one else materialized. The last thing Frank did before boarding the twin-engine plane was to toss his gun into the grass. He trusted Claudia, but only so much.

Frank sighed. He picked up the Montecristo Dorian had bought him. He pushed it out of its cellophane wrapper, smelled it, moistened the wrapping with his tongue. He took the knife and cut off a tiny portion of the tip. He used the car's cigarette lighter. He puffed a huge cloud of white smoke. He smiled. He rolled the windows down a little. He punched on one of the metal songs on the CD player. Amon Amarth roared about the twilight of the thunder god. Elliot could get rid of the cigar smell after he got the car back. He took another puff.

It felt right. He felt like he was honoring his old friend and his new one. Dorian was right. You had to indulge yourself sometimes. Otherwise why live? He pushed on through the day into the night. He wasn't hungry. He wasn't thirsty. There were things he needed to do.

85

Agent Redding waited almost an hour for the bomb squad to arrive. Talk about not being threat ready. The bomb techs were impressed with the rigging. The bomb was a shaped charge that would have leveled half the park. They talked in tech jargon about it being done by a pro and a mercury switch, and trip plates. All that mattered to Redding was that his butt was asleep and it was hard to finally stand. He was debriefed on site and told the story as close to the truth as he wanted to. The extra time had allowed him to shape it just right. He was congratulated on being a hero and patted on the back by everyone that came within reach of him. They had already found the file in his car. Forensic experts identified the body as that of the senator and not a homeless man. His car was impounded so they could search for more tracking devices. He took agents to his home and gave them the note from his bathroom. They were impressed. Redding was given three days off with pay. That was something the Bureau never did.

A new task force was formed to investigate agent Harris and his father's involvement with the Spartans. The Assistant Director was taken into custody. After they finally left, Redding got out his single-malt scotch and took off his shoes. He got comfortable on the sofa and turned on the television. It was set on the news, but he was tired of the news. He changed to an old movie channel. It was a Steve McQueen movie, *The Getaway.* He liked Steve McQueen. He was so cool. He fell asleep sometime before Slim Pickens took Steve and his wife across the border into Mexico.

DC left early the next morning. He wasn't sure what he should do. The girls told him to go. They needed to talk. Caron cried and Jenny cried. They talked about what had almost happened to them. They cried some more. They talked about what happened between Caron and DC. Caron said she was sorry. Jenny said, no, she was sorry. They avowed their lifelong friendship and love for each other. They decided they would have to talk to Frank as soon as he got back. It was the adult thing to do. They also decided they would go to college at UNC Greensboro. They wanted to stay close to home.

DC came back that afternoon and the three of them spent three and a half hours removing the broken door and replacing it. It was really pretty simple once you figured out what you were doing. And how tools worked. And what tools you needed. They were all proud of their accomplishment in the end. DC and Caron couldn't stop touching each other so Jenny left for a while.

When she returned, DC told her that the cops had caught Zack and Morgan three blocks away. They got arrested for underage drinking and possession of cocaine and marijuana. UNC had already pulled their football scholarships. Couldn't happen to nicer guys, they all agreed.

Jenny heard noises downstairs on Sunday. She was still sleeping in Frank's bed. She slipped her jeans on and got the knife. If those assholes had come back she would cut their hearts out. She crept downstairs. Someone was in the kitchen. She eased the door open. It was Frank. He was cooking.

She hid the knife in her pocket. He turned and smiled. He opened his arms and she ran into them. He hugged her hard, like he meant it.

"I missed you," he said.

"We missed you, too."

"Everything okay here?'

Jenny sighed. "It's been busy."

Frank smiled. "As long as you're safe."

"I'm fine. First, I've been sleeping in your bed."

Frank didn't say anything.

"And using your shower."

"You are welcome to all I have. I hope you know that."

"I know that here," she said touching her head, "but in here," she added touching her heart, "it seemed wrong."

"It wasn't."

"There was also some trouble with some boys."

"Oh?"

"We didn't invite them. They just showed up, but we ran them off. DC really, more than us."

"That why you have the knife?"

Jenny blushed. "Sort of."

Frank laughed. "It's a good knife. Keep it if you want. Just don't take it to school or you'll get in trouble."

"Really? I can have it?"

"Yeah. I don't need it." He paused. "It'll make me feel good to know you have it."

"Wow. Thanks. Oh, and Caron and I decided we are going to UNCG for college."

"Good. It'll be nice to have you close. Plus, they are the Spartans."

Jenny laughed. "That didn't play a part in our decision."

Frank touched his head, "Maybe not in here," then he touched his heart, "but in here, I think it did."

Jenny smiled. It was good to have him home. She seemed to notice for the first time what Frank was doing.

"What are you making?"

"Pancakes. Chocolate chip pancakes to be exact. I did a pound of bacon first. Sit down and I'll serve you."

Jenny sat. She was stunned. Frank got a plate. He put some bacon on it and a tall stack of pancakes. He got her orange juice from the refrigerator. He handed her silverware and poured the syrup over the pancakes. He got out more silverware and set three more places.

Jenny took a fork and cut a small bite. She took a tentative bite. It was good. She took another bite. It was really good. She smiled at Frank.

"I didn't know you liked chocolate chip pancakes."

"I didn't either," he said. "They are wicked good."

Jenny hid her laugh behind the paper napkin. Caron walked in. She looked shocked or scared.

"Frank! You're home."

"Have a seat, Caron. Let me get you some pancakes."

Caron looked at Jenny. Jenny shrugged.

"It's good to have you back."

"It's good to be back."

"Everything go all right for you on your trip?"

"Couldn't have been better. Try some bacon too." He handed her a plate full of food. "Hold on, I'll get you some orange juice."

Frank put the orange juice in front of her. Caron tried the pancakes. She grinned, first at Frank, then at Jenny.

"These are really good."

"Thanks," Frank said.

They heard the front door open. They all waited and DC appeared in the kitchen, carrying a box of Krispy Kreme donuts and three cups of Starbucks coffee.

"Big man. You made it."

"Looks like it."

"If I had known, I would have gotten coffee for you too."

"You can have mine," Caron said.

"Or mine. Take mine. I don't really like coffee," Jenny added.

"Don't worry about it, DC. Take a seat. I got pancakes for you."

DC sat.

"Cool. Load that bacon up, man. I love bacon. It's nature's perfect food."

Frank did and DC ate with an abandon the girls hadn't shown.

Even as they enjoyed the breakfast and Frank's return, there was an air of nervousness. Finally, DC spoke.

"There's something I need to tell you," DC started.

"Really?"

Frank sat down with a plate of pancakes.

"Yeah, man. It's about Caron and me."

Frank smiled. "I figured it out."

Caron looked at DC and then back at Jenny.

"I didn't say anything," Jenny said.

"She didn't have to. It was pretty obvious."

"Are you mad?" DC asked.

"No. You're all adults. You got to make your own choices. Just try to be discreet around me, okay?"

"Yeah, definitely. I was scared shitless about telling you. I mean…."

The doorbell rang. Frank stood and started toward the door.

"No, I'll get it," DC said. "You sit back down and have some of those cakes before they get cold."

Frank sat down and DC hurried out. A few minutes later DC came back into the kitchen.

"It's some old Mexican woman. She asked in Spanish to see you."

"If she asked in Spanish how do you know? You don't speak Spanish."

"She said something about 'hombre grande'. That sounded like you."

Frank got up and wiped his mouth. He went to the front door. Rosa's grandmother was standing there. He had never spoken to her, but he had seen her face watching him through the window a hundred times.

"Buenos dias," Frank said.

She started speaking Spanish. Frank shook his head. He held up two fingers barley apart, like he was trying to pinch something. "Un poco," he said.

The old woman hesitated. She paused searching for words. She looked at him with serious eyes.

"Muchos gracias, pistolero."

He stared back at her without expression. She extended her arms. She had a fresh baked apple pie for him. Frank looked at the pie and again at the woman. He took the pie and forced a smile. He looked left and right. He held a finger to his lips like you do to shush someone.

"No es nada," Frank said.

The woman mimicked her finger in front of her lips.

"Ssh," she whispered and smiled and then winked at him.

He had never seen her smile. It was a pretty good smile for an old broad. She probably hadn't had too many chances to practice it lately. She turned and walked away. Frank went back into the kitchen with the pie.

"Dude, she brought you a pie?"

"I guess so."

"Why?"

"I sent little Rosa a card when I heard about her accident. She was just trying to say thanks."

"Cool." DC took the pie and got some plastic wrap. He put it in the refrigerator. "We'll save this baby for dessert tonight."

"We?" Frank asked.

"I just thought. I mean we're like family right?"

"Close as I got," Frank said.

Jenny thought her heart would break. "We're all family."

"One other thing. On my drive back, I started thinking. We never take any vacation," Frank said. "It's all work or school."

The girls looked at each other.

"No, we don't do much else," they answered together.

"You get some time off school over Thanksgiving. I thought...if you want to, we would take a trip."

"Where?" Jenny asked.

"I was thinking about the Bahamas. Catch some sun. Play in the ocean. Relax."

"That would be fantastic," Jenny said.

"All of us?" Caron asked.

"Sure. DC too, if he wants."

"Man, I've never been to the islands. I don't have a passport. Do I have time to get one?"

"Don't worry about it. I don't think you need one. I'll see if I can set it up."

Jenny came over and kissed his cheek. "You are the best."

Caron came over and kissed the other side. "Thank you. For everything."

DC watched them go. "I don't have to kiss you do I?"

"No."

"Good. But I mean...I would if I had to."

86

After breakfast Frank took his bag upstairs to unpack. He locked the door. No one needed to know all his secrets. He would move the new pistol and the vests to a storage facility he rented under another name in Kernersville. He showered and changed clothes. When he came downstairs the others were all in the living room with the television on.

"Did you hear?" DC asked. "Of course not. You just got in."

"What?"

"That MS-13 crack house where they shot that little girl. Last night the Latin Kings struck back at them."

"Really?"

"It's all over the news. Four dealers got shot sometime last night. The Kings torched the place. They left some of their gang graffiti so everyone knows who took care of business."

"Any witnesses?"

"You know how these things are, Frank. No one sees nothing."

"Glad to hear it got handled."

Frank caught Jenny's eye. She knew. He didn't know how, but she knew. She smiled at him.

"I'm going to run the car back to Elliott, then I'll see if I can set up the trip."

Frank used the prepaid cell he had bought in Oklahoma at the service station. He dialed the number from memory. He didn't know if it was any good anymore. It was a private number. It was answered on the second ring.

"Hello,"

"Claudia. It's Frank."

"Frank. It's been a long time."

She didn't sound surprised to hear from him. She was always good.

"You still do private charters?"

"Sometimes. When are you talking about?"

"Thanksgiving."

"Busy time. Where to?"

"I was thinking Bahamas."

"Shouldn't be a problem. Which island?"

"Eleuthra."

Claudia laughed. "Naturally, it Greek for freedom."

"Yes, it is."

"How many traveling?'

"Four people. Two males. Two females. No passports. Off the books."

"Hotel?"

"Someplace nice. Three rooms. Big ass pool."

"I assume you'll be paying cash."

"Of course. Phil Bullington still flying for you?"

"Yes. He's still working with me. But just barely. Someone tried to shoot him down over Cuba."

"Glad he made it. I like him."

"He's still an incredible pilot."

"Same weakness?"

"He still loves the white powder. He'll probably piggyback your trip with a pickup. Double his money."

"My kind of guy."

"I knew you guys would still get along great after Costa Rica. Call me next week. I'll have the details."

"You still in Charlotte?"

"Yes. VIP Travel has a small private airfield off I-40. There's a big sign. You can't miss it."

"Claudia."

"Yes."

"I'm trusting you. I can still do that, can't I?"

"Of course. You know that."

Frank hung up. He would take precautions, but he would trust her.

Claudia hung up the phone. Frank Kane back from the dead. She wondered what his real reason was for going to Eleuthra. She knew damn well it wasn't for vacation. He was making some kind of move. Maybe he was meeting a distributor. Maybe it was a client. Maybe it was some of the old Spartan heavy hitters. It didn't matter to her. She punched in a number on her cell phone and waited.

When the phone was answered she said, "I just got a call from Frank Kane. I know where he'll be and when he'll be there."

Three weeks later, Charles Foster, a powerful attorney from Charlotte, contacted the family of little Rosa Dominguez. He explained that an anonymous donor had read about her plight. He had authorized money to cover all her medical expenses relating to a prosthetic arm and any physical therapy she required. The family was overwhelmed with gratitude. They couldn't wait to tell Frank the good news when he came to visit her.

Epilogue

Dorian was exhausted. She didn't know when the last time she had slept. She could hear the television playing in the other room. It was one of those twenty-four hour news stations. It sounded like FOX News. She turned her head, but she couldn't see it. There was a bag over her head and she couldn't dislodge it.

The television talking head was moderating between a pair of dueling pundits.

"The scene clearly proves that it was a branch of the Special Forces that intercepted the terrorists."

"I think you are mistaken. If the scene shows anything it's that nonmilitary personnel are responsible for the massacre at the house."

"Weapons found at the scene, specialized ammunition, tactics, boot marks, everything points to Navy SEALs. And it was not a massacre. It was a surgical military strike."

"If that were true, why leave the weapons behind? Why not claim responsibility? Why not confiscate the SAMs?"

"For just this reason. To confuse the issue. They probably did not want to run the risk of being intercepted with their weapons. Remember Deputy Ellisor's testimony that his assailants used military jargon? They knew he might have a BOLO out for them."

"It's all a little too pat, if you ask me. And the military just this morning announced that the weapons found on the scene were part of a stolen Navy arms shipment."

"Now they announce the weapons were stolen. We never heard a word about the theft before now."

"You didn't actually expect the military to say that one of their high tech weapons shipments had been lost?"

"What I expect is that some black op has occurred and we will never know the truth about it. All we know, all we need to know, is that some branch of our homeland security intercepted and dealt with a group of ruthless Chechen terrorists before they could act."

"Gentlemen," the talking head broke in, "this has been a lively and enlightening discussion, but we are out of time. Tomorrow we'll have an exclusive interview with Mr. and Mrs. Caudle, the couple who discovered the carnage when they returned from a month-long vacation to Europe. Authorities believe the bodies had been there for several weeks. Also, tomorrow we'll interview the first responders who…."

The television went silent. Dorian heard footsteps enter the room. A chair was pulled out. Someone pulled the pillowcase off her head. Two men in dark suits and sunglasses stepped out of her field of view. Her hair fell into her face and she tried to reach up and brush it away, but her hands were still secured to the arms of the chair. The new man, obviously the leader, leaned toward her and tucked the strand of hair behind her ear.

"Better?" he asked.

"Yeah. Thanks."

"My name is John. I am the Agent in Charge. I have a few questions if you don't mind?"

"I haven't done anything wrong. If you are going to charge me, then do it. Take me to the station or wherever, and get on with it. This is bullshit. I have rights. I want a lawyer."

John smiled. It was a soothing smile.

"Again, I apologize. I need to clarify a few elements of your statement. If you answer truthfully and completely, I'll release you. Does that sound fair?"

"I have been through this with the other agents. I told them everything."

"Indulge me, please. Just a few questions. I promise."

He smiled again. He was hard to refuse. He had a charm.

"All right."

"Excellent. According to your statement," he said, showing her the written statement she had made, "you met a man who called himself Frank Nomin?"

Dorian nodded.

"Frank claimed that he was a businessman, but you began to doubt the validity of this claim. He did not act like a businessman. In your own words, you thought he was a criminal."

"Yes."

"You say he tried to disguise his appearance."

"Yes."

"You say he had an unusual assortment of tattoos. There was what you describe as a v burned into his forearm. There was another burn on his left shoulder in the shape of the symbol Pi."

Dorian nodded.

"He had the word Spartans tattooed across his stomach. He had a full sleeve of tattoos on his left arm in what you describe as an ocean motif. You also say he had a number of scars that appeared to be from wounds. Both, as you say, from bullets and a knife wound across his abdomen."

Dorian sighed. "Yes, it's all there in the report."

"You say he was trying to meet with the owner of a lamp store."

"That's what he said."

"Did that seem odd to you?"

"Yes."

"Did you ever see him meet with this owner?"

"No."

"So it may have been a ruse to distract you from his true purpose for being in Fort Worth."

"I guess so."

"We checked this lamp store. It's closed."

"Don't you think it is odd that it would be closed as soon as he left Fort Worth? I do. Unless it was already closed or closing and he was aware of this fact."

"I don't know."

He went back to his notes. "You say he left you after about a week. And that he gave you over forty thousand dollars as a going away present."

Dorian blushed. "He liked me. He wanted to help me. He was a good man."

John nodded. "Yet before he left, you say you witnessed him murder three individuals."

"They were trying to kill me."

"So you say. Is it not possible that these men were murdered for another reason? One not known to you?"

"No. It is not."

John smiled. "Calm down. I don't mean to upset you. My associates have told you that this man's real name is Frank Kane."

"Yes."

"He is an infamous murderer. He was the former enforcer for the Spartans motorcycle club."

"That's what they say, but I'm not sure I believe that."

"The name on the business card he left you is Nomin. It is an arrogant play on the name the Greek Ulysses used to trick the Cyclops. He used the name Noman. The Cyclops was one of Poseidon's sons. Poseidon was the name given to Frank Kane."

"I don't know anything about that."

"Fair enough. Do you have any idea how we can find this man?"

"No."

"He made no plans to contact you in the future?"

"No."

"You have no idea where he might have gone or even where he was actually from?"

"I told you, no."

John neatened up the notes. "Very well, Dorian. You have kept your word. I respect that. One final question."

"What?"

"If we apprehend this man, as we will surely do at some point, are you prepared to testify against him for complete immunity for your own criminal activities?"

Dorian stared at the man. She wanted to say yes. The criminal survival part of her brain urged her to agree. It was only a white lie. She could say what they wanted to hear.

"No. I will not testify against him."

"Think carefully. That answer may be the difference between freedom and a long time in prison for your crimes."

"I will not betray him."

"You could be charged with aiding and abetting the murder of three men. In the eyes of the law you are as guilty as he is even if you did not pull the trigger or wield the knife that killed those men. I ask you once more. Think carefully. If we are able..."

"No. The answer is no. It's always going to be no. Nothing you can do or say will change that. I shouldn't have told you as much as I did. I'm done. Get me a lawyer."

John smiled. He patted her on her knee. He spoke to the men behind her. "You see what I am talking about? This is what we're up against. Frank Kane inspires unwavering loyalty."

He turned once more to Dorian. "I know I promised no more questions, but I just had an epiphany. Will you indulge me?"

Dorian sighed. "Do I have a choice?"

"Did Frank Kane have anything to do with the Russian terrorists killed near Fort Worth?"

"I don't know. How could he? There was like a million of those guys killed."

"Difficult, yes, for a normal man. Not impossible for Frank Kane. Nothing is impossible for him. The knife wound he showed you, you remember it?"

Dorian nodded.

"That wound would have killed another man."

"He isn't like other men."

John laughed. "No, he is not. I gave him that wound, did you know that?"

Dorian's face reflected her shock.

"It is true. I stabbed him. I thought I had killed him. He gave me this," John lifted his sunglasses there were a series of scars across the orbit. She noticed that the bone was not right, it was off center.

"He shattered my skull. I was lucky to survive. Doctors have done a great deal of reconstructive surgery to hide the force of his blow. As you can see there is much still to be done. It has left me with constant pain."

Dorian didn't answer.

"Did he ever mention my name? Did he say anything about his old friend, Spanish Johnny?"

Dorian shook her head, no.

"Perhaps, he mentioned Cyrus, or Helen."

"The girl he was in love with?"

"So he has not forgotten us. Good."

"He said she was dead."

"Oh, she is very much alive, I can assure you. He only hopes she is dead. If he knew how she betrayed him, he would be forced to kill her himself."

"I don't believe you."

Spanish Johnny laughed. It was a wonderful laugh. It held no malice. "I see why Frank liked you. You have fire. Unfortunately, you also have a big mouth. If you had kept it shut we never would have come looking for you."

"Fuck you."

Spanish Johnny smiled. His teeth were perfect. "Profanity is the last refugee of someone who has nothing to say. I think our work here is done. She doesn't know anything. Let's go."

"Johnny," Dorian called as he got to his feet.

"What?" he asked pulling his sunglasses back down.

"I hope he kills you when you do find him."

Spanish Johnny laughed again. "A lot of people share those sentiments, Dorian. Enjoy the rest of your life. You will never see me again."

Spanish Johnny walked past her. Dorian heard the door behind her open. She heard the footsteps leave and the door close. She waited a few seconds and started to work on the plasti-cuffs. She felt the plastic tie on her left wrist give slightly. That was where she would start. She only needed to free one hand to get the other loose. She sawed her wrist back and forth trying to stretch the plastic. She felt it cut her wrist, but she didn't care. The blood would add lubricant to her efforts. Suddenly, she felt a breath beside her ear.

"I want you to know that there will come a day when I am killed. Frank may even be the one who ends my life, but hoy ne ese dia," Spanish Johnny whispered. "Today is not that day."

He caressed her throat with the razor's edge of his knife. Dorian gasped. She felt no pain. She sat perfectly still waiting. She knew what to expect. She trembled as she waited for her severed carotid artery to spray out her life. She fought to keep her eyes open as long as possible. She had earned that. She wanted every second. It took several seconds for her to realize he had not cut her throat.

Spanish Johnny slammed the blade of his knife into the tabletop before her. Pinned beneath the knife was a card with a handwritten telephone number. The ink was red.

"I have spared you for one reason. When Frank contacts you, and he will, give him this number. Tell him I am still alive. Tell him I am coming for him. Tell him this time his luck will not save him."

She heard Spanish Johnny leave and the door close behind him. She hoped that one day Spanish Johnny would indeed find Frank Kane. She hoped Frank would make sure he was dead. She remembered Frank's perfect blue eyes and held that as her final thought as she continued to work at her restraints.

If you liked *Spartan Negotiator,* you'll love *The Last Spartan* where Frank Kane goes to Atlanta and saves Jenny and Caron from a life of white slavery. Available at **www.savpress.com** and from Amazon as a hardcover and eBook.

About the Author

John F. Saunders is a general and forensic dentist
who lives and practices in Greensboro, North Carolina.

TO ORDER ADDITIONAL COPIES OF

SPARTAN NEGOTIATOR

Call **1-800-732-3867**

or

Purchase copies online at:
www.savpress.com

Visa/MC/Discover/American Express/
ECheck/accepted via PayPal.

All Savage Press books are available through all
chain and independent bookstores nationwide.
Just ask them to special order if the title is not in stock.

Book III Coming Soon

SPARTAN KRYPTEA

Frank Kane returns in *Spartan Kryptea*. Frank heads to the Bahamas
with DC and the girls for a vacation. But it's not all palm trees and cold
beer. Mix in a few crooked cops, a violent Jamaican death cult, ancient
pirate treasure, and memories of long past Spartan betrayals. Top this
off with Helen's arrival on the same island, and you have an explosive
tropical cocktail of action, adventure, love, deceit, and violence, stirred
to a deadly intensity by Kane's invincible Spartan ethic.

All Frank and his friends have to do is survive long enough to escape
the island before the real hurricane arrives.